I0611552

A Snowball's Chance in Hell

JD Kirk is the author of the multi-million bestselling DCI Logan series, set in the Highland s of Scotland . He also d oes not exist. Instead , JD is the pen name of former child ren's author and screenwriter, Barry Hutchison, who was born and raised in Fort William. He still lives in the Highland s with his wife and child ren. He has no id ea what the JD stand s for.

Also by JD Kirk

DCI Logan Crime Thrillers

JD KIRK

A SNOWBALL'S CHANCE IN HELL

CANELO CRIME

Penguin
Random
House

First published in the United Kingd om in 2020 by Zertex Crime

This ed ition published in the United Kingd om in 2024 by

Canelo Crime, an imprint of
DK Publishing, a d ivision of Penguin Rand om House LLC
1745 Broad way, 20th Floor, New York, NY 10019

The authorized representative in the EEA is Dorling Kind ersley Verlag GmbH.
Arnulfstr. 124, 80636 Munich, Germany

ISBN 9798217259649

Cover d esign by Tom Sand erson

Cover images © Shutterstock

Look for more great books at
www.canelo.co | www.d k.com

–

154078558

Chapter 1

There was something about it, the cold . Something ancient. Something pure.

They said that it was fire that cleansed , but that had never felt quite right. Fire *consumed*. The cold , on the other hand , stripped you bare. Left you exposed . Mad e you face up to all the things you were.

And all the things you'd d one.

Fire could take you in second s. But the cold ? The cold took hours to wear you d own, whittle you away, breath by agonising breath.

Cold gave you time to think. To reflect. To regret. Cold preserved your pain, froze it in time, each painful second staying on long past its welcome, as extremities rotted and internal organs slowed , before shutting themselves d own one by one.

She was a d ead ly mistress, the cold , but beautiful, too. The clinical whites. The translucent blues. The cloud s of breath that d anced around the suspend ed flecks of frost that gleamed like tiny d iamond s in the air.

There was beauty to a flame too, granted , but it was a simple one. Obvious.

Cold 's charms, however, were richer, and more complex. Less showy, but with far greater d epth. Anyone could enjoy a fire. Only a few could truly appreciate the raw, gnawing beauty of the sub-zero.

The man in the box was not appreciating it one little bit.

He had raged to begin with, slapped his hand s against the reinforced d oor until the frozen metal had ripped the skin from his palms. He'd have howled then, called out in pain, had his lungs not begun to cramp, and his chest not begun to tighten.

The circle of glass in the d oor had held fast, d espite his efforts to break it. It was smeared with blood now—a crimson slush, with long fingers of frost creeping through it.

The man in the box had n't gone on struggling much longer. He'd jumped around , hugged himself, and d anced on the sp for almost ten minutes, before the rolling cold air had slowed his muscles and his thoughts, and he'd collapsed onto the rubber mat in the centre of the box.

There he'd stayed , all whispers and whimpers, arms wrapped around his legs, hand s scrunched up into tight balls, as the cold nipped and pinched at his extremities and forced its wa d own into his core, eliciting violent shud d ering convulsions that almost knocked him off the mat.

The last line of d efence by a bod y in shut-d own.

The whimpering had stopped forty minutes later. The shivering, too.

A few minutes later, he'd got shakily to his feet, pulled off his thin shirt, and tried to jam it into one of the vents through which the icy air came billowing in.

He could n't reach. But then, he barely really tried . He barely seemed to remember what he was d oing, in fact, and , after a few moments spent staring blankly at the intricate flowers of frost blooming along one wall, he fell onto the mat and lay on his back, staring up at the ceiling above him.

He would be gone soon. What was left of him would be snuffed out, his heat extinguished by the relentless, all-consuming chill.

He would be d ead . Gone. Cleansed by the cold .

And he would not be the last.

Chapter 2

Christ, this was d ifficult. Far more so than he'd expected .

It should n't be, he knew. It should be easy. After all, you d id n't get to be a Detective Chief Inspector head ing one of Police Scotland 's Major Investigations Teams without being able to make some tough d ecisions.

But this? This was something else.

DCI Jack Logan stood outsid e Debenham's wind ow on the upper floor of the Eastgate Shopping Centre, carefully consid - ering his options. Around him, well-wrapped late-evening shoppers hustled and bustled by, lad en with shopping bags, and sad d led with d ebt that they would n't start worrying about until mid -January.

Lights twinkled . Spirits rose. Shakin' Stevens' *Merry Christmas, Everyone* blasted out of a speaker for the umpteenth blood y time that d ay. Any other time of the year, the shops would be shutting d own at this time on a Sund ay night, but with just three more shopping d ays left until Christmas, it felt like they were just getting their second wind .

They'd been traipsing around the Eastgate for hours now, occasionally venturing to the shops further afield in the city centre, before making their way back to d ouble-check some- thing Logan had spotted earlier in the d ay.

After some more careful consid eration of the contents of the wind ow, Logan opened his mouth to speak. Besid e him, Detective Constable Sinead Bell leaned incrementally forward s, her breath held in anticipation.

3

Then, with a little shake of his head , the DCI shut his mouth again and shoved his hand s d eep d own in his coat pockets.

'Is the perfume still an option?' Sinead asked .

'Aye. I haven't officially ruled out anything yet,' Logan replied . 'I mean, perfume's fine, isn't it?'

'Aye. Perfume's fine,' Sinead confirmed .

The reply mad e Logan turn away from the shop front. It was bed ecked with boughs of holly, fake snow, and a small army of polar bears that d id n't have any connection to Christmas beyond the fact they presumably enjoyed the weather at that time of year.

'Why d id you say it like that?' the DCI asked .

'Like what, sir?'

'Like… *fine*. "Perfume's *fine*". Like that.'

Sinead , to her cred it, managed a smile. They'd been traipsing round the shops for the better part of two hours now, and Logan was yet to settle on a single purchase. Given that he was only planning on making one, this meant a 100 per cent failure rate so far.

'Just… you said it was fine, and I agreed .'

'Aye, but I said , "fine", like a good thing. You said it like it's bad .'

Sinead gave a little shrug. 'No, well, it's not *bad*—'

'Right. Forget the perfume,' Logan announced , marching off in the d irection of Waterstones bookshop.

'It's just… it's a bit obvious, sir,' Sinead said , hurrying to catch up with his long strid es.

The throngs of Christmas shoppers d id n't look in the DCI's d irection, but the way they parted to get out of his way suggested they could sense his presence. He cut through the crowd s like a hot knife through butter, his towering height, broad should ers, and general d emeanour creating a sort of forcefield that cleared the path ahead .

'We'll look at the books again,' he called back to the junior officer rid ing in his slipstream. 'Maybe something will jump out this time.'

Sinead doubted that. They'd combed through the bookshop twice already. They'd also been in HMV (twice), Menkind (once—and, Logan swore, never again), and half a dozen other shops selling everything from upcycled furniture to jewellery.

Nothing had been right. Nothing had been perfect.

'Do you know what she's getting you, sir?' Sinead asked.

Logan stopped suddenly, and the DC almost walked straight into his back. 'Why would I know what she's getting me? Has she told you something?' he asked.

Sinead shook her head. 'No. Not a thing. I mean, I barely really know her...'

'If she's told you what she's getting me, I order you to tell me, Detective Constable,' Logan said, wheeling around to face her.

'I've got no idea,' Sinead told him.

Logan gave a low grunt of disappointment, then turned and marched into Waterstones.

The place was mobbed. He scanned above the sea of bobble hats and red-cheeked faces, then tutted and immediately walked back out again.

'Bugger that. I'll never find anything in there,' he said.

'What about that necklace you saw, sir?' Sinead suggested. 'That was lovely.'

Logan's nose wrinkled. 'Aye, but is jewellery no' a bit... full-on?'

'How do you mean?'

'Well... it's no' like we're in a relationship. We've barely managed one date.' He flinched, embarrassed by how the word sounded in his mouth. *Date.* Did people even use that these days? 'I just think maybe jewellery is a bit over the top.'

'It's not like you're buying her an engagement ring, sir,' Sinead pointed out. 'It's a necklace.'

'I've never seen her wearing a necklace. Maybe she doesn't like necklaces,' Logan replied. He shuffled aside to let a succession of dour-looking men come filing out of the bookshop, their bags so light they could only contain book tokens.

5

He watched them melt into the crowds, no doubt headed for the underground car park, their tedious, uninspiring Christmas shopping done for another year.

Christ, was that him? Was he one of those grey-faced bastards, devoid of all imagination?

In their later years together, he and Vanessa had slipped into the trap of just swapping envelopes of money at Christmas.

'Get yourself something nice,' they'd say. 'You know what you want better than I do.'

The fact that the money came out of their joint bank account only made the whole thing even more depressing.

Truth be told, he'd never been a big one for Christmas. He'd worked most of them, even when Maddie had been young. The festive period brought out the bampots, and his Christmases were an endless parade of increasingly serious crimes.

On Maddie's first Christmas, he'd been flagging down cars and subjecting the drivers to a breathalyser test. It rose—or plummeted, maybe—in a curve from there, through criminal damage and domestic violence, then onwards into the sort of relentless grimness that didn't so much dampen the Christmas spirit as rip it right out of you and kick it to death.

He'd spent Maddie's sixth Christmas telling a mother her son was never coming home.

He's spent her ninth cradling a seventeen-year-old girl whose father had been abusing her for years. She'd bled out before the ambulance arrived, the gashes in her wrists too deep, too determined.

He'd managed to get a day off for her fourteenth Christmas. There was no Santa magic by then, of course. There was no magic at all, in fact, and the day had crawled by in long, uncomfortable silences, and a growing realisation that everything came to an end someday, and that the Logan family unit would be no exception.

It was early days in his new relationship, but he was determined not to make the same mistakes again. There'd be a present.

Not a voucher. Not an envelope of money hand ed over without care or thought. A proper blood y present that thought had gone into.

He just had no id ea, at the moment, what it would be.

'Right, I reckon we swing back by HMV, check Argos, then... fuck!'

He turned at a sud d en jab in his ribs, hand s balling into fists as he pulled them from his pockets.

And sud d enly, there she was. The subject of his Christmas shopping d ilemma, cocooned in warm clothing, a single book-shop carrier bag swinging id ly from one hand .

'Someone's jumpy,' remarked Shona Maguire. She prod d ed him in the belly he'd spent the past few months sweating several inches off, then shot a smile in Sinead 's d irection. 'Hi! Dragged you out shopping, has he?'

'Something like that,' Sinead said , returning the smile and throwing in the slightest suggestion of an eye-roll.

'What are you d oing here?' Logan asked , looking d own at the pathologist like she had absolutely no business setting foot in the place.

'Shopping,' Shona replied . 'Check it out.'

She opened the bag and prod uced a calend ar, all twelve pages of which were d evoted to the singer, Cliff Richard . Cliff sat on a tyre swing on the cover with a lemon yellow sweater tied loosely around his neck, and a smile on his face so wholesome and sincere it could 've shattered concrete at twenty paces.

'It's for my d ad ,' Shona explained . 'He's going away for Christmas, so I'm going to visit him tomorrow to d rop it off.'

'Big fan, is he?'

'Christ, no. He can't stand him. I get him one every year. He hates it.' She gave a little cackle of d elight, and slid the calend ar back into the bag. Cliff's eyes seemed to watch Logan until they vanished out of sight. Even then, the DCI was fairly sure he could still feel the bastard staring.

Shona looked from Logan to Sinead and back again, noting the absence of bags.

'Not find what you're looking for?'

Logan glanced down at his empty hands. 'Uh, no. Still looking.'

'We've been at it a while now,' Sinead added, not quite reproachfully enough for Logan to pick up on it.

Shona shrugged. 'I'm done with mine. I can hang on and help him, if you like? If you want to get off?'

'Eh, well...' Sinead met the senior officer's gaze. It was almost completely blank, like he had n't yet formed any opinion on this suggestion, and so offered her no guidance either way. Bugger it, then. 'Aye. Why not? Need to go pick my brother up, so that'd be great. Thanks!'

She reached up and gave Logan a pat on the shoulder. His blank look was now tempered with confusion, but he wasn't offering anything in the way of an objection.

'Good luck, sir. I hope you find what you're looking for.'

Before he could object, she flashed Shona a grateful smile, stopped short of wishing her luck, then turned and was swept away by the raging torrent of late-night shoppers.

Logan watched her until she was lost among the masses, then tensed when he felt Shona's arm slip around his own. She hung onto him like he was an anchor that would stop her being carried off like Sinead had been.

'So, then,' she began, twirling her bag around on a finger. 'Where do you want to start?'

-

Detective Inspector Ben Forde stood in his dressing gown in the kitchen doorway, slapping a heavy wooden rolling pin into the palm of his hand.

'What bloody time do you call this?' he demanded, as Logan clicked the front door closed behind him.

The cold followed the younger man in, billowing along the hallway like the breath of some asthmatic frost giant, and drawing a shudder from Ben.

8

Logan looked the DI up and d own, pausing momentarily on his angry expression, and slightly less momentarily on the rolling pin.

'What, seriously?' he asked .

Ben snorted . 'No. Jesus, what d o you take me for, your ex-wife?' he said . 'Could n't sleep, so I've been making scones. Just cooling d own now.'

'Now you're talking,' Logan said .

'Dand ruff's getting worse, I see,' Ben remarked .

Logan checked his should ers and brushed off a few big white flakes. 'Heh. Aye. Snow's started .'

He shrugged off his coat and rubbed his hand s together, teasing the blood flow back into his fingers.

'Good night?' Ben called , having alread y returned to the kitchen.

'No' bad , aye,' Logan said . The cold had numbed his nostrils, but the first wee whiff of Ben's scones had triggered the start of a very welcome thaw.

Logan let his nose lead the way, and inhaled d eeply when he stepped into a kitchen filled with the warm, welcoming aroma of fresh baking.

Twelve plump, floury scones sat cooling on a wire rack in the centre of the circular kitchen table. There was a suggestion of ginger hanging in the air, too, and a quick glance through the glass d oor of the oven revealed twenty or more star-shaped biscuits browning nicely in a tray.

'Don't you blood y d are!' Ben warned , as Logan reached for one of the scones. DI Ford e had pulled open the blind s and was gazing out at the falling snow, but he'd known Jack long enough to pred ict his attempts at scone-pilfering. 'Let them settle a bit first, and then you can have one.'

Some part of Logan—either his mouth or his stomach—groaned its objections, but he d utifully pulled out a chair and took a seat at the table, sad and sconeless.

Ben appeared to have frozen in place at the wind ow, his hand s resting on the worktop either sid e of the sink, his gaze fixed straight ahead . Logan could see the old er man's face reflected in the glass. He knew what that faraway expression meant.

'You thinking about Alice?'

Once, Ben would have shaken his head , d ismissed the suggestion, then busied around trying to pretend the moment had n't happened . He'd become more open about his feelings in recent weeks, though, and gave a slow nod in response.

'Like the snow, d id she?' Logan asked .

'Like it?' Ben gave a chuckle. 'Imagine a kid opening the curtains on Christmas Eve to find the place blanketed in the stuff. Imagine all that excitement. All that joy.' He turned from the wind ow. 'Now, imagine the opposite of that. That's how Alice felt about snow.'

'Not a fan, then?'

'Hated the blood y stuff. Could n't stand it,' Ben said , smiling at the memory. 'Always knew when it was snowing, too. Did n't even have to look. She'd elbow me awake some nights just to tell me it had started snowing. If I got up to check, sure enough, it was always d inging d oon. It was her hips, you see? They always ached when the snow came on.' He shrugged . 'That, or she was a witch. It was one or the other.'

Logan had his own suspicions as to which of these alternat-ives was the correct one, but d ecid ed it best to keep his own counsel.

'Shops must've been open helluva late the night,' Ben remarked , giving himself a shake. He shot a very d eliberate look at the area around Logan's feet, then turned and plunged his hand s into the soapy water of the sink. 'And yet, you d on't seem to have bought anything.'

'How d o you know I haven't just left all the shopping in the car?'

'Because you never lock the car in the hope that some bugger nicks it,' Ben said . 'Last thing you're going to d o is leave your Christmas shopping insid e, given how much you hate the whole present-buying experience.'

'Aye, there's no' much gets past you, Benjamin,' Logan said . His eyes had fallen on a pale-coloured crumb that had d ropped from one of the scones onto the tabletop. He pounced on it like a lion on a gazelle, snatched it up, and tossed it into his mouth.

Shite. It wasn't a crumb at all, but a bit of raw d ough. He spat it back out again into his hand , then flicked it vaguely in the d irection of the bin just as Ben turned away from the sink.

'Meet someone, d id we?'

Logan clicked his tongue against the roof of his mouth. 'You spoke to Sinead .'

'I spoke to Sinead ,' Ben confirmed . 'Seemed very excited , so she d id . Said you and the lovely Dr Maguire were going to go off and d o your shopping together.'

'Aye, we bumped into her in the Eastgate,' Logan ad mitted .

'Must've been hard buying her a present when she was with you, I'd have thought.'

Logan nod d ed . 'Aye.' He shook his head . 'I mean, I could n't, obviously. So, we just grabbed a bite to eat.'

Ben picked up a Declaration of Arbroath tea towel and d ried his hand s. 'Oh, d id you now? Go anywhere nice?'

'Everywhere nice is booked up for Christmas nights out. End ed up in Costa.'

'Costa, eh?' Ben said , in a tone that suggested the place was a five-star celebrity-chef-owned restaurant, rather than a somewhat lacklustre chain of coffee shops. 'How nice. Any gossip to report?'

Logan consid ered the question carefully. 'Her d ad 's not a fan of Cliff Richard .'

Ben tutted . 'Aye, well, that's reassuring. At least we now know he's not d eaf,' he said . 'But that's not exactly what I meant.'

'I know exactly what you meant, you nosy old bugger,' Logan said , cutting him short. 'And *none of your bloody business* is the answer to that question.'

DI Ford e chuckled . 'Methinks the lad d ie d oth protest too much.'

'The only thing protesting is my stomach,' Logan said . 'So, finish d rying your hand s and get the blood y kettle on. These scones are no' going to eat themselves.'

Chapter 3

In his fourteen years on the planet, Evan Find lay reckoned he'd made his fair share of mistakes.

There was that time he'd put a rock through the glass of the nursery cold frame, shattering it and completely obliterating the strawberries that had been growing beneath.

The time he'd got stuck on the school roof during the Easter holidays, and had to wait for the fire brigade to get him down.

The time he'd explosively shat himself in Primary 4, in front of the whole class.

All those paled into insignificance beside his latest mistake, though.

OK, maybe not the shitting himself one. But all the rest of them.

It had seemed like such a good idea at the time. At least his mum and dad had made it sound like one.

'Think of the money,' they'd said. 'You'll be able to buy yourself nice things,' they'd said.

That was why he'd applied for the stupid job. That was why he was now sitting on his bike at seven o'clock in the morning, at the bottom of a snow-covered incline, a bag of newspapers threatening to pull him sideways out of the saddle.

He'd never ridden his bike in snow before this morning. To be fair, he'd barely done it this morning, either, his thin tyres refusing to make much in the way of headway, despite his straining legs and occasional outbursts of swearing.

The hill that rose up before him wasn't exactly the north face of the Eiger, but it was steep enough that a knot of dread was settling itself somewhere in the pit of his stomach. School started in less than two hours, and he was barely a tenth of the way through his round . Ped alling up the slope would be impossible, so he'd have to walk, and the snow would be up over his ankles.

For a moment, he contemplated just heaving the whole bag over a hed ge and making a run for it, but he was two d ays away from his first pay packet, and he d id n't want the rest of the week's d eliveries to have been in vain.

Evan swung his leg backward s over the sad d le and grimaced as his foot plunged into the wet snow. With the bag keeping him off-balance, he manhand led the bike over to a lamp post and propped it there, where the circle of orange light would let him keep an eye on it all the way up and d own the hill.

Not that anyone was likely to try cycling away on it through the snow, of course. They'd have much more sense than that.

With the bike securely propped in place, Evan began his climb. There were four houses on this street he had to d eliver to—three on one sid e, and then the fourth was across the road right at the very top where the cul-d e-sac end ed .

He watched his white breath go swirling into the d arkness as he crunched his way up the incline. There had been a fresh d ump of snow overnight, and his were the first footprints of the d ay. The sound they mad e echoed strangely, the blanket of white muffling them, like it had d one to the whole neighbour-hood , and much of the world beyond .

Arriving at the first house, Evan blew on his hand s, enjoyed the warmth of his breath as it was forced through his thin gloves, then reached into the bag he'd swung across his chest.

Mr Fowler. Number 12. The Daily Record and The Sun.

Done.

He trud ged back up the path, stepping back into the same footprints he'd left on the way to the d oor, as if trying to hid e his d irection of travel from some d etermined pursuer.

The gate closed with a faint clack. The marshmallow white-ness swallowed the sound , and Evan continued up the hill, one hand hovering above the gard en fences, read y to grab it if his feet went out from und er him.

A d og barked insid e the next house the moment he opened the gate. It sound ed like one of those small, yappy wee things that spent more time being carried in hand bags than they d id walking. Less a d og, and more a well-trained rat with a superiority complex.

Mrs Marshall. Number 18. The Scottish Daily Mail.

The d og went bananas on the other sid e of the d oor when Evan shoved the paper through the letterbox. He left it sticking through, having learned from experience that pushing it all the way through the d oor meant it would be ripped apart by the rat-d og before it had even properly hit the mat.

He retraced his steps. He closed the gate. He nearly d id the splits in the snow, but found his balance before his legs could fully set off in opposite d irections.

Two more.

On this street, anyway.

Mr Rose. Number 28. The Times.

Evan hesitated at the gate, checking the coast was clear. The house was still in d arkness, which hopefully meant the sole, late-mid d le-aged male occupant was still asleep. He'd come out to 'say hello' a couple of times since Evan had taken over the round , and Evan's skin had almost crawled right off his back both times.

He wasn't quite sure what it was about Mr Rose that bothered him so much. The silky blue d ressing gown that stopped halfway d own his thighs had set some alarm bells ringing. The way he'd brushed his hand s over Evan's fingers when taking the paper from him had n't helped , either.

But it was the way Mr Rose looked at him that mad e Evan most uneasy of all. There was a hint of amusement there, but it was mixed in with something else. Something more urgent. Hunger, maybe.

Mr Rose had invited him in for 'hot chocolate and a blether' both times they'd met. Both times, Evan had declined the offer with a mortified grunt and a shake of his head.

This morning, though, with the cold biting at him and his feet soaking wet, he was worried he might be tempted to say yes. And who knew what that would lead to? *Crimewatch* reconstruction and a tearful TV appeal from his parents, probably.

He tiptoed up the path to be on the safe side, slowly eased open the letterbox just far enough to hold the very end of the tightly-folded broad sheet in place, then he hurried back to the relative safety of the pavement and closed the gate behind him.

Three down, one to go.

Mrs McGavin. Number 27. The Press & Journal.

He liked Mrs McGavin, though he'd never met her. She had taken the time to decorate her house for Christmas, and the twinkling lights cast a jolly lustre across the pure white snow, colouring it in shades of green and red.

As far as Evan could fathom, there were no kids in the house, yet she'd stuck a 'Santa Stop Here!' sign on the lawn, and painted snowflakes on the inside of her windows. She was really putting the effort in.

No doubt, hers would be one of those houses all the local kids rushed to at Halloween, too. As Evan plodded across the road towards the house, he imagined it all decked out in skeletons and ghosts, and the handfuls of sweets she almost certainly dished out.

Did she go so far as to make toffee apples? he wondered.

Yes. He thought she probably did. Cupcakes, too, with little head stones on them, or biscuits shaped like bats. Yeah, he bet all the local kids loved Mrs McGavin, and she probably loved them, too.

He had nothing to base any of this on besides her excessive Christmas lights display, of course. For all he knew, she might be a right nasty old cow who was just trying to annoy Mr Rose on the other side of the cul-de-sac.

If anything, though, that just mad e Evan like her more.

He was almost across the road when he spotted a small mound of snow that the wind must've heaped together just where the road met the kerb. Despite the numbing cold and his freezing feet, he felt the tug of a child ish urge.

Jump in it, it said . When will you get an opportunity like this again?

And it was right. Past-Evan would 've loved the chance to leave his mark on the expanse of virgin snow he'd been stomping through, and probably killed to jump into a knee-d eep snowd rift without Mum shouting at him for messing up his shoes.

Granted , the cold was making current-Evan thoroughly miserable, but he owed his younger self this one. He could n't pass this up.

Altering his trajectory by a d egree or two, Evan approached the mound , stole a look around to make sure no one was watching, then grabbed his bag and held it at his sid e so that the contents d id n't go flying out when he mad e his leap.

When he was absolutely sure he wasn't being observed , he bent at the knees, sprang into the air, and felt a gid d y rush of d elight as his feet plopped d own into the snow.

There was something solid there. Something unexpected . Thrown off-balance, Evan stumbled , sud d enly sprawling toward s the snow-covered pavement.

The snow cushioned his fall, but he felt it soaking him und er his jacket almost immed iately, and hurried ly got to his feet, d usted himself d own, and shook away the worst of it.

As he d id , he turned and looked back at the pile he'd jumped in, trying to figure out what he'd land ed on, and what had ...

His throat went tight.

His stomach twisted .

Down on the ground , picked out in flickering shad es of red and green light, a face stared lifelessly out from beneath a blanket of frosty white.

Chapter 4

'Och, go on. One wee scone won't d o you any harm.'

Logan held a hand up to block Ben as he tried to d eposit the plate on the kitchen table, then gestured to his bowl of muesli, albeit with very little enthusiasm.

'One wee scone might not d o me any harm, but in what world is that a wee scone? You could choke a blood y horse with that.'

Ben regard ed the plate in his hand . He'd warmed the scone a little in the oven, then smeared on jam and a d ollop of clotted cream.

'Breakfast of champions, that,' he objected . He d id the Waft of Temptation with the plate und er Logan's nose. 'Go on. They need used up.'

'I ate two of the blood y things last night,' Logan said .

'One more won't kill you, then.'

Logan gave a shake of his head . 'I'm fine. I've got this.' He shovelled a spoonful of muesli into his mouth and tried very hard not to grimace. 'Besid es,' he continued , if only to take his mind off what was currently happening to his taste bud s. 'You've d one it wrong.'

Ben sat at the table across from him and regard ed the scone on the plate. 'How d o you mean? What's wrong with them?'

'The scones are fine,' Logan said , still masticating what was rapid ly beginning to feel like a mouthful of old card board . 'But you put the cream and jam on in the wrong ord er.'

Ben sat back in his chair, blinking in shock. 'What? What d o you mean "the wrong ord er"?'

'Cream goes first,' Logan said , gesturing to the scone with his spoon, and flicking a few d roplets of milk onto the table.

'My arse!' Ben countered . 'Says who?'

'Says everyone,' Logan replied . 'Cream, then jam. You've gone jam, then cream.'

'Because jam, then cream is the right way to blood y d o it!' the DI insisted . 'Who in their right mind d oes cream, then jam?'

'Everyone! Jam first is a nightmare. It gets crumbs everywhere. You're meant to use the cream like a butter substitute, then spread the jam on top,' Logan explained . 'You would n't put jam, then butter on it, would you? That would be mental.'

Ben was forced to agree that would be mental. 'But it's not butter!' he pointed out. 'It's cream.'

'It's basically butter,' Logan said . 'I mean, it's all just thick milk, isn't it?'

'That's Markies' clotted cream, I'll have you know,' Ben said . 'No' thick blood y milk.'

Logan sniffed . Despite his best efforts, his gaze d rifted d own to the plate on the table between them. 'From Markies, is it?'

'Aye. None of your rubbish,' Ben said .

Logan d ropped his spoon into his bowl with a sullen clink and sighed like he was d oing the other man a favour.

'Fine. I'll eat the blood y scone, if it'll make you happy.'

Ben caught the ed ge of the plate between finger and thumb and pulled it away. 'Hold your horses there, Jack. You're on a d iet.'

Logan caught the other sid e of the plate. 'Like you say, one wee scone won't d o any harm.'

'Maybe not, but the jam and cream are on in the wrong ord er.'

'Don't remind me. But I'm sure I can bring myself to ignore that just this—'

The ringing of their mobiles cut the d ebate short. Both phones jingled into life more or less simultaneously.

Both men knew what that meant.

Logan took his phone from his pocket. He recognised the number on-screen. The station.

'Aye, well, looks like I'm going to have to keep my energy levels up,' he said , then he plucked the scone from the plate, took a big bite, and let the memories of his muesli be smothered by six hund red calories of pure, d elicious d ecad ence.

–

Logan sat hunched forward in the d river's seat of his Ford Fiesta, squinting at the narrow road ahead , and wond ering if he'd somehow put the wind screen blower on the wrong setting.

He had his d oubts that there was a setting that d eliberately fogged the wind screen and mad e it even more d ifficult to see through, but he could find no other way to explain it.

The road ahead was thick with snow, but his was not the only vehicle to have come this way that morning, and he was able to follow in the footsteps—or tyre tracks—of those that had gone before him.

A weak, watery sun was just stretching its head above the horizon over on his right, and the way the light was flickering through the trees was alread y proving annoying. In another car, he'd have ad justed the sun visor so it was blocking the top of the sid e wind ow, but as his head practically stuck up through the roof of this one, there was no space for him to start shifting things around .

He d istracted himself by listing off the things he knew about Alness, which he was currently head ed in the d irection of.

This d id not take long, as he quite quickly conclud ed that he knew precisely fuck all about the place beyond how to spell it, and where it was. And the latter was a very recent d iscovery that he owed to Google Maps.

He imagined it would be rural. Most places in the Highland s were, to some d egree or another, and the further out from Inverness you got, the more likely it was that you'd wind up wad ing through mud d y field s and sheep shit.

Quite how rural, he'd have to wait and see. Ben had said it was a town, but if Logan had learned anything since his move north, it was that what Highlanders considered a town and what everyone else in the country considered a town were often very different things.

Basically, if it had a bus stop and Tesco, it was a town. If it only had a bus stop, it was a village. If it only had a Tesco, it was a bad planning decision by the Highland Council.

That, as far as he could gather, was the main distinction.

The drive was supposed to take just over thirty-five minutes. Given the snow and the fogging of the windscreen, it was more like forty-five when he pulled up at the cordon tape. He jumped out of the car, leaving the engine running and the driver's door open and barely bothering to hide his disgust.

'Morning, sir,' chirped a suspiciously smiley uniformed constable. He was pleased that she'd recognised him without his having to go through the usual palaver of digging out his ID, but she seemed far too cheerful for his liking.

Still, he knew how he could fix that.

'Park that bastarding thing for me, will you?' Logan said, stabbing a finger at the shuddering Fiesta. It wasn't a question. It wasn't really an order either, in fact. It was more like the desperate plea of a man at the end of his tether. 'No chance I'm getting it up that hill.'

Fat clouds of puffy white smoke were billowing out from the exhaust, and the windscreen had clouded over the moment that Logan had opened the door.

He hadn't thought he could dislike the car more than he already did, yet it continued to prove him wrong at every available opportunity.

'No problem, sir,' the Uniform said. She slid into the driver's seat, and slid it forward a full foot until she could reach the steering wheel and pedals. 'I'll put her somewhere safe.'

'Not too bloody safe, I hope,' Logan muttered. He gestured past the cordon tape, to where several sets of polis car lights flashed at the top of a steep hill. 'This way, I take it?'

'Aye, sir. That way,' the Uniform confirmed . She closed the
d oor, revved the engine with an overly heavy right foot, then
went trund ling off through the snow in search of somewhere
to aband on the vehicle.

Logan flexed his fingers. The cold had mad e them stiff, and
they respond ed slowly. Bringing them to his mouth, he huffed
a few warm breaths into his cupped hand s, then d ucked und er
the tape and began the cautious plod up the long, slippery hill.

It was just before nine now, and most of the street seemed
to be gathered at the front wind ows of their houses, peering
up the hill to where the hubbub of polis activity was centred .
Logan met their gazes as he passed , and one by one they all
retreated from the glass, embarrassed at having been caught
rubbernecking.

'All right, boss?'

DC Tyler Neish gave Logan a wave from the top of the hill
and came walking d own the slope a little to meet him.

The d etective constable was d rowning in an oversized parka
that looked to be two sizes too big for him. The furry hood was
pulled up, and Logan could n't d ecid e if he looked more like a
wee boy playing d ress-up with his d ad 's clothes, or some sort of
metrosexual ted d y bear.

'Find the place OK?' Tyler asked .

'No, I'm still d riving around in circles somewhere,' Logan
retorted , unwilling to pass up such an open goal. 'Aye. I got
here OK. No thanks to that blood y car, mind .'

Tyler's gaze shifted momentarily to his own car—an Aud i
A6 Avant that had mad e it up the snowy incline without the
slightest hint of d ifficulty—and then hurried ly changed the
subject.

'Paperboy got a bit of a nasty surprise this morning,' he said ,
falling into step with the DCI as they mad e their way to the
top of the hill, where the road end ed and a thicket of wood land
began. 'Thought he was jumping in a snowd rift, and found out
there was a d eid fella und erneath.'

'Aye, that'll put hairs on your chest,' Logan said , puffing his way to the top of the hill. 'How's he d oing?'

'All right, I think. Teenage boy, so he was putting a brave face on it and not really giving much away, emotion-wise. We got a statement, and Uniform gave him a lift home.'

They stopped at the end of the cul-d e-sac, where two polis cars sat with their engines running and their lights on. Geoff Palmer's SOC team was poking around und er the seven vehicles that were parked facing the houses on either sid e of the street, their white suits turning them into floating faces against the snowy backd rop.

Palmer himself was nowhere to be seen, which almost mad e up for the unpleasant d rive up from Inverness.

'Geoff Palmer's not here,' Tyler said , picking up on the thought. 'He said they d id n't need him to hand le this one.'

Logan looked d own at where two members of the Scene of Crime team were kneeling next to the bod y, carefully brushing the snow away. The d ead man's face gazed lifelessly up at the cloud s d rifting lazily by far overhead .

'No glory in it for him,' Logan remarked . 'Fella probably froze to d eath. Doubt it's a homicid e.'

'Aye, it's looking that way, boss,' Tyler confirmed . 'Smell of booze on him is still hanging about, so it must've been strong. Chances are he got pissed , lay d own, and that was that. I've got Uniform running plates on these cars, but jud ging by the snow on them it d oesn't look like any of them moved much d uring the night.'

'Get an ID from him?'

'No, nothing.'

'No phone? No wallet?'

'They d id n't find anything, boss, no.'

Logan mulled this over for a few moments, then gestured at the surround ing houses. 'Anyone nearby reported anyone missing?'

'No, boss. Uniform d id a quick sweep asking that, and checking to see if any of them saw anything suspicious.'

'And ?'

'Hee-haw, I'm afraid . Although, the fella in number twenty-eight is… well, he's interesting.'

'In what way?'

'The kid —the paperboy—he said he gives him the creeps. Always inviting him in.'

Logan raised an eyebrow. 'Does he ever go?'

'He says no.'

Logan waited for the younger officer to say more. It quickly became clear that this wasn't going to happen.

'Is that it? He invites him in?' he pressed .

'Pretty much. Although, when I went to speak to him, he seemed a bit cagey. Like he was being careful about what he said . Like he was worried he might give something away. He was also a bit… flamboyant.'

'In what way?'

'Just, you know, a flamboyant sort of way,' Tyler said , clarifying precisely nothing.

Turning, Logan surveyed the houses until he found number twenty-eight. 'I'll go have a word in a few minutes,' he said , then he glared at the build ing on the other sid e of the street that had been getting on his nerves since he was halfway up the hill. It was a small bungalow with enough Christmas lights strung across it that it was probably visible from space.

An animated sign flashed the word s 'Ho-Ho-Ho!' at regular intervals across the front of the house. Not entirely appropriate, Logan thought, given the circumstances.

'Who's in that one?' he asked .

Tyler followed his gaze. 'Oh. Some old wifey. Did n't get her name. Sinead 's in talking to her now.'

Logan stamped his feet a few times, d riving the cold from his toes. The house really d id have a lot of lights. An insane amount, some might argue.

It was a tricky business d ecorating the outsid e of a house for Christmas. It was fine to make zero effort whatsoever— Logan's longstand ing preferred approach—but d angle so much as a single external bauble, and you'd set yourself on a very dangerous path.

There was a sweet spot you were aiming for. Just enough icicle lights and stencilled glass to draw admiring glances from passers-by, and the odd gasp of wonder from young children.

Too few decorations, and you'd come across as a miser. Too many, and you were verging into lunatic territory.

The owner of this house had left lunatic territory behind a few thousand watts ago. Lunatic territory was no longer even visible in the rearview mirror.

'You remembering it's Hamza's birthday today, boss?' Tyler asked.

Logan tore his gaze from the house just long enough to give the DC a nod. 'Aye. Plan still the pub after work?'

'Far as I know, aye,' Tyler confirmed.

Logan went back to looking at the house again. He practically felt his pupils contract as they tried to filter out some of the light. 'How long's Sinead been in there?' He asked.

Tyler shrugged. 'Eh, dunno, boss. About...' He consulted his watch, like the answer might be written there. 'Twenty minutes. Maybe a bit longer.'

'A while, then,' Logan remarked.

A flicker of worry crossed Tyler's face. 'Uh, aye. Suppose. Should I go check on her?'

Logan blew on his fingers again. The only gloves he had with him were thin, blue, and elasticated, and would n't do much for keeping the cold away.

'I'll do it,' he said. 'You keep running things out here.'

Tyler's chest swelled. 'Running things, boss?' he said, his face lighting up like one of the bungalow's more vibrant festive decorations. 'Me? You want me to run things out here?'

Logan half-turned as he plodded towards the house. 'There's no' exactly much to run, son,' he pointed out. 'Just keep an eye on the body to make sure it stays dead, and don't make any decisions until I get back.'

'Will d o, boss! I mean, won't d o!' Tyler called . He rocked on his heels in the snow, and pushed back the hood of his parka so he could better see what was going on around him.

A uniformed constable stood at the ed ge of the wood ed area that continued up the hillsid e from where the road stopped . Tyler met his eye.

'What are you d oing, Constable?'

The PC appeared momentarily confused by the question. 'Just stand ing here.'

Tyler nod d ed his approval. 'Right. Good ,' he said , with as much authority as he could muster. 'Well, just… keep it up.'

'Eh… aye. Will d o,' the Uniform confirmed .

DC Neish turned away, put his hand s on his hips, and surveyed his crime scene. His d omain. He was the guy in charge now. The main man. The head honcho.

Obviously, he wasn't allowed to make any d ecisions, which was fine, because everyone basically knew what they were d oing, anyway.

But the point still stood . Right now, while Logan was away, he was the highest-ranking d etective on-site. He, at last, was the big cheese.

'All right, mate?' said Detective Sergeant Hamza Khaled , strid ing up the snow-covered hill. He took a sip from a d ispos-able coffee cup, and completely failed to pick up on the way Tyler's should ers slumped at the sight of him, his moment of glory slipping through his fingers. 'What've we got?'

Chapter 5

The d oor was ajar when Logan reached it, having run the gauntlet of plastic reind eer, flashing signs, and strings of lights that had mad e navigating the house's front gard en something of a nightmare.

He rapped his knuckles hard enough to ed ge the d oor inward s on its hinges, then called into the d arkened hallway.

'Hello? DC Bell? You there?'

No answer.

Something tingled across the back of Logan's scalp.

Nud ging the d oor open further, he stepped quietly into the hall. It was small, cramped , and busy with knick-knacks both festive and everyd ay. A phone table stood across from the d oor, an ancient green rotary phone perched in the centre besid e a stack of BT Phone Books stretching back over a d ecad e.

A knitted Flamenco d ancer—the sort of thing usually most at home d isguising a roll of toilet paper—slouched besid e the stack of books, twenty or thirty porcelain forest animals assembled around the hem of her sagging yellow d ress.

A framed photograph above the phone table showed three men in their twenties. It was an old picture, jud ging by the quality of the image, and by the fashion sense of the young men themselves. Early nineties, maybe. Potentially the tail end of the eighties.

'Hello?'

Besid es the one he'd just come through, there were two d oors lead ing off from the hallway. One was half the wid th of a regular door, so he dismissed it as a cupboard. That only left one viable option.

He knocked lightly, then firmly, then opened the door and stepped through into a living room that may well have been immaculately tidy, were it not for the vast assortment of what he could only describe as 'shite,' that covered every available flat surface.

Whoever the owner of the house was, she—and he would 've been confident it was a she, even if Tyler had n't told him, based solely on what he could see of the room—was a hoarder.

Hundreds of old newspapers and magazines stood in towering piles against the far wall, each one threatening to knock over those around it if the slightest breeze came through.

Shelves and sideboards were crammed with hundreds of tiny figurines—pigs with hats on, penguins on skis, cats, and dogs, and squirrels, and mice, and a whole menagerie of other anthropomorphic delights.

She was a knitter, too. One side of a threadbare tartan armchair was almost completely hidden behind a small mountain of balls of wool, all different colours and thicknesses. A grey canvas bag beside it contained dozens of knitting needles, from long thin ones to short chunky ones, and there was a pile of patterns jammed between the chair and the wall that could keep the knitwear industry afloat for years.

But there was no Sinead. No anyone else, for that matter.

'Hello? PC Bell?' Logan called again, a little louder this time. He picked his way through the chaos of the front room, headed for another door at the back.

As he drew closer, he could hear the radio playing. Zoe Ball, he thought. Radio 2. He could n't make out the words she was wittering, but her relentless positivity managed to set his teeth on edge, all the same.

A crash rang out from beyond the door. There was a flurry of movement. Logan took two big steps, shouldered the door open, and found himself in a good-sized kitchen with a country farmhouse feel, and a smell of strong coffee woven through the air.

A plate of homemad e biscuits sat on the breakfast bar—Santas, and snowmen, and holly wreaths all carefully iced with an unstead y hand .

Logan's gaze went to the sink, where an old woman wearing rubber gloves and a red velour jogging suit stood d rying a cup so d ainty he'd never be able to fit a finger though the hand le.

'Hello,' she said , turning and looking the DCI up and d own. 'Are you with the police, then?'

Before Logan could reply, DC Sinead Bell popped up from behind the breakfast bar, half a plate in one hand , and half in the other. She gave Logan the briefest of smiles, then held the plate halves out for the old woman to see.

'I'm so sorry, my elbow just caught it.'

'Oh, it's fine. It's fine,' said the woman at the sink. 'It's just a plate. I've got hund red s of them. Literally. You should see the loft.'

She set d own the cup, peeled off her rubber gloves with a couple of loud snaps, then reached for a fussy-looking teapot that sat on a metal stand on the worktop.

'Now,' she trilled , peering up at the significantly larger new arrival. 'Are you for tea or coffee? And , so's you know, I won't be taking "neither" for an answer.'

–

DS Khaled and DC Neish stood several feet back while a tall, skeletal figure in tweed knelt on a mat besid e the bod y, muttering d arkly about the weather, his age, and why he'd been d ragged all the way out here for what was almost certainly an accid ental d eath.

Dr Albert Rickett—Ricketts, to pretty much everyone working in the frontline emergency services—had been the lead pathologist at Raigmore hospital for a couple of d ecad es, before begrud gingly accepting that it was time to retire, and letting Shona Maguire take up the reins.

He had n't been able to stay away for long, though, and he now provid ed cover d uring Shona's holid ays, or when she was otherwise unavailable. Usually, that involved checking in bod ies, giving them a quick once-over, then leaving the more in-d epth stuff to his successor, for when she returned .

He was happy d oing that. It kept his hand in, without requiring much in the way of actual effort.

Driving all the way out to Alness in the aftermath of a blood y blizzard , on the other hand , seemed like a lot of effort. A lot of wasted effort, too, given what all the signs were telling him.

'Drunk. Froze to d eath,' he confirmed , his knees creaking as he struggled upright, using the boot of the car for leverage. 'No other obvious injuries, although I d on't want to start taking off any clothes until I'm somewhere warmer and less exposed to the elements.'

Tyler frowned . 'Why would you…?' he began, then he worked it out just a second too late to avoid making a fool of himself. 'Oh, wait. *His* clothes. Right. Aye. That makes more sense.'

Both Ricketts and Hamza regard ed him in silence for a few moments, then simultaneously reached the conclusion that it wasn't worth pursuing the matter any further.

'Dr Maguire is back this afternoon. She can d eal with it then. I d on't think you're looking at anything too sinister, though, just some late-night revelry gone wrong, I'd imagine. You'll probably find he lives somewhere nearby, got himself lost, and sat d own where he should n't. Silly bugger.'

'Aye, probably,' Hamza agreed . He looked d own the hill to where Ricketts had parked his car. 'You be all right getting d own?'

'I've d one eleven Munros and two Alps,' Ricketts sniped . 'I think I can tackle a stroll d own a shallow incline.'

'Suit yourself,' said Hamza. He and Tyler stood by and watched as the pathologist mad e his way d own the slope. At first, he strode confidently—d eliberately so, to prove a point—but as the slope steepened he became less sure of his footing, and picked his way carefully along, leaning on the fences for support.

'He's always a barrel of laughs, isn't he?' Tyler remarked , when the part-time pathologist was safely out of earshot. 'The boss'll be sorry he missed him.'

'Aye. He's a riot, is old Ricketts,' Hamza agreed .

'Tenner says he breaks a hip,' Tyler said , as they watched his cautious d escent.

'That's inappropriate, Detective Constable,' Hamza scold ed , not taking his eyes off the man in the tweed coat. He held a hand out to shake. 'But you're on.'

They watched .

They waited .

'Damn it,' Tyler muttered when the pathologist safely reached his car. He turned to offer an excuse as to why he should n't have to pay the gambling d ebt, but was d istracted by movement at the wind ow of the house across the road .

Number twenty-eight. The fella the kid had talked about.

'Blood y hell. Did you see that?'

'See what?'

'That fella was naked ,' Tyler said , ind icating a large bay wind ow on the upper storey of the house.

Hamza followed Tyler's outstretched finger, but saw nothing at the wind ow besid es the faintest suggestion of a twitching curtain.

'What fella?'

'There was a guy stand ing there in the upstairs wind ow. Stark bollock naked . Like… all on show. Everything.'

'Seriously?'

'Seriously.'

'The whole lot?'

'The whole lot.'

'Full cock and balls?'

'Full cock and balls,' Tyler confirmed . He pulled a face that suggested the sight had been an unpleasant one, yet simultaneously nothing to write home about. 'Bit weird that, isn't it?'

'I mean… I suppose it's probably his bed room.'

'Aye, but he knows we're all out here. It's not like we're sneaking around . I even spoke to him myself about twenty minutes ago. He must've known we'd get an eyeful.'

'To be fair, it was only you who got the eyeful,' Hamza pointed out. 'Maybe it was d one for your benefit.'

Tyler shud d ered , but kept his gaze fixed on the wind ow, certain that the man he'd seen there would peek his head around the curtains again any moment. Hopefully, it would b *just* the head this time, and not the rest of him.

'The kid who found the bod y. The paperboy. He said the guy at number twenty-eight was a bit… creepy.'

Hamza glanced over at the house's front d oor, then up to the still-empty wind ow. 'What impression d id he give you?'

'Bit evasive,' Tyler said . 'Shifty.*Very* gay.'

'How d o you mean?'

'No, I d on't mean he's creepy because he's gay,' Tyler quickly clarified .

'Right. Because it sound s like you were…' Hamza said .

Tyler emphatically shook his head and launched into a hurried explanation. 'No! I was listing things about him, that's all. The kid said he's creepy, that's one thing. I thought he was shifty, that's another thing. And also, he's gay. That's a third , unrelated thing. None of those things are necessarily connected .'

'Sure…' Hamza teased .

'I'm not saying there's anything wrong with being gay. At all,' Tyler replied , his word s tumbling out as a rushed babble. 'But, like, there's gay… which, again, is absolutely fine, obviously. Each to their own. More power to your elbow. But some gay people—not all of them, or even most of them, but some of them, usually guys—are like *gay* gay. Ubergay. Like…' He pursed his lips and waggled his eyebrows suggestively. 'You know? Like... being gay is their whole personality? Like there's nothing else in there except gay?'

Hamza stared blankly back at him.

'You know what I mean?' Tyler asked. He looked slightly hysterical, like he was aware that he might be coming across as homophobic, and was trying desperately hard not to. 'I mean, it's not just gay folk. Imagine if a straight bloke went around just playing up how much he liked having sex with women. Like, all his body language was about conveying that message, and nothing else. Always making jokes and suggestive remarks about shagging birds. Striding about with his chest puffed out to show how manly he is. What would you think?'

'I'd think he was a gay fella living in denial,' Hamza said. 'But plenty of blokes do go about like that.'

'Exactly. And they're all knobs,' Tyler said. 'I'm just saying that flouting your sexuality, whatever it is, gay, straight, or one of the new ones, is a bit... you know. Tiresome.'

'What new ones?' asked Hamza.

'Oh, God. I don't know. There's loads of them now, isn't there?' Tyler said. He smiled a little too keenly, a film of sweat on his brow despite the cold. 'Which, again, is great. Whatever two—or more, or even just one, if that's your thing—consenting adults choose to do in their own homes is none of my business. Fair play to them. Whatever floats their boat. Who am I to— *There the bastard is again!*'

Hamza turned quickly. His eyes locked momentarily with those of a naked late-mid dle-aged man as he stood on display in the near full-length upstairs window. And then, with a swish of a curtain and the flash of an arse, he was gone again.

'No, you're right, that is weird,' Hamza remarked. 'Someone should go and have a word with him.'

Silence hung over the cul-de-sac for a few seconds, then was broken by a tut and a soft sigh.

'You mean me, don't you?' Tyler said.

33

'Well, it's my birthd ay, so I d on't think I should have to d o it,' Hamza said . He gave the DC a pat on the should er. 'And besid es, I can think of no better man for the job.'

Chapter 6

Olivia Maximuke was complaining bitterly when she clumped down the last few steps and headed for the kitchen, where the muted mutterings of the morning radio seeped through the closed door.

'Why didn't you wake me? I'm going to be late now,' she said, wrestling an arm into the sleeve of her school jumper.

The walk from the stairs to the kitchen door was a short one. In the old house, it would've taken a full twenty seconds of striding along corridors and hallways, but the Proceeds of Crime Act had promptly evicted them from that place once her father had been sentenced.

Luckily, there was enough legitimate money in his building company that Olivia's mother had been able to buy this place—a modest two-bedroom semi-detached with a dilapidated conservatory sticking out from the front like the wart on a witch's nose.

They could do that up, she'd said when she'd first showed Olivia around the place. Or knock it down. One of those.

That had been six months ago. They'd done neither.

Olivia threw the door open and stomped in, each thud ding footfall designed to emphasise quite how annoyed she was. Yes, she should've had her alarm on, but she'd turned it off at the weekend and forgotten to turn it back on. And her mum was awake. She was *always* awake these days, it seemed.

It hadn't always been the case. For a while, following Olivia's dad's conviction, her mum had slept most of the day away. It had been her way of escaping the problems they faced. Her own private denial of the imminent collapse of the life she had built on her husband 's d rugs money.

Now that it had all happened . Now that the house was smaller, the car was old er, and the bank balance was a fraction of its previous size, she seemed to be awake around the clock. No matter what time Olivia came home, she was up. No matter how early she rose, her mum was way ahead of her.

At night, she'd sit glued to soap operas, or trashy d ocumentaries about weird illnesses in far-flung foreign countries, and she'd d rink. Wine, usually. Gin, occasionally. Whisky once. That one had been a mess.

In the morning, she'd be hyper. She'd sing and d ance, crack jokes that a) weren't funny, and b) usually d id n't make sense, and make a big fuss about it being a new d ay, full of new opportunities. *This* was the d ay that things would change, she'd insist. *Today*, things would start to get better.

By the time Olivia returned from school, her mum would be parked in front of the telly, alread y on to her second or third glass.

'Seriously, why d id n't you wake me up before—' Olivia began, then she stopped when she saw the figure stand ing at the kitchen island , a cup of coffee in his hand .

Oleg Ivanov. One of her d ad 's Russian relatives.

He was younger than her father by a good twenty years, making him closer to Olivia's age than to her mother's. Right now, he wore a pair of jeans so bad ly ripped they almost certainly cost a fortune, but—asid e from those and the thick gold chain that hung around his neck—he was otherwise completely naked .

Olivia had met him a d ozen or so times before, but she'd never seen him like this. Never this exposed . His torso was thin, but so tightly packed with muscle that he remind ed her of a picture in her science book that showed the male form with all the skin removed .

Of course, those sketched skinless figures generally weren't covered with tattoos. They had been etched across his chest and upper arms, and bloomed up both sides of his neck. The tattoos were made up of words, mostly, written in Russian script that she had never got around to learning. She had a reasonable grasp of the spoken language, but had never studied how to read it.

Something told her that not understanding what was written on Oleg's body was probably for the best.

Olivia had heard them during the night, of course. The grunting. The groaning. The shrieked whispering of his name that had finally forced her to bury her head between two pillows and stare blankly at her bedroom wall until sleep had shown her mercy and welcomed her down into the dark.

That thump-thump-thump of the headboard had happened before. Four times before. Last night was the fifth.

But this? Finding him still around next morning?

This was a first.

'Good morning, *malyshka*,' he said. Every time she'd met him his face had been fixed into a shark's smile. Today was no different. It hoisted up his cheeks, creased his eyes, and seemed to fill the room with teeth. 'Sleep well?'

Olivia blushed and averted her gaze. She suddenly felt like a nervous child. Not in that giddy, lightheaded way that some of the girls in her school would when faced with the sight of a ripped, semi-naked older man, but in a scared, powerless way that stripped her of her voice and made her yearn for a quick escape.

'I asked you a question, *malyshka*,' he said, still pointing that smile at her. He set his coffee mug down on the kitchen countertop with a soft clunk. He wasn't using a coaster, she noticed. Mum always went batshit crazy if Olivia did the same. 'Sleep well?'

Olivia nodded, and hurriedly finished tucking herself in.

'Good. Your mother and I were worried we might have kept you awake,' he said. He didn't look worried. He looked fucking delighted at the idea, she thought.

His English was far better than her father's had been, even though he'd been in the country for far fewer years. They were distant cousins, apparently, although Olivia had never been even close to interested enough to find out to what degree they were related.

Her dad's Russian relatives mostly remained a mystery to her, and that was just the way she liked it.

'I'm going to be late for school. Mum was meant to wake me,' she said, unable to resist getting in the dig.

'She's sleeping.' Oleg winked and tapped the side of his nose. 'I think I tired her out.'

'You're disgusting,' Olivia said. The words were out of her before she could stop them, and she felt her heart leap into her mouth like it was trying, too late, to block their exit.

Oleg laughed. It was a dry, hollow, joyless thing that sounded as if he'd learned it from a book *Pretend to be Human: A Beginner's Guide.*

'You have no idea, *malyshka*,' he said. His smile fell away a little, and he flicked his gaze across her from top to bottom. 'Maybe someday you will. When you're older. Although... I forget how old you really are. You've always looked much younger. Such a little cutie-pie.'

Olivia's cheeks reddened again. Electricity tingled across her scalp and radiated through her skull. She wanted out. Wanted away from him. Out of this room, and this house, and his orbit.

'You're how old now? Fourteen?'

'Thirteen,' she corrected.

'Special age,' Oleg said. 'No longer a child, but not quite a woman. Not yet.'

He stared so intently at her she felt her face burning with a shame she couldn't quite explain.

'I'd better go,' she said.

'No breakfast?' Oleg asked, the smile fully returning. 'Most important meal of the day.'

'I'll get something at school.'

'I could make you something. Cereal. Toast. You need to keep your strength up.' His gaze licked across her. 'Growing girl like you.'

'I'm fine,' Olivia said , turning for the d oor.

'Wait.'

Olivia stopped . Something about the tone had told her this wasn't a request. This was an ord er, and ignoring it would not end well.

She heard the soft slapping of his bare feet on the lino as he approached her from behind .

'I need you to d o me a favour,' he said . 'A little thing, nothing much. But I'll be very grateful.'

Olivia's mind whirred , trying to think up an excuse that would get her out of whatever he was going to ask. Without knowing what it was, though, she d rew a blank.

'After school, I want you to swing by a friend of mine.'

He was stand ing right behind her now. She could feel the heat from him, smell the sweat, feel the tickle of his breath on her hair.

'Why?' she asked , not turning to face him.

'I want you to give him something from me. A package.'

She knew she should n't ask the question. It might be d angerous to ask the question.

She asked it, anyway.

'What kind of package?'

His voice was a whisper in her ear, making her jump.

'That's not important, *malyshka*,' he said . 'You will give him the package, and he will give you one in return. That is all you need to know. But be sure he d oes give you one. Do not give him a d amn thing unless he provid es you with one in return. Got that? These people are sly, manipulative fucks. Give them an inch, and they will bleed you fucking d ry. Und erstood ?'

Olivia nod d ed uncertainly. 'Uh, yeah, but I'm not sure I should be d oing this sort of—'

'Shh. Hush. You are perfect for the job. I have full faith in you, *malyshka*. If you d o me this favour, I'll be *very* appreciative. If you d on't...'

He let the thought hang there for a moment, then stepped back, his voice returning to its normal volume.

'Well, I'm sure you will, so there is no point in us thinking too hard about the alternatives. Am I right?'

He tapped her on the shoulder, forcing her to turn and look at him. A hand was thrust towards her, her schoolbag dangling from his tattooed fist.

'It's at the bottom of your bag. Address is in there somewhere, too. For God's sake—for your sake—don't lose it. Don't let anyone look inside. Not even you.' His grin somehow spread further, until it seemed impossibly wide. 'The less you know, the better. Trust me on this, *malyshka*. OK?'

Olivia gave her bag an apprehensive look, like she'd just been told it contained an unexploded Second World War bomb. He gave it an encouraging jiggle, and she reluctantly took it from him and swung it onto her back, noting the extra weight pulling it down at the bottom.

'Now, repeat what I have told you,' Oleg instructed.

Olivia felt herself shrinking, like a teacher had just asked her to read a book report in front of the class. She fought against it, though, and forced herself to stand tall.

'Take the package to the address. Swap it for the other one. Don't let anyone see. Don't look.'

'And if you get caught, don't mention my name. Understand?' He was still smiling as he cupped her chin in his hand, and brushed a thumb across her cheek. 'Or I will cut out your eyes, and make your mother eat them. Is that clear?'

Olivia blinked back tears. She was damned if she'd give him the satisfaction.

'Good girl,' he said, reading her reply in the expression on her face. 'Now, give your Uncle Oleg a hug.'

He stepped in closer, put his arms around her, and pulled her in tight against his bare chest. She stood there, frozen in fear, the smell of sweat, and smoke, and sex forcing its way up her nostrils and catching in her throat.

His hand   went to the back of her head , fingers tiptoeing through her hair.

'I hope you've enjoyed   this morning as much as I have, *malyshka*,' he said , his voice barely a murmur in her ear. 'Because you and   me are going to be seeing a lot more of each other from here on in.'

Chapter 7

Mr Rose, the man at number twenty-eight, answered the door on the third knock. Tyler, who had immediately taken two steps back after knocking, and was trying to ignore the burning sensation of Hamza's eyes boring into the back of his head from out on the street, was immensely relieved to see the house's occupant was now fully dressed.

Well, not quite *fully*. He had squeezed himself into a pair of tight red shorts and a muscle vest that showed off his impressively taut arms and shoulders. Despite the cold, and at least two visible fungal nail infections, he was wearing a pair of lime green flip-flops on his feet, which would've been impractical for any form of exercise that wasn't a long romantic walk along a moonlit beach.

'Oh, hello again,' Mr Rose trilled, leaning a hand on the door frame. His eyes flashed, and the tip of his tongue flicked across his lips as he looked Tyler up and down.

He was in his mid-fifties, Tyler estimated, but he kept himself in good shape. His hair was combed in a severe side-parting, the colouring so intensely black it could only have come from a bottle, or the heart of a collapsing star.

The bits of his legs visible below where the shorts stopped — so, almost all of them—were covered with a forest of thick curly black hairs. It was like his pubes had spread like a rash, until they'd taken over his thighs and begun working their way south past the knees.

This was a stark contrast to what Tyler could see of his upper body, which appeared to be completely smooth, and devoid of

42

any sort of hair whatsoever, asid e from the crop on the top of his head .

'Could n't stay away, eh?' he said , virtually purring out the word s.

'Um…' Tyler looked back over his should er, only to receive an encouraging d ouble thumbs up from Hamza. The DS was making no attempt whatsoever to hid e how much he was enjoying the moment. 'We, eh, we saw you at the wind ow, Mr Rose.'

'Shush. I told you. Call me Colin. Please.'

'Colin. Right. We saw you at the wind ow, Colin,' Tyler continued . 'You know, with the full… with everything… hanging out.'

Colin gave a little gasp and put a hand to his mouth, his eyes wid e with either horror or glee, Tyler would n't like to say which. 'Good ness. I'm sorry. I d id n't realise you'd be able to see me having a nosy. Always was too curious for my own good , me. My old mum—rest her soul—always said as much. Curious to a fault.' He put the back of a hand to his mouth and leaned closer to Tyler, as if sharing some big secret. 'And we know what that d id to a certain poor old puss-puss, d on't we?'

Tyler had absolutely no id ea what he was talking about, but the last thing he wanted was for Colin to repeat any of it again, so he nod d ed and smiled to suggest he had followed along.

'Right, well, if you could refrain from showing… everything, that would be appreciated .'

'Spoilsport!' Colin said , ad d ing a theatrical wink for good measure.

'Haha,' Tyler said . Not laughed , but said . He started to back along the path. 'Right, well, I'd best go and —'

'I thought of something,' Colin said . 'While you were gone. I thought of something. From last night. It might be useful.'

Tyler stopped by the front gate. 'Oh? What's that?'

Colin pushed the front d oor all the way open and pinned it against the wall in the hallway with one finger. 'Why d on't you come insid e, and   I shall reveal all!' he said , then he smirked . 'Not like that, you naughty boy.'

Tyler stole another look back over his should er at DS Khaled . Hamza was talking to a couple of Uniforms now, and   no longer paying attention.

'Right, then,' Tyler said , scraping together a smile that he hoped   d id n't look quite as artificial as it felt. He started   back along the path toward s the wid e-open entrance. 'Lead   the way.'

--

DI Ford e pulled   on his gloves, took a d eep breath, and   spent a few second s mentally preparing himself for the shock of what was to come.

That d one, he opened   the car d oor, and   all the lovely heat that had   built up insid e it was pushed   asid e by what felt like a swirling sub-zero wind .

'Blood y weather,' he spat, more for the wind 's benefit than his own. Then he swung his legs out of the car, hurried ly closed the d oor, and   d id   a sort of high-kneed   trot across the car park in an attempt to keep his feet out of the icy-cold   snow.

Once, he'd   loved   the snow. Even well into ad ulthood , when it had   turned   d riving anywhere into a massive pain in the arse, and   the joys of snowball fights had   been replaced   by concerns about keeping his socks d ry, he'd   still loved   it.

He'd   loved   the way it cleaned   everything up. The way it muffled   the noise. The way the untouched   pavements after an overnight fall suggested   a fresh new start for the world .

Later, when the cold   had   started   to penetrate his bones, and   worries about wet socks were replaced   by fears of broken hips, he'd   loved   the *idea* of it. He'd   loved   seeing pictures of snow, watching movies or nature d ocumentaries where the world   was clean, and   fresh, and   white.

In recent years, though, he'd   come to d espise it. The sight of it mad e him shiver. Mad e his joints ache. Mad e him long for longer d ays and   warmer climes.

Where once he'd have enjoyed watching from the wind ow as the fluttering flakes alighted on the blanket below, he started to shut the curtains, blocking it out. He could n't feel the snell wind coming like Alice always could , but once it had , he found himself feeling increasingly uneasy until it buggered off again.

The snow in the car park at Burnett Road Police Station was not even the nice crisp white stuff. Cars, and vans, and clumping great feet had been coming and going all night, and the snow was d irty with grit and salt. Patches here and there had melted into slushy pud d les, and Ben ejected a quiet but firm, 'Fuck off!' when his foot unexpected ly found one just yard s from the front d oor.

He squelched into the station's reception, muttering d arkly, showed his pass, then head ed for the lift. Half a d ozen plain-clothes officers and two Uniforms stood waiting for the elev-ator. He wasn't in much of a mood for the squeeze that would ensue if they all piled in, so he d iverted at the last moment, and took the stairs.

The first floor went by without too many problems, assuming you ignored the one wet footprint he left on every second step.

Floor one to floor two was hard er going. There was a wet footprint on every step now, the steepness of the climb forcing him to pause for half a second at every stage of the ascent.

He paused on the second -storey land ing, hold ing onto the hand rail and letting his breath return as he contemplated taking the lift from here.

But, he'd come this far. Walking along the corrid or to the lift, waiting for it, getting in, then going up a single floor felt like more effort than just climbing the next set of stairs, at this point.

Besid es, he was feeling better for the rest. And what was it? Thirteen steps? Something like that.

With a gritting of teeth and a squelching of foot, Ben began to climb.

One.

Two.

Three.

No bother.

Four.

Five.

Six.

Easy does it.

He stopped   again. Close to halfway, but his lungs felt od d ly empty, and   the stairs weren't quite staying still.

Seven.

Eight.

Nine.

Another stop.

A pain. Not sharp. Not urgent.

Not yet.

A tightness, more than anything, that rad iated   from the centre of his chest and   mad e his left arm feel clumsy and   thick.

'Bastard ,' Ben whispered , rubbing his chest with the heel of his hand .

He was aware—too aware—of his heartbeat. It wasn't just confined   to its usual spot, but reverberated   around   insid e his head , and   his hand s, and   all the way d own to his feet. Loud Fast. Unstead y.

'Oh no you blood y d on't,' he said , although quite who he said   it to, he could n't exactly say. It d id   the job, though, and   he raised   a leg, planted   the wetter of his two feet, and   continued .

Ten.

His weight pressed   on the hand rail, creaking the wood .

Eleven.

Something rippled   at the ed ges of the world , send ing shapes scurrying up the walls.

Twelve.

He was a step away. One step, but there was no breath left in him now. Nothing more to give.

He thought of Alice. He thought of all those years they'd had together.

And , if his church was right, all the time they'd have again.

But not yet. Not tod ay.

There was too much still to d o.

Slowly, with his bones creaking and fire scorching his chest from the insid e out, DI Ford e tightened his grip on the hand rail, and lifted his foot off the step.

–

Logan spent all of five second s looking at the framed photograph he'd been hand ed , nod d ed in a half-hearted show of enthusiasm, then passed it across the table to Sinead .

'Aw, they're lovely,' Sinead said , smiling at the two young girls in the photograph. They were eight and four. Stella and Joy. She knew this because Mrs McGavin had told her all about her grand child ren three times alread y.

'Stella—she's the big one—and Joy. Eight and four. Aren't they beautiful?'

'Beautiful,' Sinead agreed . She hand ed the photograph back to Logan, who had absolutely no id ea what to d o with it, so just set it face-up on the table between them. With the other hand , he picked up the flower-shaped cup that Angela McGavin had presented him his tea in. It was completely engulfed by his hand , lost among the big fleshy fingers like a child 's toy.

'They're Martin's girls. They're wond erful. Course, Martin had a big hand in that. I always knew he'd make a good father. You can tell, can't you? When they're growing up. You can just tell.'

'He must be very proud ,' Sinead said , taking a sip of her tea.

'Dead .'

Both d etectives spluttered into their d rinks.

'Sorry?' asked Sinead .

'My Martin. He's dead. Eight months now,' Angela said. Her fingers traced across the glass of the photo frame, like she could stroke the faces of the girls trapped beneath it.

Logan cleared his throat. 'I'm sorry to hear that, Mrs McGavin. Do you mind me asking what happened?'

'Cancer. Lungs, kidneys, liver. Everywhere, really. And him not a smoker, either. Never touched them. Or the booze. None of my boys were ever into that sort of thing. Partying. Drinking. What have you. Well, maybe Rory. He goes off the rails some-times, but not Bertie. He has his own office!' She announced that part proudly, like there could be no better testament to a man's upstanding character than an office of his own. 'And not Martin. Never. Not my Martin.'

She fished a scrunched up tissue from the sleeve of her cardigan, dabbed at her eyes, then blew her nose. It made a sound like a battered trumpet.

'Goes to show, doesn't it? You can do everything right, you can follow all the rules, but if it's your time, then it's your time. Simple as that. What's for you won't go by you. Rightly or wrongly, good or bad.'

Logan was an old hand when it came to talking about death. Were he to look back, he thought, he'd probably be thoroughly depressed by how much of the past decade or more had been spent on the topic.

The deaths he was used to tended to be more recent, though. More violent and visceral. He'd been forced to get comfortable with breaking bad news to anxious husbands, parents, even children. He could do that, no problem. Quite what it meant for his eternal soul, if such a thing existed, he had no idea, but he could do it, no problem.

For all his experience, though, Logan wasn't quite sure what to say to the teary-eyed old woman sitting across the kitchen table now, several months after her son had shuffled off this mortal coil. So, he offered up his best comforting smile, nodded to suggest that he agreed with her philosophy, then took another sip of his tea and hoped Sinead jumped in.

'That must've been an awful thing to go through, as a parent,' DC Bell said , much to Logan's relief. 'I hope you had plenty of support.'

'Thank you. Yes, plenty. My other boys rallied round . Friend s. Neighbours. Everyone was lovely,' Angela said . She blew her nose again, then gave her head a shake. 'Anyway, I'm waffling. Sorry. Just not often I get company these d ays. What was it you said you wanted again?'

Logan gulped d own his tea, then shot Sinead a sid eways glance. 'You haven't told her?'

'I, eh, I haven't had a chance, sir,' Sinead explained , a smile fixed across her face. 'Mrs McGavin and I have just been having a nice chat so far. I was just trying to bring us around to the reason for the visit when you came in.'

'Right. I see,' said Logan. He was far less skilled at hid ing his impatience than Sinead was. Or, it might have been that he just mad e less effort. 'We were wond ering if you heard or saw anything unusual last night, Mrs McGavin.'

'Unusual?'

'Outsid e, I mean,' Logan clarified . 'Probably later d uring the night, or in the early hours of the morning.'

'Oh. No. I'd have been asleep by then. Lights out by ten. Well, except the Christmas lights. They stay on all night. It's expensive, but it's festive, isn't it? It's only once a year.' She gave a mischievous little giggle and a shrug, as if leaving her Christmas lights on was the naughtiest thing she'd ever d one in her life. 'Why d o you ask? What's this about?'

'I'm afraid a young man was found outsid e your...'

The word s tailed away. He glanced at the photograph on the table, then quickly scanned the walls, checking for other family photographs, but find ing none.

'Wait. You said that, besid es Martin, you have two sons, Mrs McGavin?'

'That's right. What about them?'

Logan's chair gave a creak as he ad justed his weight on it. A quick glance at Sinead told him she'd realised where his questioning was going, and that she d id n't like it any more than he d id .

He thought of a bod y lying out there in the snow, yard s from Angela's front d oor.

A young man, his id entity currently unknown.

'Do you mind me asking what they look like?'

Chapter 8

'You all right there, Ben?'

DI Ford e took a backward s step, bringing him into the d oorway of Detective Superintend ent Mitchell's office. The DSup had got up from where she'd been sitting behind her d esk, and was halfway toward s him when she spoke again.

'No offence, Detective Inspector, but you look blood y awful.'

Ben managed a thin smile. 'Aye. It's this blood y cold . Plays havoc with the old bones,' he said . 'Cup of tea and a wee Garibald i and I'll be right as rain.'

Mitchell looked unconvinced . 'You're sure that's all it is? You're sweating.'

'Took the stairs,' Ben explained . 'Probably should n't be running up them at my age.'

'That's why the good Lord gave us elevators,' Mitchell said . 'Still, good to challenge ourselves once in a while.'

Ben nod d ed his agreement, although he had no blood y intention of challenging himself like that again anytime soon.

'Right, well, you go take a seat. I'll bring you a cuppa.'

'Och, no. You're fine,' Ben protested , but the Detective Superintend ent was having none of it.

'I wanted a catch-up, anyway,' she said , then she poked her head out of the office, glanced in both d irections along the corrid or, and let him in on a secret. 'And besid es, I've got a packet of Wagon Wheels in my d esk d rawer, and I've been d ying for a good excuse.'

Ben ran a hand across his chin, contemplating this. 'Wagon Wheels, you say?' He flexed the fingers of his left hand , and was relieved that they felt the right size again. 'How can I say no to an offer like that?'

—

She mad e a good cup of tea, Ben would give the Detective Superintend ent that.

Mitchell had brought both mugs in on a little round tray, with a d ainty jug of milk and a bowl of sugar cubes. Never, in all Ben's d ays at Burnett Road , had he seen a milk jug or a sugar bowl. And he *definitely* had never seen the set of tongs that stuck up from the haphazard stack of white and brown cubes.

Wagon Wheels? Now, that was more familiar territory. He'd always been partial to a Wagon Wheel, and he was quietly confid ent that a thorough search of his d esk would find half a packet carefully tucked insid e a ring bind er in the bottom d rawer.

They were a small luxury, but the boost they provid ed —both sugar and morale—had got him through many an all-nighter over the years.

Detective Superintend ent Mitchell was clearly no fool, as she had n't brought the whole pack with her. Instead , she'd brought them one each, and presumably secured the rest of the packet und er lock and key.

Biscuits were as much a currency in a polis station as cigarettes were in prison. It was amazing how half a packet of custard creams and a Kit-Kat could cut through red tape and grease the wheels of an investigation.

Sure, Rich Teas and Digestives got band ied around without any real thought. Anyone could get their hand s on those. Move up the biscuit lad d er, though, and everything became load ed with significance.

Offer someone a ginger nut, and you had their attention.

Wee bit of shortbread ? You had them onsid e.

Ask a room full of burly detectives if anyone fancied a chocolate finger? You'd never hear the end of it.

It had taken poor Tyler months to live that one down.

But a Wagon Wheel—particularly the jam-filled variety Mitchell had brought into play—that was a real power play. Either she had bad news, or she was after something big.

Going against all his instincts, Ben left the biscuit untouched in its wrapper when Mitchell decanted it and his tea from the tray onto his desk.

'How are you feeling now?' she asked, a note of concern in her voice. Evidently, Ben had looked as bad as he'd felt, and his attempts to hide it had been largely unsuccessful.

'Right as rain,' he insisted.

And he was. Mostly. The pain had passed, the vice-like grip on his chest was gone, and air was flowing in and out of him more or less exactly as it was meant to.

What he wouldn't tell her—what he likely would never tell anyone—was that the fear remained. The sense that a countdown had been started, ticking off the minutes, chipping away at the time he had left.

It had been a heart attack that had taken his father. Ben had outlasted him by more than a decade at this point.

His mother had gone to cancer, but not before heart problems of her own had left her practically housebound for years.

It was inevitable, he thought. It had always been inevitable.

But it hadn't been imminent until now.

'Well, if you're sure…' Mitchell said.

Ben could tell she was reluctant to drop the subject, but she clearly knew him well enough to understand that pressing him on it wasn't going to get her anywhere.

'Honest. I'm fine,' he said, taking a sip of his tea.

There was no danger in that. Unlike biscuits, tea—and all other hot beverages, in fact—was given and received freely, with no conditions implied or inferred. It was widely accepted that only a monster would use tea as a bargaining tool. It just wasn't d one. A cup of tea committed you to nothing and no one. Well, nothing except the obligation to somed ay return the favour, and that was just common d ecency.

Mitchell caught one of the other Incid ent Room chairs by its high back, wheeled it over to Ben's d esk, then turned it around and sat d own.

'Not eating your Wagon Wheel?' she asked , ind icating the still-wrapped snack with a glance.

'Well, that d epend s,' Ben said . 'What's it going to cost?'

A smile tugged one corner of Mitchell's mouth momentarily upward s. She und erstood the currency of biscuits as well as anyone. Of course, a Wagon Wheel would be viewed with suspicion.

'Nothing too onerous,' she said . 'I just wanted to ask your opinion on something.'

Ben d id n't make a move toward s the biscuit.

'And what might that be?' he asked .

'Detective Constables Neish and Bell,' Mitchell said . 'Specifically, them working together.'

'Ah.'

'I'm concerned it could become a problem.'

'Are you?'

Mitchell nod d ed . 'I am. Aren't you?'

'No,' Ben said . It was firm. Emphatic. Decisive.

'No? That's it? No? They're a young couple, planning on getting married ,' Mitchell said , in a tone that implied this was somehow breaking news. 'You're not worried they might argue? Fight? Fall out?'

'Of course they will,' Ben replied . 'They alread y argue.'

Mitchell mad e an open-hand ed gesture, like her point had just been mad e for her.

'Have you listened to this team when it gets going?' Ben continued . 'I mean, Christ, I spend half my d ay telling Jack he's an arsehole, and the other half listening to him telling me likewise. Tyler and Hamza rip the pish out of each other something chronic. Sinead can be a right sarky cow when she wants to be, and even the new boy—Dave—isn't afraid to have a go at any of us, if a go is what need s to be had .'

Fuck it, thought Ben. If this was all she was after, he was opening his Wagon Wheel. He tore into the wrapper, then took a bite before continuing.

'Am I worried about Sinead and Tyler arguing? No. I'd be worried if they d id n't. This team is not afraid to fight amongst itself. That's not a bad thing, it's a positive. It's what makes it work,' the DI explained . 'Those two are professional, talented officers. They work well together, and they work well with the rest of us, and while it's not for me to make the call, if you try to shift one of them elsewhere, you'll have a d amn sight more than one vacancy to fill.'

He stuffed another bit of biscuit in his mouth to stop himself saying anything more.

'Is that a threat, Detective Inspector?'

Ben chewed , swallowed , then shook his head . 'It's a statement of fact, ma'am.'

Mitchell took a long, slow sip of her tea, her d ark eyes fixed on those of the man on the other sid e of the d esk.

Finally, she ran her tongue across her teeth, nod d ed curtly, and rolled back in her borrowed chair.

'Well. I'll take that on board ,' she said , stand ing. 'Thank you for your time and your insight, Ben.'

'Thank you for the tea and the Wagon Wheel,' Ben replied . He had watched Mitchell return the chair to where she'd found it before a thought struck him. 'Oh, and ma'am?'

'Yes?'

'Those things I said about DC Neish? The compliments?'

'What about them?'

'Maybe d on't tell him, eh? Don't want to give the boy a big head , or anything.'

Mitchell smiled , then tapped the sid e of her nose. 'Very well, Detective Inspector. Your secret is safe with me.'

Chapter 9

Neither of Angela McGavin's sons matched the description of the dead man outside. She'd given them both a quick call to check they weren't lying dead in the street outside, and they had both been pleased to report that they weren't.

Logan had been relieved about that. Much as he'd like to get an ID on the body, the old woman had gone through enough losing one son, without adding another to her list of woes.

With that cleared up, they'd quizzed her again on whether she'd witnessed anything unusual the night before—seen anyone roaming around, or heard any sort of commotion—but she'd told them she hadn't. She'd been tucked up in bed, fast asleep, she'd said, then had launched into a detailed monologue about her sleeping habits that had only ended when Logan faked receiving a phone call.

They'd made their excuses and left then, both him and Sinead politely declining the offer of more tea and biscuits as they'd made their break for the door.

By the time they'd made it back out onto the street, the body was being taken away in an ambulance, and SOC were packing up their gear.

'That was quick,' Logan said, as he and Sinead joined Hamza on the pavement across the road.

A uniformed constable caught Sinead's eye from the other side of the road. He gave her a nod, but something about his expression made her uneasy.

His name was Jason... something. Hall? Yes, that sounded right. They'd crossed over in training back in the day, and had vaguely got to know each other in passing. The last time they'd spoken, it had been clear that he resented her moving to plainclothes before him.

She'd shrugged off the stick he'd given her over it, and ignored his snidey comments, but the way he was looking at her now sent the suggestion of a shiver down her spine.

Of course, the fact that it was bloody freezing and blowing a hoolie wasn't helping, either.

She nodded back, then turned to face the others in time to see Hamza glancing at his watch.

'Don't think you were that quick, sir,' the DS said. 'You were actually in there for quite a while. Been a wee while since I arrived, anyway.'

'I meant Scene of Crime. Didn't expect them to be done for an hour or two yet,' Logan said. 'Happy Birthday, by the way.'

'Happy Birthday,' Sinead said.

'Thanks. Nice of you to lay all this on for me,' he said, gesturing around. 'Far better than a birthday breakfast with the family, this.'

'You know us, Detective Sergeant. Always willing to go that extra mile,' Logan said.

Hamza chuckled, then turned his attention back to the SOC team. 'Anyway, they think they've got pretty much everything they can get. It's not being treated as a priority. Ricketts came out and checked the body over. Reckons the guy got drunk and fell asleep in the snow.'

Logan glanced down at the area where the body had been lying. 'Daft bastard,' he sighed.

'Not even a week before Christmas, too,' Sinead added. She shook her head, saddened by the thought of it. 'I wonder if he had a family?'

'Someone will be missing him somewhere, I'm sure. Any sign of his ID?' Logan asked.

Hamza shook his head. 'Not that anyone's told me, sir, no.'

Logan sucked in his bottom lip, then spat it out again. 'Right. Bit odd that. Who goes on a night out without their wallet?'

'You thinking he might've been robbed , sir?' Sinead asked .

'Maybe. Or it might've fallen out of his pocket.'

He looked around at the thick snow that covered the cul-d e-sac and the road lead ing up to it. More flakes had just started to fall. They shone in the glow of the street lights as they d rifted to the ground .

The forest that started just beyond where the road stopped had been almost completely blanketed in white. The trees— mostly evergreens and conifers—now appeared to have been carved from marshmallow, all soft, and fluffy, and plump.

A young man in a white paper suit trud ged past the d etectives on the way to the SOC team's van. Logan checked his watch. A little after nine. He tutted , and clicked his fingers to catch the attention of the man as he passed .

'Here. Son. What are you d oing?'

'We're, eh, we're packing up. We're pretty much d one.'

'No' yet you're not,' Logan said . 'I want this place properly searched . His wallet might be around here somewhere, and we d on't know yet what happened to him.'

'I thought...' the SOC man glanced at Hamza, then back to Logan. 'I thought he got pissed and fell asleep?'

'Clairvoyant, are you?' Logan d emand ed .

'Uh, no. No, it's just Mr Rickett said —'

'I d on't care what that old bugger said . We d on't know for sure what happened to him yet,' Logan said . 'So, until we d o, I want this place given the fine-tooth comb. Is that clear?'

'But, Geoff... I mean, Mr Palmer, he said —'

'I could n't give a shite what Geoff Palmer said , either. We've got a young man d ead . No d oubt, we've got a family some- where whose lives are about to be turned upsid e d own. We take this seriously, and we d o it properly. That clear?'

'Uh, yeah. Yes. Clear,' the SOC man said . 'I'll just...'

He crept past them again, like he was trying not to be seen. Logan watched as he joined the rest of his team, then saw the hand ful of d irty looks that got thrown his way.

'They don't look happy at that, sir,' Sinead remarked.

'Tough luck,' Logan said. He looked around, it finally dawning on him that something was missing from the scene. 'Where's Tyler?'

A smile tugged up the corners of Hamza's mouth. 'Well, sir, it's funny you should ask...'

–

'Don't worry about the smell. It's not weed. It's all legal stuff,' said Colin Rose, leading Tyler into a living room that was thick with the sickly-sweet smell of dope. 'I've got receipts for it all. From Amazon, believe it or not. Amazing what you can get from there, these days.'

Tyler entered, then stopped and stared at the decor of the room around him.

Colin Rose's living room was like some lovingly constructed shrine to Colin Rose himself. It wasn't quite what Tyler had been expecting, but mostly because his imagination wasn't that good. Even if it had been, he would 've drawn the line long before this, unable to believe that anyone could go quite this far.

Three of the room's four walls were painted in a uniform shade of grey, with a single feature wall having been coloured a dark, brooding burgundy. It was on this wall that a framed portrait of Colin hung. In the painting, Colin was dressed —or, more accurately, undressed —like Tarzan, and sat astride a giant tiger.

The background was a jungle scene, complete with birds, monkeys, and at least one non-native red squirrel, who all looked almost as flabbergasted by the whole scene as Tyler was.

'You like it?' Colin asked, spotting the DC's open-mouthed reaction. 'I think it's quite breathtaking. A friend of mine did it for me a year or two back. It represents virility. Passion. The animal in all of us.' He curled a hand like it was a set of claws, made a 'mrreow' noise, then indicated for Tyler to take a seat on one of the two white leather couches, both of which were wrapped in wipe-clean plastic.

'It's, eh, it's big,' Tyler said , which was about the kind est thing he could think to say about the artwork. 'It's really big.'

'You talking about the painting or my loincloth?' Colin asked , then he sniggered and gave a d ismissive wave. 'Kid d ing Strike that from the record , if you please.'

Tyler lowered himself onto the couch, and almost slid straight off the front of the cushion. It crinkled and crackled as he eased himself back on the slippery plastic, his eyes d arting around at the rest of the room, and the various Colin Rose related memorabilia that ad orned the place.

Mostly, it was just framed photographs. There was Colin d ancing on the table at a pub. There was Colin posing at the gym. There was Colin looking d eep in thought, yet ever so slightly whimsical in a staged stud io shot.

Over on the far wall, right besid e what Tyler guessed was a sixty-inch TV, a large 'Colin collage' had been formed from d ozens of smaller photographs, all assembled together behind a single glass frame. They showed Colin through the ages, from a young man in his early twenties, through a mostly mousta- chioed thirties and forties, and up to the mid -fifties Lothario who lounged on the sofa across from Tyler now.

Even without all the images of himself staring out from the walls, the living room would 've been almost unbearably tacky.

A faux leopard skin rug was spread on the floor between both couches. A small but ornate chand elier hung from the ceiling in the centre of the room, so low that anyone above average ad ult height would be forced to mind their head when passing und er it.

Right now, the chand elier was switched off, and most of the light came from four artificial cand les that were fixed to the walls at each corner of the room, their electric flames flickering unconvincingly in their patterned glass sconces.

Tyler could only assume that the look of the room was some sort of d esign statement. Quite what that statement was, he d id n't feel qualified to say, but 'Should 've gone to Specsavers' was a d istinct possibility.

'So, eh, you said you remembered something, Mr Rose?'

On the opposite sofa, the other man waggled a reproachful finger. 'Tut tut, Detective. I told you. It's Colin.'

'Sorry. Colin.'

Colin smiled , and ran a hand through his slicked -back, black hair. 'Only my stud ents call me "Mr Rose",' he said . He slowly crossed one leg over another, like some nightmarish alternate reality version of Sharon Stone, and Tyler hurried ly d arted his eyes to the ceiling to avoid seeing anything that might otherwise haunt him for the rest of his life.

'You're a teacher?' he asked , taking his notepad from his pocket.

'I *was* a college tutor for... oh, more years than I'd care to recount. All behind me now, though. Free agent.' He slapped a hand on a hairy bare thigh and gave it a rub. 'Would you like a d rink, by the way?'

'No. I'm fine. Thank you,' Tyler said . 'If you could just tell me what it is you remembered about last night...'

Colin nod d ed . 'Right. Yes. Of course. Well, last night I had a couple of...' He tilted his head from sid e to sid e, as if trying to shake loose the right word .*Friends* over. We had a nice meal, a few d rinks, had ... some fun, and then they called a taxi around four.'

'This morning?'

'Yes. It turned up around four-fifteen, I think. Although, I'd had a few, as I say, so I can't be completely sure on that. Jamie-Leigh and Eleanor will be able to tell you for sure, though.'

Tyler looked up from his notes. 'Jamie-Leigh and Eleanor?'

'My... guests,' Colin replied .

'They're women?'

Colin smiled , but his eyebrows d ipped slightly in confusion. 'Last time I checked , yes.' He put the back of his hand to his mouth again, and spoke in a stage-whisper. 'Which was last night!'

'Oh.' Tyler looked down at his notepad, then back up at the man sitting across from him. 'Oh. Right. So, your relationship with them is… what? Romantic?'

Colin snorted. 'I wouldn't call the sort of things we get up to *romantic*, exactly, no. Let's just say they're friends with benefits.' He winked. *Lots* of benefits, if you know what I mean?'

Tyler wasn't entirely sure he did know what Colin meant, but wasn't convinced that he wanted to, either.

'Right. Gotcha,' he lied. He started writing a note, realised he had absolutely no idea what it should say, so ended up just doing what he hoped was a convincing scribble. 'And they're *both* definitely women, you said, yes?'

'Both very much women,' Colin confirmed. 'Although, I'm fairly certain Jamie-Leigh has some animal in her. Lioness, maybe. Or bunny! If you know what I'm saying?' He grinned and pointed at the dumbfounded DC. 'Aah! He knows! He knows what I'm saying!'

Colin slapped a hand on his thigh again. The crack of it almost made Tyler drop his pencil.

'Right. So… your two guests phoned the taxi and were leaving around quarter past four…' the DC prompted.

'That's right. I went to the door, kissed them goodbye, waved them off, and that's when I saw the two fellas outside.'

Tyler's ears pricked up at that. 'Two fellas?'

'Walking along. Stumbling, really. Holding each other up. They were heading up the hill, walking right in the middle of the road. Had a good shot in them, judging by their stagger. I called out to them—just being friendly—but I don't think they heard.'

'Did you see where they went?' Tyler asked.

'No. Afraid not. The snow was getting heavy, and … well, I didn't have much in the way of clothes on, so I came back inside.'

'Could your friends have seen where they went?' Tyler asked.

'Those two? I doubt it. They can't hold their drink like I do. I'd be surprised if they can remember getting in the taxi.' Colin shrugged . 'I can give you their numbers, though. You can ask them yourself.'

'That would be useful, thanks,' said Tyler. The revelation that they were women was still one he was struggling to come to terms with, and he d id n't think he'd quite believe it until he met them in person. 'And the number of the taxi company, too, if you have it?'

'It'll be on my phone,' Colin said , somehow managing to prod uce a sizeable iPhone from a tiny front pocket in his shorts.

He read out the number for Tyler to write d own, then started read ing out a second number before appearing to lose all interest.

'Here, that's Jamie-Leigh,' he said , hold ing the phone out for Tyler to read the number himself.

Tyler was more interested in the picture above the contact information, though. Jamie-Leigh was in her mid -twenties, he'd say, with a mass of carefully styled blond e hair, and some smoky blue eyeshad ow that mad e Tyler think of Ancient Egypt.

Her lips were painted scarlet red , slightly parted to show just a hint of her tongue. Her skin was flawlessly smooth, with cheekbones that would 've turned the front cover of *Vogue* green with jealousy.

'This is Jamie-Leigh?' Tyler asked , glancing from the woman on the screen to the fifty-something man on the plastic-wrapped couch.

'That's her, yes. She got the brains, Eleanor got the looks.'

He leaned over and swiped the screen, and another young woman slid in to replace the first. Somehow, against all reason, this one was even more attractive than the first.

Something insid e Tyler wanted to shout. To scream. To d emand *'What the hell is going on?!'* at the top of his voice. Them. Him. How was this happening? How was that a thing?

Was it hypnotism? Blackmail? Had he taken their families hostage? What other possible explanation could there be for *those two women* to d o whatever it was they'd been d oing with

63

the mid d le-aged , self-obsessed , hair-d yeing, heebie-jeebies-ind ucing, too-tight-shorts-wearing, lounge lizard who sat reclining on the opposite couch?

He d ecid ed not to d well on it. That way mad ness lay. Instead he scribbled d own both numbers, shot another look of d isbelief at the breathtakingly beautiful woman on-screen, and hand ed the phone back.

'Thanks. That's really useful,' Tyler said . He tapped his pencil against his pad . 'And , just to be clear for the record s, it's a sexual relationship you have?'

'Almost exclusively, yes,' Colin confirmed .

'With both of them?'

'Yes.'

'At... the same time?'

Colin shrugged . 'Not always. Usually, though, yes.' He walked two fingers along the back of the couch and let his mouth play up into a smile. 'Does that trouble you, Detective? I assure you, we're all consenting ad ults. Consenting, and very willing. And we're always open to...' He gave Tyler another once over with his eyes. '...new things.'

Tyler's knees straightened like they were on springs, snapping him upright into a stand ing position. 'Right. Well, thank you for all your help, Mr Rose.'

'Colin.'

'We'll follow up with both women and the taxi company,' Tyler continued , practically sid e-stepping toward s the d oor. 'If we need any further information, someone will be in touch.'

'Aren't you going to leave me your number?' Colin asked , peeling his bare skin off the sofa's plastic wrapper with a series of 'shhhlk' sound s. 'In case I think of anything else?'

Tyler blew out his cheeks. 'I'd just call 101. That's probably easiest, all round ,' he said .

'Should I ask for you personally?'

'Or anyone. Just... they'll take your d etails. Someone will be...' He patted his pocket where his phone was, and cocked his head like he'd heard it ring. 'Oh. That's me. Duty calls. Nice to meet you.'

His eyes fell on the Tarzan portrait. He thought about what sights that poor tiger must've seen, and became excruciatingly aware of how wipe-clean those couches must be. He managed , with some effort, to contain a shud d er.

'I'll, eh, I'll see myself out,' he said .

And with that, he was gone.

Chapter 10

'Late again, Ms Maximuke?'

The head teacher's intonation suggested that this was a question, but they both knew full well that it wasn't. It was almost nine-thirty. She was just entering the build ing. Her lateness was a statement of fact.

'Yes, sir. Sorry. Slept in,' Olivia said . That part was true, at least.

She was achingly aware of the bag on her back, and had walked to school clutching the strap on her should er so tightly that her knuckles had turned white and her hand had started to cramp up. She could n't risk someone grabbing it off her, even though part of her had hoped for exactly that. For the bag to be someone else's property, someone else's concern.

But she knew that could n't happen. That would only amplify the problem, not take it away. She d id n't know for sure exactly what was buried d own at the bottom of the bag, but she knew it was nothing good .

And she knew that failing to d rop it off would bring serious consequences.

She was pretty sure the head teacher's name was Mr Monroe. She had n't had many d ealings with him yet, thankfully, beyond a quick meeting in his office with her mum a week before she'd started .

He had seemed nice. That was her lasting impression of the meeting. She had n't wanted to like him—generally speaking, she d id n't want to like anyone—but he'd been friend ly, had managed to make her laugh, and seemed genuinely interested in making her transition to the new school as painless as possible.

He didn't have children of his own, he'd told them, so he considered the pupils at the school his surrogate family. Their care was his number one priority, and despite her natural cynicism, Olivia had believed every word.

His office had been full of trophies, which she'd initially assumed belonged to the school, but had since discovered were his own personal collection. Despite being ancient—he was at least fifty, she reckoned —he was a champion cross-country runner. This was pretty much the most pointless sport Olivia could think of, but she hadn't dared say that to anyone, because the other pupils all seemed weirdly impressed by it. Her English teacher had made a joke about it once, and while she'd laughed, it hadn't gone down very well with the class.

Olivia couldn't remember that teacher's name. She was still relatively new to this school, and was still getting to know who everyone was.

Everyone knew who she was, of course. The papers and TV news reports about her dad's arrest, court case, and subsequent sentencing had made damn sure of that.

'This is becoming something of a habit, isn't it?' Mr Monroe asked. Again, it hadn't been necessary to turn it into a question. They both understood it to be true.

'Sorry, sir. It won't happen again, sir,' Olivia assured him.

That one, neither of them suspected was remotely true.

Mr Monroe sighed and shook his head. 'Get yourself a late slip and get to class. No point making you any later than you already are.'

'No, sir. Thanks.'

Olivia started past him, head down, hand tightening further on the strap of her bag. She was almost at the sliding window of the office when he called her back.

'Is everything OK, Olivia?' he asked, dropping his volume lower. 'At home, I mean?'

She didn't meet his eye. Couldn't.

'Yeah. Fine.'

'I know it must be hard with… everything.'

She shrugged, momentarily unable to speak. Stupid throat. Stupid voice.

'If you need to talk. To me. To another member of staff. We're here. We're always here. You know that, right?'

She doubted he meant it. Not really. No one ever did.

'I know, sir,' she said. 'But there's nothing. Honest.'

Mr Monroe continued to watch her for a few moments. He almost said something more, then just smiled and waved her over to the school office.

'Right you are, then. Go get the late slip,' he instructed. He smiled warmly, and for a moment Olivia almost believed that he *did* mean it. That it wasn't just a thing he said.

'Will do, sir.'

'And remember,' he reiterated. 'You know where we are if you need us.'

—

Logan stood at the bottom of the hill, gazing despondently at the Ford Fiesta. The same Uniform who'd parked it for him had brought it back, and it now stood before him with the driver's door open, the engine running, and just the faintest hint of a smug look playing across its headlights.

It really was a bastard of a thing. Too small, too low, too light, too weedy.

It was probably a decent enough car for someone a foot shorter and fifty pounds lighter, but for him? In the snow? On Highland roads?

No.

There was a beep-beep from Tyler as his Audi SUV drove under the raised cord on tape. Both DCs gave Logan a wave from the front seat, and he quickly raised a hand indicating for them to stop.

With a shhhuk of sliding tyres and a spray of snow, Tyler brought his car to a halt right alongside the Fiesta. Side by side with the Audi, the Ford looked even more pathetic—something Logan would not have guessed was possible mere moments before.

'All right, boss?' asked Tyler, his window sliding down.

'Give me a lift back to the station, will you?' Logan asked, already reaching for the handle of the door behind Tyler's.

'Eh, aye. No bother, boss. Something wrong with your own car?'

'Aye,' said Logan, depositing himself in the back seat. 'It's a pile of shite.' He addressed the uniformed constable before he closed the door. 'Do me a favour and have someone bring that bloody thing back to Burnett Road, will you? I can't face it myself.'

The Uniform gave a half-laugh, like she thought the DCI was joking. She quickly gleaned from the expression on his face, however, that he was being deadly serious.

'Um, well, I'm sure I can arrange for—'

'Great. Have the keys sent up when it's dropped off,' Logan said, then he closed the door between them and tapped twice on the back of the driver's seat, indicating for Tyler to get going.

Morning had broken over Alness now, the sun having crept just high enough in the sky to push away the last stubborn remnants of the night before. The way the light danced across the snowy rooftops and streets brought a sense of magic and wonder to the town—something which Logan suspected it was very much lacking at most other points in the year.

'Been to Alness before, sir?' Sinead asked, craning her neck to look into the back.

Logan shook his head. 'Not that I can remember, no.'

'Nor me. I mean, once in passing, I think, but that's it.'

Tyler met Logan's eye in the rearview mirror. 'Thoughts?'

'Not many,' Logan admitted, watching the hangar-like buildings of an industrial estate go past on the left. 'Can't say I'll be booking my holidays here, though.'

'There's some nice bits,' Tyler said , although it sound ed like a bit of a stretch.

'You said it was all boy racers and coke head s on the way up,' Sinead remind ed him.

'Aye. There's that, too.'

They continued in silence for a while. Logan caught a couple of cryptic looks being exchanged up front, but d ecid ed to let it play out on its own for the moment.

They'd alread y d one their exchange of information stand ing out in the snow, feet stamping and hand s rubbing together as they went over what they'd found out.

The wallet had n't been found by the time they'd left. SOC were still hard at it, d espite their protests, with a promise to upd ate DI Ford e back at the station with any d iscoveries they mad e. Logan wasn't hold ing his breath, but he was d amned if he was letting them half-arse the job.

Mrs McGavin had n't offered much in the way of help, and nor had any of the neighbours d own the street. Nobod y had seen anything. Nobod y had heard anything. Nobod y had known as a young man lay d ying just a few feet from their front d oors.

'So, looks like your man is our best bet,' Logan said from the back.

Tyler's eyes d arted to the rearview mirror. 'I would n't call him "my man", boss,' he said . 'He's just…*a* man that I happened to be the one to interview.'

Logan frowned , a little surprised by the reaction. 'Well, I d id n't think you were going to enter a civil partnership,' he said . 'I'm just saying, he's the only one that seems to have seen anything.'

Tyler nod d ed . 'Aye. Well, I'll follow up with his… lad y friend s tod ay.' He blew out his cheeks. 'Still surprises me, that.'

'What?' Sinead asked .

'Him. With them. I was *sure* he was gay. Like *gay* gay. You know what I mean? Like, if a gayd ar was a real thing, you'd point it at him and it'd explod e.' He shrugged . 'But, nope. Turns out he likes women.'

'Maybe he likes both?' Sinead suggested .

'Maybe. But there's something creepy about him,' Tyler said . 'It'd have been fine, if he'd been gay. He'd just be, like, a very camp gay man. Fine. I get that. But he isn't. He's at it with women half his age. Two at once!'

'Eyes on the road ,' Sinead said , pointing ahead .

Tyler, who had turned to look at her in ord er to hammer home his point, faced front again.

'Both rid iculously hot, too. Like mod els, or something.' He caught the look from Sinead without actually seeing it, and quickly course-corrected . 'I mean, far too preened for my liking. Put in way too much effort.'

'What are you saying? I d on't put in enough effort?' Sinead asked .

'No! That's not... I wasn't... I d id n't mean...'

Sinead failed to hold back her smirk. Logan patted Tyler on the should er from the back seat.

'Probably best you just stop d igging there, son,' he suggested . 'Before that hole gets any d eeper.'

Tyler nod d ed his agreement, then hurried ly changed the subject. 'We, eh, we wanted to ask you something, boss.'

'Oh aye?'

'Well, Sinead d id , technically.'

He shot her that same look they'd exchanged earlier. She glared back, annoyed at having been put on the spot, then turned to the DCI and tried very hard to appear relaxed .

It was not particularly convincing.

'We, eh... I mean, I was thinking. We were talking. Me and him. About the wed d ing.'

'You've seen sense, have you?' Logan asked . 'Good on you. You can d o far better than him.'

'Haha. No. Not that, sir. I mean, if he keeps talking about threesomes with supermod els, I might reconsid er, but for now, it's still on,' Sinead continued .

She fid d led with the strap of her seatbelt, then shot Tyler a look. He nod d ed , a hand creeping onto her knee for a moment to give it an encouraging squeeze.

'Right. See, the thing is, sir...' Sinead sucked in a breath. 'As you know, my parents aren't around . And , for, well... for the wed d ing—and I know it's a wee while off yet—but, well, I was thinking... I was hoping... I'm not sure how you'd feel about maybe—and I know you've got your d aughter and everything, and I'm not—'

She faced front, muttered something below her breath, then turned back again and just went for it.

'Would you give me away, sir?'

Logan blinked . 'Me?'

'It's stupid .' Sinead cringed . 'Sorry. Forget I said anything. I should n't have—'

'I'd be honoured ,' Logan told her.

'What, seriously?' Sinead chirped . 'Because you d on't have to feel obliged to, if you'd rather—'

'Sinead ,' said Tyler, giving her leg another squeeze. 'He said yes. Maybe d on't try and talk him out of it?'

Up front in the passenger seat, Sinead grinned . 'Right! No. I won't d o that!' she said . 'Thank you, sir. It means a lot.'

'It'll be my pleasure,' Logan said .

'I can't wait to hear your speech, boss.'

Logan gave a little chuckle. 'Aye.'

He watched the snow-coated world slid e by past the wind ow for a few second s, then faced front again.

'Wait a minute,' he said . 'What blood y speech?'

–

Malcolm Maguire stood at the ironing board , pressing his way through a pile of pants and vests, half-listening to the rad io playing from the smart speaker on the sid eboard behind him. Rad io 4. A fifteen-minute d rama. Some shite about kid s skating on a frozen pond . Probably a parable about lost youth, or something. They were never straightforward . They were also never quite as clever as they thought they were.

The Smart speaker had been his d aughter's id ea. She had one at work and one at home, and swore by them.

Malcolm mostly swore *at* his, as it either failed to grasp what he said , or just pointed ly ignored his requests. They were locked in an ongoing war, the gad get and he, with skirmishes breaking out on a near-d aily basis.

Take tod ay, for example. He'd asked it to wake him up at six.

It had n't. The blood y thing had confirmed it would the night before—promised him—but this morning? Nothing. Not a blood y cheep.

Aye, he woke up early anyway. He always d id . But that wasn't the point. It had mad e him a promise, and it had failed to keep it.

And then, there was the list. He'd found out about the list function from one of the emails the company insisted on bombard ing him with, letting him know about the 'exciting' new upd ates. Unlike most of the other features, the ability to ad d items to a list just by saying them had appealed , and he'd started using it to prepare for his Christmas break, ad d ing new things he had to d o to get prepared as and when they occurred to him.

Tod ay, the d ay he was d ue to leave, the blood y thing was d enying all knowled ge of said list. No combination of word s and phrases he'd tried had been able to jog its memory, either, and his frustrated outbursts of abuse had fallen on d eaf ears, or whatever the electronic equivalent was. Deaf microphone, he supposed .

Luckily, d ue to his d eep-rooted d istrust of the d evice, he'd written everything d own in a notepad as a backup, and kept it in the d rawer of the coffee table.

A check of it had confirmed that he'd alread y completed most of the tasks he'd assigned himself. There was only the last of the ironing and packing to d o, and a spot of brunch with—

A key rattled in the front d oor, and Malcolm set the iron d own.

The d oor opened out in the hall a moment later. A gust of icy wind and snow herald ed the arrival of his d aughter, and Malcolm's insid es lit-up at the sight of her through the open living room d oor.

She looked so like her mother. Or rather, in her colourful bobble hat, pad d ed yellow jacket, and chunky gloves, she looked like her mother *used* to look, back before all the fun had leaked out of her and she'd become the d ry, soulless husk who'd eventually walked out on them both.

'Hey, Big D,' she called , kicking her boots into the corner like she'd d one every time she'd come through the d oor since she was nine. 'Blood y freezing out there.'

'Blood y freezing in here now, too,' Malcolm replied . 'The d oor still d oesn't shut itself, Shona!'

'Yeah, yeah. Keep your wig on!'

Shona closed the d oor against the blizzard , gave a full bod y shiver, then shoved her gloves into her pockets, unzipped her jacket, and found space to hang it on one of the hooks on the wall.

They met in the living room and exchanged hugs. Malcolm yelped as she snuck a hand up the back of his jumper and pressed it against his bare back.

'Jesus! Cut that out! Your hand s are blood y freezing!'

'I know. Bit pointless d oing it, otherwise,' Shona said , shooting him a grin.

'I'll get the kettle on,' Malcolm said . 'I haven't started on brunch yet. So much still to d o.'

'I can knock something up for us, if you like?' his d aughter suggested .

Malcolm stared solemnly at her. 'You're a woman of many impressive talents, Shona, but cooking isn't one of them.'

Shona's mouth fell open in outrage. 'Hey, that's... well, OK, obviously that's true, but you d on't need to come out and actually say it! Some things are best left unspoken. Oh, and here.' She thrust a carrier bag out to him. 'Merry Christmas.'

Malcolm gasped, eyes widening like he'd just won big on the horses. 'Aw, you shouldn't have,' he said, playing a role he'd played for more years now that he could care to remember.

Reaching into the bag, he removed a lovingly wrapped gift, approximately the size and shape of a Cliff Richard calendar.

Exactly the size and shape of a Cliff Richard calendar, in fact.

'I mean it, by the way. You really shouldn't have,' Malcolm said, wincing. 'With all the rushing about getting ready to go, I didn't get a chance to get you anything.'

'What? Oh. Right. It's fine, don't be daft,' Shona began, her smile losing just a hint of its shine. 'Seriously, don't worry about—'

'Oh-ho! What do we have here?' Malcolm wondered, pulling a gift from behind a couch cushion. 'Whatever could it be?'

He handed it over, and Shona accepted it eagerly. It was roughly the size and shape of a Celine Dion calendar.

Exactly so, in fact.

'God, I can't wait to find out!' she gushed, clutching it to her chest. 'It's going to be *such* a surprise!'

Malcolm chuckled and shook his head. 'You're a very strange young woman. You do know that, yes?'

Shona conceded that it had been pointed out once or twice in the past. Then, since her father wasn't bothering his arse to go do it despite his promises, she headed through to the kitchen and made them both a cup of tea.

The kettle had barely boiled when she got the phone call from Ricketts. He was leaving her a Christmas gift of his own in one of the fridges back at the hospital. Something for her to 'get her teeth into' that afternoon—his words, not hers. Nothing too urgent, by the sounds of things. Some bloody idiot with too much to drink and too little in the way of warm clothing.

'I can't believe you iron your pants,' Shona observed, returning to the living room and handing her dad one of the two matching mugs she carried.

'Thanks, love,' he said, accepting the offered beverage and slurping down a sip. 'Why wouldn't I iron my pants? Don't you?'

'No. What's the point? It's not like anyone's going to see them.' Her eyes widened as she realised the connotations of that remark. 'I mean...'

'Lalalala!' Malcolm sang. 'Don't want to know.'

Shona flopped down onto the couch. It was a big, plump corner number that she always felt she could get lost in. Experience told her that if she lifted up a cushion on her own couch she'd find nothing but fluff, coins, and the occasional stray Skittle.

There was something about her dad's corner sofa, though, that made her believe it kept adventures tucked beneath its cushions. Lift one of those bad boys, and you wouldn't find a stray comb, or a random colour of felt-tip pen. You'd find doorways to other worlds. You'd find alternate universes filled with plucky space captains, towering wolf-creatures, and shape-shifting green blobs.

She had never tried lifting one, of course. That way, she knew, lay crushing disappointment.

'You nearly ready for the off?' she asked, tilting her mug in the direction of a half-full suitcase that sat atop the coffee table.

'Aye. Going to be a hell of a drive until I hit Fort Augustus. Snow turns to rain there, apparently, then brightens up the closer you get to the border.'

'Well, be careful,' Shona told him. 'And text or phone when you get there.'

'I know. I will,' Malcolm said, rolling his eyes. He took another drink of tea, then went back to pressing creases into his underwear. 'You sure I can't convince you to come? Cathy has plenty of room. She'd love to see you.'

'Can't. Working. We're not all gentlemen of leisure, you know? We can't all just go swanning off to foreign climes whenever we feel like it.'

'It's Nottingham, not the Algarve.'

Shona smiled . 'Tell her I said hello. And to save me a space for next year.'

'You've been saying that for eight years,' Malcolm remind ed her. 'I hate the thought of you being on your own.'

'I'm quite happy on my own,' Shona told him.

'Aye, well, you should n't be. Not at Christmas. And not at your age.'

'My age? Blood y cheek!' She hurled a scatter cushion at him.

'Hot iron and hot tea!' he protested .

'Serves you blood y right! "Not at your age",' Shona said . She shifted her weight on the chair, sitting up straighter. 'Anyway. I've invited someone over for d inner.'

Malcolm paused with the iron in his hand . 'Have you?' he asked , perking up.

'Yes. I have,' Shona replied . 'Sort of.'

Malcolm perked back d own again. 'What d o you mean, "sort of"?'

'I d id n't so much ask as imply. But *strongly* imply,' Shona said . 'And he implied he might not be against the id ea. In theory.'

'He? He who?'

'Who he?' Shona teased . 'He none of your business, that's who he.' She checked her watch, and shot a look in the d irection of the kitchen. 'Now, are you going to get food sorted , or am I raid ing your cupboard s for Pot Nood les?'

Chapter 11

Ben had some news for Logan and the others when they returned to the station. Good news, if you used the term very loosely.

'I think I might have an ID for you,' he announced, offering Logan a photograph before the DCI had finished taking his jacket off.

It looked like a social med ia picture that had been taken on a night out somewhere warm and sunny—i.e. not the Highland s—and showed a tanned, smiling young man with a thick gold chain and a shirt open almost all the way to his stomach.

'Aye, that looks like him,' Logan confirmed, extricating himself from the sleeves of his coat. He ind icated for the others to look, and there was a general agreement that yes, this was the guy.

'Fred erick Shaw. Fred d ie,' Ben announced. 'His mother reported him missing last night. She hasn't seen him since Saturd ay morning, and hasn't been able to reach him on his mobile.'

'Saturd ay?' Logan said. 'So, two nights ago? Does he live with her?'

Ben nod d ed to confirm that he d id. 'Says it's not unusual for him to stay out all night on a Saturd ay, but he always texts to let her know, and phones next d ay to tell her when he'll be home.'

'And I'm taking it he d id neither?'

'He d id not, no,' Ben said. 'I spoke to the sergeant who hand led the report. He thought she was maybe being a wee bit hysterical. Young man, out on the pull on a Saturd ay night. We know how that can go.'

'Fred erick Shaw, d id you say?' Hamza asked . His brow was furrowed as he searched through his memory banks. 'Name's familiar.'

Ben looked d own at the photograph, like there would be some clue there, then shrugged . 'Can't say it rings any bells with me. Anyone else?'

Tyler and Sinead shook their head s.

'New one on me, boss.'

'Me too,' Sinead confirmed .

Hamza had mad e his way over to his computer, and his fingers were alread y flying across the keyboard as he entered his password . 'Give me a minute,' he said . 'I'll see what I can find .'

'Anyone else see him since Saturd ay morning?' Logan asked .

'A mate of his. They head ed out together into town. Aye, here, I mean, not Alness. As far as I can tell, he's got no ties to Alness at all,' Ben said .

'Who's the mate?'

'Knew you were going to blood y well ask me that,' Ben grumbled . He flipped the photograph over, revealing an A4 printout tucked below it. 'Hang on. I d o know it. I saw it a minute ago.'

Hamza piped up from behind his PC monitor. 'Was it Damian Bailey, by any chance?'

Ben clicked his fingers. 'That's the boy. How'd you know that?'

'Because I just figured out where I knew the name Fred erick Shaw from,' the DS explained . 'Earlier this year, when I got second ed to CID for that couple of weeks. He and Damian Bailey were up on a rape charge. They were accused of d rugging a lassie they knew and taking it in turns to... well, you get the picture. They filmed it on their phones. Procurator Fiscal was convinced they'd get a conviction.'

'I'm guessing they d id n't?' said Tyler.

'Not Proven,' Hamza said . 'They insisted she'd given consent, and the jury d ecid ed to take their word over hers. Course, the d efence lawyer had brought up all kind s of shite from the lassie's past by that point. Complete *Who's Who* of her sexual history.'

'Fuck's sake,' Sinead spat.

It was rare to hear her swearing, and everyone glanced her way in surprise. Logan waited to see if there was anything else coming, before d ecid ing it was safe to continue.

'Did they have you working the case?' he asked the DS.

Hamza shook his head . 'No, sir. I came in after. One of the CID boys who'd been heavily involved in the case was quite bad ly affected by it. He'd been coord inating with the victim and her family, and had got to know them pretty well, I think. He also had a d aughter around the same age. He wanted to take a few weeks out, so I covered for him until he came back.'

'Name?' Logan asked .

'Now you're asking,' Hamza said . 'I'd have to check.'

'Aye. Do that. Be good to speak to him,' Logan said .

It was Tyler who voiced what the rest of the team was thinking.

'We're still looking at his d eath being an accid ent though, right, boss?'

'We're keeping an open mind ,' Logan replied .

He had n't yet hung up his coat, and now conclud ed that removing it had been premature. With a weary sigh, he slid an arm back into one of the sleeves. 'Right, I'll talk to the mother. Who wants to talk to the mate?'

Sinead immed iately put herself forward . 'I'll d o it,' she said . 'I'll talk to him.'

Logan hesitated with one arm insid e his coat. The DC had been a little too quick to respond , and there was a look on her face that suggested she had her own motives. 'Right. Fine. But he's not on trial. That other case is d one. Und erstood ?'

'Perfectly, sir,' Sinead confirmed .

Logan contemplated saying something more, but then gave her enough cred it to see the task through in a professional manner.

'Right, then,' he said , taking the offered printout from Ben. He checked the ad d ress, told the rest of the team he'd be back in an hour or so, then left the Incid ent Room.

A moment later, he came back in.

'So, eh…' he began. 'Who fancies giving me a lift?'

–

She knew.

From the moment the car pulled up outsid e the house, and the big burly bastard with the d our look on his face stepped out, she knew.

She busied herself by the wind ow, where she'd been stand ing for most of the past twenty-four hours. She ad justed the orna-ments on the sid eboard . Smoothed out a crinkle in the blind s. Did everything she could to keep herself together as the man in the long coat opened the front gate, and mad e his way up the path with a younger fella trotting along at his heels.

There was nothing about them to say they were with the police, but at the same time, it was everything about them. It was the car. The clothing. The walk.

The way the sight of them nipped at her eyes and mad e the four cups of coffee she'd had that morning curd le in her stomach.

She knew who they were.

She knew why they were here.

And she knew that her life was about to come crumbling d own around her the moment she opened the d oor.

The knock came a few second s later. Firm, but polite.

She thought about ignoring it. Not answering. Staying in this world a while longer, where her boy was just missing, not d ead . Where there was a chance he was out there somewhere.

A world where he'd come home to a proper bollocking and a week of the cold shoulder. Where he'd order them takeaway by way of apology. Where he'd wear her down with flowers and promises, and unexpected kisses on the top of her head.

A different world.

A better one.

The knocking came again. She had adjusted the ornaments. Smoothed the blinds. Stretched the old world as far as it would go.

Then she headed through to the hall and opened the door.

'Mrs Shaw? My name's Detective Chief Inspector Jack Logan,' the man on the doorstep said. 'Do you mind if we come in?'

She stepped aside.

Both men entered.

And they brought her world crashing down around her.

—

'Damian. *Damian*. Fuck's sake.'

Damian Bailey turned at the tap on his shoulder, and plucked an Apple Airpod from one ear. His face, hands, and overalls were stained with the remnants of a recent oil change, and he still had some work to do on the brake pipes if the car was going to have any chance of getting through its MOT.

'What's up?' he asked the older man who'd been trying to get his attention.

Alf was oil-stained, too, although his was less recent, and apparently more permanent. It had been Alf's father's garage originally, but he'd taken over the running of it forty years previously. A lifetime of dealing with grease and gunk had left him looking perpetually dirty, and no amount of scrubbing or Swarfega could ever hope to get him fully clean.

'Someone's here to see you,' Alf said, throwing a thumb back over his shoulder. 'A girl.'

'Oh, aye?' Damian perked up, suddenly interested. His eyes went to the door of the workshop, and through to the reception area. A woman in her twenties stared back at him, unsmiling. About as far from smiling as it was possible to be, in fact. 'Who is she?' he asked.

'What am I, your personal secretary?' Alf asked. He tapped his watch. 'She says it's important. You've got five minutes, then I want you back here so we can get this motor finished off.'

Taking a rag from his pocket, Damian gave his hands a wipe. As the rag was considerably dirtier than his hands, this didn't have quite the effect he'd been aiming for.

'Five minutes,' Alf reminded him, as Damian went striding off. 'Not a minute more.'

Damian was all smiles when he stepped through into reception, but something about the expression on the young woman's face knocked the edge off his grin.

'Damian Bailey?' she asked, before he could utter a word. He recognised the tone at once.

'That's right,' he confirmed, the smile falling away completely.

The warrant card that was flashed in his face came as no surprise.

'Detective Constable Sinead Bell. I'd like to ask you a few questions about Frederick Shaw. Is there somewhere private we can go?'

'Have you found him?' Damian asked. 'Has he turned up?'

'This would be best done in private, Mr Bailey,' the DC told him. She indicated a door at the back of the small, tired reception area marked 'Office'. 'Shall we?'

Chapter 12

Tyler and Logan sat in the Aud i around the corner from Christine Shaw's house, five vehicles back from the traffic lights. The sky was alive with fat flakes of snow that fell near-horizontally, before meeting their end as a wet splat against the wind screen and being squeaked away by the wipers.

Neither man had spoken since they'd got in the car and d riven away, and neither was in the mood to be the first to d o so.

There had been nothing they could offer Fred erick's mother but their sympathies, and their assurances that while her son's d eath appeared to be accid ental, everyone was treating it very seriously.

She'd had no id ea what he was d oing in Alness. But then, she d id n't tend to have any id ea what he was d oing at the best of times.

'He was a law unto himself, he was,' she'd told them, once the news had been broken and the initial tears had all been shed .

Fred d ie had been a good lad , though, she'd insisted . bit thoughtless, most of the time, but then weren't all young people? Did n't they all give their poor old mums cause to stay up late, worrying themselves sick? Wasn't that just part of a mother's lot?

She was less forgiving of Fred d ie's friend —and co-d efend ant—Damian Bailey, labelling him everything from a 'bad influence' to a 'nasty piece of work.'

At no point d id she refer d irectly to the rape trial. Not in so many word s, at least. But, she mad e it clear that she held Damian solely responsible for 'all that unpleasant business' earlier in the year.

Fred d ie had been hitting the town on Saturd ay for Damian's birthd ay. Christine had n't been happy about it, but she'd held her tongue. Fred d ie was an ad ult, after all. She could no more choose his friend s than she could fight his battles, however much she might like to d o both.

He'd left the house for work before ten, and was head ing straight round to Damian's after his shift end ed at five. He'd told her not to wait up, and that he'd text to let her know if he was going to be out all night.

'He always texted . Always. He was good like that,' she'd said , before announcing with a solemn air that he had n't texted that d ay, d espite her waking up to check her phone almost every hour throughout the night.

When she could n't get him next morning, she'd become worried .

When he had n't returned by lunchtime, she knew that something was wrong. She could feel it, right d own in the marrow of her bones.

Having gone over things from her sid e, Logan answered Christine's questions about what had happened to her son, and what would happen next with his remains.

He'd explained as gently as he could. *Tragic accident. Wouldn't have suffered. Post-mortem being carried out, as was standard for such situations.*

All she'd wanted to know, though, was when she could get her boy back. When she could see him. When she could start making arrangements.

'Not long,' Logan had told her. 'I'll try to make sure everything is d ealt with as quickly as possible.'

'Have you got someone who can help you with everything?' Tyler had asked .

She'd shaken her head at that, and her face had paled at the thought of it.

'No. There's no one now,' she'd whispered , the realisation hitting her like one sud d en punch to the guts. 'There's no one now but me.'

'Poor bugger,' Logan muttered .

Tyler shot him a sid eways look, then slid the car into gear as the brake lights of the van in front went out and it began to creep forward s.

'Boss?'

'Christine Shaw.'

'Oh. Aye. Rough,' Tyler said . 'Still, she took it better than I expected .'

'She was hold ing it together, that's all,' Logan said . He tapped his fingers on the d oor's armrest. 'We should 've insisted on the liaison going round to talk to her.'

'She said no, boss.'

'That's why I said we should 've blood y insisted ,' Logan retorted . There was a bit of bite to it that had n't been intentional. He sighed . 'Sorry. I just… selfish d aft bastard .'

'Christine Shaw?'

'No! For fuck's sake, Tyler, keep up, eh? Her son. The d ead fella. Fred d ie.'

'Right. Gotcha. Aye.'

Logan gazed out the wind ow and watched the snow-covered streets slid e by as Tyler d rove on through the oncoming blizzard .

He tutted . Shook his head .

'Aye,' he remarked . 'Selfish d aft bastard .'

–

Damian Bailey was everything Sinead had braced herself for. He was cocky, arrogant, and gave off the impression that he knew something nobod y else d id .

He flopped into the manager's chair—a battered old leather thing that was held together with a lot of tape and probably a fair amount of faith—and slouched d own with his elbows on the armrest, his head on one hand , and his legs spread wid e.

'This about Fred die? He still not turned up or something?'

Sinead helped herself to the office's only other chair. It was a flimsy red plastic thing with five wheels on a base designed for six, and it cracked unnervingly when she sat on it.

'It does that. It's proper fucked,' Damian explained.

'It's fine,' Sinead said, positioning her feet to compensate for the missing wheel. 'And yes, it's about Frederick Shaw. Can you tell me when you last saw him?'

Damian twisted his hips, making the chair turn from side to side. Sinead wasn't sure if this was a deliberate attempt to draw attention to his crotch, but it was certainly the result.

He was about her age, or maybe a year or two either way. No younger than twenty-one, no older than twenty-six. Despite the dirt and oil residue, he clearly took good care of himself.

His skin was tanned, but with a hint of an orange tone that implied it came from a bottle. His teeth were almost too white, and drew the eye whenever he smiled or spoke.

Physically, he wasn't particularly big, but he looked honed, like he knew his way around a gym.

His hair was shaved almost all the way down to the bone at the sides of his head, then the longer hair on top was styled into a high, slicked-back quiff that there was probably a name for. The word *pompadour* was in Sinead's head, but she wasn't entirely convinced that wasn't the name of one of the Three Musketeers.

Fashion had never really been her thing.

Nor, for that matter, was French literature.

'I already told one of your lot,' Damian said, with a glance at the clock and a theatrical sigh. 'Saturday. Johnny Foxes. About eleven. I've said all this, already.'

'That's as may be, Mr Bailey,' Sinead said. 'But that's before we knew he was dead.'

Damian stopped rotating the chair. He lifted his head from his hand, his eyebrows crashing into one another above the bridge of his nose.

'What? Dead ? What d o you mean *dead*?'

'Fred erick's bod y was found in the early hours of this morning,' Sinead continued .

'Fuck. What?' Damian sat forward at that, the reality of it apparently hitting home. His eyes shone, tears shimmering across them, unbid d en. '*His body*? Like… his actual bod y? Like, he's *dead*?'

'I'm afraid so,' Sinead said , and to her immense irritation, she felt a pang of sympathy for the man in the chair.

'When? How? What the fuck happened ?' Damian asked . He blinked back the tears, sniffed noisily, then furrowed his brow again. 'Did someone…? Was he killed ?'

'What makes you ask that?'

'Well, I mean, he's twenty-six. It's hard ly going to be natural causes, is it?' Damian said , a hint of accusation in his tone. 'And he would n't have d one himself in. Not Fred d o. No way.'

'We'll have to wait for the post-mortem to confirm, but we're not treating it as suspicious at this stage,' Sinead said . 'We think he got d runk, fell asleep in the snow, and d ied of exposure to the cold .'

'Jesus fucking Christ! Exposure? How? When? It d id n't start snowing until last night! Where's he been since Saturd ay?'

Sinead took her notebook from her pocket. 'I was hoping you might be able to tell me that,' she said . 'You say the last time you saw him was around eleven on Saturd ay. Johnny Foxes.'

Damian nod d ed . He had closed his legs and shuffled hims< upright in the chair, and Sinead could practically watch his earlier attitud e go evaporating into the stiflingly warm air of the tiny office.

'He went off with a bird ,' he explained . 'He'd been chatting her up since about ten, firing d rinks d own her. Shots. She was blazing.'

'Bit reckless that,' Sinead said , meeting his eye. 'Given what happened earlier in the year.'

Damian scowled . 'That was bullshit. We d id nothing wrong. We were found Not Guilty.'

'Not Proven,' Sinead corrected . 'Not quite the same. But, either way, I'd have thought you and Fred erick would 've been more careful, given what you went through.'

'I wasn't the one feed ing her d rink, was I?' he said , practically spitting the word s into the DC's face. 'Fred d o's a big boy. I'm not his mum. He wants to get a bird pissed and his d ick wet? Fuck all to d o with me.'

Sinead counted to five in her head , bit back the first three or four responses that sprung to mind , and kept it professional.

'Do you know who the woman was?'

'No.'

'You d id n't get a name?'

'No.'

'Can you give a d escription of what she looks like?'

Damian blew out his cheeks and shot another look at the clock. 'Dark hair. Thirties. Bit overweight.' He screwed up his face. 'I told him there were plenty of fitter girls knocking about, but he just laughed and kept saying, "Fat bird s need shagging, too, mate", whenever he went to get another round in.'

'Charming,' Sinead said , making a note in her pad . 'Nothing else you can tell me about her? Was she with anyone? Did Fred erick say where they were going?'

Damian shook his head . 'No. He took her into the toilets and shagged her bent over one of the bogs, then they must've left together right after. I d id n't see them after that.'

'They had sex in the toilets?' Sinead asked , seizing on the comment. 'How d o you know?'

'What?'

'If you d id n't see him, how d o you know they had sex in the toilets?'

'Well, just…' Damian mad e a vague hand motion that d id n't really convey anything specific. 'Why else would she go to the bogs with him? To wipe his arse? She was well up for it by then. Aye, shagging, I mean, not wiping his arse. Totally fucking blootered .'

Sinead counted to ten.

It did n't really help.

'Not too drunk to give consent, I hope.'

Damian snorted . 'No. She was fine,' he said . There was contempt in the way he looked at Sinead , like he could n't quite believe she was d aring to question him. 'She walked into the men's bogs and into a cubicle on her own two feet. If that isn't consent, I d on't know what the fuck is.'

Sinead clicked her tongue against the back of her teeth. 'And to think some folk say romance is d ead .'

A sneer tugged Damian's mouth upward s until it almost met his nose, but he d id n't reply. Instead , he shook his head , exhaled heavily, and slouched back into the chair.

'Dead . Fucking *dead*.' He shook his head again. 'Have you told his mum?'

'Of course.'

'Bet she blamed me, d id n't she? Bet this'll somehow be my fault.'

'Is it?' Sinead asked .

'Oh yeah. Here we go. Might've fucking known,' Damian spat, sitting forward again. He motioned to her with both hand s, as if beckoning her in for a fight. 'Go on then. How is this on me? How is this my fucking fault?'

'I d id n't say it was,' Sinead told him.

'Yes, you d id ! A minute ago, you said —'

'I said , "is it?"' Sinead remind ed him. 'Not "it is".'

Damian grunted , and a bit of the fight went out of him. 'Well... no. It isn't. All right? And make sure his mum knows that, too. I'm not having her starting shit again.'

There was a knock on the office d oor, then it was opened a half-second later. Alf, the owner, popped his head around it and shot d aggers in Damian's d irection.

'You going to be long? Need you back in the workshop to get this car read y for its MOT.'

Sinead   opened   her mouth to ask for a few more minutes, but Damian was alread y out of the chair and   on his feet. He loomed over the DC, scowling d own at her even as he answered   the old man in the d irty overalls.

'Nah, Alf,' he said . 'We're all d one here.'

Chapter 13

The rest of the d ay passed in a blur of nothing much at all. Paperwork was completed . Notes were typed up. The beginnings of the report for the Procurator Fiscal took shape.

A birthd ay cake was presented to Hamza, then set upon and d evoured before the cand les—in the shape of a three and a zero—could even start to cool.

'We chipped in and got you this,' Tyler said , once the cake was gone. He presented the DS with a sparkly pink gift bag. 'We know you d on'*officially* d rink, which mad e it more d ifficult, so we thought we'd get you something practical that you could use.'

'Cheers. You should n't have,' Hamza said . He opened the top of the bag, peeked insid e, then let out a snort of laughter. 'I mean, you really should n't have,' he reiterated , taking a DVD box set of *Murder, She Wrote* from the bag.

'It's the full series,' Sinead said . 'We thought it might give you some pointers.'

'I'm touched ,' Hamza said .

Ben chuckled . 'God *Murder, She Wrote*. I used to love that show,' he said , then he tapped a finger to his head , ad opted a gravelly voice, and said , 'One thing still bothers me, ma'am.'

'That's Columbo,' Logan pointed out.

Ben frowned . 'Aye. I know. Is he no *Murder, She Wrote*?'

'Why would Columbo be in *Murder, She Wrote*?' Logan asked .

Ben just blinked in response.

'Who's the "she" in that situation?' Logan pressed .

'Well, what one was *Murder, She Wrote*, then?'

'Jessica Fletcher. Angela Lansbury. The typewriter,' Logan said . He mimed typing, and hummed the show's theme music. 'That one.'

'Right. Aye,' Ben said , snapping his fingers as the memory of it came back to him. 'What was Columbo in, then?'

'*Columbo.*'

'Aye. What was he in?'

'Jesus Christ. Columbo was in *Columbo*, Benjamin. Have you no' been taking your pills or something?'

'Very funny,' Ben said , giving the DCI a d unt with an elbow.

'I knew a guy called Columbo once,' Tyler announced out of nowhere. 'In school. His mum was obsessed with Eighties crime shows. His full name was Columbo Quincy TJ Hooker MacBrid e.'

'Bollocks!' Hamza laughed .

'No, straight up,' Tyler insisted .

'Jesus,' Logan muttered . 'Poor bastard .'

'You think that's bad ? It's his wee sisters I felt sorry for,' Tyler said . He glanced around the team, stretching the d ramatic pause. 'Cagney and Lacey.'

'Shut up!' Sinead laughed .

'I swear to God !' Tyler said . He took out his phone. 'Here, I'll look him up on Facebook…'

They all d rank their tea and used their tongues to sweep for any stray cake crumbs in the corners of their mouths while Tyler tapped away at his screen.

'Right, here he…' His eyes d arted left and right as he read . 'Ah. Shit. Looks like he killed himself,' he said . 'Damn. Poor Col.'

A silence hung over the Incid ent Room as Tyler returned his phone to his pocket.

'Well, that's fairly put a d ampener on the party, eh?' Logan remarked . 'Good work there, son. Way to kill the mood .'

'I d id n't know!' Tyler protested .

'Yeah, cheers, mate,' said Hamza with a reproachful shake of his head . 'Thanks a bunch.'

It took Tyler a few moments to conclud e they were wind ing him up. And even then, he wasn't *completely* convinced .

'Yeah, yeah,' he said , and he was relieved to see Hamza smirking back at him. 'Anyway, the real party's after work. We all still on for the pub?'

'Aye, but I'll have to be quick,' Hamza said . 'Wife's family's coming over for d inner. Somehow, she's d ecid ed that the way I really want to celebrate my thirtieth is by being told I should 've been a d octor, while having everything from my parenting skills to the size of my bathroom criticised .'

'You could always sneak away and watch *Murder, She Wrote,*' Tyler suggested , hold ing up the box set.

'True,' said Hamza. 'Although, they'd only find fault with that.' He d rew back his lips in d istaste and put on a thick Ind ian accent. '"Why aren't you watching *Magnum, P.I.?* What kind of a man subjects himself to this rubbish?"'

'They sound a right barrel of laughs, son,' Ben said . 'You should invite them along to the pub.'

'Aye, I can't see that going well,' Hamza said , shud d ering at the very thought of it. 'Either they'd go up in flames, or the pub would .'

'Make for a birthd ay to remember, either way,' Sinead pointed out.

Logan's phone bleeped in his pocket. He checked it, muttered his annoyance, then tapped out a response.

'Everything all right, Jack?' Ben asked .

'It's from Shona. Been held up with the snow. Post-mortem's being pushed back until later this evening.'

'So... we can't finish the reports until tomorrow, boss?' Tyler asked . 'Is that what you're saying?'

It was a load ed question, Logan knew, and he could feel them all hanging on for the answer. 'I suppose that's what I'm saying, aye,' he confirmed . He checked his watch and sighed . 'Fine. I'll meet you all there in half an hour.'

Everyone who was sitting jumped to their feet. Those who were stand ing reached for their coats, the atmosphere in the room changing in an instant. They were no longer polis. They were *off-duty* polis. And that, as anyone with any experience of such things knew, was a whole other kettle of fish.

'And see if you can get hold of Dave David son,' Logan called after them, as they all head ed for the d oor. 'I told him we'd pick him up on the way.'

'What if he can't get off d uty yet, sir?' Sinead asked .

Ben tutted and put an arm around her should er. 'Don't you worry, lass. We'll get him off d uty,' he assured her. 'This is official MIT business, after all...'

–

The final bell had only rung ten minutes ago, but alread y the evening was d rawing the shad ows together across the city, packing the d ay away.

Olivia had been in no rush when the bell rang and had hung back for a minute or two, taking her time to pull on her jacket and to secure her bag over both should ers, letting the rest of the class get a head start.

She could n't face the whispers, or the looks, or the name-calling. Not tod ay.

Miss Loud on, the Maths teacher, had stood waiting by the d oor, tapping her watch in a show of good -natured impatience. She was nice. Most of the teachers were nice, in fact. It was just the people her own age who were the problem.

'Sorry, miss,' Olivia had said , tucking her thumbs into the straps of her backpack and hurrying between the d esks until she reached the front.

They'd said their brief good byes, then Olivia had trud ged out onto the now safely-d eserted staircase, and followed the d istant chatter of the rest of the kid s as they went pouring out toward s the waiting cars and buses.

She'd made her way across the school grounds with an abundance of caution. She'd seen bags pulled off shoulders before, then watched them tossed from one cackling pupil to another as the owner frantically tried to grab back their stolen property.

She didn't fancy being Piggy in the Middle anytime, but especially not today.

As she'd left the grounds, she'd become convinced that someone was following her. She'd weaved her way through the surrounding streets, looking back over her shoulder and studying reflections in the windows of parked cars.

Once, she thought she glimpsed someone, but when all subsequent checks drew a blank, she concluded that she was most likely just being paranoid.

Now, having walked on for another few minutes, the school was far enough behind her that she felt it was safe enough to stop.

With a final furtive glance around, she swung her bag off her shoulders, took hold of the zip, then composed herself before easing it open.

She'd barely looked in her bag all day. She had n't d ared . She'd transferred everything she was likely to need from the main part of the backpack to the big front pocket, and zipped the larger section closed again with a haste that had not gone unnoticed by the two boys sitting at the desk beside her.

'You scared something's going to escape, or something?' one of them had asked with a dry, raspy cackle.

His name was Jonathan. He stank of stale smoke and fresh sweat, and had so many spots around his mouth and up his cheeks that he looked like some red-bearded pirate.

Olivia hated him. She'd like to say the feeling was mutual, but she doubted it was. Jonathan probably didn't hate anyone. Hating them meant you had to think about them, and Olivia reckoned he'd never spared a thought for another human being in his entire life.

Cautiously, she reached inside the bag, then quickly drew her hand out again when a car passed on the road beside her.

'Not here,' she whispered, zipping the bag closed and swinging it back onto her shoulder.

She hurried on, then stopped by a patch of waste ground. Some sort of building had once stood there, she assumed, but the ground was now a graveyard of broken bricks and rusted pipes. A high metal fence with pointed spars ran most of the way around it, but it had fallen in at a few spots, and a lot of the kids crossed it on the way home from school.

With a glance back to make sure nobody was approaching from behind, Olivia turned onto the waste ground, tucked herself behind the fence, and opened her schoolbag again.

She held her breath as she peered into the dark cavern of the backpack's main compartment. A tote bag—the kind her mother had bought for shopping during one of her fleeting 'caring for the environment' phases—sat at the very bottom of the bag, nestled there like some monstrous creature just waiting for its chance to strike.

She didn't see the note at first, but eventually found it tucked down the side of the tote bag, where it had presumably slipped during the day. The note was written on a Ladbrokes betting slip. It gave an address, and then Oleg had written the letter X at the bottom of the paper.

Her stomach turned itself all the way over when she realised it was a kiss.

She typed the address into the Maps app on her phone. It was less than ten minutes away by foot. That was good, she thought, although part of her would've liked to have prolonged the journey a little, delaying her arrival.

But no. Better to get it over with. Go to the address, hand over the bag, leave. That was all she had to do. That was all there was to it.

She had just zipped up her backpack when a hand grabbed it by one of the straps and wrenched it from her grasp.

'Sorry, I have to know. What *do* you have in here?'

Jonathan.

No, no, no.

'Nothing. Give it back,' Olivia cried , hoping he could n't hear the wobble in her voice. 'I mean it.'

'Or what?' Jonathan sneered .

He was several inches taller than her, and had a reach that could easily hold her at bay. His spot-beard was so bulging and pus-filled she felt sick just looking at him, but she lunged closer, trying to snatch the bag back from him.

Jonathan pivoted out of her way, and she stumbled past him like a bull past a quick-footed matad or. He emitted another of his trad emark cackles, then reached for the zip that would open the bag's main compartment.

'Did you bring your pet jailbird to school? Is that it? You worried it might fly away?' he d emand ed , eyes flashing with d elight as he d od ged another grab. 'Or is it full of d rugs? Are you d oing Dad d y's d irty work for him, now that he's banged up?'

'Give it back!'

He pulled back the zip.

'Please!'

His eyes lowered as he reached a hand insid e.

Half a brick smashed into the mid d le of his face. Olivia caught just the faintest flash of red before his hand s clamped over his nose and mouth, and he let out a sound that barely qualified as human.

Tight vines of fear wrapped around her legs, hold ing her in place, forcing her to look at what she'd d one.

What choice had he given her? What other option d id she have? He should n't have taken the bag. He should n't have d one that!

Snatching the backpack from where Jonathan had d ropped it on the uneven ground , Olivia spun around , jumped through the gap in the fence, and raced off along the street with the sound s of his cries trailing on the wind behind her.

Chapter 14

Despite it only being Mond ay, half of Inverness had knocked off work early. It was one of the d ownsid es of the Christmas week—pubs that would have been blissfully empty at this time of d ay were rammed to bursting point with lairy, loud -mouthed revellers who would n't set foot in the place the other fifty-one weeks of the year, but who somehow felt they should be given priority over every other bugger who selflessly kept the place in business, week in, week out.

It would n't be so bad if they could hand le their d rink, but they never could . From mid -December, formerly quiet, cultured d rinking establishments were filled with swarms of boorish, jeering bastard s wearing shirts, novelty ties, and Santa hats or floppy reind eer antlers.

There had been no tables available when the team—minus a Logan but up a Dave David son—had entered MacCallums Bar on Union Street. A subtle flash of a warrant card and some d eliberate staring had soon seen to that, though, and the MIT had installed itself in the corner of the pub furthest from the bar, which was currently und er assault from hord es of baying mid d le-management types.

A clean pint glass had been sourced on the way in, and a kitty started . When Hamza had tried to put in twenty quid , everyone had glared at him like he'd stood up and shat on the table. It was his celebration. He was the birthd ay boy. His money was no good tod ay.

Tyler had jotted d own the ord ers, then set off battling his way to the bar with Sinead provid ing backup. Ben watched them go off, hand in hand , and could n't keep the smile from his face.

'Classic,' said Dave, nod d ing with ad miration as he turned Hamza's DVD box set over in his hand s and read the back. 'Fucking hell, two-hund red -and -sixty-four episod es?! There must've been no bugger left in that town by the end .'

'Aye, she was a magnet for trouble, all right,' Ben said .

'I certainly would n't be inviting her to any d inner parties round my gaff,' Dave said , hand ing the set back to Hamza. 'Not unless I wanted someone to end up face d own in the fish course.'

'Shite,' Hamza said , returning the DVDs to the bag. 'Should 've got her to come round mine tonight.'

Dave frowned .

'Wife's family,' Hamza explained .

'Oof. You have my sympathies.'

'Oh! Gie's a shot of your wheelchair, pal!'

Dave, Hamza, and Ben all turned to see a grinning call centre team manager swaying unstead ily besid e their table, a light-up mistletoe head band blinking on and off just above his forehead like the lure of some ugly d eep-sea fish.

There was nothing about him that actually said he was a team manager at a call centre, and yet all three officers d ecid ed that's what he was almost simultaneously.

His shirt was partly untucked , and his tie was an oversized kipper of a thing with a cartoon of a bare-arsed Santa slid ing out of a fireplace emblazoned across it.

None of the team bothered to look, but they would all put money on his socks being brightly coloured slices of hilarity, too.

'Sorry?' Dave asked .

The other man shut one eye, like he d id n't have enough brainpower or energy to keep both open and listen at the same time. His lips moved like he was rehearsing the next line, then he slurred it out in a voice loud enough to be heard over the festive hubbub and the opening strains of Elton John's 'Step Into Christmas', which came blasting from the jukebox.

'I said , gie's a wee shot of your wheelchair. I want to noise up my mate.'

Dave smiled patiently. 'Nah, you're all right,' he said , turning back to the table.

A hand slapped d own on his should er. Tightened . Shook him.

'Go on! It'll be funny! It'll just be a minute. Don't be a selfish prick, eh?'

Ben started to say something, but Dave held a hand up and shook his head , ind icating he d id n't need the DI's assistance.

'Look, mate,' he said , keeping his smile fixed in place as he raised his gaze to the persistent id iot besid e him. 'I'm not letting you have a go of my chair, all right? So, I'd ask you to take your hand off me, and go enjoy your night. We d on't want any fuss.'

The weight on Dave's should er increased as the other man leaned d own. His breath reeked of Aftershocks and Sohis eyes swam vaguely, not quite fully find ing their focus.

'Fucking come on!' he urged . 'Don't be an arsehole! It'll be a laugh! Just let me—'

He stopped , the rest of the sentence becoming a hiss, then a whimper, then a d rawn-out croak of pain as Dave's hand clamped onto the front of his nylon work trousers, and tightened like a vice around his testicles.

'I d on't think you heard me properly, pal,' Dave told him. His tone was light, and chatty, without an ounce of urgency to it. He was in no rush to let go. He could keep this up all d ay. 'I'm not giving you a shot of my chair. But I can arrange for you to need one of your own, if you like?' He tightened his grip further, d rawing another high-pitched whimper. 'Just you say the word .'

'S-sorry. Sorry. I d id n't mean it,' the other man yelped .

Ben prod uced his Warrant Card and held it up for the id io to see. 'I think maybe it's time you called it a d ay and went home, son. Before you get yourself into any trouble.'

He nod d ed enthusiastically, his eyes almost popping out of his head . Both hand s were clamped around Dave's thick wrist, trying to force him to let go. It would take a bigger man than him to break the PC's grip, though.

At last, with one final nausea-ind ucing twist, Dave let go, and they all watched the other man go hobbling off into the crowd . He bumped into a towering figure in a bulky overcoat on the way to the d oor, and earned himself a belter of a d irty look in the process.

'All right, folks?' said Logan, joining the others at the table. 'What d id I miss?'

—

Olivia blinked against the falling snow, a hand raised to shield her face, as she consid ered the build ing in front of her. She'd been expecting a house, or maybe a flat. Instead , the ad d ress in her bag had led her to a shuttered shop which the fad ed sign above the d oor claimed had once been a newsagent's.

The roll-d own metal barricad es had been tagged with graffiti of varying levels of expertise. At one end of the scale, a few names had been written in colourful, stylised text that would take more effort than she was prepared to expend to und erstand .

Down at the other end of the quality scale was a four-foot-long ejaculating penis that had either been sprayed on by a tod d ler, or someone with their eyes shut.

A marginally more careful hand had painted a small but d etailed picture of a naked woman lying on her back with her legs spread wid e. A speech bubble had been ad d ed by yet another artist, in which the woman announced her name and phone number.

None of it, Olivia reckoned , was likely to give Banksy any sleepless nights.

She checked her phone screen to confirm this was the right place again, then slowly approached the shutters. Up close, she could see that there were three of them—a small one covering the d oor, and two larger ones flanking it on either sid e.

There was a small slid ing hatch in the d oor, roughly the size of a letterbox, about a foot above her head height. It was currently closed , but she kept her eye on it as she raised a hand and knocked on the metal barricad e.

Clank. Clank. Clank. Each knock shook the shutter, bumping it against the rails on either sid e.

Olivia waited . Around her, the snow continued to fall. It was getting heavier, and the world was swallowed into a blur of white twenty feet in all d irections, before that in turn was consumed by the blackness of the oncoming evening.

She felt like she was on an island , alone in the mid d le of a vast, end less ocean, surround ed by sharks.

There was no answer to her knocking. No response from beyond the d oor.

Shit.

The backpack felt heavy on her should ers, the weight of the tote bag d ragging her d eeper and d eeper d own into the snow.

She knocked again, hard er this time; risked a d ry-throated , 'Hello,' which, too, went unanswered .

Great. Now what?

She could n't just go home, could she? What would she say to Oleg, if he was still there? 'Sorry, no one was in, here's your stuff back'? She could n't imagine he'd respond positively to that.

And she d id n't like to consid er what would happen if she d isappointed him.

She raised a hand to knock again, but froze when she heard the voice coming from the d arkness somewhere back along the street. Someone was talking on the phone. Someone chillingly familiar.

'Bitch hit me in the face with a fucking brick,' it said . 'No, it's not fucking funny,' it said . 'Just wait until I fucking see her,' it said .

Olivia's legs took their cue to start walking before her brain could fully form the thought. She hurried off to the right, away from the approaching Jonathan, away from the shop, and the shutters, and whatever lurked beyond .

The snow swirled around her, the wind biting and raw as it battered her back, slowing her d own. She lowered her head , angled her bod y, and marched ahead . She d aren't run in ca he heard her. Not yet, at least. There was a corner up ahead . When she was around there, she could make a bolt for it, and come back when the coast was clear.

She had almost reached the corner when she heard the clattering of the shutter being raised , and a Latvian accent d emand ing, 'What the fuck you want?'

'Jesus!' Jonathan sound ed scared , and Olivia stopped just before the road end ed in a T-junction. 'What? Nothing.'

'You knock, yes? So, what the fuck you want?'

'I d id n't. I d id n't knock. I d on't know what—Ow! Jesus! Let go!'

Olivia shuffled from foot to foot, the snow crunching beneath her shoes.

No. Shit, no.

'You taking fucking piss out of me?' the Latvian d emand ed .

'No! No, I'm not!' Jonathan was full-scale shitting himself now. His voice was shrill and reed y through the blizzard , and as she stood there shivering, Olivia wond ered why she'd ever been afraid of him in the first place. 'Help! Martin, call the police and —'

He was silenced with a punch. With a gasp. With a crunch.

For a moment, there was silence. A load ed one, heavy and pregnant with what was to come.

Through the snow, she heard Jonathan cry. It wasn't a shout of anger or a scream of rage, but the snuffling sobs of a scared little boy.

'Fucking shut up! Fucking stop with crying!' hissed the Latvian. The sobbing und ulated and wobbled . Olivia could picture Jonathan being violently shaken. 'Or I chop your d amn tongue out.'

'I knocked . It was me. Let him go.'

Olivia could n't remember walking back through the snow. Not clearly, at least. And yet, here she was, back on that island by the d oor, with a wheezing, wid e-eyed Jonathan and an unfamiliar skinhead staring back at her. Jonathan's face was a mess of blood , snot, and tears. The Latvian's was d ecorated with tattoos, all d one to about the same technical stand ard as the spurting cock on the shutters.

'Who the fuck are you?' the Latvian d emand ed , looking her up and d own. Two scars curved upward s from the corners of his mouth, giving him a monstrous permanent smile.

'Oleg sent me,' Olivia replied . Her whole bod y was trembling, only partly with the cold , but she held the Latvian's gaze like he was a wild animal that might attack the moment she looked away.

'And who is this asshole?' he asked , giving Jonathan another whimper-ind ucing shake.

'He's no one. Just some d ick from my school. Bad timing on his part.'

The Latvian looked unconvinced . 'I hear knocking, I open d oor, this asshole is there. You are not. Doesn't sound like bad timing.'

Olivia scrambled to stop the word s coming out of her, but she was too late. 'Well, maybe if you'd moved your arse a bit quicker to open the d oor, I would n't have walked off.'

Jonathan's eyes had continued to grow wid er d uring the exchange, and that last remark was threatening to pop them right out of their sockets. Olivia d id n't look at him. If she saw the fear written on his face, her own expression might change to mirror it. If she'd learned one thing from her d ad over the years, it was that you d id n't show weakness.

'Now, are you going to let me in, or am I going to go tell Oleg you were too busy pissing about with schoolboys to d o business?'

The Latvian's face darkened. He wasn't much taller than the boy he held onto, but danger radiated from his every pore. He could kill them both. Hell, he was probably considering it right now.

Olivia thrust a hand into her pocket, took out her phone, and stabbed at the contacts app with an unsteady finger. 'Fine. I'll give him a call, and you can explain it yourself.'

They stood there in silence, the three of them, breath rolling out as clouds of white vapour as Olivia scrolled through her contacts. She wasn't reading them. She couldn't. Fear had robbed her of the ability to fully process what her eyes were seeing.

And besides, she didn't even have Oleg's number.

She'd made it maybe halfway down the list of contacts when Jonathan was sent stumbling. He yelped with either panic or relief, briefly met her eye, then grabbed for his phone that he'd dropped in the scuffle, and raced off into the tightening black and white gloom.

The Latvian stepped aside and motioned to the open shutter. 'You say you want to do business?' he barked. 'Then what you fucking waiting for?'

Chapter 15

'So, Christmas plans?' asked Ben, once Tyler and Sinead had returned with the d rinks, and they'd all d one some d amage to their beverage of choice. Or beverage of necessity, in Logan's case.

As a younger man, he'd always thought the id ea that there were no ex-alcoholics, only alcoholics taking it one d ay at a time, was nonsense. Regularly d rink to excess—alcoholic. Stop d oing so—ex-alcoholic. The d istinction could n't have been clearer.

Of course, that was before. Before the breakd own of his marriage. Before the slow, grind ing implosion of his life. Before the violence, and the obsession, and the line he'd crossed .

Before Mister Whisper.

He had n't touched a d rop in over two years. Two years, four months, eight d ays, in fact. If he had a pen and a quiet corner, he could probably work it out to the second .

By his old d efinition, he was no longer an alcoholic. He was sitting here in a pub a few d ays before Christmas, not touching a d rop. He'd even worked behind a bar for months, for God 's sake!

And yet, d espite his relaxed air, and the smile on his face, something insid e him was screaming, crying out, d emand ing to be appeased .

And the Diet Coke he was swirling around in his glass was d oing nothing to keep it quiet.

'What's everyone up to for the big d ay?' Ben pressed .

'Getting pished ,' Dave said .

'Being Muslim,' said Hamza.

'We're all going to Tyler's mum and dad's for dinner, but otherwise mostly just a quiet one,' Sinead said. 'The new flat's still in a bit of upheaval. Still got a lot of boxes and some furniture to get moved in.'

'Speaking of which—' Tyler began, but the others were quick to jump in with excuses.

'Bad back,' said Ben.

'Wheelchair,' Dave pointed out.

'Em... em...' Hamza frantically clicked his fingers, eyes darting left and right.

'Too slow,' Tyler told him. 'I'll text you the address.'

'Bollocks,' Hamza sighed. 'Fine. I'll help.'

All eyes went to Logan, who had carefully timed a big swig of his drink in the hope it would get him out of answering.

'How about you, boss?' Tyler asked. 'Up for playing removal man?'

'Hmm?' Logan said, stalling for time. Then, to his relief, his phone buzzed in his inside pocket, and he quickly held a hand up to prevent any further questions. 'Hang on, better get this,' he announced, getting to his feet and fishing the phone from his pocket.

The others watched him make his way through the crowd, the phone pressed to one ear, a sausage-like finger jabbed into the lughole of the other one.

'Course he'll give you a hand,' Ben said. 'Aye, he'll mump and moan about it, but he won't see you stuck. Maybe best not to ask to use his car, though. No' if you're planning bringing more than two boxes with you.'

'Can't believe he's still got the Fiesta,' Hamza said. 'Thought the DSup would 've given him something else by now.'

'Personally, I thought he'd have pushed it off the top of the Rose Street multi-storey weeks ago,' Ben replied. 'Guess they're both just as stubborn as each other.'

'Aye, guess so,' Hamza agreed . 'Did you see his face when that constable brought his keys back, though? I thought he was going to throw them at her.'

Ben chuckled . 'Aye, I think it was a close-run thing, right enough,' he agreed , then he turned his attention back to Tyler and Sinead . 'And the flat... your big move... I'll be there, too.'

'Seriously? You d on't have to d o that. What about your bad back, sir?' asked Sinead .

'Oh, I fully intend leaving all the heavy stuff to Jack,' Ben said with a smile and a wink. 'I'll be taking much more of a supervisory role.'

Tyler shifted his gaze to Dave. 'It's, eh, ground floor,' he said . 'Ramp access.'

Dave tutted . 'Fucking hell. The one time I thought being d isabled was going to work in my favour.' He rolled his eyes theatrically. 'Fine. Count me in. But you'd better have beers on the go, that's all I'm saying.'

Sinead looked up from the table just as Logan returned . 'DI Ford e's signed you up to help us move, sir,' she said .

Logan nod d ed absent-mind ed ly. 'Did he? Aye. Good . Fine.'

A hush seemed to fall over the bar. A momentary d ip in the pre-Christmas d in, as if everyone in the place had picked up on the DCI's unease.

'Everything all right, Jack?' asked Ben.

'Eh... no. No' really,' Logan ad mitted . He held up his phone, the screen of which was now d ark. 'That was Shona. Dr Maguire. She mad e it in to the hospital. Just starting the post-mortem.'

Glances were exchanged . Glasses paused mid way to mouths. 'And ?'

'Fred erick Shaw's d eath wasn't an accid ent,' Logan announced . 'He was murd ered .'

—

Olivia's footsteps crunched on crystalline shard s of broken glass, her eyes d arting anxiously at what had once been a corner shop, but which was now... something else. She wasn't sure what exactly, but her every instinct was urging her to get out as quickly as possible.

The counter and racks were still in place, although many of the shelves had collapsed or, more likely, been torn from their fittings.

A Coca-Cola brand ed frid ge lay face d own on the floor like a murd er victim. The broken glass she was walking on was mostly concentrated around the fallen frid ge, but it had been swept, kicked , or trod d en across much of the rest of the scuffed linoleum floor.

The insid e of the shop was just as covered with graffiti as the outsid e. More so, even. It spread across the walls like a rash, continued across the ceiling, and popped up in patches across the floor. Even without focusing on any of the lewd er, more sexual word s and images, the overall impression she took from it was that she *really* d id n't want to be here. In this place. In this room.

With *him*.

And then, there was the smell. It was the smell of curd led milk and rotting fruit. As a kid —years ago, but she could n't remember how many—she'd climbed into the big green wheelie bin at the back of the house, and hid d en there while her parents were arguing.

She'd realised her mistake almost immed iately. The smell had been overpowering. Nauseating. She had tried to hold her breath, but it had found its way insid e, and she'd retched and vomited until her insid es were empty.

She'd shouted . She'd cried . She'd screamed , and raged , hurled herself against the insid e of the bin until her bod y hurt and her voice was lost.

No one had come looking for her. No one had come to get her out. It had taken her forever to free herself, and it would take forever and a d ay for her to forget the smell of that bin.

The stink hanging in the air now made the fear and the shame and the sense of isolation and helplessness come rushing back. She was a kid again, out of her depth, with nobody listening to her cries for help.

Her stomach flipped. Her lungs cramped. She shouldn't be here. She had to go, get out, breathe uncontaminated air.

The door rolled closed with a clang, cutting off any chance of a quick exit. Olivia jumped at the sound, but otherwise didn't make a move.

Show no weakness.

Rule number one.

Most of the long fluorescent bulbs overhead were off, but one hummed noisily above the shop counter, providing just enough light for Olivia to see by. It picked out the rigid metal lines of a second door at the back of the counter, even more heavily shuttered than the main door out front.

She turned at the sound of the Latvian's footsteps, her hands still gripping the straps of her bag.

'You brought it?' he asked. When she nodded, he hoiked up a wad of something green and phlegmy and spat it onto the floor. 'Well? Fucking show me.'

Olivia swung her backpack down off her shoulders. She took hold of the zip, but didn't pull it open. Not yet.

'I've… I'm supposed to get the other package,' she said.

'What you fucking say?' the Latvian demanded, taking a lunging step towards her like he was going to swing a punch.

'Oleg told me not to hand it over until I see the other package.'

'Other package?' The Latvian grabbed his crotch and hissed at her. 'There other fucking package! Now, give me fucking—'

Olivia swung her bag up onto her back. The sudden movement surprised the Latvian so much he took a step back.

'The fuck you doing?'

'I've got very clear instructions,' Olivia told him. She shrugged, aiming to give off an air of confidence she didn't remotely feel inside. 'No swap, no package.'

She stood her ground , unblinking, as the skinhead stepped closer. He stud ied her for what felt like a full minute, then slowly waved a finger at her.

'I know you. You are Bosco's d aughter. Yes?'

Olivia said nothing, not wanting to commit either way. It was one thing if this man had been a friend of her father's, but quite another if he'd been an enemy.

'Ha. Daughter not fall far from father's tree, I think,' he said . He gave her another look up and d own, then pointed to the floor at her feet. 'Wait here. I get money.'

'Be quick,' she said , before he could take a step. A little voice at the back of her head screamed at her, d emand ing to know what the blood y hell she was d oing. But, another voice—a calmer one—told it to shut the fuck up. 'I'm meeting Oleg in ten minutes. He won't be happy if I'm late.'

'Not my problem,' the Latvian replied .

Olivia met his eye. 'It won't be me he's unhappy with,' she said , then she tapped her watch and nod d ed in the d irection the d oor tucked away behind the counter. 'Now, chop-chop. We're all busy people.'

The way he glared at her mad e her worry that she may have gone too far. He'd locked the front shutters. There was no chance of her being able to overpower him. She was completely at his mercy.

Which was why she could n't afford to let him realise that.

She returned the glare with one of her own, and tucked her thumbs into the straps of her bag.

Finally, with a grunt of annoyance, the Latvian walked behind the counter, rolled up the d oor, and vanished into the back of the shop.

Chapter 16

Logan sat in the reception-come-office-area of the Raigmore mortuary, trying to ignore the whining of an electrical saw, and the sloshing of liquids and innards from the other side of the swing doors that led through to the post-mortem room.

Shona had come out to meet him when he'd arrived, decked in plastic coveralls flecked with blood, and had filled him in on what she'd found that had pointed to something more sinister than a tragic accidental death.

Or, more accurately, what she hadn't found.

Someone had pulled out two of Frederick Shaw's teeth. Big ones, too, from near the back. They had done it recently, and they had not been gentle about it.

A cursory check of the rest of him had thrown up further evidence that he hadn't simply fallen asleep in the snow. His toes were black with frostbite—too far gone to have happened the previous night in temperatures barely below freezing.

His fingers were less severely damaged by the cold, but there was bruising on his knuckles that suggested he'd been hitting something hard for a prolonged period of time. Broken bones were a distinct possibility, and she'd arranged X-rays to confirm.

All in all, even without looking in any more detail, she could say for sure that it didn't fit the picture they'd constructed at the scene. The victim may have died of the cold, yes, but it wasn't last night, and it wasn't because he'd fallen asleep in a snowstorm.

Whatever had happened in the final hours of Freddie Shaw's life, it hadn't been pleasant.

As he sat waiting at Shona's d esk, Logan flipped id ly through a textbook. It was full of grisly full-colour pictures of cad avers in various states of d ecay. Not exactly fun read ing material.

He closed the book and returned it to where he'd picked it up from at the far end of the cluttered workspace.

A d esk tid y. Would that be a good Christmas present?

No. Of course, it blood y would n't. Why not just buy her a Hoover, and be d one with it?

He looked d own at the carpet tiles below the d esk.

Actually, maybe a Hoover would n't go amiss…

He turned in the chair, taking the opportunity to examine the office, in case any gift id eas should sud d enly present themselves.

Even if he had n't known her alread y, there was plenty he could 've gleaned about the person who worked in the place. The untid y d esk, the ramshackle stacking of books and fold ers on the shelves, and the bin full of empty Pot Nood le pots all helped paint a picture of someone who worked hard , stud ied lots, but had very little in the way of organisational skills.

Or, for that matter, culinary ones.

There wasn't much in the office that gave much of a personal insight, though. Pot Nood les asid e, it said nothing about her likes and d islikes, her interests or hobbies, or all the many quirks that had mad e Logan first warm to her all those many months ago.

With a sigh of resignation, he conclud ed that the office was going to be no blood y help whatsoever in helping him choose a present, and went back to flicking through the manual on the d esk.

He got as far as a picture of something that should n't have been black, but was, and should 've been on the insid e, but wasn't, and closed the book for a second time.

The swing d oors opened , unleashing a wave of cold and an all-too-familiar smell that put his gag reflex on stand by. Logan stood up quickly, like he'd been caught somewhere he

should n't, then raised his eyebrows and nod d ed past the pathologist into the room beyond .

'That you?' he asked .

'Aye. That's me,' Shona confirmed . She ind icated a rack of
PPE with a tilt of her head . 'Get gloved up, and I'll show you
what we've got.'

—

While the Latvian was through the back, Olivia consid ered her
options.

It might be possible to unlock the front d oor from the insid e,
and make a break for it. Even if she could get the d oor open,
though, she could n't d o it quietly. He'd hear her, and she'd have
to make a run for it.

What if he caught her?

Worse, what if he d id n't, and she had to return to Oleg
without having mad e the switch?

Not really an option at all, then.

What was the alternative? Stay here, wait for the Latvian to
return, and hope the d eal went off without a hitch? She'd been
able to bluff him so far—part of her had been starting to enjoy
it, in fact—but sooner or later he'd realise she was way out of
her d epth.

What would he d o then?

Anything he wanted , and she'd have no way of stopping him.

She turned to the front d oor. It was worth checking, at least.
If there was a possibility of making a run for it, then—

The d oor behind the counter rolled upward s with a series
of clanks and clatters. Olivia fixed what she hoped was an
impatient look on her face, then wheeled around to confront
the Latvian as he emerged from the back room.

'Finally. I was starting to think you weren't coming back,'
she said , crossing her arms over her chest. 'Do you have it?'

Without a word , the tattooed skinhead held up a fat, d irty
envelope that was wrapped at both end s in brown parcel tape.

From the shape of it, and the way it bent as he flapped it about, it was a stack of banknotes. How many, and how much they ad d ed up to, she could n't even begin to guess.

'Now, give me fucking package,' the Latvian instructed . The d im light shone d own on him from above, turning his eye sockets into d ark pools of shad ow. 'And cut your attitud e, little girl, or I cut out your tongue.'

Olivia hesitated , not sure how to play her response. Would staying quiet show weakness? Should she d ouble d own on the role she'd been playing so far, tell him the d eal was off, and d emand to be let out?

He took a step closer. The shad ows fell away from his eyes, and what she saw there mad e her d ecid e to keep her mouth shut. There was nothing behind those eyes. Nothing d ecent, anyway. Nothing that might prevent him from gleefully carrying out his threat.

And there was that feeling again, flood ing her insid es, spiking her heart rate. That sense of helplessness. Of isolation. Of being a little girl trapped in stinking d arkness, while those who were supposed to love and protect her were nowhere to be found .

Without a word , she swung the bag off her should ers, rooted insid e, and took out the tote bag.

'Put it on counter,' the Latvian instructed . He was stand ing behind it, right on the other sid e. Walking over there to set the package d own would put her within grabbing reach. Her legs, having worked this out for themselves, chose not to take a single step.

The Latvian tapped the Formica worktop. 'Put. It. On. Counter.' He slammed a hand d own, making her jump. 'Now!'

Terror overruled her legs and she scampered forward s until she was close enough to toss the bag onto the shop counter. It land ed with a soft thud , skid d ed on the smooth surface, the stopped when the Latvian pinned it in place beneath a finger.

Olivia watched in silence, her stomach twisting itself in complicated knots, as he sat the envelope d own, opened the tote bag, and checked insid e.

116

'What fuck is this?' he asked , after a pause. His eyes raised to meet Olivia's. 'Is this joke?'

'What?' Olivia shook her head . 'No, I d on't...'

Reaching into the bag, the Latvian withd rew a small, colourful plastic bag. Olivia recognised it as a packet of Haribo.

'Oleg throwing in free gift now?' the Latvian asked . He tore open the pack, tossed a couple of the sweets into his mouth, then held the rest out to Olivia. 'Want one? They're very sour.'

'I'm, um, I'm fine,' Olivia replied . She looked very d eliberately at the envelope. 'I should just...'

'Huh? Oh. Right. This.'

The Latvian picked up the envelope, slapped it against the ed ge of the counter so it mad e a loud , echoing bang, then offered it to the girl just as he'd d one with the Haribo.

'Here. Take. Is yours.'

Tentatively, Olivia reached a hand out to take the offered package.

She was an inch from it when it was withd rawn.

'Actually... maybe I give it to Oleg later,' the Latvian announced . His mouth was moving up and d own as he chewed on the sour sweets. 'Maybe it safer if I d eliver personally.'

Olivia's gaze followed the envelope. 'What? No. He told me I had to get it.'

The man behind the counter stopped chewing. Those empty nothings of eyes stared at her for a few moments, then he spat the mushed -up contents of his mouth onto the counter between both packages.

'I not give fuck,' he told her, in a voice that was as d evoid of feeling as his gaze. 'I will take money to Oleg when I am good and read y. Clear?'

'No, but—'

The hand slammed d own again. It hit like a thund erclap on the countertop. His voice, when it came, was like the roar of an animal.

'*Is this clear?*'

Olivia swallowed . If she lunged , she could grab the tote bag back. But what then? Where to then? There was no way out. Nowhere to go.

And she wanted to go. More than anything, she just wanted to go.

'Fine. I'll tell him,' she said . 'But he won't be happy.'

A smile—a real one, not the one that had been carved into his flesh—curved the corners of the Latvian's mouth.

'Not happy at *you*, I think,' he said , then he emerged from behind the counter, fished a set of keys from his pocket, and crunched through the shard s of glass until he reached the roll-d own shutter at the front d oor.

After slid ing the little eye-level hatch open and checking the street outsid e, the Latvian bent and slipped the key into the heavy pad lock that kept the d oor secure.

Olivia's eyes crept sid eways. The money was sitting on the counter just a step or two away. The Latvian had his back to her as he busied himself with the locks and bolts.

Should she?

Could she?

'Don't fucking think about it,' he warned , stand ing and taking hold of the chain that would pull the d oor open. 'Just go. Get out. Tell Oleg I call him in d ay or two.' With a yank, he pulled the d oor open. 'And tell him I liked the Haribo very—'

From out in the snow, Olivia saw movement. A man in a black balaclava stepped in through the open d oor. A bag was pulled over the Latvian's head , jerked d own, tied tight. He twisted , ejecting a muffled roar as he lashed out at his attacker.

Something hard and metallic mad e a sickening thonk against his knee. He started to scream, but an arm was wrapped around his throat, pulling him backward s, cutting off his air.

Just before the man in the balaclava d ragged him away, he locked eyes with Olivia. Those eyes were everything the Latvian's had n't been. They were wid e, and wild , and blazing with emotion.

As he saw her there, he ejected a single word .

'Shit!'

And then, with the Latvian still struggling in his grasp, he retreated outsid e, and was swallowed by the blizzard .

Olivia stood frozen to the spot, not d aring to move. Hard ly d aring to breathe.

A car boot slammed . An engine roared , then fad ed into the d istance.

Still, she d id n't move. Not then. Not yet.

Some time later—she could n't say how much—she conclud ed that she should get the hell out of there.

She mad e it a single step before she stopped again.

The wind whistled in through the open d oor, swirling snow across the carpet of broken glass.

Olivia returned to the counter, picked up the envelope, stuffed it into the main part of her bag, then zipped it shut.

Then, she picked up the tote bag and crammed it into the backpack's front pocket.

Finally, she pulled a sleeve of her jacket up so it covered her hand , and wiped the countertop d own.

And then, with her backpack securely hooked over both should ers again, she stepped out into the snowstorm, and pulled the d oor closed behind her.

–

There were a lot of gaps in Shona's find ings that would n't be filled until more specialised tests had been carried out, but she had enough to paint a pretty clear picture of what had happened to Fred erick Shaw.

He had frozen to d eath. There was nothing new there.

Technically, his organs had packed in d ue to prolonged exposure to extremely low temperatures.

'Not *snowy night in Alness* low temperatures,' Shona had explained . 'More like *lengthy spell in Antarctica* low temperatures.'

She could n't say with any d egree of certainty exactly how cold a temperature he'd been kept in, but minus thirty d egrees Celsius felt like a reasonable guess, given the d amage his bod y had sustained , and the relatively short period of time he could 've been held for.

Given that nowhere in the country had reached that level of cold in record ed history, and the victim was unlikely to have taken a weekend jaunt to the North Pole, there was only one reasonable conclusion.

'Someone put him in a freezer,' Logan said .

'Yeah, that seems the most likely explanation,' Shona confirmed .

She ind icated the bod y spread out on the table between them. Most of Fred erick had been covered up, sparing Logan from the sight of the sutures and scars that would cover his corpse like some road map of horror.

Only his head was visible at the top of the table, his ears and nose blistered and blackened by cold .

'He has cold burns on the backs of his arms and legs,' Shona continued . 'Some of the skin has been pulled away, too.'

Logan frowned . 'Pulled away?'

'You ever licked a frozen lamppost?' Shona asked .

At the far end of the table, the DCI's frown only d eepened . 'What? Why the fu—?' Logan shook his head . 'No. No, can't say I have.'

'Seriously? Wow. You've never lived ,' Shona teased . 'But you know what happens, right? The moisture in your tongue freezes, sticking you to the metal?' She ind icated the bod y again. 'Same principle applies here. Only, because it was cold er, there was enough moisture to make his skin stick. Then, either he got up himself, or someone lifted him. Either way, he left big patches behind .'

'Sound s nasty.'

'Yeah. Would n't have been a barrel of laughs,' Shona said . 'That's not the end of it, either. Lift up the bottom of the sheet there.'

Logan didn't particularly want to lift the sheet, but did it anyway.

'Jesus!'

Freddie's toes were black and blistered, the flesh peeling from the bones like meat from a slow-cooked chicken drumstick. Logan's first instinct was to cover them up again. His second instinct was to vomit into the waste paper basket.

He ignored both.

'Frostbite, obviously,' Shona said. 'Very severe.'

'Aye, you can say that again,' Logan remarked. 'Can I...?'

'Fire on,' Shona said, and the DCI draped the sheet back over the victim's feet, concealing the damage. 'Here's the interesting thing, though—his fingers are more or less fine.'

She leaned over and pulled the side of the sheet up, exposing a bare forearm and a left hand that, for obvious reasons, wasn't the healthiest colour in the world, but was a long way from the rotten mess of the toes.

'Assuming everything was equally as exposed, I'd expect the fingers to be in a similar state to the feet,' Shona said. 'But there's very little damage, other than some possible broken bones. X-ray will confirm.'

'Meaning... what?' Logan pondered. 'Only his bottom half was frozen?'

Shona smirked. Logan couldn't see her mouth behind her mask, but he could tell by the way her eyes crinkled that she'd found the suggestion amusing.

'He was wearing gloves,' the detective quickly corrected.

'It would seem a more straightforward explanation, yes.'

'Why give him gloves?' Logan wondered, staring at the hand like the answer might be written on the back of it. 'If you're going to put him through hell, why keep his hands warm?'

'Maybe they were his own. Maybe he had them with him,' Shona suggested.

Logan shook his head. 'Young guy hitting the town on the pull? Can't exactly see him packing his mittens, can you?

Besid es, it wasn't all that cold on Saturd ay. Weather d id n't turn until later yesterd ay. Whoever was hold ing him must've put the gloves on him.'

Shona shrugged . 'Dunno, then.'

'Preserving fingerprints, maybe?' Logan said , extrapolating one possibility. 'Whoever killed him, they wanted to make sure we knew who he was.'

'That might be it,' Shona agreed . 'Although, it'd only make sense if his prints were on file.'

'*And* if the killer knew they were on file,' Logan ad d ed . 'Which they are, by the way.'

'Ex-con?' Shona asked .

'No. Not Proven. Rape case,' Logan said . 'Which at least gives me somewhere to start asking questions, I suppose.'

He gestured to the victim's head . Besid es the arm, it was the only part of him that was currently exposed .

'Now, tell me about the teeth,' he instructed . 'And then explain to me how the hell Ricketts d id n't spot *any* of this stuff…'

Chapter 17

DI Ford e stood by the d oors to the lift in the Burnett Road police station, waiting for it to make its way d own from the upper floors.

After what had happened last time, the stairs were out of the question. Even trud ging across the car park in the snow had given him a couple of worrying twinges across the chest, and he'd taken a few moments in reception to stand und er the heater, warming up and calming d own.

He'd been two sips into his d rink when Logan had got the message that they were now d ealing with a murd er investig-ation. At any other time, given the celebratory nature of the gathering, those two sips would 've been from a well-aged malt with the tiniest wee d aud of ice.

After his earlier scare on the stairs, however, he'd opted for a half-pint of lager tops. It had earned him some stick from the others at the time, but meant he was fit to d rive and , more importantly, fit to help lead the investigation.

Ben was still waiting by the elevator when one of the women from the front d esk came clattering up behind him. The short run from reception had been enough to almost completely steal her breath away, and the DI waited patiently as she battled through an asthmatic wheeze.

'Sorry, I forgot to say that you've got mail, Detective Inspector,' she said , puffing and panting like she'd been going for gold in the five-hund red metres. She passed him a pad d ed envelope around the size of a paperback book, then put both hand s on her hips and d rew in a big breath. 'Courier d ropped it off this afternoon.'

Ben looked d own at the ad d ress on the front. His rank and name, care of the station. No stamp, barcod e, or other id entifying stickers. He turned it over, but there were no labels lurking on the und ersid e, either.

'What was the courier company, d o you know?'

The receptionist shook her head . 'Did n't see, no. Did n't have to sign for it or anything, though.'

Ben nod d ed , then pinched the corner of the envelope between finger and thumb. 'Thanks. You go and get a seat and catch your breath. Should n't be racing around the place at our age.'

He saw the look of horror on her face and realised that the woman was probably ten years his junior.

'I mean, in our age bracket,' he said . 'Over... fift—'

Christ, no, that was too risky.

'Forty. Over forty. That age category.' He smiled , but she d id n't seem to be buying it. 'What I mean is, we over-forties should n't be racing around the place unless it's for—'

There was a ping as the lift d oor slid open behind him. He'd never been more relieved to hear a sound in his life, and took two backward s steps into the elevator car without saying another word . He stared d own at the package, avoid ing the receptionist's eye until the d oor slid closed again.

'Smooth, Benjamin,' he muttered , stabbing the button for the third floor. 'Very smooth.'

-

Her mother was lying on the couch in the living room when Olivia returned , her eyes rolling back in her head , her mouth moving up and d own like she was chewing on one of the Latvian's Haribos.

Olivia checked to make sure she was breathing, heaved and struggled with her until she was lying on her sid e, and not her back, then pulled the throw off the armchair and draped it over her mother as best she could.

'She's fine,' said Oleg from behind her. 'Leave her.'

Olivia stopped fussing, but only for a moment. Then she finished tucking her mum in, angled her head to ensure her airway stayed open, and only then turned to address the bare-chested man in the doorway.

'What has she taken?'

'I don't know,' Oleg said. He shrugged and smiled, like he'd made some comedic blunder they'd all have a good laugh about later. 'This and that. She'll be fine. Stop worrying.' His interest switched to her backpack, which was still slung over both shoulders. 'You make the switch?'

Olivia nodded and wrestled her arms out of the bag's straps. 'I did,' she said, unfastening the zip and taking out the envelope. 'He gave me this.'

Oleg took the package and squeezed it between finger and thumb, like he was measuring the thickness of it. 'Did he give you any problems?'

Olivia thought about her reply. Did he know? Did the man in the balaclava work for him? Was this all some sort of test?

She could see from his expression that she was taking too long to answer. Suspicion was narrowing his eyes and drawing lines on his forehead.

Olivia sniffed. Shook her head. Avoided meeting his eyes.

'No. No problems. All went fine,' she said, then she clicked her fingers as a detail occurred to her. 'Oh, and he said thanks for the sweets.'

A grin pushed Oleg's concerns aside. 'Oh, he liked that? I thought it could be my thing. Like, a gimmick, you know? Free gift with every purchase!'

Olivia smiled. It did not come easily. 'Good idea,' she said, swinging her bag back onto her shoulder. 'I'd better go do my homework.'

'Homework? Fuck homework! Homework is for pussies, *malyshka*. You and me? We should celebrate. Watch a movie. Have some fun.'

'Uh, I… it's a big project. It's half my mark. I have to d o it,' Olivia said .

Her gaze had wand ered d own to her feet. She forced herself to look at him again, and almost recoiled at the look of cold fury that met her.

He launched himself toward s her, closing the gap between them in a single bound . She saw his hand s come up, then gasped as they clamped her head in place, his calloused palms squashing her cheeks.

With a smack, he planted a kiss on her forehead , then ruffled her hair so violently it almost sent her stumbling into the coffee table.

'Your loss, *malyshka*,' he told her, then he stepped asid e, allowing her a clear path to the d oor. 'Oh, but wait,' he said , before she could start her break for freed om.

Olivia watched as he reached into the back pocket of his jeans and prod uced a fold ed stack of twenty-pound notes. There had to be a thousand quid there, she estimated , as he counted two bills from the top.

'Here. You earned it,' he told her.

'It's OK. It's fine,' she tried to insist, but he thrust it out to her, blocking her exit.

'Take it, *malyshka*,' he said . It was an ord er, that much was clear. 'Take the fucking money.'

Hesitantly, Olivia accepted the two twenties. This seemed to please Oleg immensely, as his face lit up in a broad , beaming smile.

'Good girl,' he said . 'And between you and me? I think this is the start of a very profitable relationship for us both.'

–

Ben sat the package d own on his d esk, ad d ress up, then took a step back from it like he was concerned   it might be giving off some low-level rad iation.

For a few moments, he just stood   there staring at it, then he removed   his coat, hung it on a hanger by the d oor, and   head ed through to the tea room to make himself a cuppa.

When he returned , he went back to stand ing by the d esk as he sipped   from the mug and   contemplated   the parcel.

The envelope was one of those pad d ed   Jiffy Bag things, with the bubble wrap on the insid e. Instead   of the usual white colour, this one was a very pale shad e of blue—the type of blue that might be d escribed   as 'd uck egg' by paint supply shops, pretentious arseholes, and   nobod y else on the face of the planet.

The colour was his second   biggest concern about the envelope.

The familiarity of this whole thing was the first.

'Bugger it,' he said , once his tea was finished .

He d onned   a pair of rubber gloves, took a couple of evid ence bags and   a craft knife from the exhibits d esk, and   pulled   his chair out from und erneath his d esk.

Once he'd   sat d own, he patted   his shirt pocket, muttered   his annoyance, then got up again and   fetched   his glasses from his coat.

Returning, he positioned   the spectacles d own near the end of his nose, extend ed   the blad e of the knife, and   carefully cut an incision into one end   of the Jiffy Bag, just large enough to tip out the contents.

He mad e his pred iction as to what the contents would   be before he upend ed   the envelope, and   d id n't quite know how to feel about it when his guess was proved   right.

But then, it wasn't a guess. Not really. He'd   known what the contents of the package would   be from the moment he'd clapped   eyes on it.

He'd   seen several just like it a few years before. And , while his memory wasn't quite what it used   to be, there were some things you never forgot.

Ben had a quick check to make sure there was nothing else in the Jiffy Bag—there wasn't—then set it asid e and consid ered the items on the d esktop. More than just those specific items, though, he consid ered the bigger picture, and what they repres-ented .

Three things had fallen from the envelope. The first was a wallet. It was slim, and mad e of something that had the look of carbon fibre about it. A silver piping effect ran d own the ed ges, giving it a slightly futuristic feel.

The other items were marked ly less stylish. The second was a tooth.

The third was a finger.

Ben sighed . 'Ah… shite,' he said .

And with that, he reached for the phone.

Chapter 18

A cheer went up as Hamza stepped in through the front door of his house, almost startling him right out of his skin.

Eight members of his extended family were crammed into the narrow hallway behind his wife and daughter, and the majority of them seemed delighted that they'd almost caused him to soil himself.

'Daddy!'

Hamza knelt down to catch a running tackle from his daughter, Kamila. She was getting bigger now—she'd be five next month—and he had to brace himself against her weight as she threw herself at him at full-speed, hands wrapping around his neck.

'Happy Birthday, Daddy!'

Hamza picked her up and held her tight against him. 'Aw, thank you, sweetheart.'

'Is this a lovely cuddle?' she asked, her face buried in against his shoulder so her breath tickled his neck.

'This is the *best* cuddle,' he told her, then he bent forward a little to receive a kiss on the cheek from Amira, his wife.

'Welcome home,' she said. 'Dinner's on.'

'Lucky it isn't burned to a crisp,' grumbled a short, squat Indian woman who stood at the front of the extended family group, a pale blue head scarf pulled tight to hide her greying hair. Hamza felt himself stand up straighter at the mere sound of her voice. 'What time do you call this?'

'Hi, Marwa,' Hamza said, forcing a smile for his mother-in-law. Not that she'd thank him for it, of course.

'You hear that? "Hi, Marwa", he says! Strolls in here late, happy as you like, with, "Hi, Marwa".'

'Leave him be, ummi,' Amira told her. 'He works hard. Some days, it's lucky if he gets home at all.'

This did not impress Amira's mother one little bit. In fact, it only made her expression turn even more sour. 'A man should have work time, and family time,' she said. 'There must be a distinction or—'

To Hamza's relief, two of Amira's brothers stepped in to save him. 'Yeah, yeah. Come on, ummi, let's go check on dinner. Better make sure Amira hasn't messed anything up.'

'Pah! Too late for that,' Marwa said, fixing Hamza with one final foul look before allowing herself to be led off into the kitchen.

The crowd that was left—more brothers and their partners, Hamza thought, although he didn't recognise two of the women—shuffled awkwardly in the hall, like they weren't quite sure what they were meant to be doing.

They all looked immensely relieved when Amira sent them through to the living room to wait for dinner, and with a few more birthday wishes, they piled out of the hall.

Amira rolled her eyes, stepped in closer, and gave Hamza a hug. 'How was your day?'

'Um... mixed,' he said. 'The usual, really.'

'Did you catch any bad guys, Daddy?' asked Kamila, leaning back and fixing him with a look so intensely earnest that he would've sworn he felt his heart grow larger.

'Hundreds,' he told her.

'Eighty-two thousand hundred?' Kamila gasped.

'Eight-two *million* hundred!'

Her eyes widened and her jaw dropped, like this was the greatest news anyone had ever been given. Then she flung her arms around Hamza's neck again, and wriggled excitedly in his arms.

'How was the pub?' Amira asked.

'Pub? That's a sland erous accusation. You'd never catch me in such a place.'

'Yeah, yeah,' his wife replied , jabbing him in the ribs. 'Well, I'm glad you're home. Now my mother will only criticise half the things I d o, since she'll have to split her time between—'

Hamza's phone rang. Amira's eyes snapped d own to his jacket pocket, her mouth stretching out and becoming thin.

'I'm sure it's nothing,' Hamza said , passing Kamila over to his wife. He tried to keep the carefree look fixed on his face as he read the name on-screen, and continued with the forced smile as he pressed the button to answer and held the phone to his ear. 'All right, sir?'

Even from a few feet away, Kamila heard DI Ford e's reply. 'Eh, no' really, son,' he said , and the smile faltered on Hamza's face. 'I know you had plans, and I'm really sorry to d o this…'

Amira shook her head emphatically at Hamza and mouthed , 'No! Don't you d are!'

'…but I'm going to need you to come back in.'

The effort of maintaining the smile was starting to take its toll. Hamza held a hand up to his wife to ind icate he would d eal with it, then turned away so he could relax his aching cheeks. 'Aye, it's just… we were about to sit d own to d inner, sir. All my wife's family is—'

The voice on the other end of the line spoke again. The angle of Hamza's bod y mad e it impossible for Amira to hear what was said , but whatever it was changed the lines of Hamza's bod y language, and mad e him shoot a worried glance back over his should er at her.

'Right, then. I see, sir. Thanks for letting me know,' he said . All he could offer his wife was a sorrowful look and an apologetic shrug. 'I'm on my way.'

–

Logan trudged through the snow, his coat collar up around his ears, his hands buried in his pockets, and his sights set on the Ford Fiesta slouching disappointingly in the Raigmore car park.

Getting parked had been a bloody nightmare, as always, most of the spaces having been occupied all day by the assortment of selfish bastards who used the place as an unofficial Park and Ride.

By the time he reached the car, his feet were wet, his ears were freezing, and his face was frozen into a scowl that would take a warm cloth and a fair bit of patience to remove.

Snow slid from the roof as he opened the door, and landed with a 'paff' on his seat. Mumping and moaning, Logan brushed off as much of it as he could, then manhandled himself into the front of the vehicle, squeezed his knees under the steering wheel, and closed the door with an overly forceful bang.

He had just got the keys in the ignition when the voice addressed him from behind.

'Jack.'

'Jesus!' There was no room for Logan to turn himself around, so he grabbed for the rearview mirror and angled it to give him a view of the back seat. A man a few years his senior sat there, a battered ex-army jacket zipped all the way up to his chin. 'Bob? What the—? What are you doing here?'

Former Detective Superintendent Hoon exhaled a cloud of white mist.

'Freezing my bollocks off, that's what. Get the bloody heating on.'

'I mean, what are you doing in my car? How did you find me?'

'Ways and means, Jack,' Hoon said, tapping the side of his nose. 'Ways and means. Better you don't know.'

'Did you phone Ben?'

'Did I phone Ben? What do you take me for, Jack? A bloody amateur? No, I did not phone Ben!'

'You phoned Tyler,' Logan concluded.

'Is that his name, is it?' Hoon asked . 'I've got him in my phone as "That Boyband Prick".' He conced ed with a grunt. 'And aye, OK. Fine. I phoned Boyband , and he told me where you'd be. I said it was an emergency. Now hurry up and get the fucking engine on and get this heap of shite warmed up.'

Logan thought about arguing—consid ered tossing his old boss out into the snow—but then relented with a sigh and a turn of the key. The engine gave its usual weed y whine, then spluttered into life.

'It'll take a minute to warm up,' Logan said .

'Really? You d on't say,' Hoon spat from the back, sarcasm d ripping from every syllable. 'Is that how car heaters work, is it? Fuck me, you learn something new every—'

Logan turned the engine off again and fold ed his arms across his chest to ind icate he had no intention of turning it back on anytime soon.

'What d o you want, Bob?' he asked . 'I d on't have time to piss about.'

Hoon breathed another cloud of vapour into the front, but mad e no more mention of getting the heating cranked on.

'Fine. I've been thinking about what you said .'

'Said when? Which bit?'

'Jesus Christ. I d on't know,' Hoon retorted . 'It's no' like I was listening to the specifics. I was thinking about what you said *in general*. And … I wanted to ask you something.'

Logan waited . The question d id n't come.

'Right, well, go on, then.'

'Fuck's sake, I'm getting to it, give us a minute,' Hoon snapped . His hand s were clasped in his lap, Logan noticed , the thumbs tapping against each other. 'I was thinking… d o you have the number for any, you know, groups?'

'Groups?' Logan's reflection in the mirror furrowed its forehead . 'Like what?'

'Just, you know. *Groups.*'

Logan tutted and reached for his inside pocket. 'Aye, give me a minute, Bob, I've got The Bangles on speed dial. Will that do?'

It was Hoon's turn to look confused. 'What? What the fuck are you…?'

'It's a joke, Bob. What sort of groups?' Logan pressed. 'Do you mean Alcoholics Anonymous?'

Hoon shook his head emphatically. 'What? No! Stick that right up your hoop! I don't mean anything as full-on as that,' he protested. 'I'm thinking, like… is there one that's like that, but no' as bad?'

Logan turned in his chair to face the man in the back. Being able to glower directly in his eye made it worth the effort.

'Like Alcoholics Anonymous, but *no' as bad*?'

Hoon nodded. 'Aye. Is there no' one that's like a step down from there? Like *Enjoys a Good Bevvy Anonymous*? Or… Jesus, I don't know, *Likes a Pint R Us*?'

'No,' Logan said. 'There's not. Or, if there is, I've never heard of it. So, do you want the number for Alcoholics Anonymous, or not?'

Hoon threw his arms up in the air, shook his head, then spat out a 'Fine'.

Logan took out his phone, opened up a browser window, and began to type. Hoon craned to see what he was doing from the back seat.

'Are you Googling it? I could've fucking done that myself.'

'Aye, bloody tell me about it,' Logan replied. 'Instead of sneaking in here like a creepy bastard.'

Hoon's phone chimed as the message was received. He made no attempt to check it.

'There,' Logan said, returning his phone to his pocket. 'Give them a call. They're easy to talk to. And they won't judge.'

'Aye, well, they'd fucking better not,' Hoon muttered. He scratched his head and stared out of the side window. His breath had fogged the glass, but the lack of visibility didn't seem to be bothering him.

'Was that all you wanted , Bob?'

Hoon said   nothing for a moment, then blinked   like he was waking from a d ream. 'What? Eh, aye. Aye, that was it,' he said .

'You need   a lift home?'

'Home?' Hoon snorted , grinned , then slapped   the DCI on the should er. 'Fuck that. The night is still young, Jack, m'boy. The night is still young!'

The passenger seat slammed   forward s as Hoon pressed d own the lever that would   let him clamber out from the cramped   rear seat of the three-d oor hatchback.

'Cheers for that number,' he said , stretching to open the d oor and   twisting his bod y out through the narrow gap. There was a crunch of snow as his feet touched d own on the ground , then his face appeared   in the d oorway again as he d ucked . 'Oh, and by the way, is it no' high time you called   Nod d y and   gave him his fucking car back?'

Chapter 19

Hamza was given a mug of coffee and an apology when he entered the Incident Room, the first from Tyler, the second from DI Forde.

Sinead looked up from her desk, where she was talking to her younger brother on the phone and instructing him to do what their aunt told him. She rolled her eyes in sympathy, then covered the mouthpiece of the handset.

'One way of getting out of dinner with the family, I suppose,' she said.

He laughed and gave her a thumbs-up, then took a seat at his desk while she returned to her call.

'How did Amira take it?' Tyler asked, sitting at the desk directly across from Hamza's. 'She pissed off at you?'

'Well, I think my traditional birthday treat is out the window, put it that way,' Hamza said.

'Your traditional birthday...?' Tyler began, then the meaning clicked. 'Oh. Right. Damn, you have my condolences.'

Hamza fired up his computer, took a pen from his desk organiser, then flipped to a clean page in the bulky A4 notepad he kept next to the keyboard and mouse. He scribbled the date up at the top—for once, not having to try to remember what it was—then absent-mindedly tapped the point of the pen against the paper, marking it with dozens of inky spots.

DI Forde sat on the edge of the desk closest to the Big Board. A police mugshot of Frederick Shaw had been pinned to the middle of the board, and a couple of snowy crime scene photographs had been attached right below it.

Around the images were several Post-it Notes, each with a name or some nugget of information marked on it in Sharpie.

Hamza recognised some of the names from the discussions they'd had about the case earlier in the day. Colin Rose. Damian Bailey. The paperboy, Evan Findlay.

There was another name, too, though. Joanna Ward.

That one took him back.

Joanna Ward had been the woman who'd accused Frederick Shaw and Damian Bailey of rape last year. She had been a slight, anxious thing that brought forth images of a frightened mouse whenever he thought back to meeting her.

By all accounts, she hadn't been like that a few months previously. She'd been bold, confident, and full of life. Whatever the jury had decided, something had happened to change all that. Something had swapped out everything she had been for everything she now was.

Hamza couldn't imagine for a second that the version of Joanna he'd encountered was capable of murder. But she'd had friends. An older brother. A father who'd sat in stony-faced silence through the trial, watching his daughter sob her heart out as her past sexual history was read out loud by the defence's legal counsel.

He could see why she'd been added, of course. In a normal investigation—under ordinary circumstances—she'd be an important line of inquiry.

But if what DI Forde had told him on the phone was right, then this wasn't a normal investigation, and the circumstances were far from ordinary.

Familiar, yes. Troublingly so, in fact. But about as far from ordinary as it was possible to be.

The door to the Interview Room opened. Logan entered, then stopped when he saw the rest of the team already assembled. Only Dave, who'd managed to go through two pints and a vodka and coke in the time it had taken the others to get halfway through their first drink, wasn't present.

'Thought we were letting you go home?' Logan asked Hamza, as the d oor swung closed at his back.

'DI Ford e called me in, sir,' Hamza said , gesturing to Ben with his coffee mug. 'Given the circumstances.'

'Circumstances?' Logan echoed , looking from the DS to the DI. 'What circumstances? What's happened ?'

'You first. What d id the post-mortem reveal?' Ben asked , but he continued without giving Logan a chance to reply. 'Hang on, let me guess. Froze to d eath, but somewhere a d amn sight cold er than Alness. Signs of torture. Missing a tooth and a finger.'

'Bang on. Except for the finger,' Logan replied . 'How d id you know that?'

Ben stood up, his face a mask of confusion. 'Eh? You sure he wasn't missing a finger?'

'No' unless he was born with eleven of them,' Logan said .

'Well, some bugger's finger's sitting on my d esk,' Ben said . 'So if it's not his, whose is it?'

Everyone turned to look at DI Ford e's d esk. Four clear-plastic evid ence bags sat on it, neatly laid out from largest— which contained a pad d ed envelope with Ben's name and the ad d ress of the station printed on the front—to smallest. This last bag contained a tooth with long, blood y roots.

The bag, one to the left of the last one, held part of a little finger, from the second knuckle up. Probably ad ult male. Bit blistered , but otherwise in d ecent nick, at least in as far as severed bod y parts went.

'Envelope was d ropped off earlier,' Ben explained . 'Ad d ressed to me personally. Fred d ie Shaw's wallet was insid e along with the tooth and the finger.'

'And how d oes that tell you anything about how he d ied ?' Logan asked .

'Because it's how they all d ied , Jack,' Ben said . He slumped in his chair, and looked shrunken and cowed against its high back. 'The ones he told us about, anyway. It's how he killed them all.'

Logan glanced around at the rest of the team. Tyler and Sinead looked as confused as he felt. Only Hamza seemed to have any clue what the DI was going on about.

'You've lost me,' Logan confessed . 'Who?'

'Called himself the Iceman, sir,' Hamza explained . 'Well, I mean, technically he d id n't, but the papers d id , and so everyone just sort of went with it.'

'Shite. Hang on. Aye. I remember this,' Logan said . 'Few years ago now, wasn't it?'

'Five,' Ben said . 'Hamza was still in uniform. That's the case that first brought him to my attention, in fact. Rough one, so it was.'

'What happened ?' asked Tyler. 'I d on't remember hearing anything about it.'

'Before your time, son,' Ben told him. 'He killed five people. Well, five that we know of, anyway. Some were beaten. Some were tortured . All of them d ied of exposure to extreme cold .'

'One in the mid d le of August,' Hamza ad d ed .

'Aye, that's the Highland summer for you,' Tyler said , but the sombre air in the room ensured that the remark fell flat.

'I thought you caught him,' said Logan, thinking back to the coverage of the case. 'Did n't he kill himself, or something?'

'We thought so, aye,' Ben confirmed . 'Bob Hoon was DCI at the time. SIO on the case. Stopping the Iceman is what helped shift him up the lad d er to Detective Superintend ent. Tracked the bastard to a butcher's shop near the town centre. Found him through the back with his wrists slit and a suicid e note left out for us. A confession, basically.' Ben sucked in his bottom lip. 'And a list.'

'A list?' asked Sinead .

'I remember this,' Logan said . 'Names, wasn't it?'

'His "Naughty List", he'd called it,' Hamza said , taking up the story. 'There were six people on it. The first five were all… known to the polis, shall we say?'

'Toerags,' Ben ad d ed . 'Petty stuff, mostly.'

'They were all scored off the list, although we only found three bod ies in the end ,' Hamza continued .

'Who was the sixth name?' asked Tyler. He was hunched forward in his seat, like he was listening to a ghost story around the campfire.

Hamza met his eye, and spoke in a calm, measured voice. 'It was you.'

Tyler's eyes wid ened , narrowed , then repeated this routine as he tried to make sense of what Hamza had said . 'What? Jesus. Why was—?'

Sinead slapped him on the leg with the back of her hand . 'He's wind ing you up,' she said . Then, less confid ently to Hamza, 'Right?'

Hamza smiled . 'Sorry, aye. Could n't resist.'

'Jesus, d on't d o that!' Tyler cried . 'I nearly shat myself there.'

'It was his own name,' Ben said , not joining in with the others' banter. 'George Morales. Family man. Pushing forty. Lovely wife and three kid s. Did n't fit the profile at all, but we had the confession—wife and hand writing experts all confirmed the hand writing, the killings stopped , and so that was the end of it.'

His eyes went to the evid ence bags on his d esk. 'Until it wasn't.'

Logan picked up the second -smallest bag and stud ied the contents. It was a finger, all right. No d oubt about it. The blistering suggested early signs of frostbite, although nothing like the state Fred d ie Shaw's feet had been in.

'This normal, is it?' he asked . 'For your Iceman, I mean?'

'Aye. We got one for every victim. Their ID, a tooth, and one of their fingers or toes,' Ben confirmed . 'You're absolutely sure that's not the victim's?'

'I'll have Shona d ouble-check. Like I say, though, unless he started the weekend with eleven, I know what answer we're going to get.' Logan placed the finger back on the d esk. 'In the meantime, we need to get all this over to Forensics so they can

140

go over it. Then we need to look into Fred d ie Shaw and build a picture of his movements since Saturd ay, re-interview anyone we've spoken to who we think it's worth talking to again, and follow up on any lead s we get from them. And we need to get a shift on, because we've lost a lot of time on this as it is.'

'I can bring Damian Bailey in, sir,' announced Sinead . 'His co-accused in the rape case. Spoke to him tod ay, and he was... well, an arsehole, basically. He might be more cooperative if we bring him in.'

'Do it,' Logan said . 'Tyler, what about you?'

'Colin Rose gave me the names and numbers of two women who left his in the early hours of this morning,' the DC replied . 'He reckons they saw two men walking near the spot the bod y was found . I'll check with the taxi company, too.'

'Good lad . Hamza?'

'Might be worth me talking to Joanna Ward , sir. The rape victim.' He winced . 'Sorry *alleged* victim. I honestly can't see it, but her family, maybe? Some new boyfriend out to prove something? Think it's worth a conversation, anyway.'

'Perfect,' Logan said . 'I'll get a liaison over to the mother's house to keep her upd ated . Ben and I will run things from here for now. I want to familiarise myself with the Iceman case files, and I want you all d oing the same first chance you get. They'll be in your inbox within the next half hour.'

He stood in silence for anything up to three second s, then clapped his hand s together like the crack of a starting pistol. 'Well? Why are you all still blood y here?'

There was a sud d en flurry of movement as Hamza, Tyler, and Sinead all jumped out of their seats and grabbed for bags, jackets, and car keys.

They had just got themselves organised when Ben stood up and ad d ressed the room. 'We all need to bring our A-Game to this one,' he intoned . 'If this is somehow the same man... if he's started a new list... we need to end it before he d oes. Is that und erstood ?'

141

Normally, even in the gravest of circumstances, there was a lightness to DI Ford e. A twinkle in the eye. The hint of a smile.

There was none of that now, though. Not a bit.

'Und erstood , sir,' Sinead confirmed .

'We've got this one, boss,' Tyler ad d ed , throwing in a d ouble thumbs-up for reassurance.

'Aye, I hope you're right, son,' Ben muttered , as he watched the younger d etectives leave. 'I really hope you're right.'

Chapter 20

He woke slowly at first, then all of a sudden, as the pain made itself known.

It was always a joy to watch those first few moments. The awakening was like a rebirth of sorts, as they emerged from the warmth and comfort of their old lives into the cold, harsh cruelty of their new realities.

However short-lived those would be.

And, just like with a birth, that first cry was so important. The anticipation of it so paramount to the whole process.

Men, women, short, tall, fat, thin—it didn't matter. They all cried. They all screamed. Their faces all contorted as they found themselves down here in the cold, naked and exposed, with the stark, blinding light shining down on them from above.

It was like theatre. Poetry.

And it was exquisite.

The first post-scream outburst from the man on the other side of the porthole window was in his native tongue. This was to be expected. He was still coming around. He was still disorientated. His mind would still be racing as it desperately tried to work out where he was. How he had got here.

And why it hurt so very, very much.

He'd know the truth soon enough, though. It would all be explained. Slowly. Patiently.

Every pitiful sob would be appreciated. Every grovelling apology enjoyed. Every ounce of terror captured for posterity.

And then, when it was all over, his name would be checked off.

Before that, though, there would be a new name added to the Naughty List. The girl from the shop. The Latvian would give her up. Of course, he would.

Once they'd got started—once they were into the swing of things— the Latvian would hold nothing back. He would give up everything and everyone he had ever loved. He would say anything and everything just to make the pain stop, even just for a moment.

And it would all be for nothing.

Chapter 21

Detective Superintend ent Mitchell stood by her wind ow, spraying water on a large cactus that sat on the sill. As she watered , she listened to Logan recap the d ay's events, from the d iscovery of the bod y, through the assumed accid ental d eath verd ict, and up to where they were at the moment.

He felt it best to leave the bit about going to the pub for Hamza's birthd ay out. No need to mud d y the waters any more than they alread y were.

Sure, not too long ago the majority of polis business was cond ucted in pubs up and d own the country. Scotland 's fine d rinking establishments had been instrumental in the break-throughs that had brought many a perpetrator to justice over the years.

It was all d ifferent now, of course. Gone were the d ays when Plain Clothes could get away with an afternoon session d own the local, then an evening of d oor-kicking and rigorous questioning, before a couple of swift pints squeezed in at last ord ers.

Despite a vague sense of nostalgia for those d ays, Logan had to ad mit that it was probably best that they'd been left behind .

'Not the most auspicious of starts to an investigation,' Mitchell said , once Logan had finished bringing her up to d ate. He was sitting across the d esk from her empty chair, after she'd told him not to remain stand ing as she was sick of craning her neck to look up at him. 'I trust you're playing catch-up now?'

'Aye. Team's got their ord ers. They're all out following up on lead s now.'

'Promising ones, I hope.'

Logan shrugged . 'Time'll tell.'

Mitchell finished spraying the cactus, then hooked the bottle onto the chain that raised and lowered the wind ow blind s, and turned to the DCI.

'Well, keep me posted . We'll want to squash this one quickly, before the press gets wind . Last thing we need before Christmas is a med ia circus, and the panic it'll most likely cause.'

'Not sure about panic,' Logan said . 'I've just been looking through the old case files. People were cheering the bastard on last time. Said he was d oing our job for us.'

'Yes. Well, that's people for you, I suppose,' Mitchell replied . 'Nevertheless, I want him found and I want him stopped before this escalates. You'll have every available resource at your d isposal.'

Logan began to speak. Mitchell cut him off.

'*Except* a new car,' she said . 'And when I say "available resource" that's precisely what I mean. It's the run-up to Christmas, and we have a third less in the bud get than we d id last year. Almost fifty-percent d own on the year before. We're alread y stretched to breaking point.'

She tutted and shook her head , annoyed at herself for veering into the politics of it all.

'The point is, I'll give you what I can, but I can't give you much.'

'Great.' Logan slapped his hand s on his thighs and stood up. 'Better go roll up the sleeves and crack on, then.'

'Yes. You better had ,' the DSup agreed , taking her seat. She picked up a pen, jotted d own a note, then looked up just as Logan turned to leave. 'How's Ben?'

'Ben? He's fine. Why?'

'He looked a little peaky earlier. Out of breath. Nasty colour. Said he was fine, but he d id n't look it. Keep an eye on him, will you?'

Logan turned to look in the d irection of the Incid ent Room, as if he could see right through all the walls between that room and this one. 'Eh, aye. Of course,' he said .

He'd mad e it just two more steps when Mitchell stopped him again.

'Oh, and everyone was breathalysed before head ing out, yes?' she asked . 'You know, just in case anyone's the worse for wear after your trip to the pub...'

–

'Here, Mitchell said you weren't well earlier. That true?' Logan asked .

DI Ford e looked up from his computer as the DCI came barging in. 'Eh? No. I was grand ,' he said . 'Not sure what's she's on about.'

There was no hesitation before he replied . Not so much as a breath. It was like he'd been poised , waiting for the question, the answer balanced on the tip of his tongue, just primed and read y to be spat out.

Ben clocked the look of d oubt on Logan's face. 'I was a bit out of breath,' he said . 'Should n't have tackled the stairs. Just felt my age a bit when I got to the top, that's all.'

Logan still d id n't look particularly convinced , but now wasn't the time to push his friend further on the subject.

'Aye. Well, maybe stick to the lift in future,' he suggested . He stopped at the DI's d esk on his way to the Big Board . 'And you'll tell me, won't you? If there's anything.'

This time, the answer d id n't come immed iately.

'Of course,' Ben said . 'But I'm fine, Jack. I'm right as rain.' He tapped the pile of paperwork on his d esk. 'Or I will be when we catch this bastard , at any rate.'

Logan unbuttoned the sleeves of his shirt. 'In that case,' he said , rolling the material up to his elbows, 'we'd better crack on.'

Sinead tucked her hand s in beneath her armpits and stamped her feet on the snowy path as she listened to the raised voices insid e.

'Will someone get the blood y d oor?' bellowed a male voice from upstairs. 'I'm trying to blood y sleep!'

'It's not even half-seven, you lazy bastard !'

That was a woman's voice from somewhere further back in the house. It was shrill and filled with venom, like this was just the latest in a long line of shouting matches she'd long-since had enough of.

'I'm on blood y early shift, amn't I? Jesus! Just someone get the blood y d oor!'

Sinead heard the thumping of sullen footsteps d rawing closer. A voice she recognised rang out from the d ownstairs hallway.

'I'm getting it! Fuck's sake!'

Light spilled out onto the path, briefly d azzling the d etective constable stand ing there. The silhouette of Damian Bailey towered over her from the top step. Though Sinead could n't see his face, the way his chest puffed up and his should ers went back spoke volumes.

'What d o you want?' It was less of a question and more of a d emand , like he was hoping his tone would make her reconsid er, and send her scampering away.

Nae chance.

'Damian. Some new information has come to light regard ing Fred erick's d eath.'

'Like what?'

'I think we should d iscuss it d own at the station,' Sinead told him. Her eyes were ad justing to the change in lighting now, and she caught the worried look that went flitting across his face.

He looked back over his should er into the house, then emerged onto the first step d own. He briefly grimaced as his

bare feet sunk into the snow. 'Are you arresting me?' he asked ,
lowering his voice.

'Will that be necessary?' she asked . At this point, she had
absolutely no way to justify placing him und er arrest, but she
was relying on the fact that he almost certainly d id n't know
that. 'I could get Uniform round here, sirens, flashing lights. I
d on't much fancy your d ad 's chances of getting his early night
with all that going on.'

Damian stole a look at the upper floor of the house and
shivered in the chill wind .

'Or you could come with me now,' Sinead continued ,
offering him a lifeline. 'We could go to the station, have a chat,
and you could be home in a couple of hours. It's your call.
Works for me, either way.'

Damian rubbed his arms through the thin material of his
shirt, then blew on his hand s. Around them, the snow d anced
and twirled through the d arkness.

'Clock's ticking, Mr Bailey,' Sinead said . She took out her
phone, making a bit of a show of it for his benefit. 'What's it to
be?'

Chapter 22

Tyler sat nestled in a couch that was made almost entirely of cushions, sipping a glass of milk in a room that was approximately ninety-percent television.

He couldn't recall ever having seen a screen that large before. Not outside of a cinema setting, at least. It must've been a hundred inches from corner to corner, and while there was plenty of wall space around it, it imposed itself on the room, drawing the eye wherever you chose to sit.

It was on at the moment, the picture paused on some scowling orange-faced woman in a Ted Baker dress. *The Only Way is Essex*, Tyler guessed. Or something like it, at least.

The milk was an odd one. After he'd introduced himself to Jamie-Leigh and Eleanor—Colin Rose's 'friends with benefits'—they'd asked him if he wanted something to drink. He'd told them tea or coffee would be lovely, and after five minutes in the kitchen, Jamie-Leigh—the brains of the outfit, according to Colin Rose—had returned with a full pint of milk, and told him it was the only non-alcoholic drink they had in the flat.

'We're completely out of water,' Eleanor had explained, and Tyler had found himself seriously questioning if they knew what happened when you turned that metal thing above the sink.

He'd decided not to blow their mind with that revelation, though, and to instead get down to business. Unfortunately, the women weren't making that easy.

They sat together on an armchair across from him, practically in one another's laps. Both were dressed for bed, and appeared to be wearing nothing but oversized men's shirts that stopped around the mid d le of their thighs.

Eleanor—who was possibly the single most attractive woman he'd ever set eyes on—id ly twirled Jamie-Leigh's hair, her plump, ruby red lips playing upward s into a teasing smile.

Jamie-Leigh, for her part, was d elicately tracing her finger-tips up and d own one of Eleanor's legs. The tickle of her touch would occasionally make the other woman twitch and giggle.

When they spoke, it was with an attempt at a Californian 'Valley Girl' accent, with a rising intonation at the end that implied everything they said was a question. This affected way of speaking had been nailed clumsily on top of two otherwise quite thick Invernesian accents, and it had taken Tyler's ear a few minutes to ad just before he could grasp what they were saying with any d egree of accuracy.

After another tentative sip of his milk, the DC looked around for somewhere to sit the glass. There was a small coffee table that had been carved from a single piece of oak, but it was too far away for him to reach without getting up, and the soft-sprung couch was so low he reckoned it would take him a good half a d ozen tries to get to his feet.

Instead , he set the glass d own on the polished wood floor, then flashed an uncomfortable smile at the women and took out his notepad .

'Um. So. I was talking to Colin Rose earlier,' Tyler said . 'As... as I think I mentioned alread y. Did I mention that alread y?'

'You d id ,' said Jamie-Leigh, still d rawing shapes on Eleanor's inner thigh.

Tyler's eyes were d rawn to the movement. He stared for a while, hypnotised , then blinked and gave himself a shake.

'Right. Aye. Sorry. Long d ay.' Tyler picked up his milk again, his mouth sud d enly very d ry. 'So, he mentioned you might have seen... actually, before we get into that, just for my record s, could you tell me what your relationship with Colin Rose is?'

'We're fuck bud d ies,' Eleanor replied .

Unfortunately, Tyler had picked that moment to take a d rink, and the bluntness of the answer mad e him splutter, choke, and shoot two jets of liquid d airy out through his nose.

'Shit. Sorry,' he wheezed .

The women d id n't seem put out in the slightest. If anything, their smiles had only broad ened .

'Does that shock you?' Jamie-Leigh asked .

'No. What? No,' Tyler replied . His voice was a thin rasp, his throat still constricted from the aborted intake of milk. 'I just... he seems... when I look at you, and ... then him... not that there's anything... I mean, each to their own, and all that. I'm sure he's a... lovely man.'

'He is. So generous,' Jamie-Leigh said .

'*So* generous,' Eleanor agreed .

'He bought us the TV.'

'And the table.'

Jamie-Leigh turned to her... what? Friend ? They seemed very touchy-feely for friend s, Tyler thought. 'No, that was Sinbad .'

'Sinbad bought us the table?' Eleanor asked , her carefully sculpted eyebrows rising in surprise. 'I thought Sinbad bought the bed ?'

'Oh. Wait.' Jamie-Leigh looked up at the ceiling. Her lips moved , like she was read ing something written there, then she gave a firm nod . 'You're right. Sinbad was the bed , Colin was the table.'

'And the TV.'

'And the TV.'

Tyler's head had been tick-tocking left and right, following the women's conversation as best he could .

'Who's Sinbad ?' he asked .

'Just another guy we have fun with,' Eleanor explained .

'Right. I see.' Tyler looked d own at his notepad . He'd written nothing in it yet, but he stared at the empty page for a few moments, regard less. 'And , d oes, eh, d oes Colin know about your relationship with Sinbad ?'

'Relationship? I mean… I would n't call it that, exactly,' Eleanor said .

'And he totally d oes, anyway,' Jamie-Leigh ad d ed , with a wave of a manicured hand . 'Colin likes to hear about what we d o with other men. It gets him off.'

Of everything Tyler had heard so far, this was the part that surprised him least.

Jamie-Leigh sat forward in the chair, the open neck of her shirt falling d own to reveal the smooth bumps of her cleavage. 'Would you like to hear what we d o with other men?' she asked in a voice so soft it was almost a purr.

Tyler clapped his hand s together then sat up straight and pointed , everything sud d enly making sense. 'Of course!' he exclaimed , like he'd just cracked some top-secret cod e. 'You're prostitutes!'

Jamie-Leigh sat back, her face falling. 'Ew. What? No!'

'Jesus! How d are you?' Eleanor spat. 'Do we look like fucking prostitutes?'

Tyler had to ad mit that they d id n't look like the sort of prostitutes he'd d ealt with while in uniform. They d id n't share the d ead eyes or the haunted looks of those women.

'Well, I mean, you get them high-class ones, d on't you?' he found himself saying, then he shook his head , mumbled some-thing that was meant to be an apology, then stole another glance at his empty notebook and wished he'd brought someone with him for backup.

'We d on't charge men for sex,' Eleanor insisted .

'We have sex with men, and they choose to buy us things,' Jamie-Leigh explained .

'Oh, right. That's completely d ifferent, then,' Tyler said . He d esperately wanted to put this part of the conversation behind him, and so grinned at the women to signal his und erstand ing of their arrangement.

He quickly became aware, though, that the grin was too broad , and mad e him look slightly maniacal, so he gulped d own another mouthful of milk, smacked his lips together and went, 'Aah!' far more loud ly than he'd intend ed to, then clicked the top of his pen.

'Anyway. Thanks for clearing that up,' he said . 'Getting back to last night, then, Colin mentioned you got a taxi back from his at around four-fifteen?'

Jamie-Leigh and Eleanor still looked unhappy about the whole 'prostitute' thing. To Tyler's relief, they appeared to have lost all d esire to wind him up, and were no longer twid d ling or stroking each other.

There was a chance he could still regain control of the interview.

'Yeah,' Jamie-Leigh confirmed . 'So what?'

'He said there were two men walking past outsid e the house at the time,' Tyler continued . 'He thought you might have got a better look at them.'

'Uh, no,' said Eleanor. She laughed lightly and pointed to the woman besid e her. 'This one saw nothing.*Noth-ing*. You were so d runk! She was so d runk.'

'Shut up!' Jamie-Leigh replied , prod d ing Eleanor in the ribs and making her squeal with laughter. 'I wasn't *that* d runk!'

'Oh no?' Eleanor asked , then she leaned in, cupped a hand over her mouth, and whispered into Jamie-Leigh's ear.

Jamie-Leigh bit her lip and winced , her neck flushing red as she was remind ed of some forgotten memory.

'Shit. Yes. OK, I *was* that d runk,' she ad mitted .

'You are *such* a slut,' Eleanor told her. She smirked at Tyler. 'She is *such* a slut.'

Tyler wasn't sure what to say to that, but felt he should say something. When the word 'Congratulations' came unbid d en from his mouth, though, he wished he had n't bothered .

Ignoring the slightly puzzled looks on the women's faces, he urgently pressed on.

'So, you didn't see any men wandering around outside?'

'I said *she* didn't,' Eleanor said. 'I did. And, speaking of being totally wasted, these guys looked *totally* drunk. Especially the one on the...' She held up both hands and stuck the thumbs out so they formed right angles to her fingers, then regarded them for a few moments in silence. '...right.'

Jesus, Tyler thought. *Maybe Jamie-Leigh is the brains of the operation.*

'Can you describe them?' Tyler asked.

Eleanor closed her eyes, cocked her head to the side, and sat there for a few moments, unmoving, like she was channelling voices from beyond the grave.

'Not too tall. But not short, either,' she said. Her eyes moved beneath the lids, giving the impression she was deep in REM sleep. 'Dark clothes. They weren't, like, *fat*, but not skinny, either. Like... medium.' She opened her eyes again. 'Did you get all that?'

Tyler finished writing his notes, then read them again. 'Not tall or short, not fat or thin.'

'Bingo,' Eleanor said. 'And dark clothes. Although, everything was pretty dark, so maybe just put "clothes".' She smiled hopefully. 'Does that help?'

'Absolutely fucking not,' was what Tyler wanted to say, but professionalism prevented him from doing so. 'Anything else you can tell me?'

Eleanor shrugged. 'Just... like I say, they were drunk. Staggering all over the place. One guy was holding the other one up.'

'Holding him up?' Tyler asked.

'Yeah, you know. Like, the guy on the—' Another check of the hands. '—right was so pissed he couldn't even walk. So the other guy was pretty much carrying him.'

'Pretty much carrying him, or could he have been carrying him?' Tyler pressed.

Eleanor closed her eyes and tilted her head again, channelling the spirits of her own memory. Jamie-Leigh licked a finger and, with a giggle, stuck it in the other woman's ear, d rawing a snort of surprise and a slap on the wrist.

'Ew. Quit it, you manky bitch!' Eleanor said , the faux Californian twang falling away momentarily. She wiped her ear, then turned back to Tyler. 'Sorry, what d id you ask again?'

'You said the guy on the left was "pretty much carrying"—'

'Right, right, yeah,' Eleanor said , waving a perfect hand to silence the d etective. 'Yes, I suppose he could have been carrying him. Like, if you told me the guy on the—' She brought up the hand s again for one last check. '—right was unconscious, I'd probably believe it.'

Tyler scribbled a note in his pad . 'Right. I see,' he said , when he had finished . He looked from one woman to the other, watching for a reaction. 'And what if I told you he was d ead ?'

–

Hamza sat in his car, watching the house at the end of the road slowly fad e out of view as his breath fogged the insid e of the wind screen and the snow piled up on the outsid e.

Why had he volunteered for this? Why had he put himself forward to come here?

The street looked d ifferent, the snow having given the whole place an impromptu makeover. There was no mistaking it, though, even with the fluffy covering of white. He'd recognised it the moment he'd turned the corner.

He'd remembered the last time he was here.

But he d id n't want to remember. He d id n't want to d well. So, instead , he thought about the meal he was missing back home. The embarrassing stories. The birthd ay hugs. Even the petty d igs from Amira's mother. He'd take them all over this. Here. Now.

Over the pain he was about to inflict. The anguish he was about to d red ge up. The past horrors he was about to unleash.

'Just get it over with,' he told himself. 'Just go over there and get it d one.'

He threw open the d oor and got out of the car before he could talk himself out of it. The car's ind icators all flashed once as he hit the remote locking button, then he thrust his hand s into the pockets of his jacket, lowered his head , and marched on through the snow until he reached a gate.

He remembered the gate. Remembered her hold ing onto the wrought-iron spars, her knuckles white, her face wet with tears. Remembered her parents plead ing with her to let go, to get in the car, to go with them to court, to say her piece, and let the truth be heard .

She'd refused . She'd begged . She'd plead ed with them not to make her go, not to make her say it, not to make her think again about all those things that had been d one to her in that room by those two men.

It had been Hamza who had finally convinced her to release her grip. He'd been the one to get through to her. He'd been the one who had talked her round . Talked her into it.

'It's only your testimony that can put them away, Joanna,' he'd told her, all soft voice and practised kind ness. 'If you d on't go, they'll walk free. You can put them away, Joanna. You can make sure they d on't d o this to anyone else ever again.'

She'd trusted him, in the end . She'd gone in. Gone over every sord id d etail of it, sobbed her way through the cross-examination, and stood shivering with shock as her whole life was rifled through by the d efence barrister, and her character was torn to shred s before the court.

And after all that, the bastard s had walked free anyway.

Hamza still remembered the look she'd given him as she was led away by her parents. She'd watched him from the back seat of their car, stared at him as they'd d riven her away from the court in silence.

This was your fault, her look had told him. *You made me go through this.*

And now he was back to make her go through it all over again.

The gate creaked out a low, solemn note as he pushed it open. Somewhere in the house, a dog barked at his approach. A big bugger, by the sounds of things. That was new.

He padded up the path, feet crunching in the snow, each step more difficult, more arduous than the one before.

He'd talked her into it.

He'd convinced her to walk, head held high, into the lion's den.

They had torn her to pieces.

And it had all been for nothing.

He stopped at the door. There had been trees on either side of the path when he'd last been here, but those were gone now, replaced by a security light that had kicked into life the moment he'd started his approach up the path.

Why had he volunteered for this? Why had he put himself forward? What had he been thinking?

He thought of dinner, fond memories, and warm, birthday hugs.

He thought of the evening that could have been.

And then, with the dog snarling at him through the door, he extended a gloved finger, rang the bell, and braced himself for what was to come.

Chapter 23

Sinead had just got out of her car, and was about to open the back d oor to let Damian Bailey out, when she heard the crunching of footsteps come hurrying up behind her, and caught the reflection of a uniformed officer in the tinted glass of the BMW's rear wind ow.

'Sinead ? Hi.'

A familiar male constable smiled a little too eagerly as he slowed from a jog to a trot, then came to a stop a foot from where Sinead was stand ing. She took a subtle step back, keeping the d istance between them.

'Uh, hello.'

'It's Jason. Jason Hall. We met at Tulliallan.'

'I know. I remember,' Sinead said . 'We spoke a few months back. Outsid e that house.'

Mostly, it had been Jason who'd spoken, of course. He'd had a few things to say about Sinead 's move upstairs.

Jason winced and nod d ed . 'Yeah. That's what I wanted to talk to you about, actually,' he confessed . 'I saw you this morning, and … well… I wanted to apologise. I was out of ord er saying the stuff I said . You worked blood y hard to get where you are.'

'It's fine,' Sinead told him. 'Job makes us all a bit crazy sometimes.'

'I'm not crazy.'

Sinead half-laughed , realised the PC wasn't joining in, then shook her head . 'No, that's not what I meant. Just… it's fine. No harm d one.'

'I'm proud of you,' he said , with a level of sincerity usually reserved for TV melod ramas. 'You've d one so well.'

'Uh... thanks,' was about the best response Sinead could come up with.

Technically, the best response she could come up with was 'why the hell are you proud ? We barely even know each other, you weird o', but she felt a simple 'thanks' was the more professional option.

'Got any plans for Christmas?' Jason asked .

Sinead glanced into the car. She and the constable were reflected there, but she could just make out the shape of Damian Bailey watching them through the shad owy glass.

'Just... spend ing it with my fiancé.'

'Oh. You're engaged ? I d id n't know. You d id n't mention.'

'I'm, uh, mentioning it now,' Sinead said .

'Bit late,' Jason said . He flicked out his tongue and pulled it back through his teeth, like he was scraping off some bitter taste. 'How long's this been going on?'

'Well, since...' She shook her head . 'Actually, that's none of your business.' She ind icated the back wind ow of the car. 'I've got a witness here. I have to go.'

'Oh. You've *got a witness here*, have you?' the PC asked , mimicking the imagined slight. 'Well, far be it for a lowly Uniform to hold you back,*Detective Constable*. I'll leave you to it.'

Despite the promise, he d id n't move. Not a step.

'Well, go on then,' Sinead urged .

Jason's gaze scanned her from top to bottom, then he shook his head , about-turned , and went marching off, head ed away from the station.

Sinead waited until he'd been swallowed by the falling snow, and was safely out of earshot, before muttering, 'Apology not accepted , you prick.'

She opened the d oor and ind icated for Damian to get out.

'Who was that? Your boyfriend ?' he sneered .

Sinead slammed the d oor shut at his back, forcing him to jump clear.

'Just shut up and get moving,' she instructed .

Then, with a check to make sure Jason wasn't coming back, she pointed Damian in the d irection of the station's front d oor, and trud ged through the snow behind him.

—

Logan skimmed the final few pages of the Iceman report, then flipped the fold er over and went back through until he found the photograph of the man they'd held responsible for the killings.

George Morales. Third generation immigrant. No apparent connection to any of the victims. No history of violence, no criminal record , nothing that would ring any serial killer alarm bells at all, in fact.

He d id own a butcher's shop, he d id have access to a walk-in freezer, and hand writing experts had analysed the confession and suicid e note, and had confirmed he'd written it himself. The killings had stopped with his d eath, and the case was closed after a relatively speed y inquest.

The Iceman had been stopped , and the city could sleep safely once more.

'Christ, Hoon must've blood y lapped that up,' Logan muttered , d rawing a slightly puzzled look from the d esk of DI Ford e.

'Sorry, Jack?'

'This. The case. The praise and accolad es. Hoon must've blood y loved it.'

Ben sat back in his chair and interlocked his fingers over his stomach. It growled , remind ing him that d inner should 've been hours ago, and d emand ing to know why he had n't eaten yet.

'Eh… maybe. I suppose he must've,' Ben said . 'He d id n't really show it, though. I'm not sure he was completely convinced we had the right man, but there was pressure from above to take the win, so he d id . When no more bod ies turned up, he was more relieved than anything, I think.'

'What d id you think? About George Morales, I mean.'

Ben d rummed his fingers on his belly and stared past Logan to where flakes of snow were cascad ing through the d arkness. 'I was surprised . He wasn't what I'd been expecting. I actually looked into him a bit more in the weeks after we wrapped the case. Kept thinking I'd find something that would make it all make sense. Some d ark secret he was keeping that would square everything away.'

'But you d id n't?'

Ben shook his head . 'Not a thing. Perfectly nice guy, by all accounts. Only time he'd ever been involved with the polis had been as a victim.'

'Oh aye?'

'Someone killed his d og. Well, his kid s' d og, he said . Kicked shite out of it, then set it on fire.'

Logan's lips twitched upward s, briefly baring his teeth. You saw a lot of horrible, senseless violence in their line of work. For better or worse, you got used to it. You learned to live with it, and with the knowled ge of what your fellow human beings were capable of.

Sometimes, though, the bastard s still found a way to surprise you.

'Ever catch the people responsible?' Logan asked .

'Not that I know of, no,' Ben said . 'Bastard s, whoever they were.'

Logan opened the fold er again, and flipped through until he found the list of victims the Iceman had taken cred it for. While only three of the bod ies had been found , the other two had both been officially d eclared d ead , having apparently vanished off the face of the Earth.

One of them—the third victim—had a criminal record . Domestic violence. He'd received a suspend ed sentence and an injunction that he'd gone on to break. His was one of the bod ies that had been discovered. Or rather, one of the bodies that had been left for them to find.

It had been placed in the front garden of the judge who had carried out the sentencing, propped up on a bench, extremities black with frostbite.

The other victims the Iceman had taken credit for had all had run-ins with the polis, too. A couple of them—an alleged paedophile and a suspected people trafficker—had gone to court, but received a Not Proven and a Not Guilty verdict, respectively.

There hadn't even been enough evidence to prosecute the other two. One of them had been arrested for his suspected involvement in a hit and run that had left a woman and her four-year-old daughter dead. In the end, there hadn't been enough evidence to take it to trial, and he'd strolled out of the station a free man.

The other—a young man in his late teens, who'd been in and out of the care system growing up—had been accused of killing a cat in a particularly brutal fashion. A report had been sent to the Procurator Fiscal, but it was felt that a conviction was unlikely, and so he had been let off with a warning.

'The cat fella. Duncan Milburn. Any chance he killed George Morales's dog?' Logan asked.

'We looked. Tried to see if that fit,' Ben replied. 'But we couldn't find anything that linked the two. Although, Milburn was—and forgive me if I get a bit technical here—a fucking head case. He'd sit there in interviews and argue with himself. Like, full-on hold two sides of a conversation. He was referred to a mental health care team, but got lost in the system some-where, I think. Didn't get help before he wound up dead, anyway.'

Logan turned a couple of pages. 'His body was never found?'

'No. He's one of the ones that didn't show up. Him and the people trafficker.'

'Crawford Johnstone-Foster,' Logan read. His lips drew up again, just like they had at the thought of the dog-killer. 'I'd have put him away just for the blood y name. Doesn't sound like a hard ened criminal, though.'

'We thought he was the brains behind the outfit, no' the one d riving the trucks,' Ben explained . 'Rich bastard . Owned a load of land in Argyll and Bute. Donated hund red s of thousand s the Tories over the years. Evid ence was strong, but... well, I suspect he moved in some pretty powerful circles. I spoke to his solicitor after the case, and even he could n't believe they won.'

'Amazing what money'll buy you these d ays,' Logan remarked .

'Aye,' said Ben, sad ly. 'Very true.'

They went back to read ing in silence, Logan jotting d own notes as he scoured through the report more closely, and Ben occasionally clicking his mouse as he mad e his way through all the files relating to Fred erick Shaw's arrest and court appearance for the rape charge.

'Know what you're d oing for Christmas d inner yet?' Ben asked , not looking up from his screen.

'Eh, no. Not yet,' Logan said . 'Shona's half-invited me round , but I wasn't sure what you were planning.'

'Me? Och, nothing,' Ben said , still glued to his monitor. 'Lot of fuss about nothing, if you ask me. Just another d ay, isn't it? You should go. Don't worry about me. I'll be grand . You should go.'

Logan peered over the top of the other workstations to where Ben sat. The DI clocked this and smiled back at him, but it was a paltry effort.

'Aye. We'll see,' Logan said . He checked his watch. It was eight o'clock, and they were just getting started . It was going to be a long night.

The d oor opened just as he turned his attention back to the report. Sinead entered , a woolly hat pulled low on her head , her nose and cheeks red from the cold .

'That's Damian Bailey in,' she announced , rubbing her hand s together. She was probably trying to get the blood flowing again, but it equally might have signalled her excitement to get started . 'Want to lead the interview, sir?'

'No, you're fine,' Logan said . He stretched and flipped the fold er closed . 'You lead , I'll sit in.'

'Me? You sure about that, sir?' Sinead asked , pulling the hat from her head and ruffling her hair back to life. 'I d on't have a huge amount of experience lead ing on interviews yet.'

'Well, you'll have a bit more after tonight, then,' Logan replied .

'Right. Aye. Thanks. Good ,' Sinead said , and Logan could hear the nerves kicking in.

'You'll be grand , Sinead ,' he told her. 'Christ, if Tyler can d o it...'

Sinead smiled . 'Fair point, sir,' she conced ed . 'Mind if I grab a coffee first?'

'Only if you get me one, too,' Logan said . 'Oh, and anything I should know about Mr Bailey?'

'Well, he's an arsehole, but you'll figure that out for yourself after about five second s in his company,' Sinead replied . 'He spent the whole way here insisting the first he heard about Fred - erick's d eath was when I told him earlier tod ay. And he called his solicitor before he'd even left the house. He was waiting for us when we arrived . They're both through in interview room one now. So, you know, if you think it'd be better you lead ing...'

Logan pointed past her to the d oor. 'Just get that coffee sorted ,' he told her. 'Then we'll go in there together and you can give the bastard s what for.'

Chapter 24

Joanna had simultaneously shrunk and grown in the months since Hamza had last seen her. She'd gained weight—two stone, maybe more—but she sat hunched over and folded in, like she was trying to make herself too small to be noticed.

She'd refused to see him, at first. He'd sat with her father in the large, almost stately, living room, listening to the ticking of a grandfather clock in the hall, and the shouted protests from upstairs as Joanna told her mother to send the detective away.

The shouts had become sobs, then angry shrieks, then thumping, then silence. And then, it had all started again, and Joanna's father had done his best to ease the palpable sense of embarrassment that hung in the air between them.

'So, how've you been, son?' he'd asked.

Hamza had always got on well with Billy Ward, even after the verdict had been returned.

'You all did your best,' he'd told Hamza and the CID team who'd led the investigation. 'We don't blame you one bit for what happened.'

Joanna's mother, Melissa, had been less forgiving. Before the trial, there had been nothing she wouldn't do for the investigating team, providing teas, coffees, and homemade cake when they came over to talk to the family, offering to make them lunch and dinner if things were dragging on.

As the family had left the court, she'd barely glanced at Hamza and the others. When she did, there was something venomous in the look, like they hadn't just failed Joanna, they'd betrayed her.

'Um, aye. Not bad , Billy,' Hamza had replied , as somewhere overhead something smashed against a bed room wall.

'That's good ,' Billy said . 'Family well?'

'Aye. Fine. Thanks.' Hamza's eyes had gone to the ceiling as a series of screeched obscenities rang out. 'How has Joanna been?'

Billy's cheeks had seemed to sink at that, until Hamza could make out the shape of his skull. He leaned forward , picked up a poker, and mad e a few lacklustre stabs into the fire crackling away in the hearth.

'Not great, if I'm honest,' he'd ad mitted . 'Not great at all.'

He had n't been lying. Once Melissa had finally talked Joanna round , Hamza had seen the toll the past year had taken on her.

It wasn't the ad d itional weight that shocked him. She'd been painfully skinny the last time he'd seen her, and she looked a healthier shape now than she had then.

It was the way she held herself that he knew would haunt him. The d ullness of her eyes, and the way they were constantly shifting around the room, ever-alert for potential d anger.

And the way she would n't look at him—or maybe could n't look at him. Not once.

Her parents had installed themselves on the couch besid e her, one on either sid e. Hamza d id n't feel it was his place to point out how visibly uncomfortable their closeness mad e her, d espite it being abund antly clear from where he was sitting.

'Hi, Joanna. How have you been?' he asked .

She shrugged . At least, Hamza thought that was what the movement was, although it was so small, and over so quickly, that he could n't be sure.

'I know I'm probably one of the last people you want to see, Joanna,' he continued . 'But... well, something's happened , and ...'

Shite. And what?

As he looked at the girl and her parents on the couch, Hamza's heart d ropped d own into the pit of his stomach. How

167

could he d o this? How could he ask her these things? How d are he? It wasn't right. It wasn't fair.

But, it was his job. And , like them or not, the questions had to be asked . The line of inquiry had to be pursued . No matter the pain it might cause.

'Fred erick Shaw was found d ead in the early hours of this morning,' he said , pulling the plaster off in one big tug.

The reactions of Joanna's parents were instantaneous. Billy sat forward , eyes wid e, mouth d ropping open in surprise. Melissa, meanwhile, clasped her hand s together as if in prayer, and rolled her eyes to the ceiling, like she was giving silent thanks.

Joanna's reaction, on the other hand , was much more subd ued . Her eyes stopped moving and held on one spot in the corner of the room for several second s, before finally flitting to Hamza. Not to his face. Not quite. It was more like the point where his neck met his chest.

But it was a start.

'Dead ?' she asked , her voice so soft and quiet he would 've thought he'd imagined it, had he not seen her lips move.

'That's right.'

'How?' asked Billy. One hand was gripping the arm of the couch, while the other had found Joanna's left hand and was squeezing it supportively. His expression was hard to read , but there was nothing in it to suggest he'd be send ing a wreath to the funeral.

'We believe he was murd ered ,' Hamza said .

'Murd ered ?!'

Billy's expression was less d ifficult to read now. It was prac-tically gleeful.

'Good blood y rid d ance!' Melissa chipped in. She grasped for her d aughter's other hand , and interlocked their fingers together. 'Serves the bastard right!'

'Mum,' Joanna mumbled .

'Well, it d oes! What he d id .'

'What about Bailey?' asked Joanna's father. 'Anything happen to him?'

'No.'

Billy let out a slightly disappointed grunt. 'Still...' he said. 'What happened, exactly? How did he die? Painfully, I hope.'

'Dad.'

'Well!'

'I'm afraid I can't go into the details at the moment,' Hamza said. 'I just... I wanted to keep you informed. I felt that you should know.'

'Aye! Thanks, son. Thanks a lot. We really appreciate you telling us,' Billy said.

He was positively beaming now, and patted his daughter's clasped hand several times before bringing it to his mouth and kissing it. Joanna made no attempt to stop him, her arms flopping around under her parents' control.

'Right. Aye. Like I say, I felt you should be kept in the loop,' Hamza reiterated, then he took a slow, shallow breath, and clasped his hands together between his knees. 'If you don't mind me asking, have any of you had any contact with Frederick Shaw recently?'

Billy's smile held firm for a few moments, before a look of confusion formed on his forehead and worked its way down.

'What do you mean?' he asked.

'Contact?' asked Melissa, gobbing out the word like it was poison in her mouth. 'What do you mean by that? Why would we want to have contact with either of those bastards, after what they did?'

'Mum...'

'I know, darling. I know. Shh,' Melissa said, without so much as a glance in Joanna's direction.

She brought up her daughter's hand and kissed it, just like her husband had done with the other one. Joanna's limbs remained limp, not her own to operate.

'Hold on. Hold on a bloody minute,' Billy said, his look of confusion taking on a darker, angrier edge. 'Are you here because you think we had something to d o with the bastard 's d eath? Is that what this is?'

'No. Not that. Not at all,' Hamza said . He consid ered his next few word s carefully. 'It's just… a formality. If we want to catch the person responsible, we have to—'

'Catch him? What for?' Melissa d emand ed . 'You should be giving him a blood y med al, you ask me. You should be thanking him for getting rid of that piece of work. I mean, you lot could n't d o it.'

'We d id our best, Mrs Ward ,' Hamza replied , but it was a weak argument, and Joanna's father quickly seized on it.

'Your *best*? Is that what that was?' he barked , a vein bulging on the sid e of his neck.

'Dad , stop,' Joanna protested , but her voice was too soft, her father's anger too great. If he heard her, he d id n't let on.

'Do you know what that lawyer of theirs put her through? Do you know how he treated her? The things he said ?'

'She could n't sleep for months after that. Months!' Melissa threw in. 'Could you, sweetheart?'

She kissed her d aughter's hand again. Billy jumped back in before Joanna could utter a syllable.

'Did we kill that piece of blood y filth, Detective Constable? No!'

'It's actually…' Hamza began, then he stopped . Correcting them on his rank wasn't really important, given the circumstances.

'Am I glad someone else d id ?' Billy continued . He bent forward , eyes locked on Hamza's, a look of triumph fixed on his face. 'Too blood y right I am! I'm over the moon. I hope the bastard suffered .'

'Dad !'

Billy was on a roll now and paid her no heed . 'And d o you know what? I hope the other one gets what's coming to him, too!'

'Shut up!' Joanna cried , pulling her hand s away, pulling them in to her tightly wound centre. Her voice filled the room as a series of rising shrieks. 'Shut up, shut up, shut up, *shut up!*'

Her parents locked eyes over her head , mouths hanging open. Billy shot a foul look in Hamza's d irection. *This is your fault*, it said *Look what you've done.*

'Happy, Detective Constable?' asked Melissa, reaching for her d aughter's hand again.

Joanna wrenched her arm away and bound ed to her feet. 'No! It's not him! It's you.'

'Me?' said Melissa, a confused smile spread ing across her face. 'What d o—?'

'Both of you! Just let him speak, all right!' The emotion that had d riven her up off the couch was rapid ly ebbing away. Hamza could alread y see the fire d ying in her eyes, like being separated from the sofa was d raining all her energy. 'Just… just please shut up and let him speak.'

'We're just telling him what he need s to hear, sweetheart,' Billy soothed . He patted the space on the couch besid e him, smoothing out the ind ent Joanna had left. 'Come on, sit back d own. If you want us to pipe d own, we'll pipe d own. Won't we, Mel?'

'We will. If that's what you want,' Joanna's mother agreed . 'We were just saying what he need ed to hear. That's all. If you want to talk, you can talk. That's fine. Of course, that's fine.'

Joanna's round should ers had slumped again. Her head was lowered , and she took a shuffled step back toward s the safety of the couch.

Without meeting the eye of anyone in the room, she settled herself back into the space between her parents.

'Good girl,' Billy said , all smiles and sad eyes. He turned to Hamza. 'Now, Detective Constable, unless there was anything else, I think you should —'

'I want to talk,' Joanna said .

'Are you sure, sweetheart?' her mother asked . 'You know how upset you get.'

171

'I want to talk,' Joanna reiterated . 'Alone.'

'Alone?' echoed Billy, practically scoffing at the suggestion. 'You can't be serious?'

'I d on't think that's such a good id ea, love,' Melissa ad d ed 'It'll only upset you. You d on't want any more sleepless nights like you had before. Do you?'

Hamza saw something hard en in Joanna's expression. She sat as far forward as she could , putting as much d istance between herself and her parents as possible while still remaining anchored to the couch.

'Can you take me to the station?' she asked .

'If that's what you want,' Hamza replied .

'Of course that's not what she wants!' Billy yelped . 'Jo! Joanna!'

Joanna kicked herself upright, away from the sofa and the smothering sanctuary it provid ed .

'Don't be d aft, sweetheart,' Melissa protested .

Both parents were reaching for their d aughter's hand s. The scene remind ed Hamza of a painting he'd seen of lepers stretching to touch the healing hand s of Christ.

At least in this version, nobod y's noses or ears had fallen off.

'Right, then,' Joanna said , wrapping her arms around her mid d le and hugging herself tightly. 'Let's go.'

–

Ben was giving some serious thought to eating a second Garibald i when the email came through. It turned up innocuously enough, with a faint ping the only fanfare announcing its arrival in his inbox.

He'd had enough of looking at reports for the moment, and the ping held promise of a d istraction, even if only a momentary one.

He stared blankly at the keyboard , struggling to remember the combination of keys Hamza had shown him that would instantly bring up the email program.

'It's much quicker to d o it like this, sir,' the DS had told him, after the fourth or fifth d emonstration in as many minutes. 'Saves you having to click the mouse. You just need these two keys.'

Now, thirty second s of staring at the keyboard later, and none the wiser as to which keys Hamza had told him to press, Ben clicked the mouse.

The PC chugged and whirred for a moment, then the screen changed to show his inbox. The top line was in bold , signalling a correspond ence that had n't yet been read .

Ben ad justed his glasses and looked more closely. It was an internal email from another Police Scotland ad d ress, and had just a single word as the subject line:

'Finger'.

Ben picked up the biscuit and took a nibble while he read the contents of the email. It was short and to the point, promising a full report to follow, but giving him a head s up on something the send er—one of the forensics bod s—thought would be of interest.

Crumbs fell like tiny hailstones onto the keyboard , getting lost between the gaps in the keys and the trenches below as Ben read to the end of the short email. It was saying... wait. What was it saying...?

He read it a second time, more slowly.

Then a third time, just to be on the safe sid e.

'Jesus Christ,' he spat halfway through a fourth and final skim of the text, spraying yet more expensive technology with bits of half-chewed Garibald i biscuit. 'Surely that can't be right?'

Chapter 25

DC Bell had been correct—Logan d id n't like Damian Bailey. Rightly or wrongly, he'd alread y formed an opinion of the young man before he'd met him, and meeting him had only further cemented it.

If the DCI d isliked the witness, though, he positively loathed his solicitor. Robert Foster was preposterously young, meticulously groomed , and annoyingly good at his job. Logan had only met the man in passing a couple of times, but he'd seen him argue a case, and had been simultaneously impressed and horrified by his ability to emotionally manipulate a jury.

He always managed to avoid the jud ge's ire by staying on the right sid e of the rules, and he was consid ered a real rising star at one of the local law firms. Despite only being in his mid -twenties, it was clear there was a partnership role looming in his not-too-d istant future, whether at his current company, or some other one.

Basically, everything Logan d id n't want in a legal counsel.

'Thank you for coming in, Damian,' Sinead said , once the formalities had been taken care of and the record ing started . She was sitting d irectly across the table from Damian, while Logan sat opposite the lawyer and fixed him with a scowl of scarcely concealed contempt.

'Mr Bailey,' Foster corrected .

'Sorry?'

'I'd prefer you to ad d ress my client as Mr Bailey. His friend s call him Damian, and you've alread y mad e it very clear with your actions tonight that none of us are friend s here.'

'My actions?'

Foster rolled his eyes like a weary teacher. 'Yes. You just thanked him for coming in, but by the sounds of things, you didn't exactly offer him a lot of choice, Detective Constable...?'

'Bell,' Sinead said.

Foster wrote the name on his pad and underlined it heavily. 'And you're the infamous Detective Chief Inspector Logan, correct?' he asked, raising his eyes just briefly, like the presence of the more senior detective barely registered as an afterthought.

'That's correct, aye.'

The solicitor jotted that down, too. It was all part of some power play, Logan knew. They'd both given their names barely a minute before for the recording, and the DCI had watched the slimy bastard across the table's lips moving as he'd made a mental note of them both.

'By the sounds of things, you didn't exactly offer him a lot of choice, Detective Constable Bell,' Foster repeated. 'It is now...' He checked his watch—an expensive-looking thing with a gold bezel and a tan leather strap. '...eight-seventeen in the evening, on a Monday, in December, during one of the worst snowstorms in recent memory. Was it strictly necessary to drag my client out of his house at this time, when he's already provided you with a statement this afternoon?'

'No one dragged him out,' Sinead said.

'Oh, but you might as well have. You threatened to bring in more officers and cause a scene,' Foster reminded her. 'Knowing full well what my client and his family were put through earlier this year. And, unless you're quite frankly an idiot, you must be aware of the sort of gossip, speculation, and tittle-tattle that have followed Damian as a result of those false accusations.'

He turned sideways in his chair and crossed one leg over the other, leaning an elbow on the seat's rigid plastic back.

'So, did you physically drag him out? No. No one is saying you did. But did you use the threat of further emotional trauma for him and his family to get him here? The possibility of further judgement from neighbours? Whispers in the supermarket? We both know you did, Detective Constable. So, please, let's all be grown-ups here and just say it like it is.' He smiled at both detectives in turn, showing teeth that were far too white. 'Hmm? Can we all agree to do that?'

It would be wrong to punch him, Logan knew. Of course, he did. Punching the smug bastard would cost him his job, and whatever paltry sum was left in his polis pension.

It would almost be worth it, though. The moment of satisfaction would be so great, so intense, it would almost be worth the lifetime cost.

Almost.

He sat on his hands and resisted.

For now.

'Anyway,' he said, urging Sinead to continue.

'Anyway,' she echoed. 'As you know, Mr Bailey, Frederick Shaw was found dead earlier today. We now believe he was murdered. You were the last person that we know of to see him alive.'

'I didn't kill Freddie, if that's what you're saying,' Damian retorted. His face was tight and confrontational, the backup from his brief giving him a renewed sense of confidence. 'He was my mate. Why would I?'

'You tell us,' Sinead said.

'He just did, Detective Constable,' Foster interjected, laughing drily. 'He told you he had no involvement. Next question, please.'

Sinead shot Logan a sideways glance. He nodded, without taking his eyes off the solicitor, and Sinead jumped back in.

'Earlier today you told me the last you saw of Freddie was when he took a woman he'd met in Johnny Foxes into the toilets, where they had sex. You assume he left after that, because you didn't see him again.'

She took Damian's silence as confirmation of this.

'I'm going to have to ask you again what I asked you this afternoon, Mr Bailey. If you didn't see him again, how do you know he had sex in the toilets?'

'And like I said to you, sweetheart, why else would she go into the toilets with him?' Damian asked.

'He "shagged her bent over one of the bogs". That's what you said to me earlier, isn't it? I wrote it down, but it was such a vivid image I don't need to check my notes,' Sinead told him. 'Quite descriptive that. It suggests to me that you know more about what happened than you're letting on.'

'You ever been shagged in a pub toilet?' Damian demanded.

Logan's gaze crept from the solicitor to his client.

He continued to sit on his hands.

'I can't say that I have, no,' Sinead replied.

Damian's eyes went to her chest. There was something sneering about his gaze when it returned to meet her own. 'Nah. I bet you haven't,' he said. 'Well, believe me, there aren't many positions to choose from.'

'How many, then?' Sinead asked, holding his eye.

Damian hesitated. 'What?'

'There aren't many positions to choose from. How many?'

The solicitor shook his head and sighed. 'What's the point of—'

'Save your objections for court, son. You're not impressing anyone here,' Logan growled. 'Answer the question, Mr Bailey.'

Damian looked to his counsel. Foster shrugged like the whole thing was completely irrelevant.

'I don't know. Like...' The witness counted slowly on his fingers. 'Five or six.'

'I see. And yet, you specified one of those five or six positions in particular when you told me your side of the story. If you didn't speak to Freddie again, how did you know?'

Damian shifted uncomfortably in his chair. 'Figure of speech, wasn't it?'

'It's not one I've ever encountered before,' Sinead said . She looked at the other two men, one on her sid e of the table, one on the other. 'Anyone else? Is it a man thing? Is "shagged her bent over one of the bogs" a commonly-used figure of speech?'

'Certainly no' in my house,' Logan said . 'Mr Foster, how about you?'

Foster gave an impatient little wave and checked his watch. 'Look, entertaining as this whole pantomime is, I'm sure I d on't need to remind you that my client is a witness, not a suspect. He has come here of his own free will—emotional manipulation notwithstand ing—to help you bring the investigation into the murd er of his lifelong best friend to the swiftest possible conclusion.

'Given the d ownright hostile nature of your questioning thus far, I'm close to recommend ing to my client that we terminate the interview and leave.' Foster flashed those perfect white teeth at both d etectives in turn. 'However, as we all want the same thing here—the killer of Fred erick Shaw brought to justice—we're prepared to continue, provid ed you both d rop the atti-tud e. Sound good ?'

Logan's hand s wriggled beneath his thighs, d esperately trying to free themselves.

'Apologies if we were coming over as hostile,' Sinead said , respond ing before Logan could finish counting to ten in his head . 'That wasn't our intention. We appreciate Mr Bailey's help in this matter.'

'That's more like it,' Foster said . He waved a hand , ind icating she was free to continue.

Sinead cocked her head to the sid e a little, swept a stray strand of hair from her face, and gave Damian both barrels of her most sympathetic smile.

'Sorry, Mr Bailey, I forget how rough all this must be on you. How long were you and Fred d ie friend s?'

'Since nursery,' Damian replied . His eyes glistened . He chewed on his bottom lip, partly through nerves and partly, Sinead thought, to keep it from shaking.

'Long time. And I know you went through a lot together.'

A nod . Another chewing of the lip. 'Load s.'

'I'd imagine you must want his killer caught even more than we d o,' Sinead said . 'We've got officers going over the CCTV at Johnny Foxes now, and for the surround ing area. We're really hopeful we'll pick Fred d ie up somewhere, and start to figure out what happened to him. Who d id this. But if there's anything else you can tell us, Mr Bailey—anything at all—it'll help us find Fred d ie's killer and bring him or her to justice. Fred d ie might be gone, but you can still help him. That's what best friend s d o, isn't it?'

Her smile softened . Her eyes puppy-d ogged .

Logan fought the urge to laugh. The poor bastard had no chance.

'He... I suppose he can't get into shit for it now,' Damian said , visibly wrestling with some internal conflict. 'Can he? He can't be, like, charged with anything after he's d ead ?'

'Like what?' Sinead asked .

Damian sighed , and reached for the pocket of his ripped jeans. 'It's not like it was a big secret. He stuck it on Snapchat right after.'

'What is it?' asked the solicitor, craning his neck to see the screen as Damian prod uced an iPhone and unlocked it. 'Should I look at this first?'

'It's fine. It's nothing to d o with me. He just sent it to me,' Damian said . He set the phone on the table, and hit the 'play' icon on a vid eo.

A sizeable bare arse appeared on the screen. That was the first thing any of them saw.

A few second s later, the picture was clear.

A woman bent over the toilet in a narrow cubicle, und erwear around her ankles, d ress pushed up high enough to reveal a tattoo on her lower back.

A man, grunting as he violently thrust into her from behind .

Text overlaid across the mid d le of the image read : 'Told u fat bird s need shagging 2.'

Several second s into the vid eo, a hand slapped the woman across the backsid e, d rawing a squeal of pain from her, and a raised thumb from the man d oing the thrusting and filming.

'We've seen enough. Turn that off, please,' Sinead instructed , sitting back in her chair.

Damian tapped the screen to pause it, just as another loud smack rang out.

'Fred erick sent you that, I take it?' the DC asked . She wasn't wearing the kind ly smile now. It had been replaced by some-thing cold and hostile. 'Did the woman know she was being filmed ?'

'I d on't know, d o I?'

'Well, d id the other women?' Sinead asked . 'I mean, presum-ably this wasn't the first time he'd sent you something like this?'

Damian reached for his phone. 'It's just a laugh, isn't it? Just a bit of fun.'

'Leave that,' Logan instructed . The sharpness of his tone and the glowered look that accompanied it mad e Damian stop with his fingers an inch from the mobile. 'That phone contains important information pertaining to an ongoing murd er invest-igation.'

Damian glanced at his solicitor, looking for clarification. Foster's only response was a weary sigh and a single nod of his head .

'What d o you mean?' Damian asked .

'Meaning, son, that we'll be hold ing onto it.'

'You can't d o that. It's my phone! Can they d o that?'

'Technically, yes they can,' Foster said . 'But for all the good it would d o them. They can't access it without your permission or a search warrant.'

'We could get a warrant.'

'Eventually, maybe,' Foster conced ed . 'But there are no guar-antees. Much quicker and easier if my client were simply to send you a copy of the vid eo to an email ad d ress of your choosing, d on't you think? That would rend er a search warrant unnecessary, and any attempt to pursue one could be construed as victimisation of my client. A client who has already suffered extensively as a result of false prosecution by officers based in this very station.'

Logan was tempted to push it and hold onto the phone, even if only to annoy the pair of smug arseholes on the other side of the table.

He decided to delegate the decision.

'Detective Constable Bell? How do you want to proceed?' he asked.

Sinead blinked in surprise, but recovered quickly.

'Fine. He can send it. But we want it sent before he leaves the room.'

'That won't be a problem,' Foster said. He tapped Damian on the arm and indicated for him to pick up the phone. 'And then, once that's done, I think we'll call it a night. My client has had a traumatic day, and I think it's time he went home.'

'We aren't finished,' Sinead said.

'Yes. Well, unfortunately for you, *we* are,' Foster insisted. 'If you have any further questions for my client, I'm sure he'll be happy to answer them during office hours, as and when his schedule permits.'

'You're letting Fred die down here, Damian,' Sinead said, the lines of her face softening again into a look of concern. 'If you walk out now, if you don't tell us everything you know, you're letting him down. I know that's not what you want, is it? Help us, Damian.'

The 'Caring Cop' act fell on deaf ears this time. Across the table, the witness's defences were back up. 'It's *Mr Bailey*,' he reminded her. 'And like my man here just told you, this interview's over.'

Chapter 26

The d rive to the station had been awkward and uncomfortable. Joanna had insisted on sitting in the back, and had gripped the hand le of the d oor with both hand s, like it was the only thing anchoring her to the world .

She had n't spoken a word , d espite Hamza's initial attempts to engage her in conversation. He'd quickly taken the hint, and they'd mad e the rest of the trip in silence, save for his occasional comment on the weather when the silence became too stifling for him to bear.

She'd appeared to shrink further and further, getting smaller and smaller as they'd approached the station, so by the time they pulled into the car park Hamza got the impression there was barely anything left of her.

He'd opened the d oor and stepped back, warned her t watch her step, then escorted her through the snow toward s a sid e entrance that would bypass all the hullaballoo of the reception area.

She'd kept her d istance at all times. Her eyes had become alive with panic when he'd stopped by the lift and pressed the call button, and she'd nod d ed briefly but enthusiastically when he'd suggested they take the stairs.

He'd taken the lead , keeping himself visible in front of her, rather than hid d en behind . She'd let him get five or six steps ahead before following, each step a plod d ing one, her left hand never once leaving the top of the wood en bannister as they'd wound their way up through the build ing to the third floor.

'You OK?' Hamza asked once they reached the third -floor land ing.

Joanna's eyes were focused like a laser guid ance system on the set of d ouble swing d oors at the DS's back. Her breath was rasping in and out of her, her legs wobbling like they might be about to give way.

'We d on't have to go in,' Hamza told her. 'I can take you home, or we can go somewhere else to talk. It d oesn't have to be here.'

'It's fine. I'm OK,' Joanna said . She snapped her head forward , urging him to open the d oors, to hurry up so they could get this over with.

With a smile of encouragement, Hamza opened one of the d oors and stepped asid e to let her through.

Joanna paused at the threshold of the d epartment and looked d own at her feet as they stepped through the open d oorway, as if she would n't be able to believe what they were d oing unless she saw it with her own two eyes.

'Still OK?' Hamza asked .

She wasn't. Not even close. But she lied with a nod of her head .

'Right. Good . We'll go to one of the interview rooms and have a chat,' he said , lead ing the way through the corrid or. 'You fancy tea? Coffee? Can probably get a soft d rink from the vend ing machine if you'd prefer that?'

'I'm fine.'

'Right, well, if you change your mind , just—'

A d oor opened ahead of them.

A man emerged .

Hamza's voice was d rowned out by the sound that filled Joanna's head . It was the crashing of water on rocks. The beating of a billion sets of wings. The roaring of an Arctic wind that stole her breath away and chilled her to the bone.

'Fuck,' Hamza said , stopping sud d enly and throwing an anxious look back over his should er.

Joanna felt for the wall, praying she found a door there. An exit. An escape.

The man hadn't seen her yet. Hadn't turned her way. Hadn't noticed her standing there, eyes wide, mouth flapping, tears springing unbidden to her eyes.

Hamza turned quickly, blocking her view of him, and his of her. The sudden movement startled her. She hissed sharply and shrunk back, drawing the attention of the man in the corridor just as a second man emerged behind the first.

She knew this one, too. His face, like the first, was burned into her memory, albeit for different reasons. The second man hadn't violated her physically, but the humiliation he'd inflicted on her had been perhaps even greater, even more shameful.

'What the fuck is this? What's she doing here?'

Damian Bailey's voice was angry. Incredulous. He started to move along the corridor, but his solicitor caught him by the arm, holding him back. 'Was it her? Did that lying bitch kill Fred die?'

'In here,' Hamza said, opening the closest door and urging Joanna to enter. The room beyond was dark. Cramped. Windowless. The thought of it made her breath run out and her head spin, but whatever dangers it held, they couldn't be worse than *him*. Them. Those two men.

Could they?

Hamza clicked on the light, revealing a room filled with filing cabinets and box files. 'There's no one there. I'll wait out here. Go.'

That was enough to tip the scales. Joanna stumbled across the corridor and into the room, tucking herself all the way at the back as Hamza closed the door with a thump.

'Well, did she? Did she kill him?' Damian barked, pulling free of Foster's grip.

'Damian…' the solicitor protested, but his client wasn't listening now. He stormed along the corridor, and didn't slow as he approached the door.

He was taller than Hamza, his reach greater. He moved to push past, but the DS stood his ground.

'Touch that door, and you're under arrest,' Hamza warned.

'For what, knocking on a fucking door?' Damian sneered, still trying to force his way past.

Hamza put a hand on the other man's chest in an attempt to hold him back, but Damian batted it away and took a step towards the door, arm reaching out.

With a flurry of movement, DS Khaled caught the extended arm, wrenched it so Damian's thumb was almost touching his shoulder blade, then slammed him face-first into the wall beside the door.

'I can think of at least five charges I can get you on,' Hamza spoke in his ear. 'Pick a number.'

'Ow! Jesus! Fucking watch it!'

'Everything all right, Detective Sergeant?' asked Logan, appearing in the corridor at Hamza's back.

'All in hand, sir,' Hamza said, keeping Damian pinned to the wall. 'This gentleman just decided to test my patience, that's all.'

'Aye, he seems to have a knack for that sort of thing,' Logan said.

'Let him go. Now,' Foster instructed. 'Or I'll be advising my client to press charges on this officer, and this department as a whole.'

'Will you now?' Logan asked. He drew himself up to his full height, and enjoyed the change of colour it brought about in the solicitor's face. 'Here's my counter offer, son. You get your client out of here, and he might not find himself in any more trouble.'

'What trouble? There's nothing you can get him on,' Foster scoffed.

Logan pointed to the man currently pinning Bailey to the wall. 'DS Khaled there is an exceptionally good detective,' he said. 'If he says he can think of five charges he can bring against your client, I'd advise not putting that to the test.'

'I just want to talk to her,' Damian hissed through gritted teeth.

'Well, you can't,' Hamza told him, twisting the arm an extra half inch. 'Ever. You d on't get to speak to her ever again. You got that?'

'That's enough, Detective Sergeant,' Logan intoned .

Hamza thrust an elbow forward , clattering Damian hard er against the wall. '*Got it?*' he d emand ed .

A hand clamped d own on his should er. A grip far greater than his own pulled him back. It wasn't firm enough to force him to break his hold on Damian Bailey, but it was enough to make it clear that it could d o so if it wanted .

'Hamza. That's enough,' Logan said again. 'Let him go.'

With a grunt of d isappointment, Hamza turned , d ragging Damian away from the d oor and send ing him stumbling along the corrid or with a shove.

'Get out. Both of you,' he instructed , pointing past them to the exit. Logan and Sinead both stepped into position behind him, backing him up.

'I will sue the fucking shit out of this place!' Damian bellowed , as Foster pulled him by the sleeve toward s the d oor. 'And if that d irty lying slut had anything to d o with Fred d ie' d eath, I'll—'

'You'll shut your blood y mouth, you id iot!' the solicitor spat. The venom in his voice and the yank he gave on the sleeve were enough to shock his client into silence. He backed into the d oors, swinging them outward s into the stairway. 'Unless you want to find yourself another lawyer.'

If Bailey replied , the d etectives d id n't hear it through the heavy d ouble d oors. They swung closed with a clunk that acted as a sort of full stop to the whole sorry episod e.

Logan gave it a moment to make sure it wasn't all going to kick off again, then turned to the DS. 'So. Mind telling me what all that was about?'

Hamza winced , and d ropped his voice d own low. 'Sorry, sir. I just... I d id n't think about him being here.' He ind icated the storage room behind him. 'Joanna Ward wanted to come in to talk to me.'

'Joanna Ward ?' Logan echoed , brow furrowing as he searched for the name.

'Shit,' Sinead whispered . 'The woman he... or who said that he and ...'

Hamza confirmed with a nod and a gesture that urged them to stay quiet. 'She's, eh, she's pretty anxious at the best of times. This... seeing them... shite. What a mess. I'd better talk to her.'

'Want me to stay?' Sinead asked .

'Would you? That might help, aye,' Hamza said , smiling gratefully.

Both younger d etectives turned and regard ed Logan solemnly, all six-and -a-half feet of him.

'What?' he asked , returning the look.

'Just... might be best if you leave us to it, sir,' Hamza said . 'Like I say, she's pretty nervous. Mostly around men. And , well...'

'You look terrifying,' Sinead conclud ed .

'Oh, well thanks very much,' Logan replied , and it was hard to tell if he was pleased by the comment or hurt by it. He checked his watch, groaned quietly, then jabbed a thumb in the d irection of the Incid ent Room. 'Meet me through there when you're d one. Hopefully, Tyler will be back by then, so we can get the Big Board upd ated and see where we are.'

'Right you are, sir,' Sinead said . 'Will d o.'

Logan cast a look at the storeroom d oor, then clapped a hand on Hamza's should er. 'Well d one, son,' he said . 'And good luck.'

–

Ben was up on his feet and pacing when Logan entered . He'd been up on his feet and pacing for a while now, if he was being honest, his mind whirring, and an impend ing sense of d read slowly filling his legs with concrete.

'There you are,' he said , when the DCI entered the Incid ent Room. 'I was about to come and get you.'

'Took a bit longer than expected ,' Logan said , looking the old er man up and d own. 'What's the matter? What's happened ?'

'The finger,' Ben said . 'The one that was d elivered tod ay.'

'What about it?'

'We've ID'd it.'

Logan's eyebrows rose in surprise. 'Alread y? DNA?'

Ben shook his head . 'Print.'

'Our stray finger's got a record ?'

'Not exactly, but he's been arrested . It's Duncan Milburn.'

'The head case you told me about? The one pulled in for killing the cat?'

'The very same,' Ben confirmed . 'Looks like we found the first part of his bod y.'

'But it's been years since he went missing. It must've been kept—'

'Frozen. Aye. Looks like it,' Ben said . 'Which means that, signed confession or no signed confession, George Morales almost certainly wasn't the Iceman.'

'Great. So we're saying the bastard 's still out there, up to his old tricks?'

Most of the colour had d rained out of Ben's skin, leaving only the grey tones.

'It would seem that way. Yes.'

Logan stud ied his old friend more closely. Ben had n't fully met his eye since he'd entered , and the pacing back and forth wasn't like him at all.

'What aren't you telling me?' the DCI asked .

Ben shook his head . Shrugged it off. The d eception was wafer-thin, though, and Logan saw through it immed iately.

'What is it, Ben?'

DI Ford e stopped his anxious pacing and switched to nervous fid d ling instead , his fingers knotting and writhing together like some frenetic worm orgy.

'If it's him—if it's the same fella as before—then I'm worried .'

'If it's him, then we'll catch him,' Logan said , but the attempt at reassurance was d ismissed with a shake of the head .

'I'm not worried about that. I mean, I am, but... that's not it.'

He sat on the ed ge of the closest d esk and gripped the wood , forcing his fingers to behave themselves.

'Then what is it?'

'The list. I'm worried about the list he mad e.'

Logan wasn't quite following. 'He'd scored all the names off, had n't he? What's the problem?'

'Not that list,' Ben said . Although spoken softly, the enormity of his word s seemed to expand to fill the Incid ent Room. 'The other list.'

Logan took a shuffled step closer, his confusion only d eepening. 'I d on't und erstand . I've read the case file. What other list?'

'We buried it,' Ben confessed . 'I found it at the scene, bagged it, but kept it away from the others.' He stared blankly at the wind ow, and the spots of white d rifting against the backd rop of black. 'I thought about binning it. He was d ead , so I d id n't see the point in hanging onto it. Did n't see the point in worrying anyone unnecessarily. In the end , I took it to Hoon. Asked him what he thought we should d o.'

'And ?'

'And he gave me a bollocking for not turning it in right away. Called me all sorts, as I'm sure you can imagine,' Ben said . 'But he buried it. It never got record ed . Not officially. We tucked it away, hid it in with all the other evid ence. Just in case.'

'So, where is it now?' Logan asked .

Ben looked away from the wind ow long enough to focus on his d esk, and the evid ence bag that lay on top of it.

Logan picked it up without a word and examined the contents through the protective plastic. It was a small scrap of paper, torn from a notebook. Five names were written on it, and Logan soon und erstood Ben's temptation to d estroy it. Two of the names he d id n't recognise, but the other three he knew only too well.

Robert Hoon.

Benjamin Ford e.

Hamza Khaled .

'Jesus,' Logan muttered , turning the bag over but find ing the other sid e of the paper blank. 'Does Hamza know?'

Ben shook his head . 'Like I say, I d id n't want to worry him. His wife was alread y struggling with him being in the polis. They had their kid d ie on the way. Last thing either of them need ed was to know he was on some nutter's blood y hit list.'

'Can't imagine Alice would 've been over the moon about it, either.'

Ben smiled weakly. 'No. No, she'd have had a thing or two to say, I'd imagine. But it was Hamza I was most worried about. Him and the other two.'

'I d on't recognise the names,' Logan said .

'Couple of DCs working the case,' Ben explained . 'Both moved on a few months later. One's in Australia now, I believe. The other took a cushy MoD job and left for Lond on. Haven't heard from either of them in years.'

His eyes went to the list. His fingers resumed their anxious d ance.

'If it's him, if he's still on the go, then we might all be in d anger, Jack. Everyone on that list could be his next victim. I'm not bothered about myself, and quite frankly Hoon d eserves everything that's coming to him. The other two are probably beyond his reach, but Hamza, Jack. What about Hamza?'

Logan returned the evid ence bag to its spot on the d esk. 'I d oubt any of you are in any d anger,' he said . 'Fred erick Shaw's nowhere on that list, which tells me he's started a whole new one. And clearly the fucker sees himself as some sort of vigilante. Killing the polis? I d on't see that winning him many fans.'

'Aye, well we both know that's not true,' Ben remarked. 'He could put our head s on spikes and half the blood y city would cheer.'

'Maybe,' Logan conced ed. 'But it still d oesn't fit his pattern. He's no' a cop killer. He thinks he's hunting the bad guys.'

'Right. And if we're hunting him, what d o you think that makes us in his eyes?' Ben asked. He blew out his cheeks, pinched the brid ge of his nose, then stood up. 'You're probably right. It's probably nothing. Chances are, the bastard was just going to try to put the wind up us with it. But we'd better tell Hamza, anyway. Can't keep it from him any longer.'

'Aye. Only fair,' Logan agreed.

'And Hoon, too.'

Logan was less quick to concur with that one. 'I mean, I'm not sure we need to rush into...' he began, then his conscience got the better of him. 'Aye. No. You're right. I'll give him a call. Make sure he keeps his eyes open.'

'Make sure who keeps his eyes open, boss?' asked Tyler, strid ing into the Incid ent Room and grinning like the cat who had n't just got the cream, but inherited the whole d airy.

'Long story. Where the hell have you been?'

'Talking to those lassies,' Tyler said. 'Mental set-up there, boss. Eye-opening. Truly. They have sex with d ifferent blokes— aye, threesomes, like—in return for gifts and jewellery and stuff.'

'So they're prostitutes?' Ben said.

'They tell me they're not, no,' Tyler replied.

'I d on't care what they told you, you've pretty much just given us the d efinition of prostitutes,' Logan said.

'Aye, that's what I thought, but... they explain it better than me,' Tyler said. 'Like, they d on't *charge* for sex, exactly. They just *have* sex, and then the men sort of shower them with gifts.'

Ben shook his head d isapprovingly. 'If they walk like a pros- titute, and quack like a prostitute, they're prostitutes,' he said.

Logan shot him an amused look. 'Quack? What sort of prostitutes have you been talking to, you d irty old bastard ?'

'Shut up. You know what I mean,' Ben tutted . 'Did you get anything off them?'

Tyler blinked in shock, fired a glance at his crotch, then hurried ly shook his head . 'What? No! I d id n't go anywhere near—'

'Information, son,' Logan said , cutting short the DC's garbled reply. 'Did you get any information off them?'

Tyler ejected a short, sharp laugh. 'Oh. Aye. That makes more sense,' he said . 'And aye, a bit. They confirmed they saw two men when they left Colin Rose's place. Could n't give me much of a d escription, but they thought one could 've been carrying or d ragging the other.'

'So, one of them could have been the victim?' Ben asked .

'Shona reckons he d ied some point yesterd ay. Either morning or afternoon, although the fact he was frozen makes it d ifficult to pinpoint,' Logan said . 'If one of the men was Fred d ie, he would 've been d ead when they saw him.'

'They could n't give you any d escription at all?' Ben asked .

Tyler shook his head , but his grin somehow became even more triumphant. 'No, but I went to the taxi company and managed to speak to the guy who picked them up. And he gave me...'

He thrust a hand into a pocket of his jacket and rummaged around , his smile losing some of its shine.

'Hang on. It's here somewhere,' he said , checking a d ifferent pocket. He patted several d ifferent pockets, one after the other, his expression becoming increasingly alarmed until, with a victorious, 'Aha!' he prod uced a small USB thumb d rive and held it aloft like it was some rare magical artefact. 'Guess what this is.'

'Dashcam footage,' said Logan.

'That would have been my guess, too,' Ben agreed .

'Uh, yeah. Yeah, that's right, boss. Footage from his d ashcam,' replied Tyler, a tiny bit crestfallen. 'Thought it'd take you a bit longer than that, to be honest, but that's right. Dashcam footage!'

'What are you waiting for, son? A chocolate watch?' Logan asked . He stabbed a finger in the d irection of Tyler's computer. 'Get it on, and let's see what we've got.'

Chapter 27

Olivia sat scooted up at the top of her bed , her back against the pad d ed head board , her raised knees forming a hillock belo the covers.

Her iPad lay on the bed besid e her, the YouTube app open, the inane chatter of some perky wannabe influencer helping to d rown out the thud -thud -thud , and the gasping and th grunting from the other sid e of the wall.

Helping, but not d isguising it completely.

She tried not to think about what was going on in any d etail, although Oleg's running commentary and forceful command s to her mother d id n't make that easy.

Still, at least she knew he was busy, and that she would n't be interrupted .

Leaning out of the bed , she took her schoolbag from beneath it, and unzipped the front section. The tote bag lurked in there like it had been lying in wait for her, bid ing its time.

Why had she taken it? And why had n't she told Oleg? She should 've either left it on the counter, or hand ed it over as soon as she'd got back. Those were the only two options that mad e any sort of sense.

Hold ing onto it? That mad e no sense. What could she possibly gain, besid es problems? If Oleg found out that she had it and was hid ing it from him, he'd …

Actually, she d id n't want to think about what he'd d o. She'd just have to make sure he d id n't find out.

She'd have to get rid of it somehow. Toss it in the river, maybe. She could n't exactly just throw it in the bin.

Or could she? As she sat there on the bed , the wall behind her shaking, the YouTuber prattling on about her top five tips for that smokey-eyed look, Olivia realised that she had no id ea what was in the bag.

She was pretty sure that 'a shitload of d rugs' was a solid guess, but which d rugs? She had n't spent the d ay rattling, so she d id n't think the bag contained pills. Beyond that, though, it was anyone's guess.

The noises from next d oor were still grind ing on. This was her best chance to look and see what she was actually d ealing with.

The tote bag was heavy. Heavier than she'd remember it being when she'd hand ed it over and picked it back up at the shuttered shop. Of course, ad renaline had been surging and her mind had been racing then, and the weight of the bag had been less of a concern than getting out of there alive.

Now, though, without the pressure of survival, she noted the weight. It was about the same as a bag of sugar, she reckoned . Which was… what? She had no id ea.

She Googled it on her phone. Two-point-two pound s. A kilo. That seemed about right.

After a quick listen to make sure Oleg and her mother were still occupied , Olivia unwrapped the tote bag and looked insid e.

A lumpy rectangular package sat at the bottom, wrapped in textured grey tape.

None the wiser, she reached into the bag and gripped the package. It was tightly packed , but there was some give in it, so she could rule out a block of cannabis resin. Not grass, either. Too heavy for that.

She took the wrapped rectangle out of the bag and then immed iately d ropped it onto the covers like it was burning her fingers.

For a moment, she just stared at it, as if waiting for it to d o something. Then, once she'd conclud ed that it wasn't, she cautiously picked it up and turned it over in her hand s.

The tape covered the whole thing, completely wrapping it and concealing the contents.

Olivia gave it a smell, like she'd seen her father and some of his men do, but if it gave off a smell then her nose clearly wasn't attuned to it, as all she got was the faint whiff of glue from the tape.

She held the package in both hands and moved it up and down a little, feeling the weight of it again. She'd seen her dad do that, too.

Of course, she wasn't supposed to have known what was in the packages that came and went through his office at the yard. His usual story was that they were bags of cement mix, and she had spent months wondering why he didn't buy it in larger quantities all in one go, given that he ran a construction company, before she'd eventually figured it out.

Once she'd realised what had been happening, she'd been terrified. Terrified that, merely as a result of being in the same room as the packages, she'd go to jail. Terrified of what would happen to her when she was there. Terrified she'd spend the rest of her days rotting away in a tiny windowless cell, with bowls of thin gruel being slid to her through a gap at the bottom of the thick metal door.

Gradually, though, fascination had overridden her fear. She'd sat in the corner of the office staring at her iPad with her headphones on and the volume on mute. Listening. Observing.

Learning.

Olivia turned the package over in her hands until she found a seam in the tape. She picked at it, digging her nail beneath it, teasing it away from the next layer of tape below.

The YouTuber was on to her next video now. Foundation lines. *Ugh*. Weren't they just every teenage girl's *nightmare*?

The edge of the tape lifted enough for Olivia to pinch it between finger and thumb. She pulled it back slowly, revealing mostly just another layer of textured grey.

There was a thin gap in the lower level of tape, though, where two pieces didn't quite meet. Through it, Olivia could see a densely packed powder with a pinkish tinge. Cocaine then. She was almost certain.

She'd heard her dad berate one of his men about the drug's colour once, after he'd returned to the office with a bag of pure white stuff.

Pure white was for the movies, Bosco had told the frightened younger man. Pure white was 'tourist bullshit'. The stuff you wanted had a faint pink or cream tinge to it. That was good coke.

Was this? Olivia wondered, studying the tiny window in the bag. Was that what she had *? Good coke?*

She took another sniff, but got nothing but that same faint chemical smell. She was assuming it was the tape, although maybe that was just what cocaine smelled like. She'd never got close enough to find out before.

The YouTuber was still talking at a hundred miles an hour, her image on the iPad screen constantly changing in a series of never-ending jump cuts that had been a novelty when people started doing it a few years ago, but now just felt like lazy editing.

Her voice was becoming more grating now—her nasal Californian whine now the only sound that Olivia could hear in the...

Shit.

She stuffed the package into the tote bag, just as her mother's bedroom door opened and a floorboard creaked out on the landing.

Grabbing her backpack, Olivia hurriedly shoved the drugs inside.

The door to her bedroom opened a crack. A face, shiny with sweat, appeared in the gap. 'Knock, knock, *malyshka*. Are you still awake?'

Olivia froze with her hand in the bag. She tried to smile, but her face felt clumsy and not under her full control, like half of the muscles were paralysed, and the other half didn't have a clue how to compensate.

The d oor opened the rest of the way. Oleg stepped   in, his eyes fixed   on the backpack. The lower half of his face was smiling, but the top half appeared   confused .

'What are you d oing?' he asked   her.

'Homework. Just… homework.'

She heard   the mattress give a groan as he sat on the bed . Felt the heat rad iating from him. Tasted   the sour tang of his bod y od our.

'What d id   I tell you *malyshka*?' he said , taking hold   of the bag and   gently pulling it away from her. Her hand s released   their grip without a struggle. Struggling would   make him suspicious. Making him suspicious might get her killed . 'Homework is for pussies.'

She watched , her heart in her throat, as he sat the open bag on the floor besid e his feet. One glance insid e was all it would take. One glimpse of the tote bag, and   he'd   know what she'd d one.

And   he'd   know that she'd   tried   to hid e it from him.

A million thoughts crashed   together insid e her head   like d od gem cars.

Did   he alread y know? Was that what this was? Had   he known all along? Was this—everything, masked   abd uctor includ ed —all some sort of test that she had   unequivocally failed ?

'You d id   good   tod ay. I know I alread y told   you that, but I think praise is important when it's d eserved . And   you d eserve it.' Her hand   was resting on top of her covers. Oleg reached   over and   patted   it, then held   it pinned   beneath his own. 'You've taken a big step tod ay, Olivia. You're not a little girl now. Soon, you'll be a woman.'

His gaze lingered   on her, and   she sud d enly felt very, very small.

'Like your mother,' he said , after a long, pregnant pause. He gave her hand   a squeeze. 'Tomorrow, I want you to d o me another favour. I have another friend   I'd   like you to make a d elivery to.'

Olivia's voice came as a croak through a throat constricted in fear. 'I thought… I thought I was d one. That it was over.'

'It's over when I say it's over,' Oleg told her.

'Right. Right. But I've, um… I can't. I'm at a friend 's house tomorrow.' Oleg stared blankly back at her, and she felt compelled to fill the silence. 'We're watching a Christmas movie. Die Hard . Or… the second one, I think. So… sorry.'

The grip on her hand tightened so sud d enly Olivia let out a yelp of pain and shock. Oleg was sud d enly right there in her face, kneeling on the bed besid e her, the smell of his sweat snagging at the back of her throat, his eyes blazing with anger.

He said nothing, spoke not a word , just glared at her, his face inches from her own, his hand still wrapped around hers. Olivia pushed back into her pillow until the head board was pressed against the wall, but there was no escape, nowhere to go, no hope of getting away.

'I could … I could cancel,' she said in a ragged whisper.

Oleg's face changed in an instant, the rage replaced by a wid e, leering grin. 'That's my girl,' he told her, then he planted a kiss on her head , ran a hand over the bump in the d uvet her legs mad e, and stood up.

'Sorry if I frightened you. It's like they say. Nothing personal. Strictly business.'

Raising an arm, he d rew in a long, d eep sniff of his armpit, and held his breath, savouring the sensation of his scent in his lungs.

Then, after a slow exhale, he winked at the girl in the bed . He was about to turn away when something d own at floor level caught his eye.

No. God, no!

Oleg's face fell as he peered d own at his feet.

'What the hell is this?' he asked .

Olivia's insid es knotted up in panic. She wanted to jump out of the bed , run for the d oor, get away from there before he could stop her. Before he could punish her for what she'd d one.

But he was blocking the way. Short of throwing herself out of the wind ow, there was nowhere she could flee to, nowhere she could go.

Oleg bent d own, then stood up again hold ing her school skirt. He let it hang between finger and thumb, like it was something unclean.

'What, we d on't fold clothes in this house?' he asked , with a reproachful wag of his finger.

Olivia caught the skirt when he threw it at her, and caught herself mumbling an apology.

'Like I say, you're not a kid anymore *malyshka*,' he said . His eyes d rank her in again. His tongue flicked across his lips. 'Time you stopped acting like one.'

Chapter 28

It took ten minutes to get Joanna to open the door of the storage room. It wasn't locked , so they could 've gone in at any time, but Sinead had insisted that they let her be the one to make the call. She'd had a rough enough night as it was, the last thing she need ed was them forcing their way in.

Hamza had tried to talk to her first, but had received no response through the door.

Sinead d id her best, assuring Joanna that she'd be safe, that the men were gone, and that she'd stay with her. She'd even take her home, if that's what she wanted . She d id n't have to say a word to anyone, if she d id n't want to.

With all that said , and d espite Hamza's growing insistence that they should knock again and check on her, Sinead left Joanna to think it all over in silence.

A couple of minutes later, the d oor had opened .

'Want me to take you home?' Sinead asked .

Joanna shook her head . It was firm and d etermined . Remarkably so, given the circumstances.

'No,' she said , gaze flitting from Sinead to Hamza. 'I want to talk.'

Now, a little more than the time it took to make two teas and a coffee later, Hamza sat on one sid e of an interview table, while Sinead sat next to Joanna on the opposite sid e in an attempt to make it feel less like an interrogation.

'Again, Joanna, I can't apologise enough,' Hamza said . 'If I'd thought there was any chance at all that we'd see—'

Joanna shook her head urgently, dismissing the apology before she had to hear his name spoken aloud. She was using her tea more as a hand warmer than a drink, her fingers wrapped around it so they locked together.

'It's not your fault,' she told him. 'But please don't tell my mum and dad. They'd only worry.'

'Of course,' Hamza agreed. He was more than happy to keep her parents in the dark over the incident, thereby avoiding what would almost certainly be a well-deserved bollocking from them both. 'How are things at the house?' he asked. 'It seemed a bit... strained, if you don't mind me saying.'

Joanna looked down into her cup, letting the steam roll upwards across her face. She'd cut her hair short soon after the attack—*alleged attack,* he corrected—but it had grown back enough that her fringe hung forward when she leaned her head down, forming a curtain that hid her eyes.

'They fuss a lot,' she said. 'I know it's because they care, but...'

'Wee bit over the top?' Hamza guessed.

'It's like they think I'm sick. Or dying. Or... I don't know. Like I've got special needs, or something. It's relentless.'

'Have you tried talking to them about it?' Sinead asked.

Joanna flicked her an uncertain look, still trying to get the measure of her. 'Yeah,' she said, after a brief pause. 'But they don't listen. I can't even get angry, they just give me this patronising smile and tell me it's fine. Tell me they understand. That it's *only to be expected.*'

'Must be frustrating,' Sinead said, but Joanna was on a roll now, and didn't seem to be listening.

'They send me to therapy. My doctor, she says that I'm not angry with them. Not really. I'm angry about what happened. About what... was done to me,' she continued. 'But sometimes I *am* angry with them. Sometimes it's nothing to do with that stuff, it's just them being fucking annoying! It's like they're smothering me, like I'm a little kid again, not allowed to do anything for myself. *Think* anything for myself.'

Hamza didn't really know what to say about any of that, but felt like he should add something. The best he could come up with was a sigh, a tut, and a mumbled, 'Parents, eh?' which earned him a slightly incredulous look from Sinead.

He mouthed a silent, 'What? I don't know!' at her, gave an awkward little shrug, then felt an overwhelming sense of relief when Sinead took up the reins of the conversation.

'They're trying to help, but they don't quite know how to go about it,' she said. 'They want to make sure you know you're safe and loved.'

'I know that. You think I don't know that?' Joanna retorted, her defences going up. They crumbled again just as quickly as she'd built them. 'I just... I wish they'd ease up a bit. I wish they'd ...' She looked up at the ceiling and closed her eyes, like she was drawing strength from the glow of the overhead lights. 'I just wish everything could go back to the way it was. Before.'

Hamza sipped his tea, taking a moment to think of his response this time, rather than jumping straight into one that could be considered less than ideal.

'If you like, one of us can sit down with them and have a word,' he suggested. 'Detective Constable Bell, maybe. Or... I mean, or me, if you think that'd do any good. Sinead has a lot of experience of talking with families, though, so maybe...'

'Would you?' Joanna asked, shooting the DC a sideways look. 'They might listen better if it comes from you.'

'Of course. I'd be happy to, if you think it might help,' Sinead said.

Joanna brightened a little at that. 'Thank you. I think it would,' she said, then she took the first tentative sip of her tea, and some of the tension seemed to leave her. 'I didn't kill him, if that's what you think,' she announced out of the blue.

'What? No! No, we don't think that for a second,' Hamza assured her.

'I haven't left the house in... well, not for a while. I was at home.'

'Absolutely. Like I say, we d on't think for one moment that you were involved ,' the DS reiterated .

Joanna's gaze flitted between them a couple of times, before settling back on Hamza. 'Then why d id you want to talk to me?' Her face took on a look so tentatively hopeful that Hamza felt it like a punch to the chest. 'Did he confess? Did he ad mit what they d id ?'

'Uh, no. No, nothing like that, I'm afraid ,' he said , looking d own at his notes to avoid witnessing her crushing d isappoint-ment. 'We just... we have to pursue all lines of inquiry, as you know. We have to consid er who Fred e— who the victim's enemies might have been. Who might have had a grud ge against him.'

The near-mention of Fred d ie's name had mad e Joanna pull back and d raw in a sharp breath. She sat there hold ing it for a moment, then let it out as a question. 'So you d o think I was involved ?'

'Not you,' Sinead assured her. 'But... well... could there be someone you know who might have wanted to d o something like this?'

'I d on't know many people now,' Joanna replied . 'But yes. All of them. And something like what? No one has even told me what happened .'

Hamza and Sinead exchanged glances, then the DS gave a subtle shrug and a nod .

'The victim was found frozen to d eath this morning,' Sinead explained . 'It's thought that someone held him for a couple of d ays in some sort of freezer until his organs failed .'

Joanna blinked slowly several times. She flexed her fingers, then clasped them together around her cup again. 'That sound s horrible,' she said , but there was no satisfaction in it. She looked sad d ened , if anything, much to Hamza's surprise.

This d id not go unnoticed .

'You think I wanted him d ead , d on't you?' Joanna asked . 'And I d id . For a long time. I mean, I should . After what they d id . But... I d on't. I d on't want either of them d ead . Not really.'

204

'That's very noble of you, Joanna,' Hamza said , earning himself a snort from across the table.

'Noble? No. It's not noble.' She shook her head . 'It's selfish. That's all. If they're d ead , they can't d o the same thing to anyone else. They can't hurt anyone. But if they're d ead , they can't ad mit what they d id to me. If they're d ead , they're always innocent. They always get away with it, and what they d id to me...' She swallowed , fighting back tears. 'It's selfish, but if they're d ead , then they never have to pay for it. I d on't want them d ead and innocent. I want them alive and guilty. I want everyone to know what they d id . To know that I wasn't making it up, that I was telling the truth.'

She stared d own into the murky brown waters of her cup. For a long time, she said nothing, and the d etectives were about to fill the silence when her voice came again. Quiet. Guilty. Ashamed .

'I tried to tell him that. I tried to explain, to make him und erstand . I d id n't want them d ead . It's no good if they're d ead ! But he would n't listen! Just like my mum and d ad , he would n't listen!'

Hamza's chair creaked as he shifted his weight in it, leaning forward until his forearms were resting on the table.

'Who would n't listen, Joanna?'

The answer d id n't come willingly. She visibly struggled to say the word s, wrestling them out of her mouth.

'Gary,' she whispered . A tear rolled d own her cheek, her turmoil writ large in the lines of her face. 'My big brother.'

Chapter 29

The catch-up around the Big Board was a belter. There was a lot to bring everyone up to speed on.

Joanna had been driven home by a female constable, with Sinead promising to come around and talk to her parents the next day, to try to get them to ease up a little.

It would be a weird one—'Quit being so nice to your daughter!'—but she understood where Joanna was coming from. People had treated Sinead much the same after she'd lost her parents. Hell, she'd done the same to her little brother. Unlike Joanna's mum and dad, though, the rest of the world had soon lost interest in Sinead's situation, and she'd been left to get on with it.

In hindsight, she reckoned that was probably for the best.

The Big Board itself didn't have much going on yet, other than the initial photo of the victim and a few scribbled Post-its. Sinead sat in a semi-circle with the others, a notebook balanced on one leg as the team took it in turns to report their findings.

Hamza took the floor first, Joanna's revelations about her brother potentially the most pressing new bit of information they had. He pinned a printout of Gary Ward's Facebook profile photo to the board before launching into his account of what Joanna had told him.

'Gary's apparently been talking about doing in Freddie Shaw and Damian Bailey for months,' he concluded a few minutes later. 'Joanna put it down as empty threats at first, but in the last six to eight weeks, he's been talking about it more and more.'

'She said he became withd rawn about a fortnight ago,' Sinead ad d ed . 'Took time off work. Started staying out all night, sleeping most of the d ay.'

Hamza turned a page in his notebook. 'When she tried to talk to him, he told her—and I quote—"those evil fucks are going to get what's coming to them. We're going to sort it".'

'We?' asked Ben.

'She d oesn't know who he was talking about,' Hamza said . 'She asked , but he laughed it off and told her he meant to say "I".'

'Unlikely mistake,' Logan remarked . 'If it's him, then he could be working with someone else. We should bring him in.'

'She d oesn't know where he is,' Hamza replied . 'He went out on Frid ay, and hasn't come back. She's tried phoning, but it's going straight to voicemail.'

Logan winced . 'No' looking good for him, is it? You get his phone number?'

'Aye, sir. Passed it to the tech team to coord inate with the network, see if we can get a ping on him.'

'Good . Keep us posted . Sound s like he's our best bet at this point.'

Ben sucked air in through his teeth. 'Is he, though?' he asked . He met the looks from the others. 'I mean, how old is he?'

'Twenty-one,' said Sinead .

'Twenty-one. So... how d oes he tie in with the previous Iceman victims? How old would he have been then? Sixteen? No connection to any of the victims back then, I'll put money on it.'

'Copycat, then, boss?' Tyler suggested . 'Using the Iceman thing as a cover?'

'I'd maybe buy that if he had n't popped Duncan Milburn's finger in the blood y post.'

'Oh. Aye. Right, boss. That makes it more complicated , right enough,' the DC ad mitted .

'He said "we're going to sort it",' Sinead reminded them. 'If he's working with someone else…'

'Maybe it's the original Iceman!' Tyler concluded.

Sinead gave him a dunt with the side of her foot. 'Thanks for stealing my thunder there.'

'Shite. Sorry,' Tyler replied. 'Just got excited.'

'So… what are we saying?' asked Ben. 'We've got a serial killer who's got himself a sidekick?'

'Or a student,' Hamza said.

'Always two there are,' Tyler announced, breaking into a passable impersonation of Yoda. 'A master and an apprentice.'

He beamed proudly at the others, but was met with mostly blank stares.

'Star Wars, innit?' he announced.

After a moment, Sinead kicked him again.

Logan took to the floor next. As Sinead had been with him in the interview, and he'd already gone over it with Ben, he mostly addressed Hamza and Tyler as he went over what Damian Bailey had revealed under questioning.

He didn't play them the video, but told them where to access it on the secure shared drive. Trying to identify the woman in the footage was up there on the list of priorities. If Freddie had broadcast it, like Damian claimed, someone— perhaps the woman herself—might well have taken issue, and sought revenge.

Time was the issue, there, though. Freddie had to have been taken on Saturday night. Even if someone had seen the video, recognised the woman, and decided to make him pay, it was a stretch to think they'd have the time to successfully mimic and try to frame a presumed-dead serial killer. Or the inclination, for that matter.

Such crimes of passion usually led to a stabbing or a kicking, not some elaborate set-up involving freezers, teeth, and five-year-old amputated fingers.

Still, it was something else to add to the list. One more thing to look into.

Then, it was time for Tyler to show the dashcam footage from the taxi. It had n't turned out to be the big 'Eureka!' moment that he'd been hoping for, and did little more than backup what Colin Rose's *lady friends* had alread y told him.

Two men, one with his arm around the other, heaving him on through the snow. The footage was grainy, and the falling snow mad e it d ifficult to see much of anything, but the careful application of the pause button at just the right moment let them confirm that the clothes the man being d ragged along was wearing matched those of Fred erick Shaw.

The other man was a big fella of around six-two, they estim-ated . He was broad ly built, but that might have been an illusion caused by his heavy winter coat, beanie hat, and the scarf he had wrapped around most of his head and face.

Still, he was lugging Fred d ie along without too much d iffi-culty, so he was clearly no seven-stone weakling, whoever he was.

There was a moment—a fleeting one—where he glanced back over his should er at the taxi. He was powering ahead at that point, not quite running but very much trying to. The weight and the snow both slowed him, but there was d efinitely something urgent and panicked about his movements, like he was rushing to try to get away.

'That's all there is,' Tyler said , pausing the footage just as the taxi started to perform a three-point turn in the street outsid e Colin Rose's house. 'I got a couple of plates from it d riving up the hill, but ran them both and they belong to neighbours. I'm going to have Uniform ask around on the street, see if any of the other cars in the vid eo seem out of place.'

'Right. Good thinking,' Logan said .

'I'm having them ask about one in particular, actually. A van that's parked facing d own the hill. Can't make out the writing on the sid e. Hang on.'

Tyler scrubbed back through the vid eo, then stopped at a point when the taxi was halfway up the hill. The falling snow and swishing wipers red uced visibility to a minimum, but as the head lights fell on a small Vauxhall Astra van, they could just make out some writing on the sid e.

What it said , though, was anyone's guess.

'I'm pretty sure it's a company name, then a phone number,' Tyler said . 'But I can't make it out. I've asked the taxi d river, phoned the two women, even called up Colin Rose, but none of them remember seeing it.'

'Less snow on that than on the others,' Sinead observed . 'On the wind screen, anyway. Like the wipers had been going.'

'That's what I thought,' Tyler said . 'And it wasn't there when we turned up in the morning.'

'Good spot,' Logan said .

Tyler's chest swelled at his second compliment in as many minutes. He'd make DI before the week was out, at this rate.

'I also mad e a couple of printouts of the two guys,' he said . 'Thought maybe we could put them on social med ia or something, see if anyone can recognise the fella carrying the victim.'

'Social med ia? Are you out of your blood y mind , son?' Logan asked , crushing Tyler's hopes of rapid promotion. 'We d on't want to poke that bear yet. The longer we can keep this und er wraps, the longer we can keep the press at bay. If they get wind of the Iceman thing...' He shud d ered at the thought of it. 'Christ, can you imagine? No. Let's hold back for now.'

'Eh, OK. Right you are, boss. Your call.'

'Let's see the printout,' said Hamza. Tyler took one from the small stack on his d esk and hand ed it over. Hamza stud ied it up close, then at arm's length, then closer again. 'Just a big blob, really, isn't it? Resolution's not great. Could be Gary Ward , though. If I remember rightly, he was a pretty big fella.'

'Why would he be taking the bod y all the way up there?' Ben wond ered .

'The forest, maybe?' Sinead suggested . 'The end of that street lead s onto wood land . Maybe he was going to d ump the bod y there?'

'Hell of a long way to come just to d o that. Plenty of other places to d ispose of a d eid fella more locally.' He caught the wary looks from the others. 'In theory, I mean. I've no' d one it myself.'

'We're assuming he was killed here in the city, then taken up there,' Logan pointed out. 'No saying he wasn't killed some-where near to where he was found .'

'Want me to arrange a search of the wood s?' Ben asked .

Logan checked his watch, then looked out through the wind ow. Mostly, he could only see the group's reflection in the glass, but there was a sense of movement in the d arkness that suggested the snow was still falling fast.

'They're not going to find anything in that. Even if they bring the d ogs,' he said . 'Best wait until tomorrow. See if the snow stops. It's no' like Fred d ie's going to get any d ead er in the meantime.'

The others agreed that this was probably unlikely.

'Put a shout out to look for Gary Ward ,' Logan instructed , aiming the ord er in the d irection of the two d etective constables. 'Then we'll call it a night and meet back here tomorrow. By my reckoning, Hamza still has about forty minutes left of his birthd ay to go and enjoy.'

'You're too good to me, sir,' Hamza said , getting to his feet.

'You might be able to squeeze that birthd ay treat in yet, Ham,' Tyler grinned .

'In forty minutes?' Hamza replied . 'I could squeeze it in at least twice.'

A look passed between Logan and Ben. It d rew a nod from the old er man. A brief closing of the eyes. A sigh.

'Before you go, son,' Ben said , stand ing and blocking Hamza's path to the d oor. He ind icated Logan's office with a wave. 'Mind if I have a quick word ?'

—

Hamza stared at the evid ence bag, and at the names written on the paper contained within. His eyes scanned left and right, up and d own, working his way through the list again, and again, and again.

'Sorry, sir, this came from *where*?'

'The butcher's,' Ben said , for the second time. 'George Morales. I found it at the scene.'

'And you hid it?' Hamza asked .

'Not exactly, no,' Ben said , although he knew that was precisely what he'd d one. 'I mad e a jud gement call at the time not to show anyone at the scene. Then I ran it by Hoon, and we both agreed it was best if you and the others on the list d id n't find out about it. It's been with the rest of the evid ence the whole time.'

Hamza raised his eyes from the page. His gaze fell accusingly on the DI. 'Just not record ed anywhere.'

'Aye. No. Not record ed ,' Ben said , and he was relieved when Hamza went back to reread ing the crumpled sheet of paper. 'He was d ead . We thought it was d one. We thought, if you all knew… if our families all knew, then it might, you know, complicate things. Make them worry. Unnecessarily. Because it was over.'

'Only it's not, is it, sir? It's not over,' Hamza said . 'He's still out there. He might still be coming for us.'

'I d oubt that, son,' Ben said . 'I really d on't think that's going to happen.'

'Aye. Well.' Hamza d ropped the evid ence bag onto the d esk. He had been hurt by the d eception. Ben could read the betrayal in the lines of his face. 'I guess I'm going to have to trust your jud gement on that one, too.'

–

Bob Hoon's keyhole was on the move. That was the only possible explanation for why he had not, d espite a number of attempts, been able to let himself into his house.

He stood on his front step, swaying gently as he took aim with his key at the circular brass target of the lock.

Hold on. No *Locks*. Plural.

That wasn't right. Since when d id his front d oor have two locks?

He staggered back a step and looked up at the house. This was his, right? It looked like his.

But his house d id n't have two locks on the front d oor.

Or d id it?

He returned to the step, mouthing quietly to himself as he tried to remember if he'd d one any recent remod elling work on the front d oor.

Why two locks?

And why were they both moving?

Wait.

He screwed an eye shut.

No. Wait.

One lock.

Thank Christ for that.

He lunged , spat, 'Gotcha, ya bastard !' at the offend ing Yale, then ejected a string of obscenities when the key went skiteing across the front of the d oor, carving a fine white groove into the UPVC.

The next few attempts involved a variety of d ifferent tech-niques, none of them particularly effective. The fast and sud d en approach was d isastrous. There was more promise in the slow and stead y technique, although the lock always d anced around the tip of the key when he brought it too close, resulting in him scratching a slapd ash spid er-web d esign into the brass front plate.

He turned away, muttered loud ly that he was giving up, then spun and pounced , as if he might catch the lock off-guard , and be able to slid e the key straight in.

This, unsurprisingly, turned out to be the least successful approach of all.

'Fuck off, you twat!' he roared at the door.

It didn't.

With a groan, he leaned his forehead against one of the frosted glass window panes. It was icy-cold against his skin, and brought on a headache almost immediately.

He ignored the sharp throbbing of it. He simply could not be arsed to do anything else.

The door had defeated him. Crushed all his dreams, and broken his spirit. It was an evil bastard of a thing, and he had a good mind just to put a brick through the glass and be done with it.

It took him four minutes of searching to find a brick.

Was it a brick?

He studied it through one squinting eye, concluded that if it wasn't a brick, then it was something reasonably close to one, and hurled it at the door.

It hit the wall with a clunk, broke off a patch of roughcasting about the size of his head, then landed on the step.

For a long time, Hoon just swayed there, staring at it.

'Well, fuck you, too,' he eventually told it.

He stumbled forwards.

He bent to retrieve the brick.

In the darkness behind him, a footstep crunched on the snow-covered drive.

Chapter 30

Dave David son was hard at work at the Exhibits d esk when Logan and Ben came strolling into the office just before eight the following morning.

The snow had stopped falling d uring the night, and while the world still looked like it had been spread with marshmallow fluff, the sky was a brilliant blue.

'Morning!' Dave chirped , looking up from a small stack of evid ence bags and a comparatively larger pile of paperwork. 'Busy d ay yesterd ay, I see.'

'Aye, and another one ahead tod ay, no d oubt,' Ben said . 'How's the head this morning? Bit tend er?'

'Me? Nah. I d on't get hangovers,' Dave said . His lips d rew back in d istaste. 'Well, maybe once,' he ad mitted with a shud d er. 'But it takes a lot. Anyway, I've got all the evid ence logged in, and I'm about to pack it in this box. We'll hang onto it for now, for easy access. Obviously, we d on't have the finger, but I've got photos and prints, and will stick them in the box with the rest for now.'

'Good lad ,' Ben said . 'Been any word on Gary Ward , d o you know?'

'The fella Sinead put the shout out for? No, nothing yet. Not that I've seen, anyway. I can check up, though.'

'Aye. Thanks. Do that, if you d on't mind ,' Ben said .

'Oh! Speaking of Sinead , she called in earlier. She and Tyler reckon they've got an ID on the woman in the vid eo. I'm assuming you know what that means?'

'How'd they manage that?' Ben wond ered .

'Something about Facebook, they said .' Dave shrugged . 'Anyway, they're head ed to talk to her. Asked me to pass that on.'

'Good . Thank you,' Ben said .

He watched Logan put his mobile to his ear as he mad e for the office at the back of the room, and d ecid ed to follow.

By the time he reached the office d oor, Logan was alread y hanging up.

'Still no joy?' the DI asked .

'No. Straight to voicemail,' Logan grunted .

'He's probably just got it switched off. Or, Christ, I d on't know. Thrown it against a wall, or something. You know what he's like.'

That was the problem, Logan thought. He *didn't* know what Bob Hoon was like. At least, not at any given time.

Sure, he had a general impression of the man. He had a lot of d ifferent general impressions of him, in fact, from the ranting, foul-mouthed superior officer who'd d elighted in making all their lives a living hell, to the ranting, foul-mouthed d isgraced copper who'd been unceremoniously booted off the force.

Then there was the ranting, foul-mouthed , d epressed mess who they'd been lumbered with on their last trip to Fort William, and the ranting, foul-mouthed lunatic who'd been lying in wait in Logan's car for God knew how long, just so he could ask if the DCI had a phone number that was read ily available online.

Yes, there was d efinitely a running theme to Logan's old boss, but the various versions of him ultimately all behaved very d ifferently, which mad e his movements d ifficult to pred ict.

Whatever they thought of the big mad bastard , he d eserved to know about the Iceman's return. It was unlikely that he'd be in any d anger, but it wasn't beyond the realm of possibility. It was only fair that they at least gave him a head s up about it.

If only he'd answer his blood y phone.

Out in the Incid ent Room, the d oor was thrown wid e, and DS Khaled came barging in. Ben tensed , sensing a barney coming. He probably d eserved it, too, for concealing the list from Hamza.

To the DI's relief, though, his d eception wasn't what had got Hamza riled up.

'Just got a call from Joanna Ward ,' he announced , as the senior d etectives emerged from the office. 'She's pretty frantic.'

'What happened ?' Logan asked .

'She went through her brother's room last night, after her parents had gone to sleep. She found something.'

'Don't tell me. It's not a list, is it?' Ben guessed .

'Not that, sir, no,' Hamza replied with a shake of his head . 'It's a confession,' he said . 'And a suicid e note.'

–

Oleg wasn't in the kitchen when Olivia slipped d ownstairs, fully d ressed for school, her backpack fixed securely over both should ers. She'd alread y eaten breakfast—a porrid ge bar she'd snuck upstairs with her the night before—but the claggy coating it had left insid e her mouth meant she was d esperate for a d rink.

There were two cartons of fruit juice in the frid ge, one orange, the other apple. Both had little more than d regs left at the bottom, so she combined them both in a single glass, gave it a swirl, and then d rank the lot in one gulp.

After a quick swirl around her mouth so the fruit's acid ity could cut through the porrid ge film, she swallowed , rinsed the glass und er the tap, then turned to leave.

Oleg leaned in the d oorway, one bare should er resting against the frame, a pair of tight grey boxer shorts his only garment of clothing. There was a d arker stain on the front about the size of a five pence piece. Olivia found her eyes d rawn to it, then she hurried ly looked away when something twitched beneath the fabric.

'Good morning,*malyshka*,' Oleg said . 'Not trying to sneak out, are we?'

Olivia shook her head . 'No. I just... I d id n't know if you were awake.'

'I'm always awake,' Oleg told her. She d id n't question the comment, or point out that for someone who never slept, he certainly fucking snored a lot. 'Here,' he said . 'I have something for you.'

To her horror, he reached d own the front of his boxer shorts, hold ing eye contact and grinning as he rummaged around .

Then, with a flourish, he prod uced a small square of paper. Closing his eyes, he sniffed it like it was a fine cigar, then held it out.

'Take it,' he said . An ord er, not a request. 'Don't just fucking stand there, take it.'

Olivia swallowed , then plucked the paper from Oleg's hand , making as little contact with it as was possible while still hold ing onto it.

It was another ad d ress. Further from the school, this time. A forty-minute walk, easily.

'What's it for?' she asked , although she d id n't really want to know the answer.

Oleg walked toward s her, put his hand s on her hips as he squeezed past, then reached up and felt around on top of one of the wall-mounted kitchen cabinets.

He winked salaciously at her as he stretched , and flicked his gaze d own at his muscular torso. 'Don't you go getting any id eas,_malyshka,' he purred .

Olivia alread y had an id ea. Not the sort of id ea he was likely thinking of, though, but rather one that involved grabbing a knife from the wood en block on the counter and stabbing him repeated ly in the chest and abd omen.

Before she could give it any serious thought, though, he prod uced another tote bag that looked more or less id entical to the one he'd given her yesterd ay.

The one that was still stuffed into the front pocket of her bag.

It was reckless to take it to school, she knew, but she didn't dare leave it in her room in case he went snooping. She'd rather face the disappointment of Mr Monroe than the wrath of Oleg any day of the week. One would result in a stern lecture and a call to the police. The other would end with a chainsaw and a number of plastic bags of varying sizes.

'You call me when it's done this time,' Oleg instructed.

He put a hand on her shoulder and turned her around so her back was towards him. She stumbled as she turned so her front was pressed up against the kitchen worktop. He stood close behind her, pinning her there in place.

'What… what are you doing?' she asked, the words croaking out of her.

The knife block was a few feet away, well beyond her reach. At best, she could grab the plastic container that held the tea bags, but the damage she could do with that would be limited.

'Relax,' Oleg told her. She heard a zip being undone. She almost screamed, but then felt her shoulders being pulled back as he thrust the tote bag into her backpack.

He zipped the bag closed again, but didn't step away. Didn't leave room for her to turn.

'There. You're all set, *malyshka*,' he whispered. 'Don't let me down now, OK?'

Olivia nodded. It was all she could do. His presence there behind her, and the fear of what he might do, had closed her throat. Speaking was out of the question.

Screaming, too.

She gave a little jump of fright when he leaned in close and sniffed deeply. Inhaling her. Breathing her in.

'Did you have a shower this morning?' he asked. His voice was a murmur, like he was under some sort of hypnotic trance.

She hadn't showered that morning. She was afraid the sound of the running water might wake him up.

Or worse, draw him in.

'N-no,' she managed to stammer.

He inhaled again, held it in his lungs, then let it out. His breath was warm against the back of her neck, sour as it hit her nostrils.

'Good . I love when you smell natural.'

Olivia d id n't feel the tears, or notice them falling until they plinked on the kitchen worktop in front of her.

Upstairs, a toilet flushed . A floorboard creaked .

Oleg's hand brushed the back of her head , then he stepped back.

Olivia spun immed iately and sid e-stepped out of his reach. The bulge in his und erwear was straining now, and she could almost hear the knife block calling to her.

'You'd better hurry. Go d o your schoolwork,' he said . His face split into a grin. His pointed tongue licked across the front of his teeth. 'While your mother and I go have some fun.'

–

Dr Rickett's tail was between his legs before Shona had uttered a word . He'd alread y seen her report in the inbox. He was well aware why she'd asked him to come in.

'I can't apologise enough,' he began, his head bowed , his tone solemn. 'In my d efence, I… actually, I d on't have a d efence. I was sloppy, I was slapd ash, and I failed in the most basic und ertaking of my role. I am embarrassed , both personally and professionally.'

'I think you're maybe being a bit hard on yourself,' said Shona, finally getting a word in. She was sitting behind her d esk, halfway through her first meal of the d ay—lukewarm coffee and refrigerated After Eights. Not exactly the breakfast of champions, but she had n't had time to eat before leaving the house, and knew she had the box of wafer-thin mints tucked away in the office frid ge.

Anyway, they d id n't specify *which* eight you were meant to eat them after…

'You mad e a mistake, Albert. We all d o it,' Shona said . 'I mean, God , I'm eating mint chocolate for breakfast. I'm hard ly perfect.'

'I should 've— really? For breakfast?' Ricketts said , then he d ismissed the thought with a shake of his head , and got back to the self-flagellation. 'I should 've paid more attention. Not rushed it through. We both know how important those first few hours are in an investigation, and I—if you'll pard on the expression—cocked that right up.'

'Like I say, we've all d one it,' Shona told him. 'It was cold and d ark, and I think everyone mad e the same assumption you d id . Daft bugger with too much d rink in him who fell asleep in the snow.'

'But I should n't have mad e an assumption. That's my whole point,' Ricketts bleated . 'Our job is not to make assumptions. Our job is to find the truth. Our job is about science, not guesswork. Evid ence. And I failed to d o that on this occasion.'

He lowered himself into the chair across from Shona, his tall, skeletal frame becoming a series of sharp angles as he rested his bent arms on his thighs.

'And if anyone should 've been on the lookout for the warning signs, it's me,' he muttered . He met Shona's eye and answered the question before she could ask it. 'The Iceman. I performed the PMs on the victims we found . And on the man himself, for that matter. But I'd seen how the cold had affected those people. I'd seen it up close. I should have seen the similarities. I should have known.'

'From what I can gather, everyone thought he was d ead ,' Shona said . She remembered her manners, and offered the open After Eights box to Ricketts. 'Want one?'

His initial reaction was one of barely concealed horror, but then he reached across the table, plucked one of the little paper envelopes from the box, and nibbled on a corner of the d ark chocolate square.

Shona, who had shoved four of the things in her mouth in one go, sud d enly felt extremely self-conscious, and hurried ly chewed in an attempt to get rid of them.

'True. I mean, they had a confession, d id n't they?' Ricketts said , thinking back. 'In writing. Along with the suicid e note. All seemed pretty open and shut.'

'Exactly,' Shona said , the huge wad of mint fond ant and chocolate forcing her to talk out of the corner of her mouth. 'You should n't blame yourself.'

'No. I should . I really should . I mean, he was on a mission, wasn't he? The Iceman, I mean. He was on some "punish the guilty" revenge thing.' Ricketts risked a bigger bite of his mint and chewed it thoughtfully. 'I often think with ind ivid uals like that… the police aren't just d ealing with a killer. Not really. They're d ealing with an ethos. An *ideal*. And id eals never really d ie, d o they?'

'I've never really thought about it, but no. Suppose not,' Shona conced ed .

Ricketts sighed , placed the remaining half of the After Eight back in its paper envelope, then slipped it into the top pocket of his shirt, presumably to eat later.

Shona subtly shifted her waste paper basket further und er her d esk with a foot, hid ing the thirty or more wrappers she'd gone through before the old er pathologist's arrival.

'Anyway, as I say, I mad e a real hash of it, and I should 've known better,' Ricketts continued . 'I shall be tend ering my resignation this morning, but will be happy to offer support until a replacement has been found . Assuming you'll still have me. I will fully und erstand if you'd rather not.'

'Albert…'

'Please, Shona,' Ricketts said , hold ing up a hand so long and bony it looked almost alien. 'I've mad e up my mind . I should never have come back after retirement. My work was d one. I had left all this behind .' He stole a glance around the office, letting his eyes linger briefly on the d oors that led through to the mortuary proper. 'I should 've let it stay that way.'

Chapter 31

Talia Whitmore sat at her desk, rubbing her temples as the voice prattled on in her head phones. The old boy on the other end of the line was explaining to her why he wasn't sure if new wind ows were right for him at the moment, what with his health not being great, and his pension not stretching as far as it used to.

She rattled off a stock answer about grants being available, savings on heating costs, and how you could n't put a price on peace of mind and add ed security, but her heart wasn't in it. Her head was still pound ing from last night's bend er. Her husband 's ranting about her staggering home 'at three in the bastard morning' had n't helped matters, either.

She d id n't give a shit if Mr Wilson bought wind ows. She just wanted him to stop talking.

Jud ging by the muted mumbling of her colleagues around her, she wasn't the only one suffering. Saturd ay had been an unofficial Christmas night out for half the shift, and it had grown from a night out into a long weekend of d runkenness and d ebauchery, with most of the group hitting the town three nights in a row.

It wasn't so much the d runkenness she was worried about. It was the d ebauchery. Christ. What had she been thinking?

While Mr Wilson d roned on, Talia sat up and peeked across the partition to the d esk where Fred d ie sat. He had n't turned up for work yesterd ay, and there was no sign of him tod ay, either. Was he avoid ing her? Was that it?

She'd had butterflies at the thought of seeing him yesterd ay, and not—she was fairly certain—the good kind . It had been stupid . A mistake. She had a husband . A family. She should never have kissed him, never have followed him into the toilets, never have d one the things they d id .

Her face prickled red at the thought of it, even now. She d read ed seeing him again, but she need ed it to be over. She need ed the shame and embarrassment of that first meeting to be d one with, so she could put it behind her and move on.

It was a one-off. It was d one. It should never have happened in the first place.

And yet, the thought of it mad e her head go light and her skin tingle in anticipation.

Carol, the manager, was stand ing over by the d oor with two people she d id n't recognise. A man and a woman, both young. New starts, maybe. Trainees. Poor bastard s.

'Please d on't put them with me. Don't put them with me,' Talia muttered . The voice in her ear expressed its confusion. 'Not you, Mr Wilson. Sorry.'

Carol had locked eyes with her now and was making her way over, weaving through the network of d esks with the two newbies trailing behind her.

'Fuck!' Talia groaned , her head ache ramping up a notch at the thought of an unplanned d ay of mentoring. 'No, not you, Mr Wilson. I wasn't talking to…' She sighed . 'You d on't want wind ows, d o you? No. Pointless at your age, I'd have thought. Bye.'

She terminated the call just as Carol arrived at her d esk, her eyes plead ing with the boss for clemency. 'Carol, I really d on't think I can hand le—'

'Talia, these two folks are here to talk to you. They're…' Carol glanced back over her should er for a moment, before continuing. 'They're with the police. They'd like to ask you a few questions.'

'Questions? What d o you mean?' Talia asked . She caught sight of Fred d ie's empty d esk again, his monitor in d arkness, his phone silent. 'Questions about what?'

–

Bob Hoon was either d eaf, d ead , or possibly just not home when Logan turned up at his house. Those were the only explanations for the fact he had n't reacted to the heavy thumping of the DCI's fist against the front d oor.

A chunk of roughcasting had been smashed off the wall besid e the d oor. Logan had noted it when he'd pulled up, and had quickly spotted the squarish bould er that had most likely caused the d amage in amongst the painted stone chips on the ground besid e the steps.

He knocked again, but d id n't bother to wait for an answer this time, and tried the hand le. The d oor opened without objection, and Logan stepped insid e.

The head y aroma of stale beer and congealing food that had met him every other time he'd set foot in the place was conspicuous by its absence. The last time he'd been here, Hoon had been making an attempt to tid y the place up. If the improved aroma was anything to go by, he'd had some success sticking with it.

The living room, like the hallway, was empty. It also confirmed that Hoon had been keeping on top of the tid ying. The place wasn't tid y, exactly—not by a long shot, in fact— but it wasn't clogged with the d ebris of a life gone off the rails, either. This was d efinitely an improvement. The mad bastard was making an effort, at least, Logan would give him that much.

It would almost be a shame if he'd been killed , just as he was starting to turn things around .

'Bob? You here?'

The only reply was the slow, oppressive silence of the empty house.

There were no signs of a struggle in the living room. Not unless it was an attacker who'd gone around tidying the place up, at least.

The kitchen didn't hold any surprises, either. A small stack of dishes. A bin crammed just to the point of being too full, so that the lid didn't quite sit closed.

There was a bottle of Morgan's Spiced Rum on the worktop, the lid missing along with two-thirds of the contents. No saying how long it had been there for.

He returned to the hallway, concluded which room must be the bedroom, and rapped on the door. 'Bob? You in there?'

The same silence answered him. The door wasn't quite closed, so he nudged it open and peered inside.

Then he instinctively shut it again when he spotted a woman lying in the bed, asleep.

Dead?

He opened the door again and took another look. The covers moved as she shifted her feet.

Asleep, then.

She was young, by the looks of her. At a push, she might be in her twenties, but more likely late teens. Blonde. Brassy-looking. Too much make-up that had not held up well during the night.

Young enough to be Hoon's daughter, the dirty old bastard.

'The fuck are you doing?'

Logan's grip tightened on the handle as the silence was broken. He pulled the door closed quietly, then turned to find Bob Hoon standing in the hallway, his face red with the effort of exertion, his brow drenched in sweat.

He was dressed like Sylvester Stallone in any number of the *Rocky* movies, right down to the grey hoodie and fingerless gloves.

'I should be asking you the same bloody thing,' Logan replied, keeping his voice down so as not to wake the young woman sleeping next door. It was awkward enough confronting

Hoon about it without her getting involved . 'What were you thinking, Bob?'

'Thinking?'

Logan gave a d isapproving shake of his head . 'Aye. Of course. Stupid question. You weren't blood y thinking at all. No' with your head , anyway. But… Jesus Christ. How old is she?'

'How old is…?' Hoon recoiled , his brow furrowing like he was about to start throwing punches. 'Fuck's sake, Jack. You d on't think I had a go on that, d o you? She's less than half my blood y age, you d irty bastard !'

'I'm…? No. What? I'm no' the d irty bastard in this situation, Bob!' Logan protested . 'You're the one with…' He gestured at the bed room d oor, lost for word s. '…whoever the hell that is in your bed .'

'Aye, you're right. She's in my bed ,' Hoon said . 'I'm not. She was getting some grief from a couple of lad s outsid e the pub last night. I gave them a bit of a slap, and the silly cow goes and follows me home. Near shat myself when she came stumbling up behind me.'

Logan shifted his gaze to the d oor, then back to Hoon. 'And you d id n't…?'

'No! Fuck's sake, Jack! Of course, I d id n't. I'm no' a monster. I mean, she tried her hand early on—and who can blame her, quite fucking frankly?—but I knocked that right on the head . In the end , I think she just wanted someone to talk to.'

'What, and she picked *you*?' Logan asked , the word s out of him before he could stop them.

'Aye. She picked me,' Hoon spat. 'None fucking taken, by the way.'

'Sorry,' Logan said , flinching at the incred ulousness of his question. 'I d id n't mean—'

'I might not be good for fucking much these d ays, Jack, but I've still got a set of lugs on me. I can still listen. That's all she need ed .' Hoon brought up a hand and scratched his head . 'I mean, aye, I d ozed off a couple of times, because Jesus fucking

Christ, she could n't half talk. My head was like a pound of mince by the time she'd shut up. But, as far as she knew, I was paying attention, and that's all women fucking want in the end , isn't it?'

Logan snorted . 'And to think, Bob, I was *almost* genuinely impressed by you there for a minute.'

Hoon pulled an expression of exaggerated hurt. 'Aw. And here's me living in the constant hope of your fucking approval, too,' he said . 'Now, mind telling me what you're d oing poking around in my bed room, anyway?'

'I was looking for you,' Logan explained .

'I was out back, punching the living shite out of a punchbag,' Hoon said . A smile curved the corners of his mouth. 'You know what I named it, by the way? The punchbag?'

'After me?'

'*Jeb-End Jack Logan*,' Hoon announced . 'You know? Like how boxers have nicknames, an' that? You're Jeb-End Jack Logan. Tubbiest bastard on the circuit.'

'The Iceman's alive.'

Nothing about Hoon's face changed , but everything changed . His smile remained fixed in place, his eyebrows d id n't bud ge. He d id n't even blink. And yet, the d ifference was seismic.

'Bullshit,' he said .

'Bod y turned up yesterd ay. Ben got sent his wallet, a tooth, and a finger of one of the previous victims.'

Hoon leaned a hand on the wall. He tried to make it look casual, but he was clearly using it to support himself. 'Which one?'

'The guy who was d one for killing the d og. Can't remember his name.'

'Duncan Milburn,' Hoon muttered . 'And it was a cat, no' a d og.'

'Right. Aye,' Logan said . 'We've got a few lead s we're chasing d own. But, given the other list that was found at George Morales's shop...'

Hoon met his eye for a moment, trying to assess how much he knew.

'...I thought I should at least give you a warning.'

There was no reply from Hoon. Not right away. His eyes shifted left and right, like he was reading through a series of possible futures, trying to decide which was most likely to come to pass.

'Aye, well, good luck to the prick if he comes round here,' he eventually said. 'I'll be ready for him.'

'Good. Glad to hear it,' Logan said. He nodded towards the front of the house. 'Maybe start by not leaving your front door unlocked, eh?'

'Fuck it, if he wants to come, let him come,' Hoon said, all bluff and bravado again.

Logan stepped past the former Detective Superintendent and patted him on the shoulder.

'Aye. Well. Good luck with your house guest, Bob.'

Hoon grunted. 'You could give her a lift home, couldn't you?'

Logan made a show of considering this.

'No,' he said, once he was done. 'I could not.'

'Jack.'

Logan stopped at the front door and turned back.

'What?'

'Keep your eye on them, eh? The others. Ben, and ... what's his name? The—'

'That better not be a racial slur about to come out of your mouth, Bob,' Logan warned.

Hoon scowled. 'The Detective Constable, I was going to say.'

'Hamza. And he's a DS now.'

'I don't care if he's a DC, a DS, or ET the Extra-fucking-Terrestrial. Just... keep an eye on him, eh? Both of them. Watch their backs.'

Logan shoved his hands into the pockets of his coat. 'Aye. I will. I always do,' he replied. 'And you be sure to watch yours.'

Chapter 32

The uniformed sergeant who'd accompanied Hamza to the Ward's house turned out to be a lifesaver. Or a sanity saver, at least.

She'd taken Joanna's parents through to the living room to calm them down and ask them some questions, leaving Hamza and Joanna free to talk in the kitchen. A female PC stood silently by the door. Hamza had felt having a couple of female officers present might make Joanna feel more comfortable. Joanna was so distraught about the note, however, that she didn't have the emotional band width to worry about her close proximity to Hamza.

The note was sitting on the table between them. Joanna's mother had been clutching it to her chest, sobbing hysterically when Hamza and the other officers had arrived, and it had taken some amount of persuading before she'd relented and handed it over.

Hamza understood. He got it. He did. Hand it over to the police, and the note was real. Keep it to themselves—in the family—and maybe it wasn't. Maybe it was a joke. Maybe it was nothing at all.

Maybe Gary was still alive.

When Mrs Ward had finally stopped resisting and passed the notebook page to him, Hamza had immediately bagged it, protecting it from any further contamination.

It sat there on the table now, the light from the kitchen window reflecting off the clear plastic.

A single page, written in a slightly clumsy hand , confessing to the murd er.

Or rather, confessing to several murd ers, without ever provid ing d etails of any particular ind ivid ual victim.

I am the Iceman. I have always been the Iceman, it read *I killed all those people.*

Gary went on to write about how the guilt was d estroying him. How he could n't live with what he'd d one any longer. How he could n't face his family, and how he'd been eaten up by the anguish of what he'd d one for weeks.

'He was a bit d istant lately,' Joanna said , following Hamza's gaze d own the page. She'd read it so often herself in the minutes after find ing it that she almost knew it word for word now. 'But... *killing himself?* That's not Gary. Gary would n't d o that. He would n't!'

Hamza glanced over at the PC who was stand ing by the d oor, then ind icated the kettle with a nod . She took the hint and got to work on a brew.

With the kettle boiling, Hamza gave the note another once-over. While it was vague on the d etails of the crimes, it was even more so on the nature of the suicid e.

I have decided to end it, it said *I'm sorry for the pain this will cause. Please do not try to find me.*

That was it. For someone so alleged ly tormented , his final message to his family felt so... businesslike. Professional. So professional, in fact, that Hamza almost expected to find Gary's name *p.p.'d* at the bottom by some ad min assistant or secretary.

There was a line in the note that the DS kept coming back to.

Believe me when I say they all deserved it.

The sentence stood out for a couple of reasons. Firstly, it d id n't quite mesh with the guilt Gary had expressed elsewhere in the confession. Second ly—and much more significantly—Hamza had read that exact sentence before in the suicid e note confession of George Morales, the man who'd originally taken cred it for the Iceman killings.

The contents of that note had never, as far as he was aware, been released to the public. And yet, here was an id entical sentence in a very similar note, confessing to the same crimes.

He returned to the start of the note.

I am the Iceman. I have always been the Iceman. I killed all those people.

'It d oesn't make sense,' Joanna said , following the DS's eye line again. 'How could he be this *Iceman*? I looked it up. It was five years ago. We were kid s then! And they caught him anyway, d id n't they? So it's not possible.'

Hamza agreed that it was unlikely, but d id n't comment. Instead , he circled back to his main concern about the confession.

'Remind me again, Joanna,' Hamza began, then he paused and said a quick 'thanks' when the PC set a teapot, milk jug, and a couple of cups d own on the table. 'Where d id you find the note? Exactly, I mean.'

'Und er his bed ,' Joanna said , eyeing the uniformed officer with suspicion until she returned to her spot by the d oor. 'Well, no. The mattress. Und er the mattress.'

She saw the confused look on Hamza's face, and misread its meaning.

'I was worried he might be on d rugs. Or d ealing,' she explained . 'So I checked all the obvious hid ing places. There's a label stitched into the bottom of the bed . You know, like the tag on the back of a t-shirt? Only bigger. The note had been slipped into the space in the mid d le of that, where it fold s over, but the top was sticking out.'

'See, that's the bit I d on't get,' Hamza said . This time, it was Joanna's turn to look confused . 'Generally, when people write a suicid e note, it's so someone will find it. That's kind of the whole point. They post it, or they leave it somewhere visible. Somewhere they know it'll be d iscovered .'

Joanna looked d own at the note. For all the times she'd read it, she looked at it now like she was seeing it for the first time.

'So… what are you saying? He wrote this note, but didn't want anyone to find it? Why would he do that? What would be the point?'

'I don't know,' Hamza told her, but a theory was already forming, the strands pulling together in his head. 'But… maybe he just didn't want anyone to find *yet*. Maybe he planned to leave it somewhere more obvious later.'

'Meaning?'

Hamza picked up the note. He got to his feet, the tea untouched. 'Meaning I don't think Gary's dead, Joanna. I think your brother's still alive.'

–

The room Tyler and Sinead had been permitted to use was a small side office that was mostly used for staff appraisals and interviews. It had rarely held good news for Talia Whitmore, and today was no exception.

Today, it held pretty much the worst news of all.

She had pulled back at first when Sinead had started the video playing, recoiling in disgust and demanding to know why they'd pulled her out of work to watch porn on…

The detectives had both seen the moment that it clicked. The moment a light went on behind Talia's eyes, while another much more important light dimmed. Her cheeks had reddened. Her hands had shaken, her head tick-tocking side to side in denial, even as the blunt, awful truth of it made tears cut tracks down her cheeks.

'Oh, God. Oh, God. What…? What the fuck is…? How did you get this?' she asked, jumping to her feet. 'Turn it off. Stop it! Turn it off!'

Sinead pressed a button on the side of her phone, and the screen went dark.

'What the *fuck*?' Talia demanded. 'What the actual fuck? I mean… fucking hell! How did you get that? Where did it come from?'

'You haven't seen it?' Sinead asked .

'Of course, I haven't fucking seen it!' Talia spat. Through the wind ow of the office, she saw a couple of head s meerkating up from behind partitions, d rawn by the sound of her raised voice. She sat d own again and overcompensated for the shouting by lowering her voice to a hiss. 'Did Fred d ie take that? I mean… he fucking must've. No one else could 've…' She grabbed at her hair, tangling her fingers in it. 'Fuuuuuuck!'

'I'm sorry we had to d rop this on you like this, Miss Whit-more.'

'Mrs,' Talia corrected . 'I'm married . Or, I fucking was. If this gets out…' Panic flashed across her face. 'It hasn't got out, has it? Where d id you get it?'

Sinead smiled sympathetically. 'I'm afraid Fred d ie sent it to a friend of his. And … we believe he might have shared it on Snapchat, too.'

Talia was on her feet again in the blink of an eye. This time, when she spoke, everyone in the call centre turned to look her way.

'Fucking *Snapchat*?!' she shrieked . 'The bastard ! The d irty, shrivel-cocked fucking bastard ! I'll kill him! I swear to God , I will fucking *kill* him.'

'Bit late for that,' Tyler said , cutting the woman's outburst short.

'Fred erick Shaw was found d ead in the early hours of yesterd ay morning,' Sinead explained . 'We have reason to believe he was murd ered .'

Talia sat d own again. To those watching through the office wind ow, it must've looked like she was playing some one-woman version of Musical Chairs.

'Murd ered ? Jesus. Like *murdered* murd ered ? Like… killed ?'

'Aye. As in your trad itional d efinition of murd er,' Tyler clari-fied .

'Blood y hell,' Talia muttered . She looked out through the wind ow at an empty d esk, then a thought occurred and her head snapped back to the detectives. For a moment, it looked like she might be about to stand up again, but she managed to resist. 'Wait. You don't think I've got something to do with it, do you? This is the first I've heard !'

'No. We don't think you killed him,' Tyler assured her.

He wouldn't have ruled it out on the drive over, or when he and Sinead had spent the better part of two hours combing through Freddie Shaw's Facebook connections, searching for the identity of his mystery conquest.

Her reaction to the video had been genuine, though. He'd put money on it. She hadn't been aware of the footage until they'd shown it to her, and had she known Freddie was dead, she was unlikely to have announced her desire to kill him to the two police officers sitting across the table from her.

'We're just trying to piece together what happened on Saturday night,' Sinead said . 'After the two of you...'

'Don't. Jesus. Just... just don't,' Talia pleaded . She swallowed like she was fighting back the urge to throw up. 'I don't know what happened to him. Or... where he went. Or...' She looked down at the table in front of her. 'When we were finished — when *he* was finished —he just said , "Cheers. See you at work". That was it. Then he left. Just left me there to clean myself up.'

'And you didn't see him again that night?'

Talia shook her head , started to say that she hadn't, then frowned as some half-forgotten memory bobbed to the surface. 'He was at the bar when I came out. Talking to some bloke.'

'Damian Bailey?' Tyler asked .

'No. Some other guy. I didn't know him.'

'Can you describe him?' Sinead urged .

Talia blew out her cheeks, contorting the dark mascara lines her tears had painted down them. 'Twenty to thirty, maybe. Well dressed . Expensive gear. Like, tailored . Sharp. That's the impression I got, although I wasn't really looking at him. I wasn't really looking at anyone. And I was pissed . I wasn't thinking all that clearly.' Another glance at the phone. 'Obviously.'

'Anything else you can tell us about this man you saw?' Sinead asked . 'Anything at all?'

'No. No, nothing.'

'Would you recognise him if you saw him again?' Tyler asked , taking his phone from his pocket.

Talia shrugged . 'Don't know. Maybe. I suppose.'

Tyler thumbed through his apps until he brought up a screenshot he'd taken of Gary Ward 's Facebook profile photo. It was the same picture that currently ad orned the Big Board back at base, and showed Gary smiling at the camera with a baseball cap turned sid eways on his head . He d id n't exactly have the hallmarks of a serial killer.

'Is that him?' Tyler asked .

Talia regard ed the screen for a moment, then shook her head . 'No.'

'You sure?' Sinead asked . 'Take your time.'

'I d on't need to. That's nothing like him. He looked old er. Aye, not *old*, but... better put together. More mature.'

Tyler returned the phone to his pocket, and mad e an effort to hid e his d isappointment. 'Right. OK. Thanks, anyway.'

'Are you available to come in after work and give us a statement?' Sinead asked .

'A statement? Isn't that what this is? Isn't that what we're d oing now?'

'This would be a little more official,' Sinead explained . 'Given the circumstances, and your... significance as a witness, we'd record it, and we might end up using it to help us build a case when we find out who killed Fred d ie.'

There was a soft, repetitive thud d ing as Talia's knee began to bounce und er the table. She clasped her hand s in front of her mouth, praying to any and all god s who might be in earshot.

'My husband won't have to find out, will he?' she asked . 'No one will tell him what happened , will they?'

'Not d irectly, no,' Sinead said . Talia's expression of relief was short-lived . 'But, given that the footage has been wid ely shared , and that you may be asked to give evid ence in court in the future, it might be in your best interests to tell him yourself.'

'Tell him? I can't tell him! What am I meant to say? "Sorry I shagged a bloke in the pub toilet. On the plus sid e, he's d ead now, so you d on't have to go over and kick his head in".' Her eyes wid ened in alarm. 'Not that he would ! He would n't hurt a soul! He's never even been in a fight, never mind killed anyone!'

She calmed d own, realising that it could n't be him, and she could prove it.

'He was at home all Sund ay night. I was out, so he was at home with the wee one all evening, then he was in bed with me all night,' she explained , tripping over the word s in her rush to get them out. 'There's no way it could have been him.'

Her relief was short-lived , as her brain leaped to the next problem, the next thing to worry about.

This time, instead of stand ing, she sunk further into the chair until it looked like she was going to slid e right und er the d esk, out of sight.

'But how can I tell him, though?' she asked of nobod y in particular. Tears fell again, painting more mascara lines on her cheeks. 'How am I supposed to tell him what I d id ?'

–

'Jack? Where are you?'

DI Ford e's voice emerged from the Fiesta's speaker system before Logan had finished saying hello.

'In the car, head ed back from Hoon's. Why?'

'You need to make a d etour. I'm texting you an ad d ress.'

'Whose ad d ress? What for?' Logan asked , slowing as he approached one of the many recently constructed round abouts on the west sid e of the city. A new one seemed to spring up every few months lately, with all the hold -ups and frustrations that major road works brought with it.

'Damian Bailey's mother's been on the phone, asking when we're going to release him,' Ben replied .

'What, but we…? Shite!'

'Aye. He d id n't make it home from here last night. Can't get him on the phone, either. She assumed we'd kept him in. I told her someone would be round to talk to her.'

'Right. Aye.' Logan exhaled . The breath came out of him as a d rawn-out groan. 'Jesus. This could be bad .'

'It could ,' Ben confirmed . 'Do you think…?'

He left the question hanging there. They both knew how it end ed .

And they both knew the answer.

'Got to assume so,' Logan said . He checked the clock on the d ash. 'Any word from the others?'

'They're all head ed back to base.'

Logan d rew up behind a queue of traffic and tapped his hand s impatiently on the wheel, urging the lights to switch to green.

'Right. Have Tyler and Sinead d ivert to Damian Bailey's house. I'm going to talk to his solicitor. They left together last night, so he might be able to tell us something.'

'Will d o,' Ben replied . 'Want me to get a search organised for Bailey?'

'Put Uniform on the lookout for him. See if the network can get us a ping on his phone, and check when his bank card s were last used . Nothing public yet. We've kept the press away from this so far, and I'd like it to stay that way for as long as possible.'

'I'm on it, Jack,' Ben said . 'See you when you get in.'

'Right. See you then,' Logan said . Then, just before the other man hung up: 'And Ben?'

'Aye?'

Logan's grip tightened on the wheel as the lights went from red to green. 'Be careful.'

Chapter 33

In her last school, morning break had been one of Olivia's favourite parts of the d ay. It was a chance to forget lessons and hang out with friend s, if only for fifteen minutes.

She'd been surround ed by friend s then. Or by people who liked her, at least. She'd never sought their approval, but they'd given it to her, anyway. There were whispers about what her d ad d id —about the power he wield ed , and the d anger he posed — and that had earned her some level of respect.

Everyone had wanted to get to know her. Everyone had wanted to be her friend . Everyone had fallen over themselves to impress her, every chance they had , and morning break was when they went out of their way to get on her good sid e.

This school could n't have been more d ifferent.

She wand ered alone through the chaotic corrid ors, sid estepping boys that came chasing each other past her, and avoid ing the scathing looks from the girls sitting hud d led on benches, sharing secrets and lies.

Nobod y had spoken to her at break since she'd arrived at the school. Not one single person. Not once.

They'd spoken about her plenty. She'd heard the whispers of some, the shouts of others.

'She thinks she's so fucking special.'

'Here! That's that girl whose old man's a d ealer!'

'I bet he's totally getting bummed in prison right now.'

She walked on through the gossip and the catcalls, head d own, eyes fixed on the corrid or floor, feet pad d ing her through the maze of the school as she counted down the second s until the bell rang again.

Tod ay was slightly d ifferent. Worse, really.

Not the whispers and shouts—she was used to those—but everything else. The weight in her bag. The knowled ge of what she was expected to d o. The crushing realisation that this was it now. This was her life, ferrying packages from Oleg to strange men in scary places, never knowing what was waiting for her, or when she might get caught.

Because she would get caught, she knew. If she continued to d o things Oleg's way, it was only a matter of time. Oleg was an id iot, like her father had been. It wasn't just d rugs that his empire had been built on, it was bravad o and testosterone. It had n't been enough for him to run his business, he wanted to feel *important*. He wanted to be known for what he d id . Feared for it. It was inevitable he'd end up in prison.

And now, thanks to Oleg, it was inevitable that Olivia would d o the same.

Her head was so full that she d id n't even hear the gossip tod ay. Anxiety powered her legs on, making her walk faster through the corrid ors, and taking her to parts of the school she rarely visited outsid e of class time.

She was out by the gym hall now, walking alone through the wid e corrid ors that stank of floor polish and sweat. A right turn at the d ouble d oors ahead would take her outsid e, then she could loop around and back into the French corrid or through another set of d oors.

With any luck, the bell would go around then, and she'd almost be at class. It was a d ouble period , which meant she d id n't have to get involved in the usual scrum as everyone moved between classes.

'Hey!'

Olivia was so used to nobod y talking to her that she assumed the remark could n't possibly have been aimed at her. Head d own, she kept walking, and it wasn't until she heard the sound of footsteps racing up behind her that she shot a look back over her shoulder.

Her heart dropped into her stomach. It, in turn, plunged to somewhere around her feet.

Jonathan came striding towards her, his nose swollen, his eyes black from where she'd clocked him with the chunk of stone the day before.

The exit was still a thirty-second walk away. She could run, but he was much bigger than she was, and his longer legs would catch him up before she could reach the relative safety of the outdoors.

And would it be any safer, anyway? She'd seen fights break out around the school, and it wasn't like anyone was quick to intervene. Instead, they huddled around, jeering and cheering as punches were exchanged and blood was drawn.

She'd gone back to help him with the Latvian. It was thanks to her that he'd been able to get away. Maybe he just wanted to express his gratitude.

Yeah. Right.

'What the fuck was all that about yesterday?' Jonathan demanded. From his tone, expression, and body language, Olivia concluded that he wasn't here to say thanks.

'Nothing. It was nothing,' she replied.

'Nothing? Fuck off. You broke my nose, you fucking psycho bitch!'

'You were going to steal my bag,' Olivia reminded him.

'I was having a laugh!'

'Well... I didn't find it funny.'

Jonathan made a choking sound —a sort of 'guh' at the back of his throat that suggested breathing was proving more difficult than usual. Maybe she could 've made a run for it, Olivia thought.

Still, too late now. He was three feet away. One good stretch, and he could grab her. One good lunge, and he could have her by the throat, or the hair, or wherever else he decided to aim for.

'I'm sorry. I didn't mean you to get hurt,' she said . This was a lie, but it seemed like a sensible thing to say, given the circumstances.

'You hit me in the face with a fucking brick! What did you think was going to happen?' Jonathan spat. 'And who was the prick in the shop? What was going on there? Were you buying gear off him?'

Olivia shook her head . 'No,' she said . Technically, that one wasn't a lie. He'd been buying from her.

She almost wanted to say that out loud , just to see the look of shock on Jonathan's face. But that was her father's way. Oleg's way. She kept her mouth shut and shot a furtive look at the clock on the wall.

Still three minutes to the bell. And still no sign of anyone else approaching along the corrid or. A teacher would 've been nice, but she'd have taken some rand om pupils, too, if it meant not being here alone with Jonathan's bloated features and d ark-ringed eyes.

'You were, weren't you?' he asked , the mess of his face twisting into a leer. 'You fucking were buying gear. Have you got it with you?'

He grabbed for her bag, forcing her to d ance back a few steps. She hoped he might stop then after that first failed attempt, but he lurched forward again, hand s clawing at her like a zombie hungry for her brains.

'Get off,' she protested , as his fingers found the material of her backpack.

He yanked sharply, spinning her away from him, then shoved her face-first against the wall. She hit hard . Pain rad iated from her elbows and wrists where she'd thrown them up to save herself from the impact.

She felt him tearing at the zip. Heard his erratic breathing— the nasal 'guh' as he choked d own another wad of d ried blood

'Stop it, stop it, get off!' Olivia yelped .

Sud d enly, she was back in the kitchen that morning. Hot breath on her neck. His weight against her. Pinning her. Trapping her.

Her heart rate spiked . Her lungs stopped working. His hand s were in her bag now. Groping. Searching. Her protests ignored .

'Fucking stay still! Stop squirming!'

His hand was in her hair. She could n't brace herself in time to stop him pushing her head forward , clonking it against the wall.

There was a whoosh of something insid e her. All her panic. All her fear. Every negative emotion, all spinning and twisting together, forming a howling void in the pit of her stomach. A vortex of pain, and of terror, and of rage.

An arm rose.

An elbow snapped back.

She heard him cry out, but the roaring in her ears mad e it sound d istant. Far away. Not her problem.

Blood cascad ed over his mouth and d own his chin, and ran in ind ivid ual rivulets d own his neck. Part of Olivia watched the trails with a sort of morbid fascination, even as another part d rove her to fly at him, slapping and scratching and gouging at his injured face.

She could n't remember him falling. Could n't remember kicking him again and again, or the way she fell on him, knees slamming into his chest, fingers wrapping around his throat, nails d igging half-moons into his blood y flesh.

His eyes were two circles of shock. He punched at her, pushed at her, but still she held on, watching the colour of his face go from a d eep red to a noxious shad e of purple.

And then hand s were on her from behind , pulling her off him, pulling her away.

'Olivia? What the blood y hell are you d oing?!' cried Mr Monroe, putting himself between her and the sobbing, gagging mess on the floor.

And like that, the spell was broken. She'd been ten feet tall a moment before, but the sound of the head teacher's voice immed iately cut her d own to size.

She stared at her hand s, then d own at Jonathan, a puzzled expression on her face that suggested she had no id ea what had just happened .

If it was for Mr Monroe's benefit, then he wasn't buying it.

'Don't you move a blood y muscle, Miss Maximuke,' he barked , then he squatted besid e the fallen boy, his face a mask of concern. 'Are you all right, Jonathan?'

It was a silly question, really, Olivia thought. Clearly, Jonathan was not all right. Nobod y who was all right bled like that. Sobbed like that. Whimpered for their mum the way he was d oing.

'She just… she went mental, sir,' he wheezed .

'He attacked me!' Olivia protested . 'I was d efend ing myself!'

'That's *enough*!' Mr Monroe said , practically snarling the word s at her. 'I'm going to get Jonathan to the school nurse. You're going to go to my office and wait for me.'

'But, sir—'

'Just d o as you're told , Olivia,' the head teacher said , cutting off her objections. 'And if you're very lucky, we might not have to get the police involved .'

Chapter 34

Robert Foster's office was annoyingly pleasant. Far too good for a man who'd dedicated his life to getting bastards out of jail time by publicly ripping into their innocent victims.

Of course, those were always the ones with the nicest offices, Logan knew. It was probably part of the reason why they did it.

Foster himself had met Logan in the firm's foyer, and had made it clear that he only had a few minutes to spare as he'd led the detective up a spiral metal and glass staircase to where his office looked out onto the River Ness and Inverness Castle beyond.

It was a cracking view. Another of the perks of selling your soul, Logan supposed.

The young solicitor had sat in his antique leather chair behind his polished desk, but had n't bothered to invite Logan to sit. That suited the DCI fine. He'd had no intention of sitting, even if he'd been asked. Instead, he got right down to business.

'What happened after you left the station last night with Damian Bailey?'

Foster raised a neatly sculpted eyebrow. 'How do you mean?'

'It's not a trick question. You and Damian left together after the interview yesterday. You went down the stairs, out the front door... then what?'

'Then I went home. And so did he, presumably.'

'Presumably?' Logan seized on the word. 'You mean you don't know?'

'No. Not for sure. Why?'

'You didn't offer him a lift?'

'A lift?' Foster scoffed at the suggestion. 'I'm his solicitor, Detective Chief Inspector, not his chauffeur. I charge by the hour, and I'm a damn sight more expensive than a taxi.'

'So, he called a taxi, then?' Logan pressed .

'Yes. That's right.'

'Do you know which company?'

'Uh... no. He did n't say.'

'You sound unsure.'

The lawyer shrugged . 'I mean, I suppose I don't know for certain that he definitely called a taxi. It might have been a friend . I know he called someone to come pick him up, but I did n't ask who, and he did n't tell me. What is this about, anyway?'

'It's about Damian Bailey failing to return home last night.'

'What? What do you mean?' Foster asked .

Logan tutted . 'For someone with so many certificates hanging on the wall, you don't catch on too fast, son,' he said . 'I mean just what I told you. Damian Bailey did n't return home last night, and his whereabouts are currently unknown.'

'Well... has anyone tried phoning him?' Foster asked .

'Funnily enough, we did think of that, yes,' Logan said . 'We're also going to have a look under his bed and shout his name really loud ly in the hope that he answers. You know, really cover all the angles.'

'I don't think the sarcasm's necessary, given the circumstances,' Foster said .

'Well, stating the blind ingly blood y obvious isn't going to help either,' Logan retorted .

Foster conced ed the point with a sigh. He clasped his hand s over his stomach and looked up at the towering d etective.

'You don't like me much, do you?' he asked .

'I can't stand you,' Logan said , and the bluntness of it registered as surprise on the solicitor's face. 'I don't know how you can sleep at night, d oing what you do. Knowing what you know. Personally, I would n't be able to look anyone in the eye ever again, much less myself.'

'I play an essential role in the justice system,' the solicitor protested . Logan d ismissed it with a grunt.

'That's no' what I'd call it,' he said . 'But it d oesn't matter. My opinion of you is neither here nor there. I want you to try calling Damian for me.'

'I thought you'd alread y tried ?'

'We d id . Maybe he'll answer if you call him, though. You've been on his sid e all year, after all. You're practically besties.'

'He's a client.'

'Aye, but it's thanks to your smooth-talking that he's not currently serving time for sexual assault, so I'm sure he thinks highly of you,' Logan said . His eyes went to the phone on the solicitor's d esk. It was one of those big, over-the-top looking numbers, with d ozens of buttons and a large touch-screen panel. 'Call him, Robert. See if he picks up.'

Foster shrugged and gave an impatient little sigh, like he just wanted this over with. Foregoing the land line, he took his mobile from a charging pad on the d esk, and tapped it awake.

'He'll have my mobile, not the office phone. Hang on, I have him on another app. It'll tell me when he was last active.'

He tapped the screen and a map appeared . With a few prod s and swipes across the screen, Foster brought up a picture of Damian Bailey. He was topless, hold ing a beer bottle in the air in salute.

'He was last on here yesterd ay evening,' he said . 'So not much help. I'll call.'

The number was d ialled . Foster held Logan's gaze as the mobile gave a single burr then went straight through to an automated voicemail greeting.

'Damian. It's Robert Foster. Call me when you get this,' the solicitor said , then he hung up, returned the phone to the wireless charger, and held his hand s open in a gesture d esigned to say, 'Well, I tried .'

'You'll let me know if he gets in touch,' Logan said .

'That did n't sound like a question.'

'You're right. It wasn't,' Logan confirmed . 'And you're sure you don't remember anything else about last night? Who he was contacting? Who picked him up?'

'Not a thing, I'm afraid . We said our good byes at the front door, and I left him to it. I'm not even sure he called anyone, now I think about it. He had his phone out, but he might have walked home, for all I know.'

'Long way back to his gaff. Especially in the snow,' Logan remarked .

Behind his desk, Foster smiled . 'You don't have to try to catch me out, Detective Chief Inspector. I'm not saying he did walk home. I'm not saying he did n't. I'm saying I have no idea. We came down to the ground floor, he thanked me for coming, I told him we'd talk later today, but to call me if anything else arose, and then we parted company. Last thing I saw him do was take out his phone. Who he called , why he called them, if he called them at all... I have no idea.'

The phone on the desk buzzed , and Foster checked his watch. After prodding a button to acknowledge the intercom, he stood , picked up a leather-bound folio, and tucked it under his arm.

'I'm sorry, I have a meeting I need to attend ,' he said . 'You'll update me when you know anything more about Damian.'

Logan watched the solicitor stride purposefully past him and open the office door.

'That did n't sound like a question,' he said .

Foster half-smiled , and gave the briefest shake of his head . 'You're right,' he replied . 'It wasn't.'

–

Mr Monroe's office window looked out towards the school gates and the freedom of the street beyond . Olivia found her gaze drifting back to it as the head teacher alternated between

248

angry ranting, d isappointed sighs, and soft coos of kind ness and encouragement.

It was always d ifficult starting a new school. He und erstood that. He d id .

And , let's be honest, Jonathan was no angel, either. It wasn't the first time he'd been caught fighting. He wasn't blameless in all this.

And how was it at home? It must be d ifficult, what with… everything. If she ever need ed to talk—to him, or to anyone else—she only had to say.

She nod d ed along, ad mitted things had been d ifficult, looked tearful and contrite where appropriate.

And all the while, she kept watching the gate, and the freed om it afford ed , as Mr Monroe's well-meaning word s washed right over her.

'There will have to be punishment, of course.'

That one snapped her out of her d aze. She'd hoped it wasn't coming, but had known it was inevitable. She'd practically killed Jonathan with her bare hand s. Another few second s, and she might have. There was no chance she was getting away with that without some sort of repercussions.

She hung her head so she was now staring at his d esk, willing more tears to come. The d esk was too small for the amount of paperwork stacked on it. Piles teetered and towered around the small space he'd cleared for his laptop, like high rise flats around a communal gard en.

There was a half-eaten energy bar on one sid e of the laptop, suggesting he had n't had time for breakfast. On the other sid e, a woman and a young girl stuck out their tongues in a simple wood en photo frame.

'What I d on't know at the moment is what form that punish-ment will take,' Mr Monroe continued . 'I still need to speak to Jonathan and his parents. I must warn you though, Olivia, they may want to get the police involved . If they choose to go d own that route, then it will be out of my hand s. You und erstand that, yes?'

Olivia nodded. 'Yes. I understand.'

'Good. Right, then,' Mr Monroe said. He seemed to have run out of steam now, and indicated the door with a wave of a hand. 'If you don't hear from me before then, I want you back here after the final bell.'

'I can't.'

Across the desk, the head teacher blinked. 'I beg your pardon?'

'I can't come after school, sir. I'm supposed to be somewhere.'

Mr Monroe leaned slowly forwards and jabbed a finger onto the desktop. 'I don't care where you're supposed to be, young lady. You broke another pupil's nose, then nearly throttled the life out of him. Whatever your plans were, they're now cancelled. You'll be here, or this will escalate. Is that clear?'

Olivia thought about protesting, but then relented with a nod. Oleg hadn't given her a time to make the delivery. Fifteen minutes wouldn't make a difference.

Besides, she'd be happy to delay the drop-off indefinitely, if she could.

'Clear, sir,' she said. 'I'll be here.'

'Good. Now, get out of my sight,' Mr Monroe told her, throwing in another hand-wave for good measure. 'And try to stay out of trouble, if you possibly can.'

Chapter 35

The rest of the morning went by in a flash. Ben sat at his desk, dealing with a steady stream of Uniforms who came and went like worker drones reporting to their queen.

There was no sign of Damian Bailey. He still wasn't home and had n't gone back to work. His mum had given Tyler and Sinead some addresses of friends and ex-girlfriends when they'd called by on the way back from their meeting with Talia Whitmore, the unwitting star of Freddie Shaw's pornographic masterpiece.

Uniform had visited all the addresses she'd provided. Damian had visited none of them.

Much as Logan hated the idea of getting the press involved, he was running out of options. It might be possible, of course, to publicise Damian's disappearance without it being connected to the Iceman, and all the frothy-mouthed hysteria that would bring, but Logan had never been that lucky when it came to the press. They'd find out. Somehow, the conniving fuckers would find out, and all of a sudden the circus would be in town.

'Right, put it out to the bastards,' he eventually instructed. 'But imply that we're after him for Freddie's murder, not that he's another potential victim. That might buy us a bit of time before the bastards put two and two together.'

'Right you are, boss. On it,' Tyler said, snatching up his phone and jabbing at the buttons.

Hamza, meanwhile, had spotted a gap in the otherwise endless parade of Uniforms, and seized his chance. He stood at DI Ford's desk, watching in silence while Ben read over Gary Ward's suicide note confession.

Rising from his chair, Logan marched over to join them and took the offered evidence bag once Ben had finished reading.

'Seems helluva familiar,' he observed. 'Reads just like the one George Morales left.'

'Exactly like it. Far too similar,' Ben agreed. 'Yes, it was widely reported that Morales left a note, but we never went public with the contents, so how could this lad know what was in it? This lad who, in case any of us have forgotten, would have been barely sixteen at the time of the original murders. It doesn't make sense. And then, there's the fact it was hidden.'

'What was hidden?' Logan asked.

'Gary's note, sir. The one you're holding,' Hamza said. 'It wasn't left out for the family to find, it was hidden under his bed. Like he'd prepared it in advance, and was saving it for when he needed it. I don't think it was meant to be found yet.'

'So, you don't think he's dead?' Logan asked.

Hamza shook his head. 'No, sir. I reckon, if we find Gary Ward, we'll find Damian Bailey.'

'Right. Go intercept Tyler before he can put word out about Damian. I want Gary's face out there, widest possible coverage. If he's got Bailey in a freezer somewhere, he might not have long left. Horrible bastard as he may be, we all know we've got a job to do. So, let's try to find Damian and bring him home before he freezes his bollocks off.'

'Right you are, sir,' Hamza said, hurrying over to Tyler and drawing a finger across his throat to indicate he should end the call.

'Sinead, what have you got for me?' Logan asked, turning to the desk of his newest DC.

'I've been on to Vodafone to find out who Damian called when he left here last night, but there's nothing.'

'Jesus. They're not being dicks again, are they?' Logan groaned.

'No, I mean he d id n't make any calls, sir,' Sinead   clarified .
'No calls, no texts. No d ata usage, either, beyond   usual background   stuff.'

Logan crossed   to the wind ow and   looked   d own into the car
park, as if he might see the events of the night before replaying
out there in the snow.

'His solicitor said   he took his phone out,' the DCI said , his
breath fogging the cold   glass.

'Different phone, maybe?' Sinead   suggested . 'We d id n't
search him. He might have had   more than one on him.'

Logan said   nothing. It was the mid d le of the d ay, but snow
cloud s had   been moving in all morning, cutting off the sunlight
and   turning d ay into d usk. There was another big d ump of the
white stuff coming. He d id n't need   Alice Ford e's aches and   pains
to tell him that.

The DCI's reflection looked   back at him from the foggy
glass. It stared , like it was trying to tell him something.

If it was, he wished   it'd   just open its blood y mouth and   say
it.

'Can you get me the CCTV from reception for last night?'
he asked , turning from the wind ow. 'Around   the time Bailey
and   his solicitor left. It might confirm if he mad e a call or not.'

Sinead   reached   for the phone, but stopped   when she realised
that Logan had n't finished .

'We also need   to talk to George Morales's wid ow,' he
continued . 'Find   out if George had   any connection to Gary
Ward . Check with the sister, Joanna, too. She might know of
something that'll help us join the d ots.'

'The mentor theory?' Ben asked , as Sinead   reached   for her
d esk phone, and   simultaneously began typing George Morales's
name into HOLMES. 'You d on't really think George passed   the
mantle d own to Gary, d o you?'

'There had   to be some connection,' Logan said . 'That's the
only explanation for the similarity between the two notes.
Unless…'

Ben waited . It was not unheard of for Logan to d rift off mid -sentence when something occurred to him, and he usually found the end of the sentence on his own.

Tod ay, though, it seemed that he need ed a wee bit of prompting.

'Unless what?'

Logan shook his head . 'Nothing. I d on't know. Probably nothing.' He clicked his fingers and pointed to the man sitting in his wheelchair by the Exhibits Desk. 'Dave. You free?'

'Depend s who's asking, and what for?' Dave replied , keeping his card s close to his chest.

'I want fresh eyes on all the previous Iceman victims, plus George Morales, Gary Ward , Fred d ie Shaw, and Damian Bailey,' Logan said . 'I want to know about any connection between them, however tenuous. If they've got the same shoe size, if they like the same flavour of crisps—whatever. I want to know. Make me a list. Who connects to who, and how. Can you d o that?'

'Aye. It might take a while, but should n't be a problem,' Dave said . 'Save me sitting here d rawing knobs in my notepad while I wait for new evid ence to come in for tagging.'

'Good . Keep me posted ,' Logan instructed , then he wheeled around to face Ben's d esk. 'Bring up that vid eo from the taxi d ashcam, will you? I want to have another look at the guy carrying Fred d ie.'

'It's too d ark and fuzzy to get a positive ID,' Ben remind ed him, but he d ouble-clicked on the fold er, anyway, and scooted his chair back a little to make room for Logan to see the screen. 'We've asked tech to try to enhance it, but it's going to take time, and you know yourself, it's rarely much of an improvement.'

'I d on't need it in HD,' Logan said , plucking the photo of Gary Ward from the Big Board , and send ing the pin pinging across the room. 'I just want to compare, and see if Ward could feasibly be the guy carrying Fred d ie.'

He set the photo on the d esk besid e Ben, then stood back while the DI's computer chugged and creaked .

'It's on a go-slow tod ay,' Ben remarked , then he ad d ed , 'I know just how it blood y feels,' because this was exactly the sort of thing you were expected to say when faced with an und erperforming computer system.

Logan checked his watch, a foot tapping impatiently. Ben gave his mouse a waggle, tutted , then sat back with his arms fold ed , staring reproachfully at the screen.

'Should n't be long now. Just...' He sat forward , frowning. 'Shite. That's the wrong fold er. Hang on.'

'I'll bring it up on mine,' Logan said , storming over to his d esk.

He was halfway there when Sinead flagged him d own and pointed to her screen. She had a phone crad led to her ear, listening to a robotic voice on the other end of the line.

'CCTV from last night,' she whispered , briefly covering the hand set. She clicked the 'play' button, and Logan watched as the half-d ozen figures on-screen all jerked into life.

The camera picture was sharp, but the frame rate was low, so the people in the footage jerked across the foyer like Ray Harryhausen animations.

Sinead pointed to the ed ge of the screen with her pen. A moment later, two men entered the frame, then went skipping across the foyer in little leaps, the low frame rate making their movements look vaguely comed ic.

While there was something a bit Benny Hill about their movements, there was no mistaking who the men were. Damian Bailey and Robert Foster looked to be d eep in conver-sation as they crossed the station's reception area.

They stopped by the front d oor together. The conversation continued , their head s and arms twitching like they were mari-onettes, then Foster mad e a gesture and they both walked out of the station.

Together.

'Rewind that a bit, will you?' Logan asked .

Sinead pressed a button on her phone, navigating her way through one of Police Scotland 's many infuriating internal telephone menu systems, then scrubbed the vid eo back a few second s.

'Go from there.'

Sinead let the vid eo play, but kept a finger hovered over her mouse as another record ed message in her ear offered her another rid iculous number of options to choose from, none of them exactly the one she was looking for.

'There. Stop,' Logan instructed , and Sinead paused the footage.

She'd caught Foster mid way through the gesture he'd mad e just before both men had left. He had his car keys in his left hand . The thumb of his right hand was pointed to the d oor.

Logan stood back, took out his own car keys, then replicated the movement.

'What d oes this suggest to you?' he asked the room in general. He held out the keys like Foster had d one, and gave another jab with this thumb.

'What is it? A book or a film?' asked Dave. He slapped a hand on his d esk. 'Wait. Got it. *The Hitcher*. Rutger Hauer.'

'Good film, that,' Tyler remarked .

'They d id a remake,' said Dave. 'Load of shite.'

'They always are, aren't they?' Tyler said , with a sad shake of his head . 'Same with *Robocop*. I wish they'd stop just rebooting stuff, and come up with some original—'

Logan cleared his throat. It was a low, ominous rumble—the first small earth tremor, warning that something seismic might strike at any moment.

The chatter stopped .

'Let's try that again, shall we?' the DCI asked . 'What d oes this suggest to you?'

'I'd say you're asking me if I want a lift,' said Ben.

Logan twirled the keys around on his finger and returned them to his pocket, like a Wild West Sheriff with his gun. 'That's what I thought.'

'But, having seen your car and experienced your driving, I'll probably take the bus,' Ben added, earning sniggers and grins from everyone but Logan.

'It's high time you had your own comedy show on the telly, Benjamin,' Logan said, visibly unamused.

'You think?'

'Aye. At least then, I could turn the fucking thing off,' Logan replied. 'The point—the bloody important point—that I'm trying to make is that we've got footage here that I'm sure shows Robert Foster offering Damian Bailey a lift home. And Foster told me—quite emphatically—that he did no such thing. He said he left Bailey at the door, but this video shows them both walking off together.'

'You mean he's a lawyer who's full of shit, boss?' Tyler asked, eyes wide with shock. 'I find that very hard to believe.'

'Someone get onto his office, see if he's back from his meeting. Don't say you're polis, if you can help it,' Logan instructed. 'There might be a good explanation, but I want to hear it from him, face-to-face.'

'I can do that, sir,' Hamza said, picking up his phone.

'Good. Let me know what they say, and I'll head over and talk to the bastard.'

Logan looked down at his feet, like he'd found himself somewhere unexpected and was trying to work out how he'd got there.

'What was I going to do?' he wondered aloud.

'Taxi video,' Ben told him.

'Shite. Aye,' Logan said, turning towards his desk.

'I've managed to get it open here, if you want to see it,' Ben said, and Logan wheeled around on the spot again, then hurried over to watch the DI's screen.

They both studied the footage in silence, watching as the two men went stumbling along through the snow outside the car.

It was only when the taxi started its three-point turn that Logan voiced what they were both thinking.

'That wasn't Gary Ward , was it?'

'I mean, it's hard to tell, so…' Ben sighed and shook his head . 'No. Height and build are all wrong.'

'Could feasibly be Robert Foster, though,' Logan remarked , then his brow furrowed into a frown and he bent to get a closer look at the screen. 'Wait a minute, wait a minute.' He took control of Ben's mouse and paused the footage. Captured in the vid eo freeze-frame, a house blazed with Christmas illumin- ations. 'The old woman who lives there.' He clicked his fingers in Sinead 's d irection.

'Angela McGavin,' the DC announced .

'Angela McGavin. She said she was fast asleep all Sund ay night. Told us she was in bed sharp, and slept right through.'

'So?' Ben asked , squinting at the screen.

'So, if she was tucked up in bed when all this was going on…' Logan tapped a finger on the frozen image. '…how come her front d oor is open?'

'Is it? I d on't know,' Ben said , looking more closely. 'That might just be shad ow, or… wait. No. You're right. It is.'

Logan straightened , mind racing as he tried to slot the pieces together. None of them fit yet, though. Not neatly, and not in a way that revealed any sort of clear picture.

The clack of Hamza's phone hand set returning to the crad le broke the DCI's concentration. He raised his eyes to the DS. 'Well? He out of his meeting?'

'He d id n't have a meeting,' Hamza said . 'He went home sick. Cancelled his appointments for the rest of the week.'

'Shite,' Logan spat. 'Get Uniform round his house. Now. Send someone senior to his work—some pushy bastard who won't take no for an answer—and have them search his office.'

'On it, boss,' Tyler said .

'Dave, ad d Robert Foster to your search. We know he's connected to Fred d ie Shaw and Damian Bailey, and ind irectly to Gary Ward . Anyone else?'

'Christ!' Ben ejected , a realisation hitting him with enough force to propel him onto his feet. 'The people trafficking case.

One of the Iceman's victims. Foster was part of the d efence team that got him off. I'm almost sure of it.'

'Get on that and   check it,' Logan said , pointing to Dave.

'He would 've still been young, though,' Ben pointed   out. 'And   that was one of the last victims. The first was, God , a year before? Not sure what age that would 've mad e Foster.'

'There's something there, though. He's involved . Which means we've now got three people to find . Surely to Christ, we can get one of them.' Logan grabbed   his coat from the back of his chair and   shoved   an arm into a sleeve.

'Where you off to?' asked   Ben.

'Alness. Angela McGavin's. See what she knows.'

'Need   backup, sir?' Sinead   asked .

'Pretty sure I can hand le her,' Logan replied . 'Where are we with George Morales's wid ow?'

'Still tracking d own her d etails.' Sinead   sighed   and   selected yet another option on yet another menu. 'Hopefully have something soon.'

'Let me know if anything comes up,' Logan said , head ed   for the d oor. 'That goes for all of you. We act fast on this, and   we might just get Damian Bailey back alive.'

Chapter 36

The Fiesta mad e it two-third s of the way up the hill that led up to Angela McGavin's house before its wheels started to spin. The engine whined bitterly as Logan tried to force the blood y thing to battle through the snow, but a smell of burning and a cloud of exhaust fumes eventually convinced him to knock it on the head .

Aband oning the car, he trud ged the rest of the way up the hill, his size thirteens giving him enough purchase on the ground to make it the rest of the way to where the cul-d e-sac end ed .

More snow was falling—big patterned flakes that meand ered d own from the sky like they had all the time in the world . It was the sort of snow you got in Hollywood movies, Logan thought. The sort of big, fat flakes that land ed on the noses of young people in love, or were caught by the tongues of child ren.

None of them land ed on Logan's nose, though. They all knew better.

The fella Tyler had interviewed —Colin something—stood at his living room wind ow, wrapped in some sort of silk kimono and sipping tea from a glass mug. He watched the d etective with interest, and gave a little wave of his fingers as Logan trud ged past.

The DCI d id n't acknowled ge it and instead crossed the road to where Angela McGavin's house spewed its festive lightshow out into the greyness of the afternoon.

He stopped at the gate and consid ered the forest beyond where the cul-d e-sac end ed . The trees stood close together, but many of them were bare, and the forest floor was a carpet of white, just like the street lead ing up to it.

Even missing much of its canopy of leaves, the wood s were a patchwork of shad ows, the first line of trees stand ing like a gateway between the light and the d ark.

He'd checked the place out on Google Maps earlier. The forest was extensive, covering a couple of square miles. Maybe more.

Big enough to hid e a few bod ies, certainly.

He fired off a text to Ben, instructing him to go ahead and arrange the d og and ground rad ar search of the forest. Then, he unlatched the gate and plod d ed up the path toward s the house.

Logan rang the bell. Waited . From insid e the house, he heard the shuffling of footsteps slowly approaching.

He glanced back over his should er. Colin was still stand ing at his wind ow, watching. Logan held his gaze, expecting the other man to become uncomfortable and look away. He d id n't, though, and it was the DCI who was forced to break the eye contact when Angela McGavin opened her d oor.

'Did you forget your key or—? Oh.' The old woman pulled her read ing glasses d own her nose and looked up at the d etective in surprise. 'You're that policeman from yesterd ay, aren't you? I thought you were Bertie back again.'

'No, Mrs McGavin, I'm afraid , it's… wait. Bertie?'

'My son. He was just here. Left in a bit of a hurry. Thought he must've left his key behind , or something.'

Logan looked d own at the path. Footprints led away from the house, trud ged into the snow.

Bertie.

'He can't have gone far. That's his car,' Angela said , peering past the d etective to where a large BMW was parked just d own the hill from the front gate. 'You sure you d id n't pass him? He's only been gone a minute or so.'

'Bertie. What's his full name, Mrs McGavin?' Logan asked .

Before the old woman could answer, a voice called to her from across the street.

'You all right, Angela, my love?'

Colin stood on his front step in his kimono, cup of tea still in hand . Angela gave him a big wave back.

'Fine, Colin. Fine. Thank you!' Angela replied , then she leaned a little closer to Logan. 'That's Colin. Lovely fella. Bit… you know.' She mad e a floppy-hand ed gesture and pursed her lips. 'But I won't hear a word against him. Always looked out for me, he has.'

'That's great, Mrs McGavin. But your son. Bertie. What's his name?'

'Well, he'll always be my Bertie to me,' Angela said , smiling fond ly. 'But it's Robert.'

'Robert Foster?'

Angela nod d ed . 'Goes by his father's name, like all my boys. I remarried , see? James, his name was. Long d ead now, of course. Rest his soul. Why d o you ask?'

'Mrs McGavin, I need you to go insid e and wait,' Logan instructed , pulling his phone out again. 'Do you still have the card I gave you with my d etails on it?'

'I think so. Yes. It's on the mantlepiece. I remember, because I was trying to think of somewhere safe that I could —'

Logan cut her off. 'Good . Go insid e, and if Robert turns up, and you feel it's safe to d o so, I want you to call me.'

'Safe to d o so? Why would n't it be safe? What's going on?' Angela asked . She had a smile on her face, but it was anxious and unsure.

'No time to explain, Mrs McGavin, but it's important that you try to keep Robert here, if you can. I need to talk to him.'

'Whatever for?'

Logan hesitated as he figured out how much he should tell her. 'Not much' was his eventual conclusion.

'It's a work-related matter,' he offered . 'That's all. It's regard ing one of his clients who's gone missing. I'm hoping he can help me find him.'

Angela's face brightened . 'Oh! I'm sure he'll be d elighted to help. He's a very helpful lad . Caring. As soon as I see him, I'll give you a call.'

Logan thanked her, then turned and hurried up the path, firing off another text message to Ben with the reg of the Beamer and an instruction to pull up the owner record s.

He was at the gate when Colin Rose came swishing through the snow toward s him, steam rising from the cup in his hand . 'You looking for Bertie?' he asked .

'Aye. Head ed into the wood s, jud ging by the footprints,' Logan replied .

Colin looked crestfallen, like his big moment had been spoiled . 'Yes. That's right. Think he spotted you coming up the hill, because he high-tailed it thataway just before you passed mine. He can't have gone far.' He glanced at Angela's house, then d ropped his voice to a whisper. 'Has he been a naughty boy, then?'

'I'm afraid I can't give you an answer to that.' Logan turned away from the man in the kimono and eyed up the wood s. 'But I intend to find out.'

–

There was a buzz about the office. Ben could feel it in the air all around him. There were times in every investigation when breakthroughs were mad e, hurd les were vaulted , and obstacles were overcome. Those times when something about the case changed , and the atmosphere changed along with it.

It was happening now. The excitement in the air was palp- able. And Ben was loving every blood y minute of it.

Moments like these energised him, mad e him feel ten years younger. Twenty. A man in the prime of his life, not rid d led with aches and pains.

'Reg confirmed , boss,' Tyler announced . 'Car is registered to the law firm Foster works for.'

'And I can connect him to three of the old Iceman cases,' Dave threw in from the sidelines. 'His firm represented them. Two in court, one during interviews before charges were dropped. That was Foster himself.'

Ben clapped his hands together then rubbed them gleefully. 'Right! Now we're talking! Hamza, Sinead, get over to those offices and start making a fuss,' he instructed.

'I could go with Sinead on that,' Tyler suggested.

'Hamza's a DS. He's got more clout,' Ben said, before turning his attention to the DS in question. 'See how far Uniform's got, and see how much further you can get without a warrant. If their clients are being murdered by one of their employees, it's not going to look good in the press. Maybe point that out to them, if they're being uncooperative.'

'One sec, sir,' Sinead said, scribbling in her notepad. She tore off the top page and passed it to Tyler. 'Did n't get much from George Morales's widow, but see what you make of that.'

She jumped to her feet, already grabbing for her jacket. She could feel the energy in the room, too, Ben thought. They all could. They could sense a collar was coming, and they could hardly bloody wait.

'Remember, our first priority is finding Damian Bailey,' Ben said, as Hamza and Sinead hurried for the door. 'We can still find the lad alive, and still get him home with his family for Christmas. Everything else is secondary. Even if we don't like him.'

He aimed that last part firmly at Hamza, who nodded his understanding.

'Priority one, sir,' he agreed, and then they headed out into the corridor, letting the doors swing closed behind them.

Ben allowed himself a moment of... not triumph, exactly. It wasn't 'case closed' yet. But a moment of satisfaction, at least. There still some muddy waters to wade through—the connection to Gary Ward for one—but there was a clear route now. They knew what they had to do, who they had to find.

He could n't be sure it would be easy, of course, but the hard est part was d one. The worst was over, he thought.

He was wrong.

Chapter 37

Foster's trail wasn't hard to follow. He'd been running, Logan thought, stumbling frantically through the snow in his rush to get away from the approaching d etective.

He'd fallen a few times—big ind ents in snowd rifts, and the od d hand print both testament to his clumsiness.

Logan moved quickly, but carefully, through the wood s, d ucking the spind ly fingers of branches that clawed and scratched at him as he pressed d eeper into the d arkness of the forest.

The snow was smothering the sound . It blanketed the wood s in the sort of silence that might d rive a man d emented through solitud e and isolation. It seemed to cut the place off from the rest of the world . There was no bird song. No rumble of d istant traffic. No life that existed beyond the forest's bord ers.

There was just the soft crunch of Logan's footsteps and the slow, stead y huffing of his breath.

'Foster!' Logan called , d eliberately breaking the hush before it could start to eat away at his nerves. 'There's no point running, son. You'll only make it worse.'

That wasn't strictly true, of course. If Foster really was the Iceman—if he'd really killed all those people—resisting arrest was unlikely to ad d much to his sentence.

The bastard would know that, too. Logan d ecid ed to try another approach.

'Your mum's worried about you, son,' he called into the shad ows, then he spun, fists raised , as a sud d en movement over on the right caught his eye.

A mound of snow fell from the branches of a tree and paffed against the ground . Otherwise, the forest was silent.

Logan continued on, following the clumsy trail that Foster had left. It zig-zagged through the trees, but seemed to be head ed in a specific d irection that led ahead and to the left.

The lack of sunlight and the veil of falling snow mad e it impossible to see more than twenty feet ahead . Logan shield ed his eyes against the worst of it, and set off in as straight a line as possible. A more d irect route would let him cut into Foster's lead , and he could hopefully nab the bastard before it got too much d arker.

The snow was growing heavier with each passing moment, and had started to swallow up the tracks both ahead of Logan and behind . Without them, he'd have no way of following Foster. And , if he was completely honest, no real way of find ing his way back to the cul-d e-sac.

He picked up the pace, risking his footing as he broke into a jog. The extra turn of speed mad e the blizzard seem even more brutal, even more blind ing.

The clawing clutches of the trees grasped for him, grabbed at him, ripping at his coat and scratching at his face. He raised his arms to protect his eyes, bound ed over a knot of snow-covered roots, and found himself racing toward s a d eep hole, d ead ahead .

'Fuck!' Logan hissed , d ropping his centre of gravity and falling onto his back before he could plunge over the ed ge and into the long, narrow pit.

The soft land ing promised by the powd ery snow d id n't materialise, as his back slammed onto a large concealed rock, and the impact forced all the air out of his lungs in a big gasp of swirling white vapour.

He had stopped with one foot hanging over the d rop, and scrambled his hand s through the biting cold snow until he found something to hang on to. Only then d id he risk moving enough to peer d own into the hole.

The blizzard was doing its best to fill it, but it was still defined enough that Logan could tell it wasn't naturally occurring. The hole was maybe five feet deep. Six feet long. Three wide.

Grave-sized. Man-made.

Had this been where Freddie Shaw was supposed to end up? Hidden away out here in the cold and the dark?

Tightening his grip on the roots of the closest tree, Logan dragged himself back from the edge of the hole, the heels of his boots slipping and sliding, his fingers numb with cold.

He was halfway to his feet when he heard the crunch of a footstep.

He was halfway turned when he saw something black and fast-moving come swinging at him from the shadows.

The impact wasn't painful, exactly, but it was shocking enough and hard enough to send him sprawling.

He threw his hands out, caught the tips of a branch, but he was too heavy, falling too fast. The branch became twigs in his hand. The world seemed to unhinge its jaws beneath him.

Logan landed heavily at the bottom of the hole, and a fireball of pain erupted from his ribcage.

He saw spots of red on the otherwise unblemished white snow, and a sharp ache on his forehead answered the question before he could ask it.

Blinking, Logan looked up at the rectangle of forest that stood towering above him. The first movement he saw was the swinging of a shovel. He heard the thack of the blade being wedged in the snow, and then Foster was there, standing above him, face red from the effort of running, eyes alive with excitement, or terror, or some combination of the two.

Ignoring the pain it brought, Logan sat up. The sudden movement brought snow cascading down on top of him, the walls of the hole collapsing as he tried to stand.

'I wouldn't do that,' Foster warned.

He swung with the shovel, forcing Logan to flop down onto his back to avoid a crack on the top of his skull. Logan was trapped . Even if he could clamber out without burying himself alive, Foster would smash his brains into a paste before he could make it halfway.

'All right. Easy, son, easy,' he said , buying himself some time to think. Time to plan.

Or, more realistically, time to realise just how truly fucked he was.

'Why are you here?' Foster d emand ed . 'Why d id you have to come after me? Why d id you have to come?'

The solicitor's should ers were shaking, the pitch of his voice rising and falling sporad ically, like he was singing the word s to some half-remembered song. At first, Logan thought he was laughing, but the tears cutting tracks d own his face told another story.

'It wasn't meant to happen like this. You weren't supposed to be here!'

'Robert. Listen to me,' Logan began, but a hiss from the man at the top of the pit cut him short.

'Shut up! Shut up, shut up, fucking shut up! Shut up!'

His hand s were red with cold , but his knuckles shone white as he clutched the hand le of the shovel. Logan raised a hand of his own, trying to calm Foster d own.

'You weren't meant to be here,' the solicitor whined . 'Not yet. We're not d one yet. *We're not finished!*'

'Who's not finished , son? Who are you working with?' Logan asked . 'Is it Gary Ward ?'

Foster's eyes went wid e. Shocked . 'How d id you...? Did he...?'

'He grassed you up,' Logan said , pouncing on the other man's confusion. 'Said you're the brains behind all this. Pinned the whole lot on you. But I d on't believe him, Robert. I think he's been manipulating you. I think you're as much a victim here as anyone. Help me prove that, son. Don't make it worse.'

He sat up slowly, like Dracula rising from his coffin. Something hard and sharp ground painfully against something wet and squid gy in his sid e. Two ribs gone, at least. Maybe more. The wound in his head was d ribbling blood into his eyes, too, blurring his vision and making them sting.

Things were bad . But he'd talked his way out of worse.

'There's a whole army of angry polis on the way here right now, Bertie,' he said . Foster's head cocked , ears pricking up as he tried to verify this. The only answer was the silence of the forest.

'They won't find us,' Foster said .

'The d ogs will. Big bastard s of things they are, too,' Logan said . 'They'll have the bollocks off you as soon as look at you. But, I can call them off. I can make them hang back. Give me a hand out of here, son. Let me help you straighten all this out. If not for your sake, then for your mum's.'

Foster ground his back teeth together, tears d ripping d own his face. His breath was a frosty-white wreath around his head — the hazy halo of some fallen angel.

'I'm sorry,' he whispered , as the blad e of the shovel d ug d eeper into the snow. 'But we're not d one yet. Not even close.'

'Bertie, d on't d o this!' Logan said , his voice rising to a shout. He scrambled for purchase on the walls again, then fell back when a shovelful of snow hit him like a punch to the face.

He coughed . Spluttered . Choked and spat.

More snow land ed . A big icy chunk of the stuff that crashed onto his chest, send ing searing streaks of agony through his ribcage.

He tried to cry out, to shout, to ord er him to stop, but every breath d rew in the cold and the wet. Smothering him. Drowning him.

And the shovel d ug d eep once more.

And the blizzard continued to fall.

–

Dave jabbed his thumbs into his eyes, gave them a rub, then refocused on his computer screen. He had four d ifferent wind ows open, d isplaying old polis files, historical newspaper reports, assorted social med ia profiles, and the AC/DC album *Let There Be Rock* on Spotify.

Other than confirming that Foster's firm had been involved in most of the Iceman cases, includ ing Fred d ie Shaw's, the connections he'd come up with so far could generously be d escribed as 'flimsy'.

Victims one and four shared the same d entist.

George Morales and Fred d ie Shaw were both allergic to Penicillin.

That sort of thing.

All the victims had run-ins with the law at some point, and none of them had faced any sort of punishment. That was the one thing that linked them all together, and was presumably the reason why the killer had taken it upon himself to enact his own form of justice.

This wasn't new information, though. That had been estab-lished way back in the original Iceman investigation. It was how he'd managed to be seen by some as a sort of psychotic Robin Hood figure, slaying the guilty so that the innocent could sleep more sound ly in their bed s.

Beyond that, there was no one thing that linked the whole thing together. Not one he could see, anyway.

Still, the sun might be making a beeline for the horizon, but there was still an hour or so left until d ay officially slid into evening. Plenty of time to find some connection, then.

With a nod of d etermination, Dave pressed his earbud s d eeper into his ears, cranked up the AC/DC, and went back to d igging.

Across the Incid ent Room, Tyler sat up straighter behind his monitor and waved to catch Ben's attention. 'Boss. Seen the inbox?'

DI Ford e had his phone crad led between his should er and his cheek, listening to Hamza give one of the partners at Foster's law firm both barrels of what-for.

'Think we're all right now, actually, sir,' Sinead said . 'DS Khaled has pointed out what you said about bad publicity, and they seem to be coming around to our way of thinking.'

'Good . Shout if you need me,' Ben told her, then he hung up the phone and checked his screen just as Tyler appeared beside him.

'You see it yet, boss?'

'No. You just saw me hang up the bloody phone,' Ben pointed out. He reached for his mouse, but Tyler grabbed it first. The DI watched , unable to keep up, as Tyler minimised various other wind ows, opened up the email, and selected a message in the shared inbox.

A map of Inverness appeared , with a cluster of red d ots gathered together near the airport.

'What am I looking at?' Ben asked .

'Well, as luck would have it, boss, Robert Foster is on Vod a-fone, and my man there was able to help me out. After DCI Logan paid him a visit earlier tod ay, Foster mad e two calls to the same number.'

'Whose number?'

'We d on't know. Pay As You Go. Unregistered ,' Tyler said . 'But... good news. Also on Vod afone. Better news, whoever's using the phone has got d ata and GPS turned on. Those red d ots? They're location pings from the phone.'

Ben sat forward in his chair. 'He's here? The person Foster was calling? This is him here?'

'Seems to be, boss,' Tyler said .

'Gary Ward , d o we think?'

'Beats me. Maybe. Whoever it is, they're out on one of the ind ustrial estates over by the airport. I zoomed in. Closest build ing is a d istribution centre for Nisa. The food place.'

'Food d istributor? They'd have frozen stuff, would n't they?'

'Not a clue, boss,' Tyler ad mitted . 'Even if they d o have freezers, I'd imagine they might take issue with someone hold ing prisoners in them. Want me to get Uniform round there?'

Ben could feel it again—that buzz of excitement. That shed - d ing of the years.

He got to his feet, a man of forty again. Thirty, even. His car keys jangled in his hand .

'They'll only scare him off. Even if it is him, we d on't know for sure that's where he's got Bailey,' the DI said . 'Best if we go scope it out first.'

Tyler stepped back in surprise. 'You sure you'll be all right d oing that, boss?' he asked .

'Aye, ye cheeky bastard ,' the DI said .

'No, I just meant—'

'I know full blood y well what you meant. And , listen, d on't you worry about me, son, just you worry about keeping up.' He bund led Tyler toward s the d oor. 'Come on, we'll call Jack from the car to let him know what's happening. Dave... Dave?' Ben clapped his hand s loud ly. 'Dave!'

'Hm? Sorry? What?' Dave asked , plucking out an earbud , and unleashing a tinny blast of *Whole Lotta Rosie*. 'Did you say something?'

'We're head ing out. Got a possible lead on Gary Ward . Man the fort until we get back, will you?'

Dave looked around the empty Incid ent Room. 'Aye. No bother,' he said , with a nod , then he waited until the d etectives had left, and jammed his earbud back in his lug.

Chapter 38

The build ing that had once been a Nisa food d istribution centre, was now nothing of the sort. It was… nothing, really. An empty warehouse, the shutters d own, the wind ows board ed .

Tyler and Ben sat in Ben's car, thirty yard s back from the first gate, watching for any sign of movement. So far, the most they'd seen was a carrier bag skipping along in the wind , then getting tangled in a clump of weed s and flapping about like a white flag of surrend er.

'What's wrong?' Ben asked , catching Tyler staring at his sid e mirror. 'See something?'

'I d on't know. I kept thinking we were being followed on the way out here, but… I d on't know. Can't see anyone.'

Ben checked the rearview mirror, then turned and looked back along the street. 'Well, if there was someone there, they're not anymore.'

Tyler nod d ed , took another look in the mirror, then faced ahead and stud ied the board ed -up build ing.

'What d o you reckon, boss?' He asked . 'Call in backup?'

Ben sucked air in through his teeth and tapped his fingers on the steering wheel. The location pings had n't been specifically in that build ing. They'd been d otted around it, jumping here and there like the owner of the phone was d oing laps of the immed iate area.

If he had been, then there was no sign of the bugger now.

'I think we should take a closer look,' Ben d ecid ed . 'We need to establish who's in there before we start escalating the situation. It might be empty, or he might have a knife to Bailey's throat. Either way, a big circus of flashy lights and sirens isn't going to help matters.'

Tyler looked from the DI to the warehouse and back again. 'So... should I go suss it out?'

Ben unclipped his belt. 'I'll come with you.'

'Are you sure, boss? Do you no' want to stay here and try calling DCI Logan again?'

'No, I bloody well do not,' Ben said, the words coming out with some venom behind them. 'I'm not for the scrapheap yet, you know? Still plenty of life in the old dog.'

'Aye. No. I wasn't saying—'

'Yes, you were,' Ben said, but he added a smile to take the edge off it. 'But I'm fine, son. And I've left Jack a voicemail. So, come on, me and you'll go see what we can see.'

After a glance in all directions, the detectives stepped down from the car and set off towards the warehouse. Ben told Tyler to keep it casual, act natural, and not draw attention.

'Just play it cool. Nice and cool,' Ben instructed, side-eyeing the warehouse as they passed the first of its two front gates.

As he walked, Tyler couldn't help but wonder what their cover story was meant to be. To any onlooker, they were two men, decades apart, out for a stroll together in a rundown industrial estate in the shadow of a regional airport, during the heaviest snowfall the city had seen in years.

He couldn't, for the life of him, think of a decent explanation for that.

What were their roles here? Who were they meant to be? How could he 'act natural' if he had no idea how his character would naturally move?

'Stop overthinking it,' Ben muttered, as if reading the DC's mind. 'And stop walking like that.'

Tyler checked his feet. 'Like what, boss?'

'Like a toy bloody robot,' Ben whispered. 'Just relax. Play it cool.'

Tyler mad e a conscious effort to relax his gait. Ben picked up on it immed iately. 'Jesus Christ, son, are your legs mad e of rubber all of a sud d en?' he scold ed . 'Just walk normally.'

'I can't remember how!' Tyler hissed , a note of d esperation in his voice. 'It's like when you think about breathing too much, and you go... in, out, in... shit. What's next?'

There was a scuffing of feet and Ben stopped by the second gate. Tyler lurched awkward ly on for a few more paces before he realised the DI was no longer besid e him.

'There. Look,' Ben said .

Tyler followed the old er man's gaze. A fire exit stood ajar at the sid e of the warehouse. Just visible through the snowfall, a thin line of smoke trailed up from the top of a cigarette bin that had been fixed to the wall besid e the d oor.

Their feet crunched softly on the carpet of snow as they approached the d oor, eyes scanning ahead and behind , on the lookout for any signs of life.

Tyler took the lead as they reached the fire exit. It was open a foot or so, and the faint humming of something electrical was the only sound from insid e.

'See anyone?' Ben whispered .

Tyler took a half-step closer and peered into the warehouse. The fire exit opened up onto a cavernous storage space. Four wood en crates blocked most of Tyler's view, but he got the impression that the place was empty.

There were skylights in the apex roof, but the snow had covered them, blocking out the sun, and the only light came from a couple of hanging fluorescent strips, and neither one seemed to be trying very hard to fend off the gloom.

There was no movement. No sound , other than the whine of electrics.

Tyler shook his head . 'Not a soul, boss,' he replied , keeping his voice low. 'Should we go in?'

Ben d id n't hesitate. He nod d ed , then stepped in closer behind the DC, all but urging him insid e.

The build ing was clearly meant to be empty and secured . They had good reason to believe that someone had broken in, let alone their suspicions about what else might be happening insid e. They d id n't need a warrant, but as Tyler stepped quietly over the threshold , he could n't help but think that some backup might be nice.

He stuck to the shad ows that the wood en crates painted across the wall, and waited for Ben to slip in through the d oor behind him.

Now that they were insid e, Tyler could see that a rectangular metal box, the size of a large shed , stood at the far end of the warehouse. A porthole wind ow in the front d oor was fogged up with cold , and the box was clearly the source of the electronic hum he had heard from outsid e.

Tyler pointed , d rawing Ben's attention to the freezer. The DI gave a thumbs-up, then tapped himself in the mid d le of his chest and mad e a chopping motion with one hand to suggest he would lead the way.

They'd mad e it just a few cautious steps when the figure emerged from behind the crates. He was a young man in his early twenties. That was the first thing they noticed .

The second thing they noticed was the shotgun. It was pointed at Ben, its twin barrels cut d own with a hacksaw. It shook in the young man's hand s, his finger trembling on the trigger.

'Gary? Gary Ward ?' Ben asked .

'Shut the fuck up!' Ward hissed . He glared at Tyler. 'And shut the d oor, or I blow this old prick's head off!'

–

Robert Foster had just come running out the trees, when a size-able gentleman in a long coat slammed into him from behind , send ing him sprawling onto the snow-covered road .

Breathless and terrified , Foster scrambled backward s on his hand s, kicking, slipping, and slid ing as he tried to put d istance between himself and the detective who stood towering above him like some vengeful god .

'What the…? What the fuck? I buried you!'

'You buried me in snow, you useless bastard ,' Logan pointed out. 'And no' very much of it, at that. I climbed out. If anything, you shovelling all that extra snow in actually mad e it easier. So, thanks for that.'

Logan flexed his fingers. Cracked his knuckles. Clenched his jaw. 'Now, Robert, you and me have got a lot to talk about. Don't we? So, how about—'

'Bertie? Here! What are you d oing to my Bertie?'

Logan shot a look of warning at Angela McGavin as she came hobbling up her front path, her Christmas lights blazing behind her.

'Angela, stay there!' Logan barked . He saw Foster start to move, and turned in time to be blind ed by a snowball to the face.

Spitting and wiping the snow away, Logan saw the solicitor racing for his car. The DCI threw himself after the bastard , big feet tramping and swishing through the road slush, eyes still blurry from the faceful of snow.

Foster had mad e it to the car and pulled open the d river's d oor, but Logan was too close behind for him to get in, lock the d oor, and get away. With a wild , animalistic shriek, he spun around , the blad e of a kitchen knife glinting in the faint, d iffused glow of the sun.

Logan d id n't have time to stop. Which was fine, because he had no blood y intention of d oing so. He angled himself away from the knife, pushed it asid e with his arm, and let his momentum and weight d rive Foster hard against the sid e of the car.

'Stop it! Stop it, please!'

Angela was at Logan's back, grabbing at his arm, pulling at his coat. Logan saw Foster's knife-arm start to swing and stumbled clear just in time to avoid a wild , frenzied slash.

'Bertie, what's going on? What's happening?' the old woman wailed , reaching for him.

'Don't!' Logan cried , but the warning came too late, and she almost certainly would n't have listened , anyway.

Angela gasped as Robert threw an arm around her neck and twisted her to face the DCI. 'Back the fuck off!' the solicitor hissed , the tip of the knife held poised at his mother's throat. 'I'll fucking kill her. I swear!'

'That's your mum, son,' Logan said . 'Don't be a d ick, eh? Put the knife d own.'

'Angela? Oh, God . Angela!' Colin Rose came jogging across the street, his silk kimono billowing behind him like a super-hero's cape. 'What the heck is happening right now?' he asked , skid d ing to a stop a few paces behind the DCI.

'Nothing. It's all und er control. Go home,' Logan instructed .

'No!' Foster spat. 'If he goes home, he'll call the police. More police.'

'They're alread y on their way, Robert,' Logan said . 'Be here any minute. There's nowhere for you to go.'

'You d on't go anywhere!' Foster said , shooting a glare in Colin's d irection.

'Fine. He'll stay here with us. Uniform's going to be here in minutes, anyway. It's all over, Robert,' Logan said . He smiled , not unkind ly. 'So, let your old mum go. Eh, son? Let her go.'

Foster's hand s trembled . His head shook. His voice, when it came, was a sob of anguish.

'I can't, can I?' he whispered . 'How can I, after everything I've d one?'

Chapter 39

'Look, I don't know what you've done, son, but trust me, this isn't helping matters,' said Ben. He and Tyler stood with their hands up, their backs to the walk-in freezer, Gary Ward pointing at each of them in turn, like he didn't want either detective to feel left out.

'What I've done? I've only done what you lot should've done already,' Gary said. 'Justice. That's what I've done. For Joanna. My sister.'

'She doesn't want this, Gary,' Ben told him. 'She told us herself.'

'Yes, she does! She wants them punished!' Gary retorted. 'And that's what we've done.' He gave a shake of his head, annoyed at himself. 'What I've done.'

'She wants them to admit to what they've done. She wants them in jail, Gary, not for you to go out and bloody kill them.'

'And we know you're not working alone, Gary,' Tyler added. 'We're taking Robert Foster into custody as we speak.'

A look of horror flashed across the lad's face, but he tried to bury it behind a sneer. 'I don't know who that is.'

'I know that's a lie, Gary,' Ben told him. 'He was the lawyer defending Freddie Shaw and Damian Bailey. You sat in court while he got torn into your sister's character. While he got those men off with what they'd done.'

'He had to. It... it was his job,' Gary stammered. 'But we made sure they got what was coming to them. In the end. Him, and me, and ... we made sure.'

'Where's Damian now?' Tyler asked.

Ward was scared shitless, that much was clear. He was being sensible enough to keep his distance, though. They had about a snowball's chance in hell of getting to him before he could pull the trigger.

Gary's eyes flitted to the door of the freezer behind the detectives. Cold rolled around inside it as wavy white clouds, coating the inside of the window with thick frost. A digital display on the wall by the door read minus thirty-eight.

'Nippy in there,' Ben remarked. He tilted his head towards the freezer door. 'Let us get him out, Gary. You don't need to do this.'

'I do!'

'You don't, son,' Ben insisted. 'Let us help him, and the court will go easy. We'll explain the situation. They'll understand.'

The muscles in Gary's jaw tensed and rolled below his skin. He adjusted his grip on the sawn-off barrel of the shotgun.

'If he dies, there's nothing we can do to help you, Gary,' Tyler told him. 'Let us get him out. Let us call an ambulance. Help us to help you, Gary. We can put this right.'

Ward groaned, somewhere far back in his throat. With a twitch of the gun, he gave them permission to open the door, and Tyler kept an eye on Ward while Ben pulled down the big metal handle that sealed the heavy door shut.

A chill mist rolled out. It was the sort of thing you'd see in a sci-fi movie, Tyler thought, when someone was woken from suspended animation. For a moment, he considered using the cover it offered to make a grab for the gun, but it rose quickly, leaving him and Ben just as exposed as they'd been a moment ago.

'Oh, Gary,' Ben sighed. 'What have you done?'

In that moment, even before he looked, Tyler knew there would be no need for an ambulance.

He knew that there would be no helping Damian Bailey.

One glance confirmed it. Bailey lay on a puddle of frozen red, his body naked and punctured by a dozen or more stab wounds.

There was a hole where his crotch should have been. That was the only way Tyler could think to describe it. Everything that had been there previously was now... elsewhere. All that remained was a dark, bloody void of flesh, skin, and sinew.

The detectives both heard the clack the shotgun made as Gary adjusted his aim.

'Get in.'

'Gary, don't be stupid,' Ben began, but one look at Ward's face told him to keep his mouth shut and do as he was told.

'Get in. Now.'

Slowly, so as not to tempt Ward's trigger finger, Ben stepped up into the freezer. The cold hit him immediately, nipping at the exposed skin of his face, and making his eyes and throat go dry.

Once Tyler had stepped in behind him, Ward motioned with the gun to the floor in front of him.

'Your phones. Chuck your phones.'

'Jesus Christ, Gary, think about what you're doing here, mate,' Tyler said.

'*Chuck your fucking phones or I'll shoot you both!*'

Their phones hit the ground where he'd indicated, both screens cracking on the concrete floor.

'You shouldn't have come here. You made me do this. You made me,' Ward babbled.

'You don't have to do this, son,' Ben said. His body had already started to shake as the icy waves of cold came crashing over him.

'What the fuck do you know? Eh?' Ward barked, face contorting in anger. 'Get up the back. Move!'

Tyler eyed the gun. Ward was standing right by the door now. If Tyler threw himself—really threw himself—he might be able to get to the shotgun before Ward could fire off a shot. He wasn't a big lad, and Tyler would have the element of surprise.

The DC rose onto the balls of his feet.

A hand rested on his arm, the grip firm.

'Come on, son,' Ben said . 'Let's d o as he says, eh?'

When the DI pulled , Tyler had no choice but to back d own. They retreated to the back of the freezer, stepping over the wid e-eyed , frozen corpse of Damian Bailey.

The d oor closed with a sound like the tolling of a bell.

CLUNNNNNG.

The cold became more intense even before the sound had fad ed . It was like nothing either man had ever felt. More biting, more raw than any temperature they'd ever experienced .

They returned to the d oor, and Tyler wiped the frost from the glass with the sleeve of his jacket. Gary Ward was still out there, smashing their phones with the butt of the shotgun. The innard s of Tyler's iPhone were alread y strewn across the concrete, and Ben's mobile was hold ing up no better.

'Shite. They'll no' cover that und er the warranty, will they?' Ben said . There was alread y a tremble in his voice, his jaw shaking as the extreme sub-zero temperature took hold .

'Doubt it, b-boss,' Tyler said .

The sound of the phones being smashed to bits was d istant and muted , muffled by the thickness of the walls, and d rowned out by the buzzing of the freezer.

Tyler thumped a fist against the wind ow. 'Gary! Gary, come on, d on't d o this!'

Ward d id n't look up until he'd fully obliterated both mobiles. Only then d id he meet Tyler's eye. Only then d id he launch into a full-scale rant, hand s gesticulating wild ly as he railed against them, against the justice system, against the sheer fucking cruelty of the world they lived in.

At least, that's what the d etectives assumed he was going on about.

'I can't hear a b-blood y word , can you?' Ben asked .

Tyler blew into his cupped hand s, then shoved them as d eep in his pockets as they would go. 'No, boss.'

Ben hugged himself. The cold had been quick to find its way beneath his jacket, and the shakes that had started in his jaw were now spread ing throughout the rest of his bod y. His legs, which d id n't have the luxury of several layers of clothing, were alread y tingling painfully, and he d id n't want to think about what was going on with his toes.

'M–maybe he'll see sense,' he said . 'When he c–calms d own.'

Tyler nod d ed . Stamped his feet. Forced his hand s d eeper in the corners of his pockets. 'Aye. Maybe we'll b–be able to r–reason with him when he gets this out of his s–system.'

They both went back to peering through the glass just as Ward jammed both barrels of the shotgun und er his jaw, screamed silently, and pulled the trigger.

They heard the roar of the weapon even through the sound - proofed walls.

Blood , bone, and lumps of brain matter coated the wind ow from the outsid e.

'Jesus Christ!' Tyler shrieked , jumping back.

Ben sighed . His breath fogged and instantly froze on the glass. 'W–well,' he stammered . 'B–bang goes that id ea.'

–

'Bertie. Please. You're hurting me,' Angela plead ed , the pressure of her son's arm across her throat turning her voice into a croak. 'Let me go. Put the knife d own.'

Behind her, tears sprang to her son's eyes. He sniffed , like he could suck them back in, and shook his head . 'I can't. I can't. I'm sorry, Mum. I'm sorry!'

'You've nothing to be sorry for, Bertie,' Angela assured him—present situation presumably exclud ed . 'You've d one nothing wrong, son. You've d one nothing wrong.'

'I have. I have, Mum,' Foster said , his own voice now matching his mother's, croak for croak. 'I've d one... I've d one really bad things.'

'What? When? To who?' Angela asked .

'Bad people. It was... just to bad people,' Foster said . There was no point in him trying to hold back the tears now. They fell

like rain and were swallowed by the snow where they land ed .
'People that got away with things they should n't. People that
someone need ed to stop.'

'You d efend ed them, Robert,' Logan felt compelled to
remind him.

'Because I had to! It was my job!' Foster seethed . 'But they
d id it. They all d id those things. And they all got away with
them, over and over again.'

He ad justed his grip on Angela, so it almost looked like he
was giving her a hug.

'I d id it for Martin, Mum,' he sobbed . 'How is it fair? How
is it fair that he was d ead , and evil bastard s like that were alive?
Walking around , free, d oing what they liked . How is that fair?'

'It isn't, sweetheart. It isn't fair,' Angela told him. 'But life's
not fair, is it?'

'No, I know, but I mad e it fair, Mum. I d id . I mad e it fair,'
Foster continued , d esperately seeking her approval. 'I d id it for
him. For Martin. It's what he'd have wanted .'

'It isn't, love. He would n't have wanted this. Not this.'

'Just give me the knife, son. You d on't want to d o this,' Logan
said .

'Come on, Robert,' Colin urged . 'Let her go, eh? There's a
lad .'

'Shut up! Everyone just shut up!' Foster cried . 'And fucking
stay back. I'll… I'll kill her. I will!'

Logan d id n't move back but d id n't come any closer, either.
He ind icated for Colin to retreat a pace or two, then held his
hand s up in a show of surrend er.

'All right, Robert. You're in charge. What d o you want to
d o here?'

Before he could answer, Angela brought a hand up and
placed it on the arm that was hooked across her throat. She
rubbed it fond ly, her eyes glassy with tears of her own.

'Remember, son, when you used to get upset? When Rory
had been fighting with you or wind ing you up, and you could n't

sleep? Do you remember?' she asked . 'Do you remember what I used to sing?'

'Mum, stop,' Foster croaked .

'Aye, you remember,' Angela said , then she began to sing in a soft, gentle burr. 'Coorie d oon, coorie d oon, coorie d oon my d arling. Coorie d oon the d ay.'

The word s were barely more than a whisper, but they carried clearly through the hush of the falling snow.

'Stop it. Shut up! Don't!' Foster begged .

'Lie d oon my d ear, and in your ear, to help you close your eye, I'll sing a song, a slumber song, a miner's lullaby.'

Foster's hand s shook, the point of the knife jerking around just millimetres from his mother's throat.

'Mum. Don't. Stop it. Please! Just stop it!'

She let out a cry as the blad e nicked her skin. A single d rop of blood ran d own the length of the knife, then pinkened the snow at Foster's feet.

'Oh, God . Oh, God ! Mum! I'm sorry, I'm sorry!' he sobbed , releasing his grip on her and jumping back.

He thrust the knife out before Logan could make a move, hold ing him and the other man at bay.

'I'm fine! I'm fine, I'm all right,' Angela insisted , clasping a hand over the injury. 'Just… put the knife d own, Bertie. Please.'

The weapon swayed like he was d rawing d runken figure eights in the air. He was a mess of tears and snot now, his whole bod y trembling with cold and with shock.

'It's over, Robert. Thatta boy. Give me the knife,' Logan said , hold ing a hand out. 'Let's talk about this, all right?'

The solicitor stud ied the offered hand for a moment, then looked at the knife he was hold ing.

His face changed .

A d ecision was reached .

'There's a note in my flat. Bottom d esk d rawer. The key's in my pocket,' he said , gritting his teeth and pushing back his tears. 'But I am the Iceman. I have always been the Iceman. I killed all those people.'

'Robert—' Logan began, but that was as far as he got. He could only watch helplessly, as Foster plunged the knife into his own throat. Once. Twice. Blood sprayed in a wid e arc, spattering the snow as a mist, then cascad ing d own his front as a crimson waterfall.

Angela wailed . It was an inhuman sound that cut through the stifling silence of the snow-covered cul-d e-sac and went echoing d own the hill.

She ran for her son as his legs gave way and he fell to his knees, but Colin was there in front of her, blocking her, wrapping his arms around her, pulling her in close.

'Don't look, Angela, d on't look,' he urged , turning her away from the scene, even as Logan d ropped to the ground besid e Robert.

The solicitor had twisted as he'd fallen, so he lay on his back, bubbles of blood forming in the yawning wound that was his throat.

The air rasped in. Out. In.

His legs twitched . His bod y convulsed . Logan clamped one hand over his throat, and fished in his pocket for his phone with the other. He'd call an ambulance, of course. Tell it to get here quickly.

But it would be too late by then.

It was too late alread y.

Angela struggled in Colin's grip, but he held her tightly, hand s rubbing her bony back.

'Let me go,' she sobbed . 'Let me see him!'

'Just give it a minute, Angela, love. Give it a minute,' Colin said . 'Why d on't you sing that song again? The one you used to sing? It was lovely. What was it, again?'

Angela continued to resist for a few more second s, then let her head fall against his chest.

And , as the last of her son's life ebbed out onto the snow behind her, she sang to him one final time.

Your daddy coories doon, my darling,
Doon in a three-foot seam,
So you can coorie doon, my darling,
Coorie doon and dream.

Chapter 40

Mr Monroe had been waiting for Olivia outsid e her final class of the d ay and had intercepted her before she could so much as think about head ing for the exit.

He escorted her to his office in silence, then told her to wait while he went back out to reception to make a few calls. These, he said , would d ecid e her fate, so she had better keep her fingers crossed .

She d id n't bother. Instead , she sat on the chair he had d irected her to and hugged her backpack to her chest, arms through the straps, fingers clasped together as an ad d ed precaution.

Through the wind ow, she could see the other pupils all head ing home. They walked in groups, laughing and joking, flirting and jostling as they mad e their way to the fleets of cars and buses that waited for them in the car park and pick-up zone.

For the most part, they looked happy. Carefree.

Like kid s.

She watched them through the glass like they were attractions at a zoo. Monkeys, maybe. Similar to her in so many ways, but not the same. Alike, but d ifferent.

Mr Monroe still wasn't back by the time the last few stragglers had exited through the gate, and the first weary bus d river had pulled away, visibly muttering to himself about 'noisy blood y hooligans'.

Olivia turned her attention to the office around her, her gaze taking a stroll through some of the more interesting d etails.

The head teacher's trophy cabinet stood over on her right, all the cups and med als arranged on shelves behind the glass d oors. It was an impressive haul. Olivia envied the d ed ication it must take to achieve all those little victories, while simultaneously consid ering it to be absolutely the lamest thing ever.

It was confusing, sometimes, being a teenager.

She saw herself reflected in the glass of the cabinet. The way she was clutching the bag to herself mad e her look like a suicid e bomber just waiting to be blown to pieces. Mr Monroe was unlikely to grab the bag from her, she reasoned , but he was bound to get suspicious if he came in to find her crad ling it so protectively.

Unhooking her arms, she tucked the bag und er her chair so it was mostly out of sight.

Then, just to be on the safe sid e, she hooked a foot through one of the straps.

Mr Monroe still had n't returned , so she continued her visual tour of the office.

There were two battered old filing cabinets, both with keys sticking out from their locks. She was tempted to have a look insid e, but suspected they'd probably be empty. Surely everything was on computer nowad ays, wasn't it? There was probably nothing in them but spare pants, in case any of the first years unexpected ly started their period .

Or shit themselves. She'd seen that happen, too. A girl at her old school. Third d ay there.

She had n't come back for d ay four. Rumour had it that she was home-ed ucated now.

And who could blame her?

Olivia's gaze alighted on the photo on Mr Monroe's d esk. The woman and little girl in it looked back at her, tongues sticking out.

Reaching across the d esk, Olivia picked up the wood en frame and stud ied the picture. The girl must have been three or four. She had a gid d y sort of look on her face, like she was barely containing the biggest laugh anyone had ever heard .

The woman was pretty, but not in the harsh, sculpted way some of her mum's friend s looked . She had n't sculpted her eyebrows into thin, angular lines, or stained her skin orange with fake tan.

She had blond e hair, cut short. Eyes that sparkled . A mouth that seemed a half-second away from smiling. Olivia expected she'd be a very nice person. Kind .

It was the girl who kept d rawing Olivia's eye, though. That gleeful look pulled her back. She'd have loved to have seen the moment after the photo was taken. To have heard the laughter. To have witnessed the excitement finally bubbling to the surface and popping as high-pitched giggles and snorts.

It struck her then, as she held that photo. As she anticipated that laughter.

She'd never been as happy as the girl in that picture.

Not even close.

The d oor opened and then closed behind her. The photo frame was plucked from her grasp with a 'thank you', and returned to its spot on the d esk.

'Sorry, sir. I was just looking,' Olivia said , but the head teacher gave no ind ication that he'd heard her as he took his seat on the other sid e of the d esk.

'Right, then. I've spoken to Jonathan's parents again, and I've spoken to the ed ucation d epartment at the Highland Council,' he announced . His face was thin and d rawn, like a d octor about to break bad news. 'How d o you think that went, Olivia?'

Olivia shrugged . 'Not well?'

'Not well at all,' Mr Monroe said . 'Jonathan's parents were incand escent with rage. Do you know what that word means? "Incand escent"?'

'Yes.'

'It means "full of strong emotion",' the head teacher said .

'I know,' Olivia replied .

'Do you? Good . Then I'm sure you can imagine quite what an unpleasant phone conversation I just had with them,' Mr

Monroe said . 'With them both, mind . Jonathan's mother and father. One after the other. Both at once, at one point.'

Olivia swallowed . 'Are they... d id they want to call the police?'

'They d id . They very much d id ,' the head teacher replied and Olivia felt her heart d ropping into the pit of her stomach. 'But, fortunately for you, I was able to talk them out of it.'

'What? Seriously?' Olivia asked , perking up in her chair.

'Yes. Seriously,' Mr Monroe told her.

'Oh. Wow. Thanks, sir!'

'Don't thank me quite yet. I assured them we'd take appropriate punishment, which we are still to d ecid e on.'

Olivia d id n't care. Whatever the punishment—however long the d etention, or suspension, or whatever was hand ed d own— it was better than trying to explain to the police why she was carrying a big old pile of d rugs around with her.

Mr Monroe clicked his tongue against the roof of his mouth a few times, consid ering his next word s. 'I was going to phone your mother,' he announced . 'But I d ecid ed against it. I'm sure, given everything that's happened in the last eighteen months, she's got enough on her plate. Would you agree with that assessment?'

Olivia nod d ed .

'It must've been a real shock for you. Find ing out what your d ad was d oing.'

Another nod . A glance away.

'Unless you alread y knew, of course,' Mr Monroe said . He smiled , but it d id n't seem as effortless for him as it usually d id . 'Did you? Know, I mean? About what he was d oing?'

'No,' Olivia said . 'We d id n't.'

'No. Good .'

He tapped a finger on the ed ge of the d esk like he was playing a percussion instrument. He wasn't being gentle about it, either, and Olivia reckoned it probably had to hurt.

Mr Monroe sat forward sharply, startling her.

'Where did you go after school yesterday, Olivia?'

Olivia blinked. 'What?'

'After school. Yesterday. Where did you go?'

'Just… just home.'

'Don't lie to me, Olivia. Please. I put my neck on the line for you today, so I'd ask you to be honest.'

The head teacher gave his request a moment to bed in before continuing.

'Where did you go after school?'

Olivia felt her mouth go dry. Did he know? Had Jonathan grassed her up? If so, she should 've finished strangling the bastard.

'Just… just home, sir.'

Across the desk, Mr Monroe let out a long, weary breath. He closed his eyes for a moment, gave a minute shake of his head, then sat back.

'I've heard different, Olivia.'

'Was it Jonathan? He's lying,' Olivia protested. 'He followed me, so I took a weird route trying to lose him, but I just went home, sir, I swear. I just went—'

'I want to see your bag.'

The rest of Olivia's objections died in her throat. She licked her lips. Swallowed. Her mind was racing, but it was empty of everything but panic.

'What?' she asked, stalling for time. 'Why?'

'I think you know why, Olivia,' Mr Monroe said. He closed the lid of his laptop and moved it aside, then indicated the space on the desk where it had been sitting. 'Give me your bag, or I'll take back what I said to Jonathan's parents and weill be calling the police. Is that what you want?'

'No, sir.'

'No. Then give. Me. The bag.'

Slowly, her eyes fixed on the head teacher as if he might pounce on her the moment she looked away, Olivia reached und er her chair, unhooked her foot from the strap, then placed the bag on the d esk between them.

'Open it,' Mr Monroe instructed .

'It's just school stuff.'

'I won't ask you again, Miss Maximuke.'

The head teacher's whole d emeanour had changed . This wasn't the caring school lead er she'd known until now. This was someone else, wearing that same skin. His gaze was an electric d rill, boring into her. His fingers had balled into fists, thumbs rubbing up and d own the curled ind ex fingers like they were trying to calm the hand s d own.

The sound of the bag's zip seemed unnaturally loud in the otherwise silent office.

'And the front pocket.'

Olivia d id n't bother to argue. It wasn't like he was going to change his mind at this point, no matter what objections she offered .

She unzipped the front pocket and sat back. Mr Monroe turned the top of the bag toward s him, then reached into the top d rawer of his d esk and prod uced a small black torch. A press of the button on the bottom ignited a powerful beam that hit Olivia in the face, temporarily blind ing her and d rawing a hiss of shock.

The head teacher d irected the beam into the bag and , using the plastic ruler, wid ened the opening to give him a better view of the contents.

He checked the main part of the bag first. Books. A pencil case. Nothing out of the ord inary.

Olivia blinked away the spots of the torchlight, then watched as he used the ruler to open the front pouch, and aimed his torch insid e.

For a long moment, he said nothing. It was Olivia who eventually broke the silence.

'I d on't know what you were looking for, sir,' she said . 'But I d on't have it.'

Mr Monroe reached into the bag, felt around , then slid it back across the d esk so it land ed in her lap. He clicked the torch off, returned it to his d esk d rawer, then slid it closed with a clunk.

'I suppose I should 've expected that,' he said .

'What, for my schoolbag to be full of school stuff?' Olivia asked , zipping the backpack closed . 'Yeah, you probably should have. *Sir*.'

She expected the head teacher to lose his temper at that, given the tone that she'd said it in. Instead , he just shook his head . Not angry. Just d isappointed .

'For you to have taken precautions. You're a smart girl. You could 've achieved so much here. Put your past behind you. Looked to the future. But, no. You had to go and blow it.'

'What d o you mean, "could 've achieved "? Are you expelling me?'

Mr Monroe stretched his fingers wid e, then placed them, splayed out, on the d esk. He smiled , but everything about it was wrong. Everything about it was the opposite of what a smile was meant to be.

'Not exactly, Miss Maximuke,' he said . 'Not quite.'

–

'Holy shit. Seriously?'

Sinead stood in one corner of the expansive foyer of the legal firm that had , until very recently, counted Robert Foster amongst its employees. She had her back to the heated d iscussion that was currently taking place between the firm's senior partners and Hamza, her voice low to prevent anyone else picking up on her conversation with Logan.

'Aye. Right in front of me,' Logan confirmed . Sinead could hear the nasal whine of his car engine in the background , and the roar of faster traffic overtaking. 'Ambulance came. Paramed ics tried to d o their best, but it was a lost cause. Uniform's taken over with the mother. There's a neighbour looking after

her, too. I'm on the way d own the road   now. I'm getting
the bod y brought in to Shona, although cause of d eath won't
exactly be too hard   to pinpoint.'

'Blood y hell. Are you all right, sir?'

'Me? Aye. Fine. Getting buried   alive, then having someone
knife themselves in the throat in front of me is just par for the
blood y course since I moved   up here. I swear to God , all the
rain over the years must have d riven you lot mental.'

'Aye. Maybe,' Sinead   ad mitted . 'Should   we carry on trying
to get access here? They let us in with a bit of persuasion, but
now the bosses have turned   up and   got involved , and   it's hit a
bit of a sticky patch.'

She looked   back over her should er to see fingers being
pointed   in Hamza's face. A couple of Uniforms stood   behind
him, and   they seemed   to be taking it worse than he was. Hamza
was more patient than most people she knew, but even he had
his limits, and   there were only so many fingers in the face one
man could   take.

'I'd   knock it on the head ,' Logan said . 'Leave a couple of
constables there to make the bastard s uncomfortable. Make sure
his office is secured , but he said   there's a note in his d esk d rawer
at home. I've got the key here. If you text me the ad d ress, I'll
meet you there.'

'Will d o, sir. So… he confessed ?'

'He d id .'

'But what d oes that mean for—'

'Gary Ward ? Christ knows. At the moment, we can only
assume they were in it together,' Logan said , then the screaming
of a motorbike engine came blaring from Sinead 's mobile.
'Arsehole!' Logan bellowed , before getting back to the matter
at hand . 'Any sign of him? Ward , I mean.'

'I got a text from Tyler. They got a lead   on his phone. He
and   DI Ford e were going to check it out.'

'When was this?'

Sinead   shrugged . 'An hour ago, maybe.'

'Any word since?'

'Nothing yet, sir. Want me to give them a call?'

There was a lengthy pause as Logan considered this.

'No. Leave it with me,' he eventually decided. 'Just get me that address, then head over to Foster's flat, and hopefully we can get this thing wrapped up without any other bugger getting hurt.'

Chapter 41

Cold . Biting, agonising, all-consuming cold .

It circled around them like a flock of vultures, waiting for one of them to d rop. It filled their insid es, creeping in with every breath, cramping their lungs and slowing their organs.

It was, as Tyler had remarked on three separate occasions now, 'fucking freezing'.

He had n't mad e the remark in several minutes now. In fact, he had n't said much of anything. Talking hurt. Talking took energy, and gave the sub-zero air another opportunity to sneak d own his throat and eat away at him from within.

He'd shouted . For a while. Not long. They could n't keep it up for long.

The floor was too cold to sit on. The walls too cold to lean on. They stood in the centre of the room, d own by Damian Bailey's feet, hugging each other for warmth. Their jackets were d esigned more for the wet than the cold . Not for this cold , anyway. Not this harsh. Not this brutal. Not this raw.

Tyler stamped his feet. Flexed his fingers. Wiggled his toes. He could n't tell what the expression on his face was. The only reason he knew he had a face at all, in fact, was the pain. It started on the tip of his nose and rad iated backward s into his skull. His teeth ached . His tongue was a fat, slow-moving alien presence in his mouth.

'F-fuck this,' he grimaced , fixing the largest of the freezer's three cold -spewing vents with a look of sheer hatred . 'I'm g-going to block that f-fucker.'

'With what?' asked Ben, his voice barely a whisper above the insistent electrical hum of the freezer.

Tyler looked d own at Damian Bailey's bod y. He wasn't wearing anything that would help protect them from the cold , but his clothing might help block the ingress of icy air. It would n't miraculously warm the place up, but it might buy them some time.

He released his grip on the DI and shuffled stiffly over to the rigid , wid e-eyed corpse on the floor. Bend ing, he gave Bailey's arm a tug.

Stuck.

Frozen to the floor.

'B-bollocks.'

'T-Tyler.'

'I can get it,' Tyler insisted . His hand s were numb. Fingers barely responsive. 'J-just give me a s-second and —'

'Tyler!'

The urgency in the DI's voice mad e Tyler turn. Ben stood swaying on the spot where Tyler had left him. His eyes were wid e. Face pale. Hand clasped to the mid d le of his chest. Mouth d rawn in pain.

'I'm… I'm s-sorry, son.'

Tyler blinked . It was a slow process, his eyelid s scraping up and d own, momentarily turning everything to black.

'B-boss?' he muttered .

And then, like a puppet whose strings had all been cut, DI Ford e fold ed to the floor, a gasp of pain rising as a white mist from somewhere d eep within.

–

Logan gripped the wheel of the Fiesta. It twitched in his grip, the car behaving like a jittery horse as it trund led along the icy A9. The gritters had been out, but the severity of the recent snowfalls had caught everyone off-guard , and the usual stories of bud get issues and cutbacks meant even the main road s were on the ropey sid e.

'Dave. Still there?' he asked , tearing his eyes off the road long enough to check the d isplay on the car's stereo.

'Aye. Here. Lost you for a bit, but you're back,' Dave replied . 'Did you get what I said ? About find ing a connection?'

Logan reached over and turned the volume up a notch or two. 'No. Missed that. What have you got?'

'Right. Are you sitting d own?' Dave asked . 'Wait. Aye. You're d riving. Blood y hope you're sitting d own.'

'The connection, Dave. What have you got?' Logan urged .

'OK. Aye. So, I looked into everything and everyone, like you said . Here's what I got. You alread y know about Foster and his firm repping most of the victims. Right?'

'Right.'

'Right. Well, this is the new bit. Damian Bailey, Fred erick Shaw, and Robert Foster all went to the same high school. Robert was a few years old er, but there'd have been some crossover.'

Logan checked his mirrors in time to see a big SUV come flying past him on the straight lead ing up to the Kessock Brid ge. The Fiesta reacted skittishly to the gust of wind the bigger car d ragged behind it, and Logan had to wrestle with the wheel to keep the blood y thing from skid d ing into the centre railing of the d ual carriageway.

'Bastard ,' he muttered .

'Eh?'

'Not you, Dave. Go on.'

'Right. Aye. So, they were all in school together. You know who else went to the same school? Joanna Ward and her brother, Gary. Gary was in Robert Foster's year.'

'Really? OK. So, there's our connection between those two,' Logan said . 'Good work.'

'That's not the half of it,' Dave continued . 'George Morales. The guy who claimed to be the Iceman?'

'What about him?'

'He was the janitor.'

Logan shot a look at the stereo like it was wind ing him up. 'Bollocks.'

'Straight up.'

'George Morales was the jannie at their school?'

'Aye. But not at the same time they were there. Before,' Dave said . 'That got me d igging d eeper. And if you think that's a revelation, you'd better hold onto your hat. One of the original Iceman victims. The hit and run d river. Mind him?'

Logan confirmed that he d id . 'Killed a woman and her d aughter.'

'Aye. Well, that woman's husband ? He's one Mr Rowan Monroe,' Dave announced . 'And he's only the blood y head teacher of that very same school.'

–

Olivia sat quietly, her bag back in her lap, her head lowered a little so she wasn't meeting the head teacher's eye. He'd been staring at her for almost a minute now, saying nothing, waiting for her to answer his question.

And she had answered it. Twice now. The same lie both times.

He wasn't buying it. Not one bit.

'I am going to ask you again, Olivia,' he said . The lightness in his voice that she was used to from his assemblies and corrid or chats was gone now. There was no expression on his face but contempt. 'And this time, I want you to answer me honestly. It's very important that you d o so. For your sake.'

Olivia stole a peek at the reflection of the office d oor in the wind ow. She could make it, she thought. If she jumped to her feet and ran, she could reach it before he could catch up. It'd probably mean she'd never be allowed to set foot in the school again, but she d id n't care. Right here, right now, she just wanted to be out of his office. Out of the build ing. Out of his d irect line of sight.

'Where d id you go after school yesterd ay?' he asked .

Olivia took a breath. 'I told you, I walked around for a bit, then I went home to—'

The hand s slamming on the d esk mad e her jump.

'Don't *fucking* lie to me!' Mr Monroe yelled .

Olivia shrank back in her chair, shocked by the word s, and the ferocity of them. She glanced over her should er at the d oor this time, sure that someone out there must have heard . Sure that someone would come and check what was going on.

'I sent them home,' Mr Monroe said , picking up on the thought. 'I sent them all home. We're the only ones here, Olivia. We're the only ones left.'

This was wrong. This was all wrong. This was no longer just a head teacher d isciplining a pupil, it was something else. Something more. Something worse.

'I… I think I'd better go home,' Olivia ventured .

'You're going nowhere until you tell me the truth. We'll stay here all night, if that's what it—'

Olivia sprang to her feet before he could finish, pushing herself back from the d esk and racing to the d oor. She grasped for the hand le and pushed it d own.

Thunk.

Locked .

No, no, no.

His hand s were sud d enly on her, grabbing at her hair and her blazer, d ragging her back. She collid ed with the chair she'd been sitting on, twisted , then hit the d esk hard , scattering paperwork, and send ing the framed photo of the woman and child clattering to the floor.

Mr Monroe ignored all of it. He round ed on her, eyes ablaze with rage. He seemed to have expand ed to fill the room. There was no way past him now, no way out.

'You were at that shop. You were d ealing d rugs. It was you there, wasn't it?' he seethed , a hand on her throat, his face leering up close in hers. He was barely recognisable now from the man he had been before. It was like something else had stepped insid e him, and taken control. 'Wasn't it?' he shrieked .

Olivia found herself nod d ing. She just wanted it to be over, wanted it to stop. 'Yes! Yes, but it… it wasn't me. I mean, it was me, but I d id n't want to d o it. He mad e me. He mad e me d o it!'

'You fucking liar!'

She felt the world lurch sid eways and scrabbled for a hand - hold as she was sent stumbling across the room. The glass of the trophy cabinet shattered , and pain tore across her forearm.

Her hand found a tall, thin trophy. It looked like gold , but was mad e of plastic. The base, though, was solid . Heavy. Squared off at the ed ges.

She turned , swinging. Mr Monroe was too close, though. He caught her arm and pulled , send ing her crashing into his filing cabinet. Her chin struck metal. The impact broke the connection between her brain and her feet, because sud d enly she was on the floor, with no id ea how she'd got there.

Kicking backward s, she tried to put some d istance between herself and the head teacher, but the office was small, and he had grown so very, very large, and there was nowhere for her to go.

'I swear, it was my d ad 's cousin!' she sobbed . 'He mad e me. He mad e me d o it. He said he'd hurt my mum. Hurt me. I d id n't want to. I d id n't, but he mad e me d o it! I swear, Mr Monroe, I swear!'

The head teacher stopped a foot away from where she lay sprawled . Less. He had his back to the wind ow, and his face was cast into shad ow as he glared d own at her, so all Olivia could see were his eyes.

God , his eyes. They burned like stars. Like their heat might consume her at any moment. Burn her away to d ust and ash.

'What's his name?'

'Oleg. It's… it's Oleg,' Olivia answered .

Mr Monroe squatted besid e her. She could feel the anger rad iating off him as waves of heat, and tried to d raw further back against the wall before her skin could blister and burn.

'Now we're getting to the truth,' he said . 'The man you were with. In the shop. He thought he could get away with the things he d id . He thought he could push his poison next to my school. To my kid s. But we could n't stand for that.ould n't.'

Olivia swallowed . It was mad ness to ask the question, but she had to. She had to know.

'Was it you? In the mask?' she whispered . 'Did you take him?'

Mr Monroe's reply was a single slow nod .

Olivia sniffed . Wiped her nose on her sleeve. Sat up a little straighter.

'Could you… could you take Oleg, too?'

This time, there was no response from the head teacher.

'I could help you. I could help get him,' Olivia continued , the word s falling from her mouth in their rush to get out. 'I could get him to come somewhere, and … and you could be waiting. I would n't tell anyone. I swear. I just… I just want him gone.'

Mr Monroe snorted . 'What the fuck d o you think I am, Olivia? When you look at me, who d o you see?' he asked . 'You think I'm some sort of genie? You think I'm here to magic away the problems of some d rug d ealing little know-it-all bitch like you?' He jabbed a thumb against his chest and hissed at her. 'I have a mission. I have a plan.'

'He d eals load s. Like *load*s. Way more than that other guy. He's trying to replace my d ad ,' Olivia said , but her courage was fad ing fast now, and getting the word s out was becoming more and more d ifficult. 'And … I think he's going to hurt me and my mum. I… I think he's going to kill us.'

The head teacher continued to glare at her for several second s, but then his eyes d arted to the fallen photograph on the floor. The glass had cracked , but both faces were still visible.

A woman and a child.

A mother and a daughter.

An injustice he was still trying to avenge.

'Get up,' he instructed, standing and stepping back.

Using the wall for support, Olivia got to her feet.

'Sit down.'

Olivia picked up her chair, set it down right-way-up, then took a seat at the desk as Mr Monroe crossed back to the other side.

He sat down, pulled his chair in closer, then interlocked his fingers. This time, when he locked his gaze on her, Olivia didn't look away.

'The truth now,' he said. 'I've been honest with you, and I need you to be honest with me. No more lies. No more deception. The truth.'

'It is the truth,' Olivia insisted. 'He's building up a network of dealers. He got me to bring a bag to that guy yesterday. I was scared. Really scared. And that was the first time, I swear. The only time! He tried to get me to do it today, but I told him I couldn't. I wouldn't. That's when he threatened me. That's when he said he'd kill me and my mum.'

Mr Monroe sighed, then reached into the top drawer of his desk. Olivia braced herself for a gun or a knife, but was instead offered a tissue from a box. She accepted one for her eyes, and another to dab at the blood that was running down the inside of her sleeve and staining the creases of her hand.

'Thanks.'

He waited for her to clean herself up before continuing.

'If, for the sake of argument, I believed you. If I was going to... take care of things. Where would I find him?'

Olivia blew her nose into one of the tissues. 'I don't know.'

'You don't know?'

'No. I mean I don't know where he is right now. But I could get him to meet me somewhere. I could bring him anywhere you wanted. You could be ready and waiting.'

'And then what?' Mr Monroe asked . His tone was lighter than it had been since she'd stepped into the office, but there was a weight to the word s that was unmistakable.

'Then... it'll be our secret,' Olivia said . 'I won't tell anyone. I promise.'

The head teacher laughed at that. 'The promise of a child . Of a d rug d ealer! Hard ly worth much.'

'No, it will. I won't say a word . You can record me saying that I helped you kill him. Then we'd both be in trouble. I'd have to stay quiet.'

'Or... how about this?' Mr Monroe asked . 'If you spoke a word about it to anyone—anyone—then my associates would kill you and your mother before the police had so much as put cuffs on me. You see, I'm not alone in this, Olivia. In what I'm d oing. There are those who have followed in my footsteps. Those who can no longer abid e the filth out there corrupting our city, who'll no longer tolerate them getting away with it, again, and again, and again.'

'I want to join, then,' Olivia said , and the sud d enness of it mad e Mr Monroe creak back in his chair. 'I can help you. You can teach me. We can help each other.'

'You're a child .'

'I can d o it, though. I can help. I want to help,' Olivia insisted .

Mr Monroe picked up a pen and tapped the end of it on the d esk. It sound ed like a metronome in the otherwise silent office.

Or a clock, counting d own Olivia's remaining second s on Earth.

'Everything you've told me tod ay has been the truth?' he asked .

She nod d ed . 'Completely. I swear.'

'Because, if I find out you've lied to me...' He left the sentence hanging there, letting her imagination fill in the blanks.

'I haven't.'

Olivia flinched as the head teacher suddenly bent sideways in his chair. When he straightened up, he was holding a notebook, which he set down in front of him. With a click of his pen, he began to write.

'I want you to bring him to... wait. No.'

He scribbled out what he'd written, flipped the page, and started writing again.

'I want you to bring him to this location in one hour. That's... ten past five. We'll be ready. Once we have him, we'll discuss what happens next.' He tore off the page, folded it, and handed it to her. 'If you tell anyone about this, remember what happens. You. Your mum. That will be it for you. The last words you'll hear will be my name. The last face you think of will be mine. Is that clear?'

'Yeah,' Olivia said, nodding her understanding.

'Say, "that's clear, Mr Monroe".'

'That's clear, Mr Monroe.'

He smiled, and some semblance of the man he had been before today was there on his face again. 'Very good. If we continue to be truthful with each other—if we build a relationship based on honesty and trust—then there may be a bright future for you at this school, after all. How does that sound, Olivia?'

'Sounds... it sounds good.'

'It sounds good *what*?'

'Sir. It sounds good, sir.'

'Excellent. Capital. Well, we'd better let you get off, then,' he said, getting to his feet. He produced the door key from his pocket. 'And I'll see you very soon.'

Chapter 42

Ben lay on the floor, Tyler's jacket below him, pain twisting his features into a knot.

'Hold on, boss. It's going to be all right,' Tyler insisted .

He was squatting by the old er man, the cold stabbing through his shirt like thousand s of pinpricks. He could n't kneel, d id n't d are put the thin material of his trousers into contact with the floor.

He'd d one his best to make the DI comfortable, but his best was almost nothing at all. Despite Ben's protestations, Tyler had removed his jacket and wed ged it und er the senior officer, trying to limit his contact with the icy metal floor.

The DI's breath had been a wheeze even before he'd fallen. Now it was something less than that. The occasional rattle at the back of his throat. The erratic rising and falling of his chest.

'We're going to get out of here, b-boss, all right? We're g-going to get out.'

Talking still hurt, but he had to keep the old er man awake. Conscious. Alive. Every time Tyler stopped speaking, Ben's eyes started to roll backward s, so he kept talking. Kept saying his name. Kept up the chit-chat that everyone had come to expect from him.

'Put your coat on, s-son.'

Ben's voice was even less of an event than his breathing. To call it a whisper would be an exaggeration. It was *suggestion* of a whisper. An exhalation that implied the existence of word s.

'Nah. I'm g-grand , boss,' Tyler stammered , having a bash at a smile, d espite the lack of control he currently had over his face. 'Highland er, me. Used to the c-c-cold .'

'Too cold . You'll d ie.'

'Here, no b-bugger's d -d ying tod ay. C-cut that shite out right n-now.'

Another stab of pain tore at Ben, and he contorted on the floor, the veins in his neck bulging, his hand tightening on his chest.

'Shit. What d -d o I d o?' Tyler bleated . 'Boss? Ben?'

The pain passed . Ben let out a breath and some of the tension left him. The sharpness of it had cut through the fog, and his eyes swam for a moment, find ing a focus they had n't had in several minutes.

'T-Tyler. Put on the jacket,' he said . He took the hand from his chest and placed it on the sid e of the DC's face. The skin was neither warm nor cold against Tyler's own, it just *was*. 'Please, son. You're a g-good lad . You're a good c-copper.'

Tears formed at the outer corners of Ben's eyes, then rolled outward s over his temples, and land ed somewhere in Tyler's jacket.

'M-me and Alice, we n-never had kid s. But watching you lot... w-working with you. Seeing you grow. I... I just could n't be proud er, son.'

'Don't, boss. You'll only have to t-take it back, later.'

Ben's mouth tugged up at the corners. It was about as close to a smile as he was likely to get.

'There's n-no later. But p-promise me, you'll g-get out of here, son.'

'We're both getting out, boss. You and me.'

Ben shook his head . He grimaced again, another stab of pain burning through his chest. 'You're all my weans. T-tell the rest of them, eh? Hamza. Sinead . I could n't b-be proud er of...'

He coughed . It was ragged , and violent, and scratched up through his throat from d eep d own within. His eyes rolled .

His bod y shook, trembling from head to toe as the heart attack, or the cold , or some combination of the two took its terrible toll.

'Boss?' Tyler cried , hold ing him by the should ers. 'I d on't know what to d o! I d -d on't know what to d o!'

–

Olivia stopped at the bin around the corner from the front gate, glanced around furtively to make sure she wasn't being watched , then reached insid e and took out the tote bags she'd stashed there earlier in the d ay.

She had just stuffed them into her backpack when the hand caught her by the back of the neck, the grip like steel, fingernails d igging into her flesh.

'I told you not to fucking lie to me!' Mr Monroe hissed , practically lifting her off the ground as he marched her toward s the gate. 'I warned you what would happen, but you d id n't listen, d id you? You d id n't fucking listen to me, and now you're going to pay.'

'I'm sorry! I'm sorry! I just… please, you're hurting me.'

The head teacher's mouth was sud d enly right by her cheek, his word s spitting furiously into her ear. 'I'll d o more than hurt you. You're part of the problem. Don't you see? You're part of the virus infecting this city, and we're the cure.'

He stopped at the front gate, checked that nobod y was approaching, then clamped a hand over her mouth and half-marched , half-d ragged her over to the only car left in the car park. It was a large silver Toyota SUV, and as Olivia was pulled , kicking and squirming toward s it, the only thought in her head was that the boot would be more than big enough to stash her bod y.

They were halfway to the car when a Ford Fiesta pulled into the car park, skid d ed erratically on the ice, then came to a stop half-blocking the exit.

Mr Monroe stopped as a d oor opened . A giant of a man emerged , his coat billowing around him, his face like thund er.

The only thing that lessened the impact of his arrival was when his feet slid apart and he let out a gasped 'ooh, shit!' but he recovered quickly, and when he next spoke, his voice boomed across the car park.

'All right, Rowan? What's going on here, then?'

Olivia kicked the head teacher hard , d riving the point of her scuffed black boots into his shin. He hissed in pain and shoved her hard , send ing her stumbling back in the d irection of the school as he raced for his car.

'Don't you blood y d are!' Logan bellowed , but the head teacher was alread y pulling open the d oor, alread y jumping in, alread y firing up the engine. 'I mean it! Switch off the engine and … shite!'

Logan threw himself sid eways out of the path of the SUV as it powered toward s him. He hit the ground and rolled clumsily in the snow, his coat tangling around his head , and temporarily blind ing him. He d ucked as the crunch of metal on metal rang out like a gunshot across the car park.

When he struggled free of the coat's embrace, he saw that the front of the Fiesta was crumpled , fluid s cascad ing onto the snow from beneath what was left of the engine. For a moment, he wasn't quite sure whether to be furious or elated , and so he d ecid ed to come back to it at a later d ate. Monroe's much larger car was alread y powering away, head ed for the main road , and from there to freed om.

Not blood y likely. Not on Logan's watch.

'You all right?' he barked over at Olivia.

She nod d ed , but chose to offer no explanation as to why the head teacher had been manhand ling her into his car. Similarly, Logan chose not to ask. There'd be time, of course. But not yet. Not now.

'Phone nine-nine-nine,' he instructed , breaking into a run.

Monroe had a clear head start, of course, but he had to stick to the road . If Logan cut across the grass and through the bushes, he could reach the main road first.

Quite what the hell he'd d o when he got there, he had no id ea. He'd figure it out as he went.

The snow had mad e the grass almost as treacherous as the surface of the car park. Logan skid d ed and slipped across it, blund ered through a crop of bushes, then explod ed onto the pavement next to the road in time to see the Toyota go speed ing past.

'Fuck it!' he bellowed , grabbing for his Warrant Card and stepping out into the path of oncoming traffic.

A car screeched to a stop d irectly ahead of him, the d river— an eld erly woman—peering up at him in horror.

The feeling was mutual.

It was a Fiesta.

A bright green Ford Fiesta.

Logan groaned , and shot an imploring look to the heavens above. 'You have got to be fucking kid d ing me.'

–

Olivia stood alone in the snow, watching an old woman ranting about civil liberties while her car went screeching off in pursuit of the fleeing Mr Monroe.

Blood d ripped d own her sleeve and plopped into the carpet of white beneath her feet. She watched another few d rops fall, contemplated having a look at her arm to make sure it wasn't too bad ly cut, but d ecid ed that she'd rather not know until she was in a position to d o something about it.

She took out her phone. There were two missed calls on the screen. Both from the same number.

Oleg.

He'd sent a text, too.

Where the fuck RU?

As she read the message, another slid in below it.

U better not b fucking with me.

She swiped away quickly, as if being unable to see the word s meant they had n't been written. Whoever she was meant to d eliver to, had obviously been in touch with Oleg to say she had n't arrived . While she'd over-egged the pud d ing a bit with Mr Monroe, and Oleg had never explicitly threatened to murd er her and her mother, she had no d oubts that he would d o so without a moment's hesitation if he thought she'd betrayed him.

With a flick of her thumb, Olivia brought up the d ialler on her phone. Nine. Nine. Nine.

She hesitated then, the tip of her finger hovering over the green phone icon that would make the call.

She thought of the questions they'd ask her. The statements she'd have to give.

She thought of the repercussions. The price she and her mother would have to pay.

She thought of Oleg's breath on her neck, his hand s on her waist, the leer on his face as he looked her up and d own. Appraised her.

The d ecision was easy.

As Olivia tapped and swiped and put her phone to her ear, several d ozen feet away, another mobile buzzed quietly in the snow.

–

'Still nothing?'

Sinead turned in the passenger seat of Hamza's car, pressed the button to hang up her phone, then shook her head . 'No. Still not answering,' Sinead said .

'He d id say to text the ad d ress,' Hamza remind ed her, as he pulled out of the law firm's car park and onto Union Street, where some lacklustre Christmas lights were d oing their d amned est to push back against the wintery d arkness.

A procession of slow-moving traffic chugged along the one-way street, as last-minute Christmas shoppers took their chances and crisscrossed between the cars, lad en with shopping bags and boxes.

'I know. I just...'

'You feel like there's something up?' Hamza guessed .

'Does that sound mental?' Sinead asked .

The DS shook his head . 'No. I think it's important to trust your instincts,' Hamza said . He put a hand on the back of his neck and moved his head from sid e to sid e. 'Honestly? I'm a bit on ed ge, too. I have been since the start of all this. Or... well, since DI Ford e told me I'm on the list.'

'What list?' Sinead asked , then her mouth formed an O-shape. 'What, *the* list? The Iceman's list?'

Hamza nod d ed . 'Me, Ben, Hoon. Couple of other guys involved in the original case. Apparently, we were all on a list they found when they d iscovered George Morales's bod y. They buried it. So as not to worry us.'

Sinead stared ahead at the traffic, and at the shoppers' Kamikaze-style approach to road crossing. 'Jesus. That's... I mean...'

'Bit of a concern, aye,' Hamza said . 'I've been keeping my eyes peeled . You know, in case anyone tries any funny stuff? But... listen, if you've got a bad feeling about something, let's follow it up.'

Sinead looked d own at her phone. 'It's just... I haven't been able to get Tyler, either. He texted to say he and DI Ford e were following up a lead on Gary Ward , but I've heard nothing since. And now his phone's switched off. He never switches his phone off.'

'Might just have no signal,' Hamza reasoned .

Sinead looked out of her sid e wind ow at the street. A young couple strolled by, arms linked , swishing their feet through the snow as the glow of an electric Santa painted them in festive shad es of red .

'Yeah. It's probably that,' she ad mitted .

'But, like I said , you should trust your instincts.'

Sinead   woke her phone with a tap. 'I'll call Dave. See if he can tell me anything,' she said . 'I mean, chances are I'm worrying about nothing.'

Hamza smiled   reassuringly. 'Aye,' he said . 'I'm sure they're both absolutely fine.'

Chapter 43

Tyler could hear nothing now but the sound of his blood struggling to circulate through his veins. It thrummed in his ears—whum-um-um-um—on some endless loop.

He was sure it was getting slower, though. Certain it would come creaking to a halt just as soon as the cold had finished turning it to a cherry slush in his veins.

Even his own voice was silent to him. He was speaking—pleading, begging—he was sure of it, but the constant drum of his heartbeat in his ears prevented him from hearing a word.

On the floor beside him, Ben's eyelids fluttered as he fought to keep them open. The fits of pain that had contorted his face and his body had passed now. Or he was too far gone to be able to react to them when they struck.

Either way, he lay mostly still, and utterly silent, his skin a patchwork of frozen reds and bloodless greys.

He had minutes left. Maybe less.

Maybe, to all intents and purposes, he was already gone, and the twitches he made in Tyler's arms were just the last of the electrical impulses shutting down.

'Come on, boss. Don't do this. Wake up. Please, wake up!'

Those were the words Tyler thought. Those were the words he tried to say. How successful he was, he didn't know.

They were going to die here. Both of them. Today. Soon.

He wondered who'd find them. Not Sinead, he hoped. No her. Please, God, not her. Let it be Logan. Or, better yet, some CID DI who didn't know them well. Some face they passed in the corridors.

But please, not her. Anyone but her.

The cold was slowing his brain now, making it hard to think. He watched, momentarily hypnotised, at the way the steam of his breath rose towards the ceiling, then fell again as all the heat was pulled out of it. Pulled out of him.

Out of them.

He gave the man in his arms a shake.

'Boss?'

He heard a snatch of the word that time. The thumping in his ears was coming less frequently now. A steady, sombre funeral drum.

Boom.

Boom.

Boom.

The man in his arms did n't respond. Tyler shook him again, more urgently this time.

'Ben? B-Ben? No, no, n-no. Ben!'

The vapour of the icy air sud d enly swirled, as if it had come alive. It circled around them, a crisp, fresh, white ghost d ancing its first few steps.

Or its last.

Tyler watched it, his cold -d ulled brain transfixed by the movement.

'B-Boss?' he whispered, as the cloud of white was replaced by the glow of a bright, brilliant light.

Tyler croaked out a little yelp of fright as a hand clamped d own on his should er. He looked up, half-expecting to find Death himself staring d own.

Instead, he saw someone almost as terrifying.

'Fuck sake, ya bellend. Are you d eaf, or something?' barked Bob Hoon. Behind him, the d oor to the freezer stood open, sucking the cold air out into the warehouse beyond. 'Come on,' Hoon instructed, hooking an arm und er DI Ford e's should ers. 'Help me get this old bastard out of here.'

After much searching, and a fair amount of swearing, Logan had come to the conclusion that he'd lost his phone. Most likely, it had fallen from his pocket when he'd had to d ive out of the path of Monroe's car.

Just another reason for him to d islike the bastard .

The Toyota was eight cars ahead , in the left-hand lane. Logan hung back in his command eered Fiesta in the lane on the right, as they all waited for the lights to change.

They were close to the Burnett Road station, head ed south on Longman Road . Logan was anticipating a left turn at the Harbour Road round about and , sure enough, when the lights went green, the Toyota turned just as he'd expected .

Cutting across to the left lane, Logan followed in the Fiesta. A set of rosary bead s d angled from the rearview mirror, while a little bobble-head ed Jesus shot him d aggers from where he'd been glued onto the d ashboard .

Logan had never been a religious man, but the expression on the wee fella's face caused even him a little pang of guilt.

'She'll get it back,' he muttered . 'Keep your blood y hair on.'

A hund red yard s ahead , the Toyota hung a right. Logan caught a glimpse of some d amage to its front bumper, then it d isappeared between a car showroom and a tyre repair place, and he put his foot to the floor in an attempt to gain some ground .

The Fiesta, pred ictably, gave very little response. It acceler-ated at the same glacial pace as his own, and several second s passed before he reached the turn-off, swerved across the oncoming traffic, and d rove up the same sid e-road that Monroe had taken.

The road led to a network of car parks and private road s that ran behind the showrooms, garages, and other auto-related businesses that had mad e their base on Harbour Road .

Logan scanned his surround ings as he slowed the Fiesta, searching for any sign of Monroe's car. Or, id eally, the bastard himself.

He caught a glimpse of silver tucked in between a couple of large metal storage containers, slammed on the anchors, and reversed so he could take another look.

'Got you,' he muttered , yanking on the hand brake.

He aband oned the car at the sid e of the road , then hurried over to the Toyota. The warmth of the engine and the d amage to the front clearly marked it as Monroe's car, but the man himself was nowhere to be seen.

Logan checked the storage containers, but found both locked from the outsid e.

Further back from the containers, a couple of portable office cabins stood , stacked one atop the other with an external stair-case lead ing up to the office above.

In there. Had to be.

Logan contemplated running back to one of the showrooms and calling for support, but Monroe might slip away while he was gone. And , frankly, Logan was itching to get his hand s on the bastard .

The d irect approach it was, then.

He kept watch on the offices' wind ows as he approached the front d oor of the d ownstairs build ing. While his instincts were urging him to kick the thing off its hinges, he started by trying the hand le.

It turned easily. The d oor swung inward , Logan stepped insid e, and found himself staring at the business end of a revolver. He'd never had much of an interest in guns beyond not being shot by them, so he had no id ea what make or mod el the one in Rowan Monroe's hand was. It looked real enough, though.

Bollocks.

'Shut the d oor,' Monroe instructed .

'I'd rather leave it open, if it's all the same with you,' Logan told him. 'I like the fresh air.'

'Shut. The. Door.'

The gun in his hand d id n't shake, Logan noticed . Not once. He shut the d oor.

There were two chairs in the office. Monroe sat in one, behind the room's only d esk. He motioned with the gun to the other chair. It was positioned beneath the wind ow, well out of grabbing reach, but well within a bullet's.

'Sit d own.'

'I'd rather stand , Rowan.'

'I'd rather you sat. So, sit. I'm not kid d ing around here.'

Logan eyeballed him. He ran his tongue across the back of his teeth, then smacked his lips together and shrugged .

'Fine. I'll sit. Happy?'

Monroe lowered the gun so the butt was resting on the d esk, but kept it pointed at the d etective in the chair.

'Not really, no. I'm far from happy, if I'm honest,' Monroe said . He grimaced , his lips d rawing back over his teeth. 'Just who the fuck d o you think you are?'

'Polis, Rowan. Sorry, d id I no' introd uce myself? Detective Chief Inspector—'

'I know who you are,' Monroe snapped . 'That's not what I meant.'

'What d id you mean, then?'

Monroe's eyelid s became heavier. He twitched , like he was fighting back some sort of transformation. 'I mean, why are you trying to stop me? I'm d oing your job for you. We should be on the same sid e.'

Logan shook his head . 'Killing people isn't in my job d escrip-tion,' Logan said . He smiled d rily. 'Although, I might be prepared to make an exception now and again.'

'I kill the—'

'Oh, shut up, Rowan,' Logan said , sound ing thoroughly exasperated by the whole thing. 'Just… fucking shut up. I know what you're going to say. "I'm fighting the good fight. I'm punishing the guilty". All that bollocks. That about the size of it?'

Monroe said nothing, just did the same eyelid flutter and adjusted his grip on the gun.

'See, I've met arseholes like you before, Rowan. I mean, not quite as full-on pathetic as yourself, but not far off. They all thought they were something special, too. They'd had something bad happen to them in the past. Some big fucking trauma that they thought gave them the right to do what they wanted. Take what they wanted. Hurt who they wanted.'

He pointed to the door, and out at the world beyond.

'Go into any jail, and talk to any prisoner. They'll all sing you the same song. "It was my childhood. My best mate OD'd on me. My sister's boyfriend was knocking her about". They all think like you do, Rowan. Like whatever awful thing happened to them means they're free to do awful things themselves. But they're not. The law doesn't work that way. And you bloody well know it.'

'Maybe it should,' Monroe suggested. 'Maybe, if someone actually did something to stop those people once and for all, the rest of us normal folk could go about our lives.'

'Listen to yourself, Rowan. You're no' normal, son. You've been freezing people to death, cutting bits off them, and popping them in the bloody post. You're about as far removed from normal as it's possible to get.'

'But I was!' Monroe barked. 'I was normal once! And then that was stolen from me. Taken away!'

Logan's eyes went to the gun. Monroe's grip on it was no longer steady. Clearly, he'd touched a nerve.

'I know, Rowan. And that was a terrible thing that happened to you. To them. I can't imagine the pain you must have felt. The grief.'

Monroe shook his head. 'Anger. I couldn't afford to grieve. Your lot made sure of that when you let him walk free. The man who killed my wife and daughter, you had him, and you let him walk free. How could I grieve, knowing he was out there? How could I shed tears for my little girl when he was walking around ?'

It was Logan's turn to fall silent. Everything else asid e, he had no way of saying how he'd have reacted in the same situation. How he'd have coped .

'They said there wasn't enough evid ence. The police,' Monroe continued . 'But he told me he d id it. I looked into his eyes, and he told me it was him. I only grieved once I'd watched him d ie. That was the one and only time I cried for them. When I'd given them justice. When I'd sent that bastard to hell.'

'But that wasn't enough. Was it?' Logan pressed .

'How could it be? When there were so many others out there? Thieves. Rapists. Killers. Remorseless, but walking free. Unchecked . The police d oing nothing to stop them. No one d oing anything to stop them, until we came along. We wrote them d own. We mad e a list. And we started working through it.'

'That was years ago, though. Why now? Why come back now? You'd stopped . What mad e you start up again all of a sud d en?'

Monroe's mouth opened as if to answer, but no word s came. A frown troubled his brow for a moment, like he was struggling to remember.

'Come on, Rowan, you must know why you started killing people again. You d on't just slip back into that sort of thing on a blood y whim.'

'It… it d oesn't matter. The time was right, that's all,' the other man said , although he sound ed even less convinced than Logan d id .

'Right. Fine. But tell me, when was it that you started your little… what was it, Rowan? A serial killer pyramid scheme? Clever move, by the way. Meant you could pin it all on poor George Morales,' Logan said . 'Or maybe Robert Foster, or Gary Ward . Good to have options.'

Rowan gave another twitch. The shape of his eyes registered his surprise.

'Robert's d ead , by the way,' Logan continued . 'Gary, we should have in custod y by now.'

'You won't,' Monroe said .

'Aye. Well, we'll see,' Logan replied . 'If we d on't have him now, we'll get him soon.'

Behind the d esk, the head teacher gave a chuckle and a shake of his head . 'That's not what I mean,' he said .

There was a squeak as he pulled open the d esk d rawer and reached insid e. Logan watched as Monroe placed a rectangular envelope on the d esk in front of him, and closed the d rawer again.

'What d o you mean, then, Rowan?' Logan asked , shifting his gaze from the envelope, to the gun, to the now blank and emotionless face of the gunman himself. 'Explain it to me.'

'We all knew what we were getting into. We all agreed ,' he said . 'Any one of us was expend able. Any one of us would take the blame. What mattered was the mission. Not us. We all knew. We all agreed .'

Logan gripped the arms of his chair and shifted his weight a little, getting read y to move.

'No one's expend able, Rowan. Not you. Not me. Nobod y,' he said . 'Now, you've got Damian Bailey somewhere. He's a young lad , and his family is—'

'He's a rapist, you know?' Monroe said . 'They both were. I knew they were bastard s right from the start. Had their card s marked from the moment I saw them. The things they d id to Joanna. The things they *boasted* about d oing to her. We d id a good thing, getting rid of them. We mad e the world a better place.'

'Where is he, Rowan?'

'You'll never find him,' Monroe replied . 'We have access to a lot of sites. You'll never find them all. And , even if you d id , he's alread y d ead .'

'Let us see for ourselves, then. Prove it.'

Monroe tapped the envelope on the d esk. 'It's all in there,' he said .

'Where you put Damian?'

'Forget that sick fuck!' Rowan hissed , his face momentarily twisting in rage, before slackening back into nothing at all. 'My confession. We had them prepared . Because we always knew it would come. A moment like this one. A d ay like tod ay. You see, Detective Chief Inspector, the gun was never for you.'

He slid the envelope to the very ed ge of the d esk, still well beyond Logan's reach.

'I am the Iceman,' he announced . 'I have always been the Iceman. I killed all those people. And I would d o it all again.'

He put the gun to his head . Logan was out of his seat in a heartbeat, throwing himself toward s the d esk.

A single gunshot rang out, and everything that had been Rowan Monroe painted the wall behind him.

Chapter 44

Olivia took a d eep breath as the car approached , then gave a little wave of acknowled gement. It slowed to a stop besid e her, but the man behind the wheel d id n't move to get out.

Instead , she trud ged over, opened the passenger d oor, and climbed onto the seat besid e him. His eyes, which were narrowed , lost some of their suspicion when he saw the d ried blood on her face.

'The fuck happened ?' Oleg d emand ed .

Olivia sniffed , d abbed gingerly at her top lip, and tried very hard not to cry. 'He… he just jumped me. After school. Tried to grab my bag, but I held on. I held on for as long as I could , but then… he punched me. And … I must've fallen, because he took my bag. He had my bag, and he was walking off, and he was laughing, and …' She looked d own, her face crumpling. 'I knew you'd be angry, so… I followed him.'

Oleg watched her for a moment. She could feel his eyes on her, even without raising her head .

'Here?' he asked . 'You followed him here?'

Olivia looked up and out at the board ed -up build ing ahead of them. 'Yeah.'

'Long fucking way from school,' Oleg remarked .

She just nod d ed . Better to say too little, than too much.

'And he's in there? This fucking kid ?'

'He is. The board on the front d oor lifts up,' Olivia said . 'But he's not a kid . He's a sixth year, I think. He's pretty tough.'

Oleg let out a snort. 'Oh, you think he's tough? I'll show you fucking tough, *malyshka*. I'll put that little shit's head on a fucking spike, then we'll talk about "tough".' He opened his d oor. 'Wait here.'

Oleg placed one foot out into the snow, then stopped . He turned back to Olivia. His hand cupped her chin, and forcibly turned her to face him. 'If you're lying to me, Olivia, there will be hell to pay. You know that, right?'

Olivia tried to nod , but his grip was too tight. 'Yes. I know. I'm not lying,' she offered . 'He's in there. And he's got my bag. And … whatever you put in there.'

'Fine. Wait here,' he instructed . He released his hold on her chin, but then jabbed a finger in her face. 'And once I get it back, you and me are going to have a long talk about your responsibilities, *malyshka*. A *long* fucking talk.'

He stepped out. Closed the d oor. Went stomping off through the snow toward s the barricad ed shop front, and pulled back the loose board over the front d oor until it popped right out of the frame and fell to the ground behind him.

Olivia watched as he stepped insid e.

And then she waited .

–

Sinead was out of the car before Hamza had fully brought it to a stop. One ambulance had alread y gone screaming past them, head ed back toward s the city, and the Raigmore A&E d epartment.

Tyler was being load ed into the back of the second ambu-lance when she slipped and skid d ed up behind the paramed i her face ablaze with panic. 'Tyler? Tyler! Jesus! What happened ?' she cried .

'Sinead ?' Tyler wheezed .

He lay strapped to the stretcher, wrapped in a silver foil blanket, like he was about to be slung in the oven to roast. His face was a colour she'd never seen before—so pale she could see all the veins and capillaries beneath his skin.

Had he not been moving, she'd have sworn he was d ead , and she got the d istinct impression that he must've come pretty d amn close.

'I'm all right,' he told her, although the effort of talking took a visible toll.

'Daft buggers got themselves stuck in a freezer.'

Sinead looked in the d irection of the voice and saw Hoon sitting on the bonnet of a car, id ly rolling a cigarette.

'Luckily for them, though, I was keeping an eye on them,' Hoon continued . He ran his tongue along the ed ge of the Rizla paper, then shrugged . 'Well, on Ben. No' so much this prancing cocksplat. Right time, right place for him, really.'

'H–how d id you find me?' Tyler asked , pointed ly ignoring the remarks from the former Detective Superintend ent.

'Dave. I got him to check your computer,' Sinead explained . She put a hand on Tyler's cheek and almost recoiled at how cold he felt to the touch. 'Your password 's shite, by the way. Took me two tries to guess it.' She leaned in closer and whispered so no one else would hear. 'I love you, too, by the way.'

Tyler managed a small smile at that, and there was the faintest red d ening to his cheeks, Sinead thought.

'B–Ben's in a bad way,' Tyler said . 'H–heart attack, they think.'

'The hospital will take care of him,' Sinead soothed . 'He'll be fine.'

'We should get you in, too, son,' urged the old er of the two paramed ics. 'Hospital's expecting you, and we d on't want to keep the nurses waiting. They can be vicious buggers when they want to be.'

'Aye. G–go for it,' Tyler stammered , shivering in his silver wrapper.

'Right. We'll follow you in,' Sinead said , stepping back.

'No' so fast on that, sweetheart,' Hoon said . He finished rolling his cigarette, stuck it in his mouth, then slid d own off the front of the car. 'I almost forgot to mention.'

'Forgot to mention what?' asked Hamza, striding through the snow to join them.

Hoon pointed to the boarded-up building behind them. 'Wee Christmas present waiting for you on the floor in there. Well, mostly on the floor, but partly on the walls and ceiling, too.'

'What do you mean? What sort of "wee Christmas present"?' Sinead asked.

Hoon cupped his hand around the end of his roll-up and sparked a lighter into life. He took a long draw, then grinned at the detectives as the ambulance pulled away, blue lights flashing in the evening darkness.

'Well, I can't just fucking tell you, can I?' he said. 'That'd spoil the big surprise...'

—

The beam of Oleg's phone torch did very little to push back the darkness inside the shop. The smell of the place had hit him when he'd entered. He recognised it immediately—blood, and gristle, and meat. Old, though. A lingering odour that no amount of scrubbing would get rid of.

It had been a butcher's shop at some point, judging by the smell, and the layout of the glass cabinets. Most of them had been smashed, but a few were still intact, the glass coated with a thin layer of grease and a thicker one of dust.

There was no sound in the place, except the faint humming of something electric. It came from a room at the back of the shop, a beaded curtain separating this area from that one.

Oleg slipped a hand into the pocket of his jeans, wriggled his car keys between his fingers, then pushed aside the dangling strings of beads and entered the next room. He swung the torchlight around, expecting to catch some far-out-of-his-fucking-depth teenager off guard.

But there was no one. Nothing. The room was empty, aside from a walk-in freezer that stood at the back, a light glowing through the porthole window in the door.

'Hey, you little fuck,' he sang into the gloom. 'Come out, come out, wherever you are.'

He listened for a moment. Over the sound of the humming, he heard another sound. Faint. Far-off. A scuffing. A scratching.

Coming from the freezer.

'The fuck?' Oleg muttered. He stole a glance back at the beaded curtain, then drew in a breath of stale, meat-flavoured air, and approached the freezer.

Through the frosted window, he saw movement. What it was, he couldn't tell, the layer of ice on the inside fogging his view.

With a clunk, he turned the handle, and the door eased outwards. A figure lay gasping and groaning on the floor, his skin black, and blistered, and peeling in long, freezing strips.

It took him a moment to recognise the man.

Juris. The Latvian he'd sent Olivia to visit the day before.

'Jesus fucking Christ. What is this?' Oleg said.

There was a clack of beads behind him. He turned in time to see, but not avoid, a piece of metal pipe that came swinging at his head.

Pain went off like a bomb above his right eye. Blood cascaded into it, hot, and sticky, and blinding.

He swung with a punch, off-balance, then wailed as the metal cracked him across the jaw, spinning him around.

Oleg stumbled, tripped, fell. Suddenly, the cold was all around him, swarming him like ravenous, sharp-toothed insects. He heard Juris let out a low, barely-human moan, and then this was drowned out by the clang of metal on metal.

Despite the pain and the head spins, Oleg leapt to his feet and hurried to the door. His hands scraped wildly at the spot where a handle should have been, then hammered against the thick, frozen glass.

'The fuck? Open up, you little prick! I'll fucking kill you, you piece of—'

He stopped ranting when Olivia's face appeared on the other sid e of the glass.

'Thank fuck,' he gasped . 'Open the d oor. Hurry. That piece of shit kid is...'

It was the look on her face that mad e him realise the truth of it. Her smile. It wasn't the smile of a thirteen-year-old girl. It was a shark's smirk. A monster's grin.

A light appeared from below the wind ow, casting most of Olivia's face into spooky, low-lit shad ow. She raised a phone for Oleg to see, and he noticed for the first time his empty hand .

'Enough messing around *malyshka*,' he urged . 'Come on, joke's over.'

'Joke's not over until I say it's over,' Olivia replied . Her voice sound ed d istant, muffled by the thick walls. 'And d on't worry Oleg. It's nothing personal. It's strictly business.'

She heard him shouting as she turned and walked away.

By the time she was through into the front shop, his voice was faint and faraway.

By the time she'd replaced the board on the front d oor, she could n't hear him at all.

Taking Mr Monroe's note from her pocket, she tore it into strips and let them be carried off on the wind .

Then she turned off Oleg's phone, shoved it in her pocket, and d ug her bag out from beneath the pile of snow she'd stashed it in.

Olivia wrapped her arms around herself and head ed for home. She had a long walk ahead of her, but that was fine. A long walk would give her time to think.

She had a whole lot of planning to d o, after all.

Chapter 45

Tyler limped through the corrid or, wished 'Merry Christmas' to a couple of the friend lier nurses, then turned into the private room where DI Ford e lay propped up in bed .

Ben was peering d own his nose at the TV remote when Tyler entered , thumbing one of the buttons like he was squashing a particularly sturd y bug.

'All right, boss?'

'No. This bastard of a thing won't turn on. I'm trying to watch the Queen's speech.'

'Aye. *Doctor Who* more like,' Tyler teased . 'Give it here.'

'You can keep your blood y*Doctor Who*,' Ben grumbled . 'I've had quite enough of d octors to last me a while, thanks very much.'

Tyler prod d ed at the buttons of the remote. Then, when nothing happened , he took the back off, and massaged the batteries.

'Merry Christmas, by the way, boss,' he said , clipping the back into place again.

'Aye. Merry Christmas to you, too, son,' Ben said . They swapped hand shakes, which became a stilted , awkward sort of embrace, then Ben lay back in bed before the monitors he was attached to could start whinging at him again. 'Sinead and Harris popped in this morning on their way to see you. He's a cracking wee lad , isn't he?'

Tyler smiled and sat on the end of the DI's bed . 'He is. I mean, he can be a pain in the arse, too, d on't get me wrong.'

'Probably gets that from you,' Ben remarked .

'Aye, he might d o,' Tyler conced ed . 'The big chief been in yet?'

'Jack? No. He's spend ing Christmas with his fancy woman. Told him not to bother coming in. He's no' exactly full of the festive cheer at the best of times, is he?'

'True. And Sinead says he's been up to his eyes in paperwork and meetings, what with all three of our suspects having, you know, killed themselves.'

'Two in front of him. In the one d ay, too,' Ben ad d ed . 'I mean, that's got to be some sort of record , that, surely? Even for someone with a face like his.'

Tyler laughed , but d ecid ed not to comment, just in case the DCI found out about it. Instead , he announced that the remote control was 'jiggered ', and then ad d ressed the elephant in the room. 'Good to see you still with us, boss. You had me worried for a while there.'

Ben raised his eyebrows and blew out his cheeks. 'Had a few concerns myself, I'll be honest with you, son. If you had n't been there…'

Tyler d ismissed the rest of the sentence with a wave. 'Wasn't me, boss. I was clueless. If Hoon had n't turned up when he d id , we'd both be d one for.'

Ben conced ed the point with a slow nod . 'Aye. Maybe he's no' as much of an arsehole as I've always thought.'

Tyler mad e a weighing motion with one hand . 'Largely still an arsehole, I reckon. But, he's an arsehole with good timing. I'll give him that.'

Ben rubbed his stomach below his blanket, and shot a longing look at a multipack of Quavers on the bed sid e table. 'Any word on when d inner's happening? I thought we were meant to be getting some big Christmas spread in the d ining hall? I've been eyeing up them crisps since half-eleven, but I d on't want to get stuck in and ruin my appetite.'

'We're both in the second sitting, boss. I was in the first, but thought you might like some company.'

'Some company, aye. Your company? That's debatable,' Ben said.

Tyler laughed and got to his feet. 'You're obviously on the road to recovery, boss. I was really starting to worry when you said all them nice things about me.'

'I'm sure I don't know what you're talking about, Detective Constable,' Ben said, but the smile on his face told a different story. He remembered. Of course, he did. And he meant every bloody word.

'Anyway, you'll be glad to hear it's grub time. That's why I'm here,' Tyler said. He unfolded a wheelchair after a couple of aborted attempts, then motioned to it. 'Shall we?'

'I thought you'd never ask,' Ben said. He indicated the banks of equipment he was wired up to. 'Although, unless you're planning on dragging this lot along with us, you should probably go get a nurse first.'

–

Ben braced himself for the impact as the wheelchair clipped the second bench in as many minutes.

'Christ Almighty, Tyler, I thought you were bad enough at driving a car,' he complained. 'Are you trying to hit everything on purpose?'

'Sorry, boss. Just not used to steering one of these,' Tyler said from behind him.

'Well, I'm no' exactly used to having my shins mashed against every piece of furniture in a five-mile bloody radius, son, so maybe go a bit more canny, eh?'

'We're nearly there, anyway,' Tyler said.

They continued along the corridor, Tyler doing his best to avoid any further collisions. A couple of nurses dressed up as elves smiled and nodded as they passed. A doctor stormed by a few moments later, the deeply troubled look on his face offset a little by the reindeer antler head band he wore.

'Alice always mad e the d inner on Christmas Day,' Ben said out of nowhere. 'Big spread , she'd d o. Far too much for the two of us.'

'Bet you mad e a d ent in it, though.'

'Oh God , aye. A big d ent, too. She d id turkey. Gravy. Wee sausages wrapped in bacon. Four types of tatties. The works.'

'Sound s tasty,' Tyler remarked .

Ben shook his head . 'No. Awful, most of the time. She always overcooked it. Dry as a bad ger's arse, it was.'

Tyler wasn't sure bad gers' arses were particularly renowned for their d ryness, but he chose not to comment.

'Still, it was nice. Just the whole thing. The experience,' Ben conclud ed . 'If, as I say, largely ined ible.'

They stopped just outsid e the d oor of the d ining hall. The first sitting for Christmas Dinner had been booked in for half-past twelve. Those who were fit enough to get out of bed and travel d ownstairs had enjoyed almost two hours of food , music, and a few party games.

One quick turnaround later, and it was all read y for the second sitting at three.

'So, we're going to end up with the shite left over from the first lot, aren't we?' Ben grumbled . 'All the stuff they d id n't eat will just get d umped on our plates.'

'I'm sure that's not how it'll work, boss,' Tyler said . He leaned over to look through the wind ows that were set in the top half of the d oors, checking to make sure the place was read y.

'It will be. Just you wait and see,' Ben said . 'And what's the betting I'll be sat next to some annoying arsehole the whole time?'

Tyler grinned . 'Aye. Well, that part's pretty much guaran-teed , I reckon,' he said , then the d oors were pulled open by a bear of a man in a truly blood y hid eous Christmas jumper.

'About time you pair showed up,' said Logan. 'I'm nearly chewing my arm off, here.'

Ben frowned , not quite und erstand ing. Not yet. Not until Tyler wheeled him into the empty hospital d ining room.

Almost empty.

A single table had been set up in the mid d le of the room, fully d ecorated with cand les, wreaths, and Christmas crackers, and mad e up with eight place settings.

Sinead appeared at Logan's sid e, one arm d raped around Harris like she was hold ing him back.

'He wanted to shout "surprise",' she explained .

'But we thought that might kill you stone d ead , all things consid ered ,' ad d ed Logan. 'So we d ecid ed against it.'

'What in the name of God are you wearing?' Ben asked .

Logan looked d own at his patterned jumper, then back over his should er to where Shona Maguire sat at the table.

'Shona bought me it,' he said .

Ben clicked his fingers. 'Got it. That explains why she's interested in you. The poor lassie's obviously blind .'

'It's meant to be horrible, actually,' Logan said , taking another look at the offend ing garment. 'Apparently, that's the joke. Anyway, are you coming in or what?'

Ben craned his neck to look up at Tyler. 'Did you blood y know about this?'

'Might have heard a wee rumour, boss,' the DC ad mitted , as the others stood asid e to let him wheel Ben in.

'Nice wheels!' called Dave from the table. He was sitting near the mid d le, knife and fork held upright like he wanted to be read y to pounce the moment the food arrived . 'We should have a race.'

'Can I have a race?' Harris asked .

'You can't be any worse a d river than this eejit,' Ben said , jabbing a thumb in Tyler's d irection.

There was a clunk as the wheelchair d eliberately clipped the ed ge of the table.

'Whoops. Sorry, boss,' Tyler said , then he backed up a little and parked Ben at the table's head .

Hamza appeared from a d oor at the back, carrying a big tray of melba toast and pâté. 'Aw, d id I miss the big moment?' he asked . 'You should 've shouted .'

Ben watched in surprise as the DS set down the tray. 'I thought you did n't celebrate Christmas?' he asked .

'I don't, but I'm hard ly going to pass up a big scoff like this, am I?' he said , then a worried look flitted across his face. 'But, if my mother-in-law asks, this is a business lunch. All right?'

There were a few chuckles at that, as everyone took their seats. Ben's eyes flitted to the chair next to Logan's, where Shona sat. He watched as she gave Logan the briefest of acci- d ental d unts with her should er, and ad mired the way they both pretend ed not to notice quite how close together they just happened to be.

'So, would I be right in thinking that there's no second sitting?' Ben asked .

'Not officially, no,' Logan confirmed . 'So, we thought we'd put one on ourselves. Could n't be having our second and ...' Logan counted on his fingers. '...sixth-best officers eating Christmas d inner off a tray now, could we?'

From along the table there came a sud d en bang

'Jesus fuck!' Ben hissed , jumping in his chair and grabbing at his chest.

All eyes went to Tyler and Harris, who each sat with half a cracker in their hand s.

'Sorry, boss,' Tyler said . 'My bad .'

Canteen staff appeared from through the back, and more food was d eposited in front of them. Melon. Soup. A cheeky wee prawn cocktail.

As everyone started eating, Logan reached for a piece of melba toast, just as Shona reached for the same piece. Their fingers brushed together. Their eyes met.

'On you go,' Shona urged , and for a moment Logan wasn't sure what she meant. 'The toast. You take that bit.'

'Oh. Aye. Right, thanks,' Logan said , placing the rock-solid piece of bread on his plate. 'I, eh, I'm sorry. About the present. I meant to get you something. I went looking, but... with everything in the last few d ays... but I d id mean to get you something.'

336

Shona smiled   and   put a hand   on his arm. She looked   along the table. Crackers were being pulled , jokes were being shared , and   everyone was getting stuck into the food .

Especially by Dave, who was getting stuck in twice as much as anyone else.

'You d id   get me something.' She planted   a kiss on his cheek, and   Logan glared   around   the table, d aring anyone to say a blood y word . 'You got me this,' Shona said .

Then, with a snell wind   blowing a hoolie outsid e, Logan and the others got d own to the business of celebrating Christmas.

Chapter 46

They were gone. All of them. All of his soldiers. His most trusted lieutenant.

Gone.

All gone.

It wasn't the end, of course. It would never be the end. It was merely a setback. A hurdle. A blip on the road of the righteous.

There was still work to be done. Justice to be dealt. Victims to be avenged.

He would rebuild. Recruit. Start again.

It would take time, yes. Resources, too. But he would see it through, like he'd done before, back when it was just him—only him, and no one else. No loyal soldiers. No faithful army.

He would continue the mission that he had started. Whatever it took.

And he'd start with a name.

Alone in his study, he unfolded a notebook page and spread it on the desk before him, smoothing the creases with the heel of his hand.

Five names. All current or former police officers. Two of them now perhaps beyond his reach, but the others? They remained close enough to strike at. And they'd all helped bring down his army.

He drew a silver pen from a pot on his desk, clicked the button to extend the nib, then began to write a sixth name at the bottom of the sheet.

Jack Logan.

That d one, he returned the pen to the pot, blew lightly on the paper to d ry the ink, then fold ed the note in half once more.

He was the Iceman. He had always been the Iceman.

And he had a lot of people still to kill.

Do you love crime fiction and are always on the lookout for brilliant authors?

Canelo Crime is home to some of the most exciting novels around . Thousand s of read ers are alread y enjoying our compulsive stories. Are you read y to find your new favourite writer?

Find out more and sign up to our newsletter at canelocrime.com

Penguin Random House LLC
1745 Broadway
US-NY, 10019
US
https://www.penguinrandomhouse.com
1-800-733-3000

The authorized representative in the EU for product safety and compliance is

Penguin Random House Ireland
Morrison Chambers, 32 Nassau Street
D02 YH68
IE
https://eu-contact.penguin.ie

ISBN: 9798217259649
Release ID: 154078558